Little Witch Academia

3

Contents

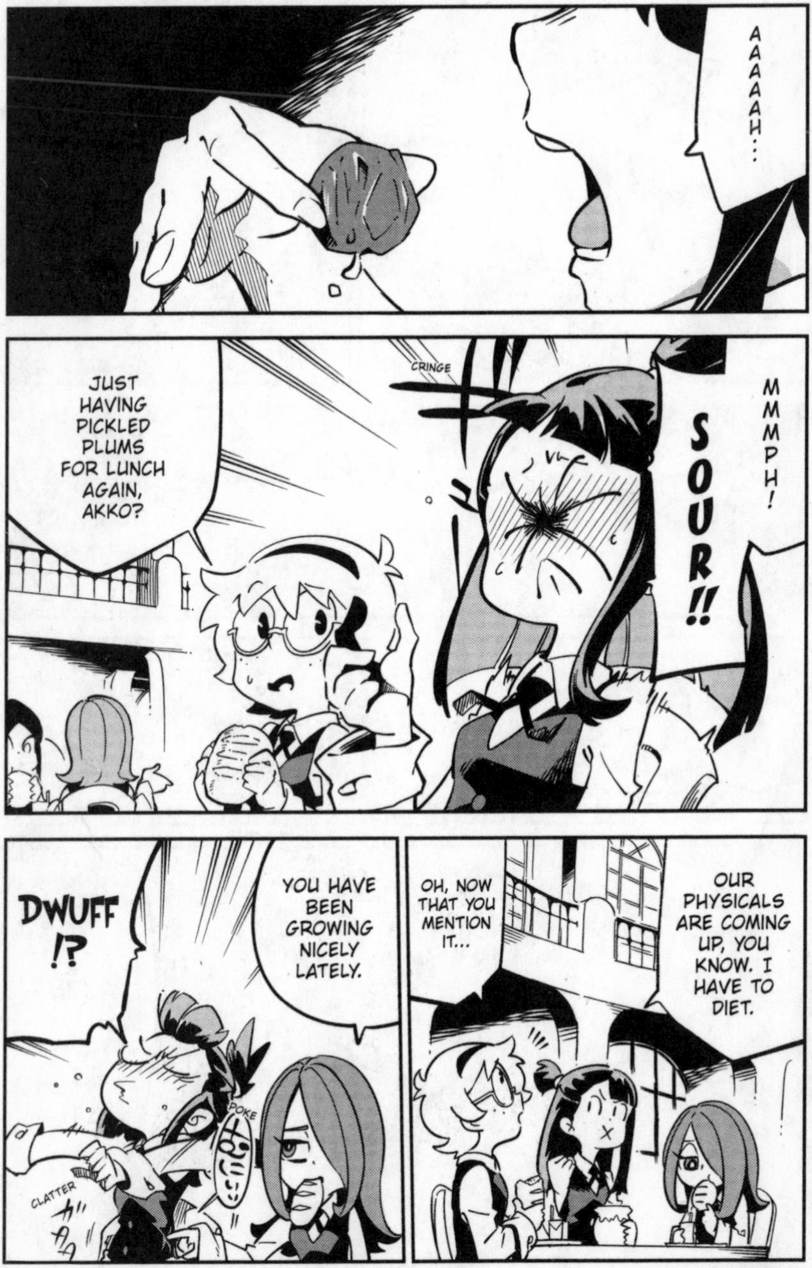
AAAAAH...
MMMMPH!
SOUR!!
CRINGE
JUST HAVING PICKLED PLUMS FOR LUNCH AGAIN, AKKO?
OUR PHYSICALS ARE COMING UP, YOU KNOW. I HAVE TO DIET.
OH, NOW THAT YOU MENTION IT...
YOU HAVE BEEN GROWING NICELY LATELY.
POKE
DWUFF !?
CLATTER

Chapter 12

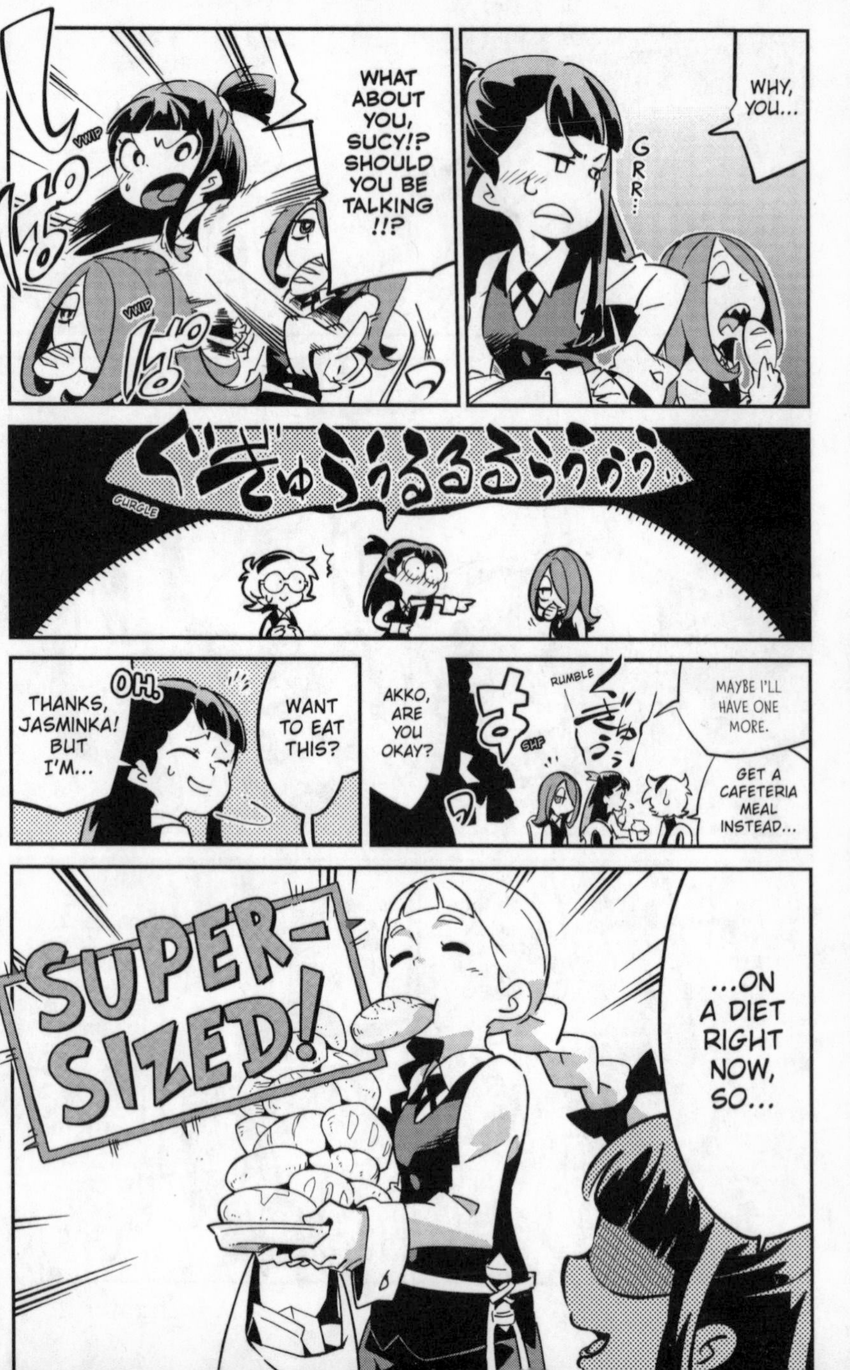
WHY, YOU...
GRR...
WHAT ABOUT YOU, SUCY!? SHOULD YOU BE TALKING!!?
YWIP
YWIP
GURGLE
MAYBE I'LL HAVE ONE MORE.
GET A CAFETERIA MEAL INSTEAD...
RUMBLE
SHF
AKKO, ARE YOU OKAY?
WANT TO EAT THIS?
OH.
THANKS, JASMINKA! BUT I'M...
...ON A DIET RIGHT NOW, SO...
SUPER-SIZED!

Chapter 12 I EAT, THEREFORE I AM

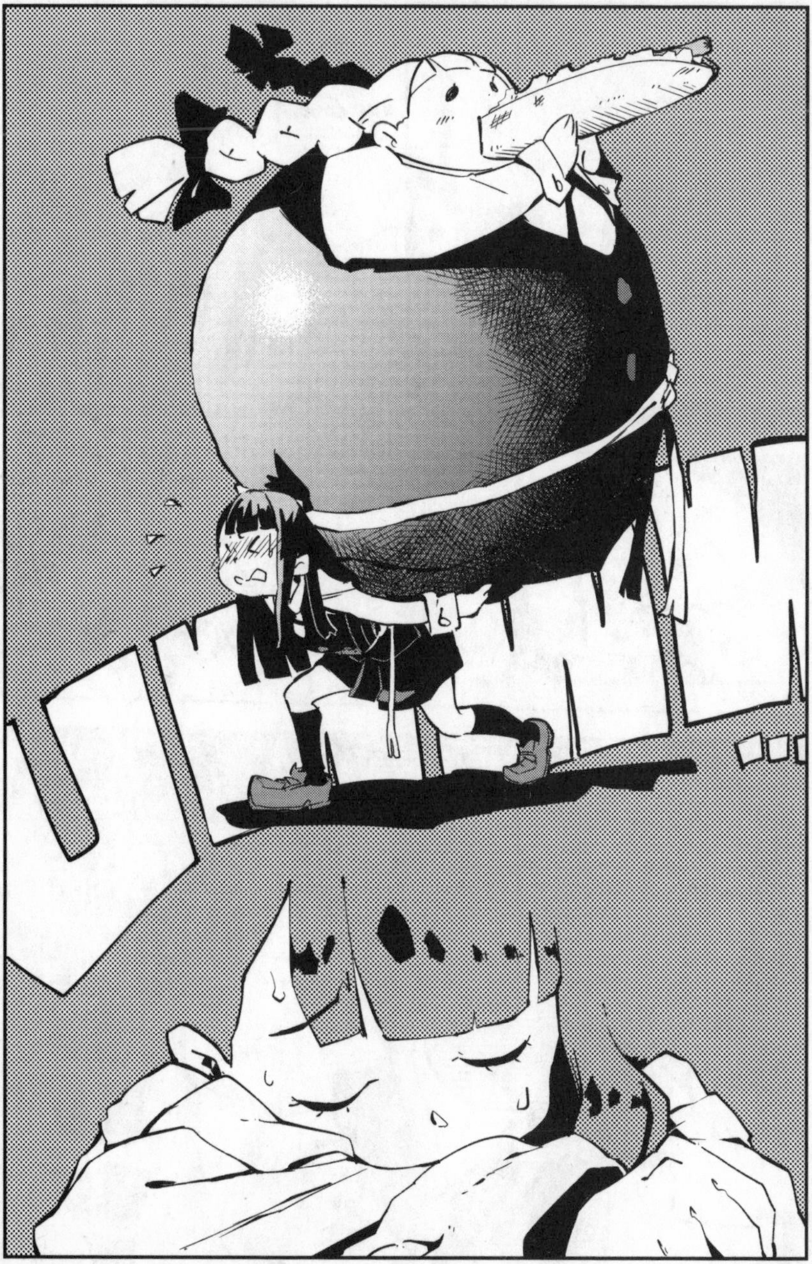

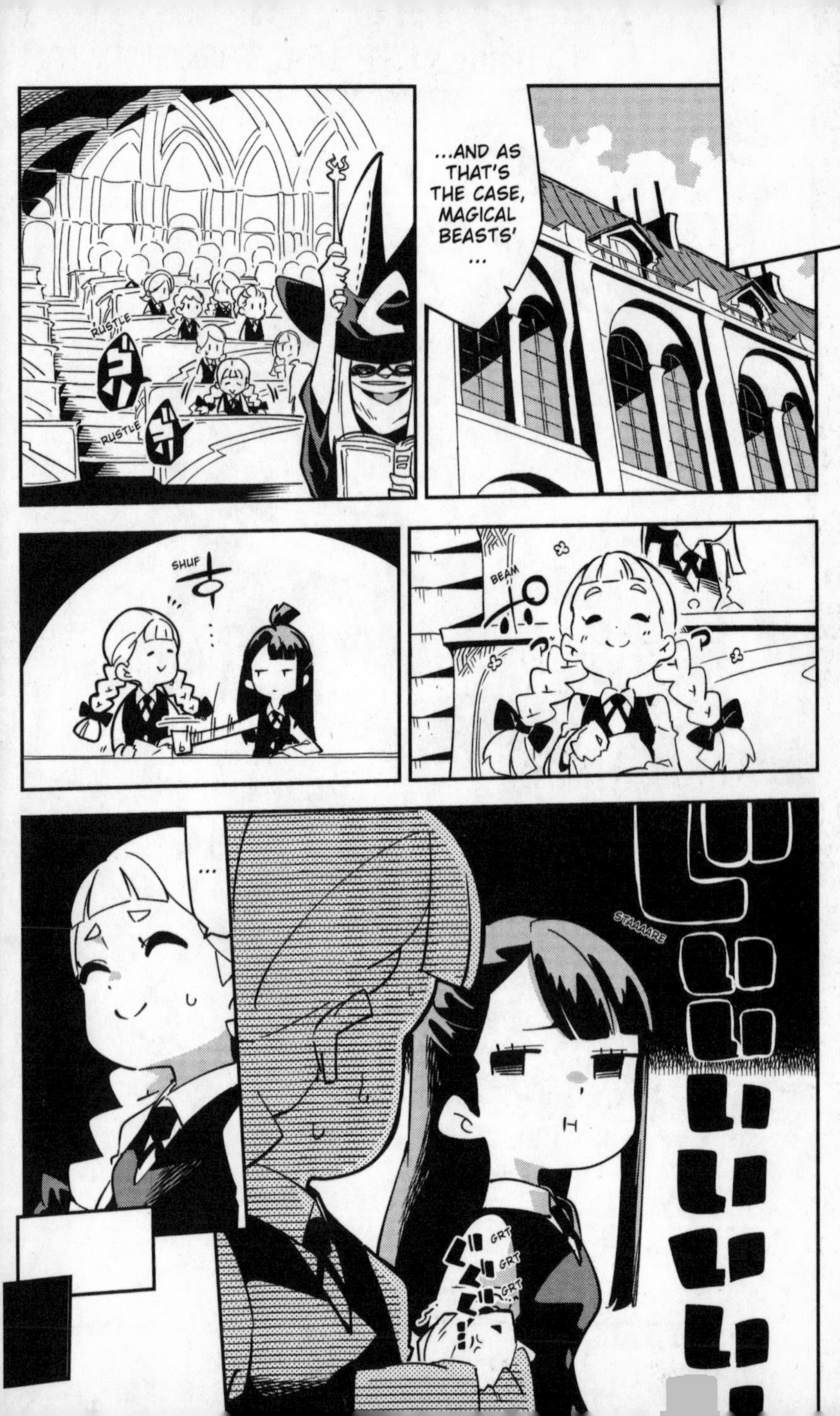
...AND AS THAT'S THE CASE, MAGICAL BEASTS' ...
RUSTLE
RUSTLE
BEAM
SHUF
...
STAAAARE
GRT
GRT
GRT

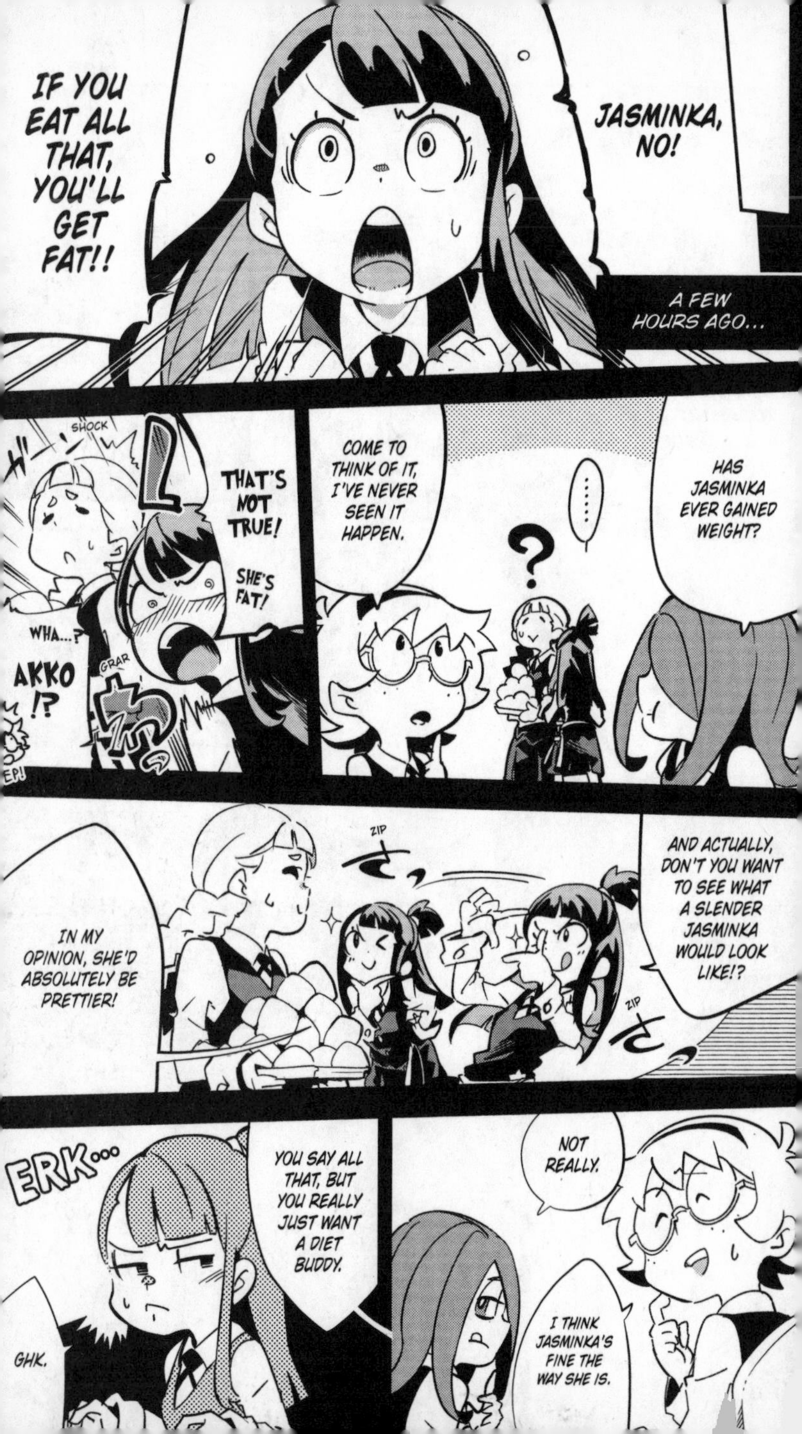
JASMINKA, NO!
IF YOU EAT ALL THAT, YOU'LL GET FAT!!
A FEW HOURS AGO...
HAS JASMINKA EVER GAINED WEIGHT?
......
?
COME TO THINK OF IT, I'VE NEVER SEEN IT HAPPEN.
THAT'S NOT TRUE!
SHOCK
SHE'S FAT!
WHA...?
GRAR
AKKO!?
EP!
AND ACTUALLY, DON'T YOU WANT TO SEE WHAT A SLENDER JASMINKA WOULD LOOK LIKE!?
ZIP
ZIP
IN MY OPINION, SHE'D ABSOLUTELY BE PRETTIER!
NOT REALLY.
I THINK JASMINKA'S FINE THE WAY SHE IS.
YOU SAY ALL THAT, BUT YOU REALLY JUST WANT A DIET BUDDY.
ERK...
GHK.

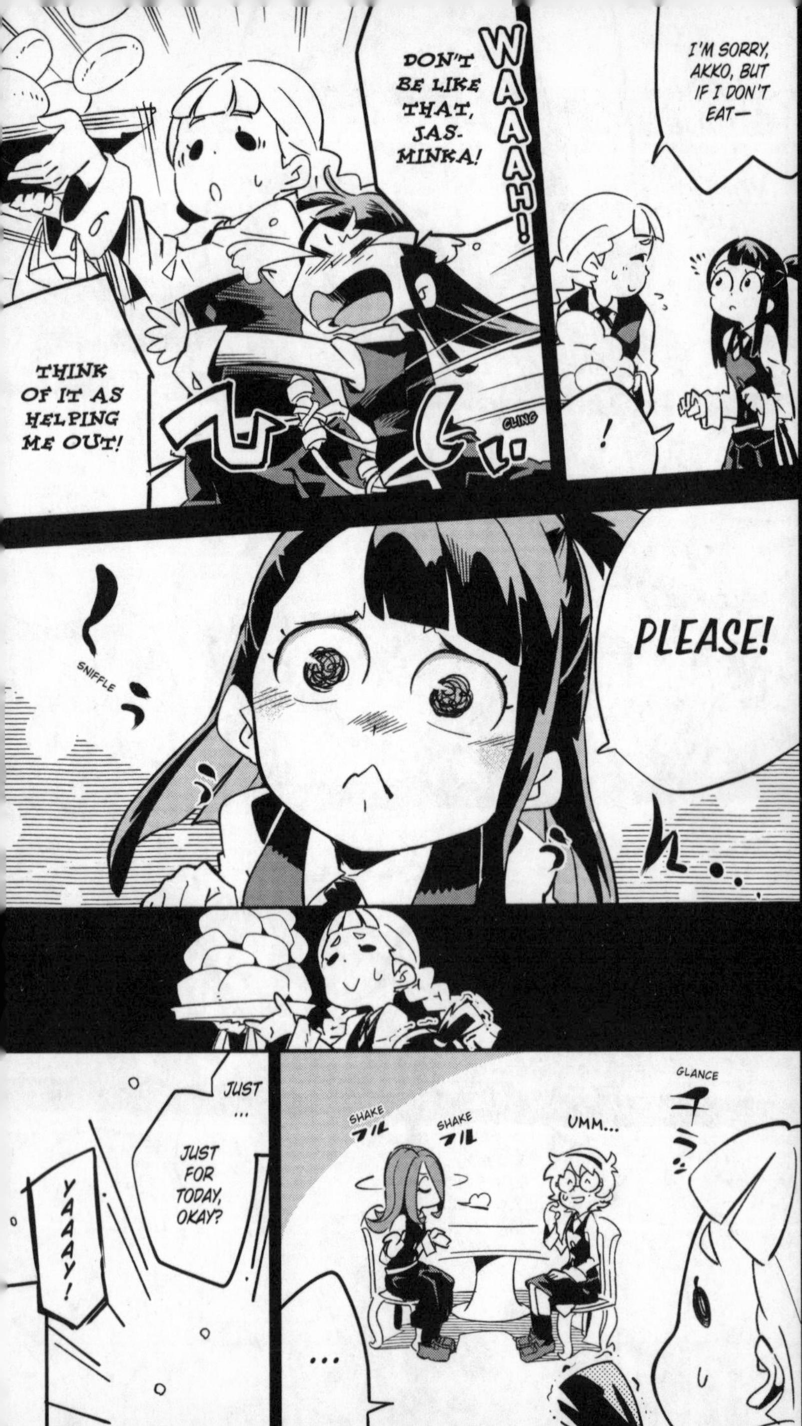
I'M SORRY, AKKO, BUT IF I DON'T EAT—
!
WAAAAH!
DON'T BE LIKE THAT, JAS-MINKA!
CLING
THINK OF IT AS HELPING ME OUT!
PLEASE!
SNIFFLE
GLANCE
UMM...
SHAKE
SHAKE
JUST ...
JUST FOR TODAY, OKAY?
YAAAAY!
...

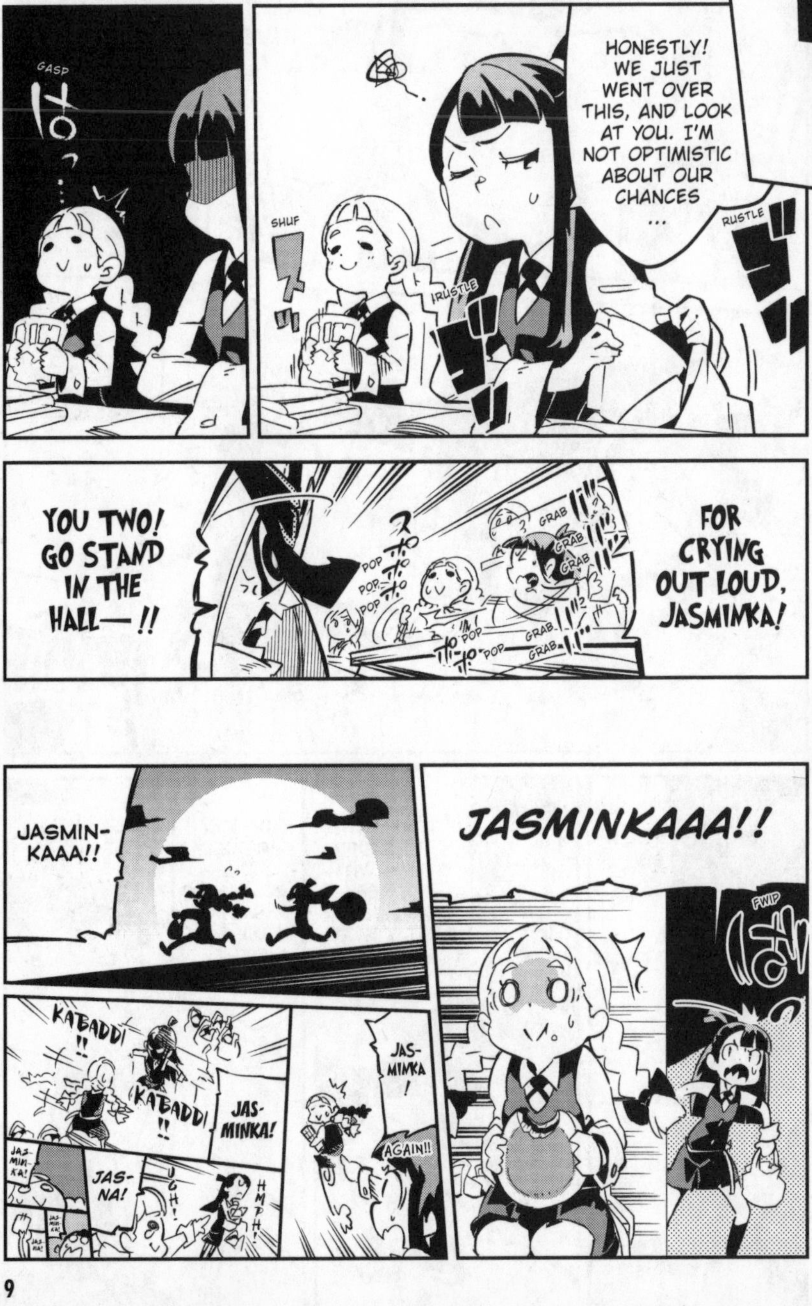

HONESTLY! WE JUST WENT OVER THIS, AND LOOK AT YOU. I'M NOT OPTIMISTIC ABOUT OUR CHANCES ...
RUSTLE
RUSTLE
SHUF
GASP
FOR CRYING OUT LOUD, JASMINKA!
GRAB
GRAB
GRAB
GRAB
GRAB
POP
POP
POP
POP
POP
YOU TWO! GO STAND IN THE HALL— !!
JASMINKAAA!!
FWIP
JASMIN-KAAA!!
JAS-MINKA!
AGAIN!!
JAS-MINKA!
KABADDI !!
KABADDI !!
JAS-MIN-KA!
JAS-NA!
UGH!
HMPH!

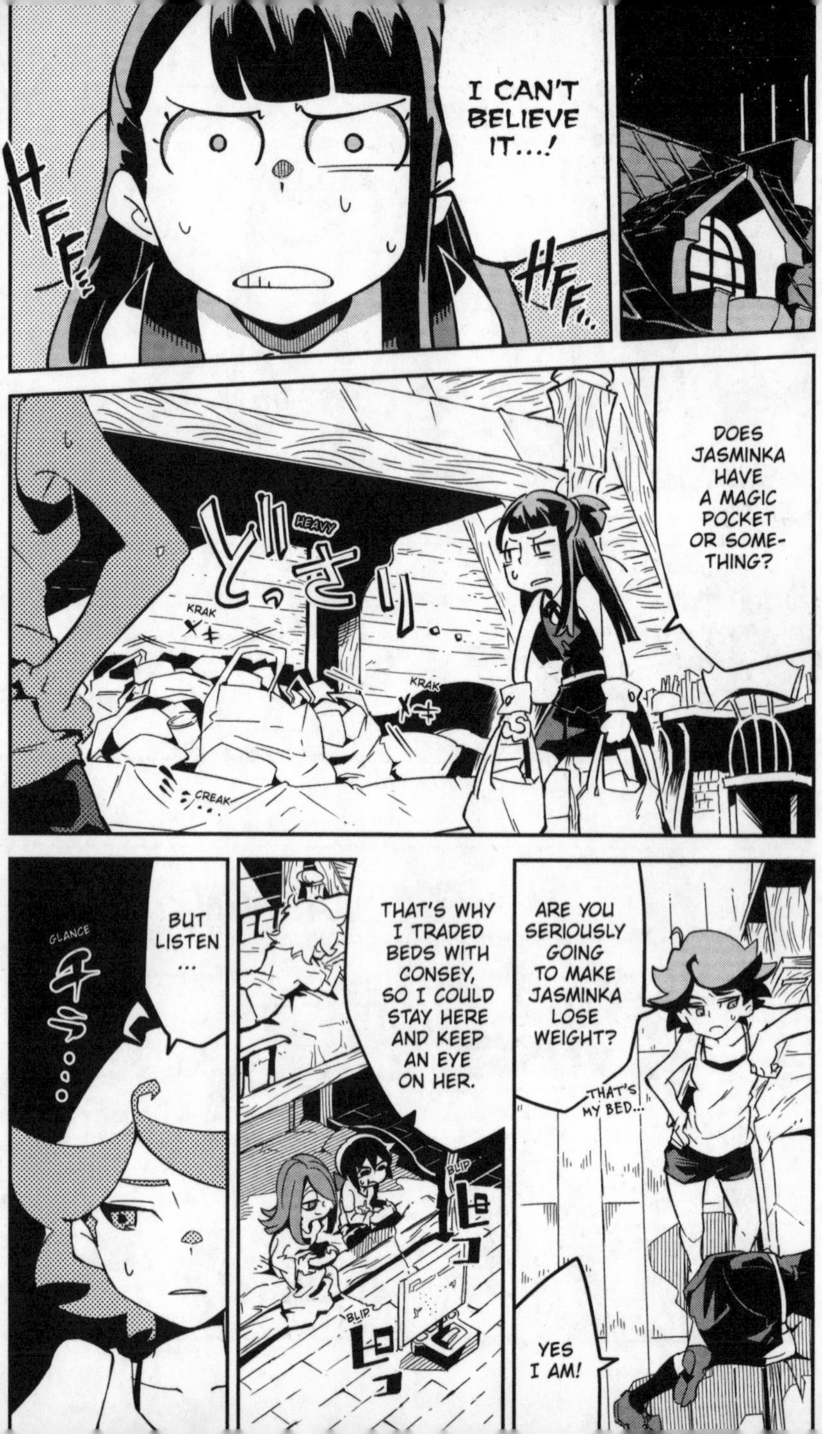
I CAN'T BELIEVE IT...!
HFF
HFF...
DOES JASMINKA HAVE A MAGIC POCKET OR SOME-THING?
どっさり
HEAVY
KRAK
KRAK
CREAK
ARE YOU SERIOUSLY GOING TO MAKE JASMINKA LOSE WEIGHT?
THAT'S MY BED...
YES I AM!
THAT'S WHY I TRADED BEDS WITH CONSEY, SO I COULD STAY HERE AND KEEP AN EYE ON HER.
ピコ
BLIP
ピコ
BLIP
BUT LISTEN ...
チラ○○○
GLANCE

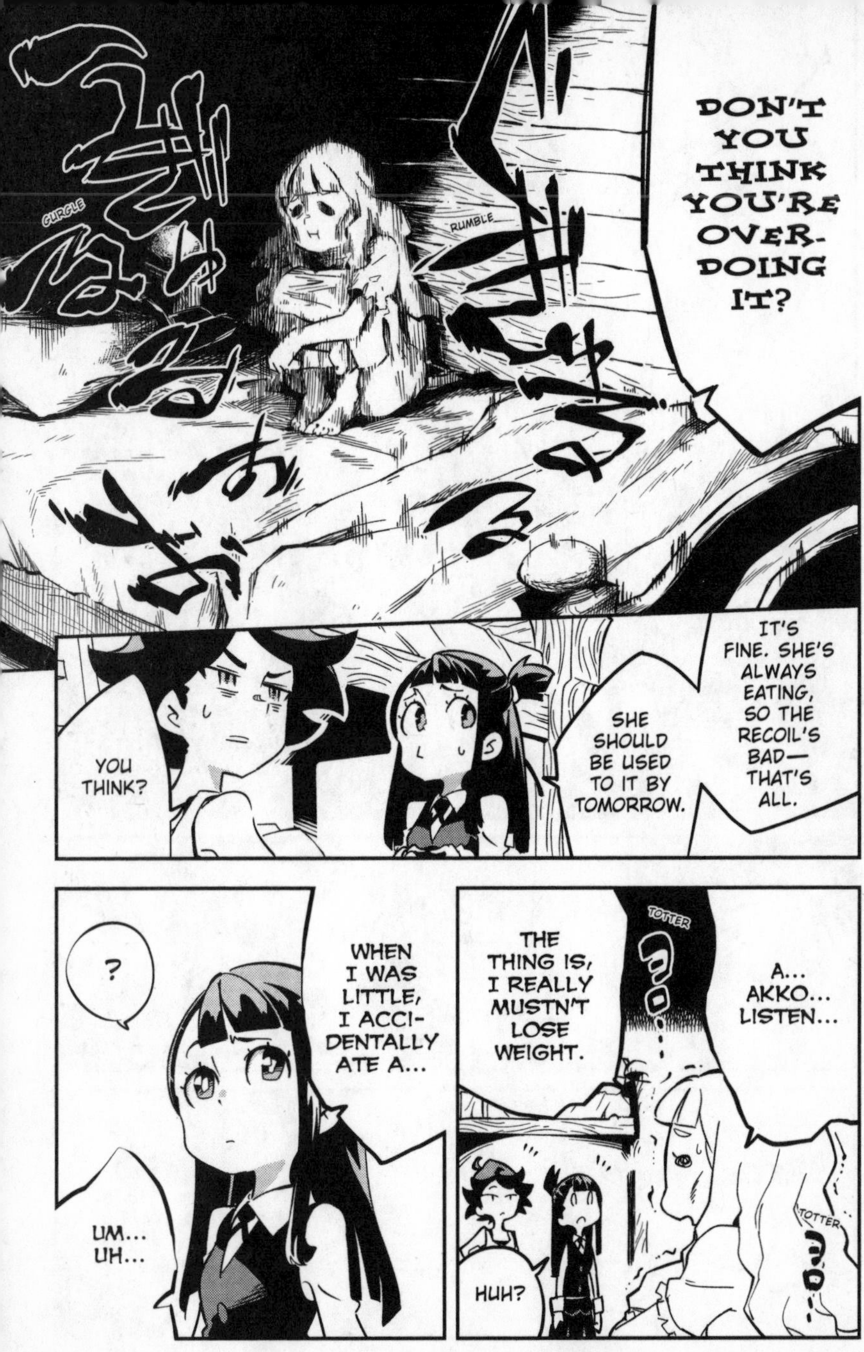

DON'T YOU THINK YOU'RE OVER-DOING IT?
RUMBLE
GURGLE
IT'S FINE. SHE'S ALWAYS EATING, SO THE RECOIL'S BAD—THAT'S ALL.
SHE SHOULD BE USED TO IT BY TOMORROW.
YOU THINK?
A... AKKO... LISTEN...
TOTTER
THE THING IS, I REALLY MUSTN'T LOSE WEIGHT.
TOTTER
HUH?
WHEN I WAS LITTLE, I ACCI-DENTALLY ATE A...
?
UM... UH...

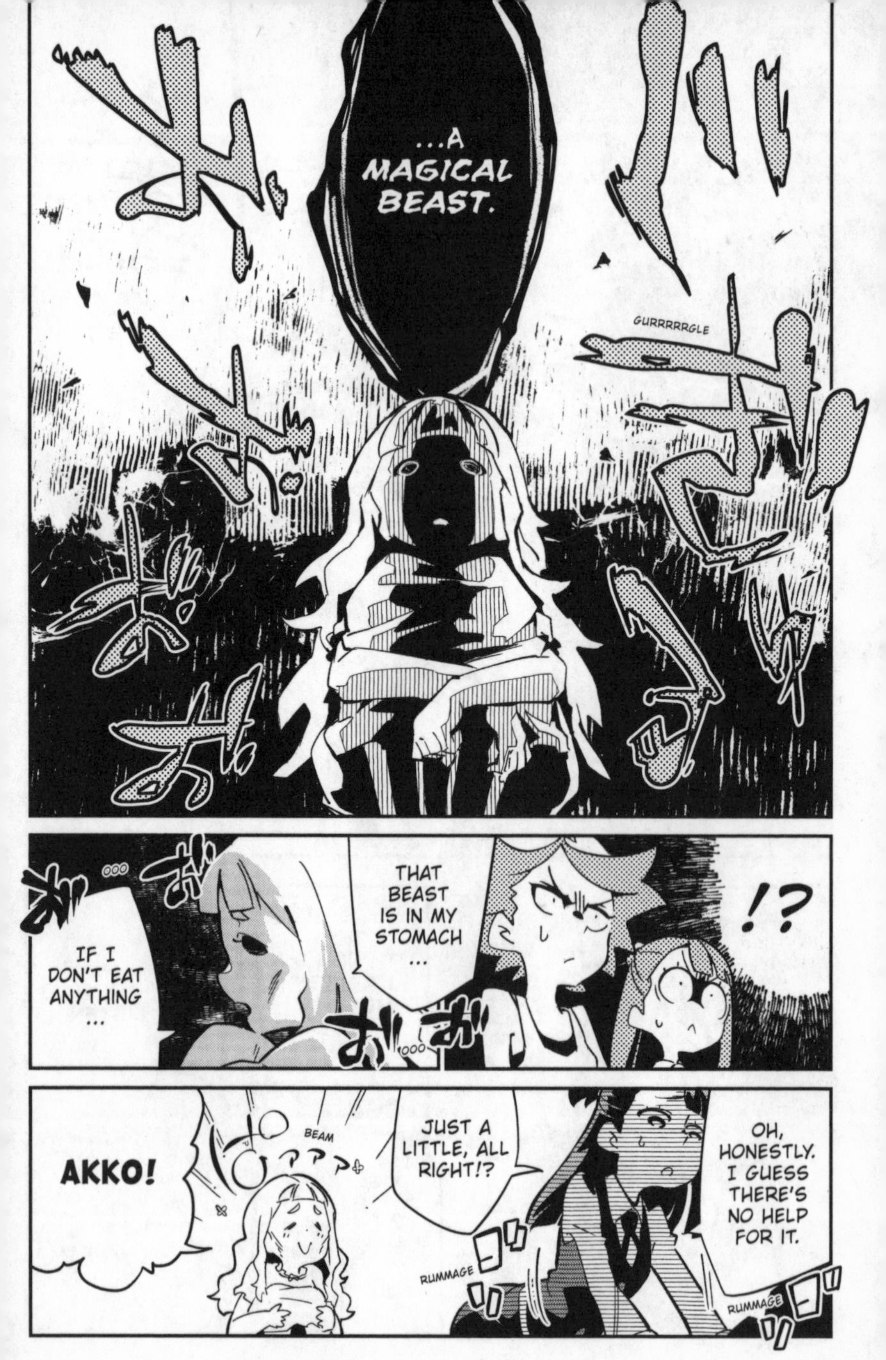
...A MAGICAL BEAST.
GURRRRRGLE
!?
THAT BEAST IS IN MY STOMACH ...
IF I DON'T EAT ANYTHING ...
OH, HONESTLY. I GUESS THERE'S NO HELP FOR IT.
RUMMAGE
RUMMAGE
JUST A LITTLE, ALL RIGHT!?
BEAM
AKKO!

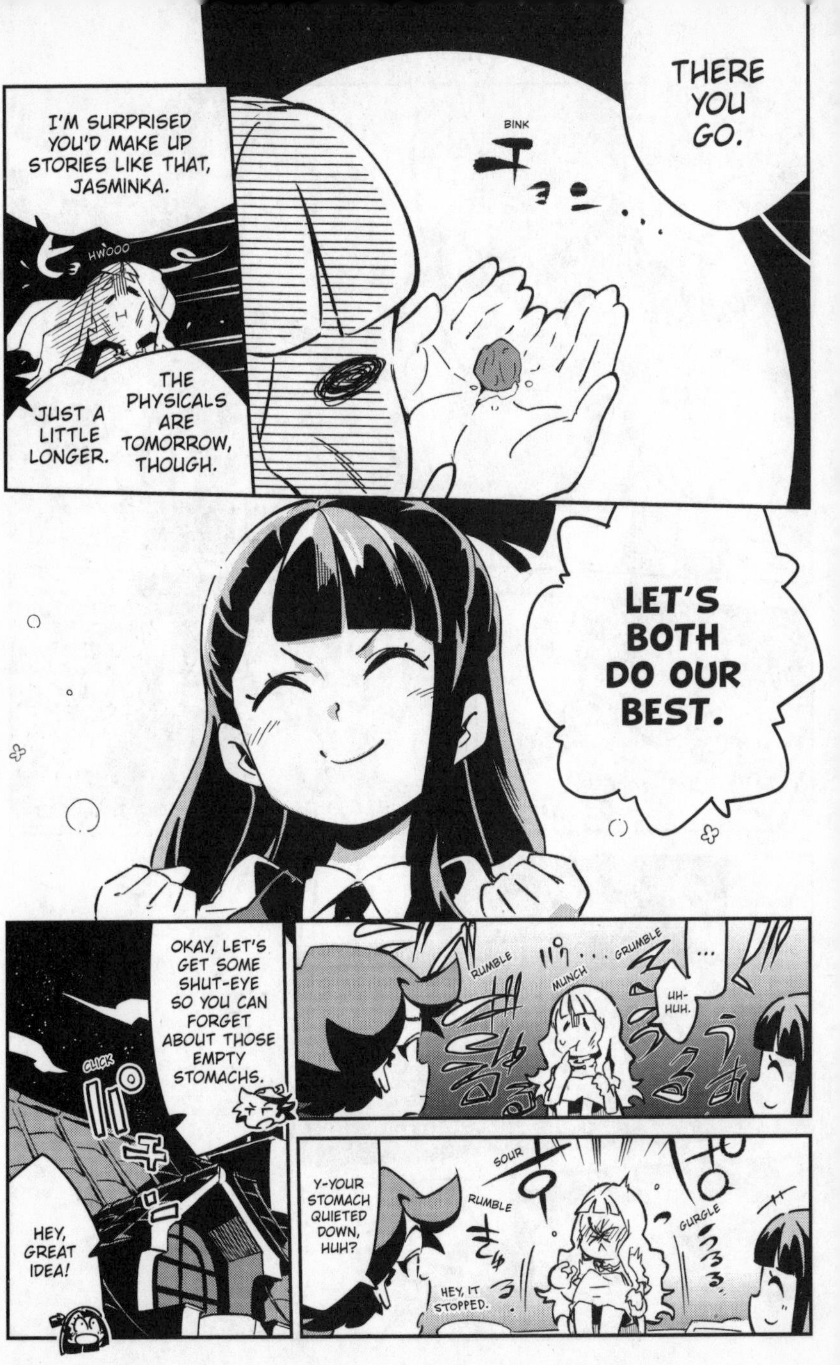
THERE YOU GO.
BINK
I'M SURPRISED YOU'D MAKE UP STORIES LIKE THAT, JASMINKA.
HWOOO
THE PHYSICALS ARE TOMORROW, THOUGH.
JUST A LITTLE LONGER.
LET'S BOTH DO OUR BEST.
...
UH-HUH.
GRUMBLE
MUNCH
RUMBLE
SOUR
GURGLE
RUMBLE
Y-YOUR STOMACH QUIETED DOWN, HUH?
HEY, IT STOPPED.
OKAY, LET'S GET SOME SHUT-EYE SO YOU CAN FORGET ABOUT THOSE EMPTY STOMACHS.
CLICK
HEY, GREAT IDEA!

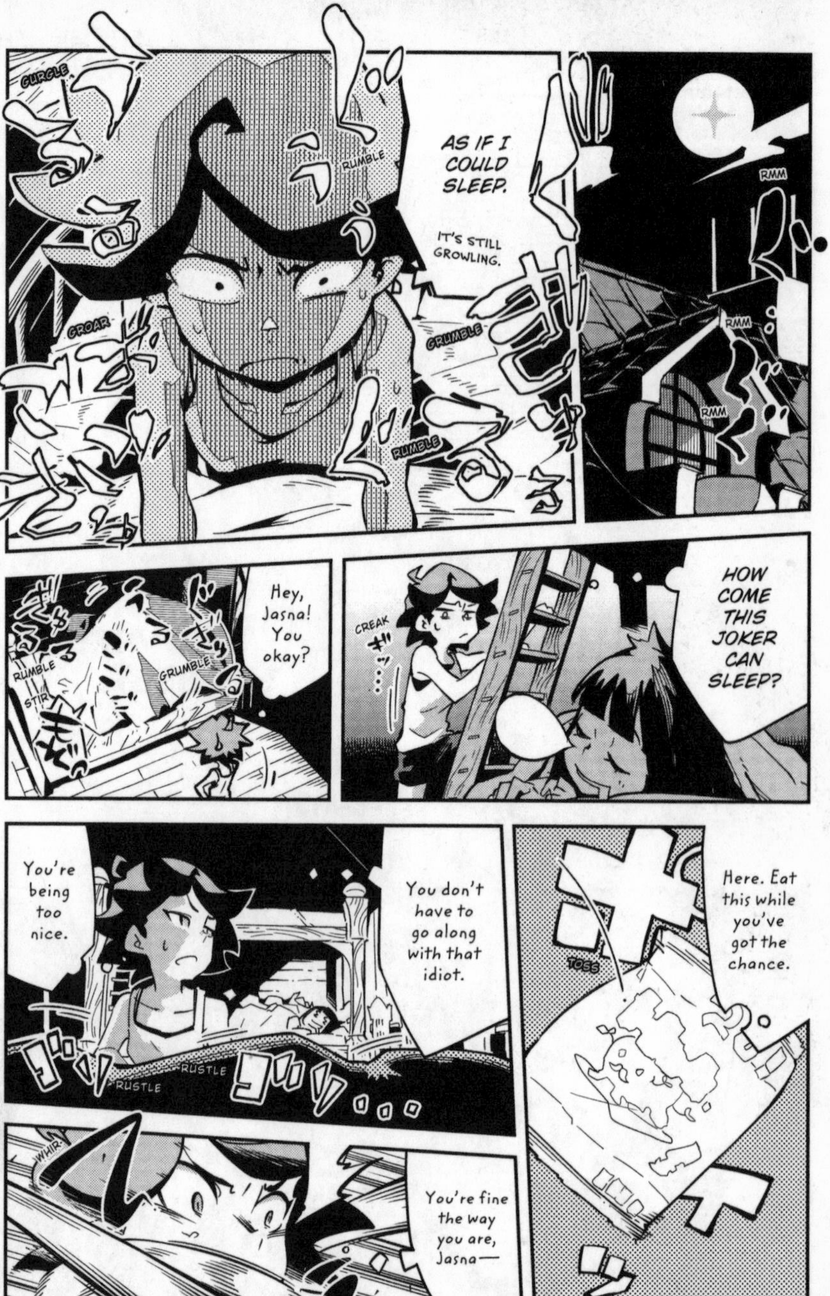
RMM
RMM
RMM
AS IF I COULD SLEEP.
IT'S STILL GROWLING.
RUMBLE
GURGLE
GRUMBLE
GROAR
RUMBLE
HOW COME THIS JOKER CAN SLEEP?
CREAK
Hey, Jasna! You okay?
GRUMBLE
RUMBLE
STIR
Here. Eat this while you've got the chance.
TOSS
You don't have to go along with that idiot.
You're being too nice.
RUSTLE
RUSTLE
You're fine the way you are, Jasna—
WHIRR

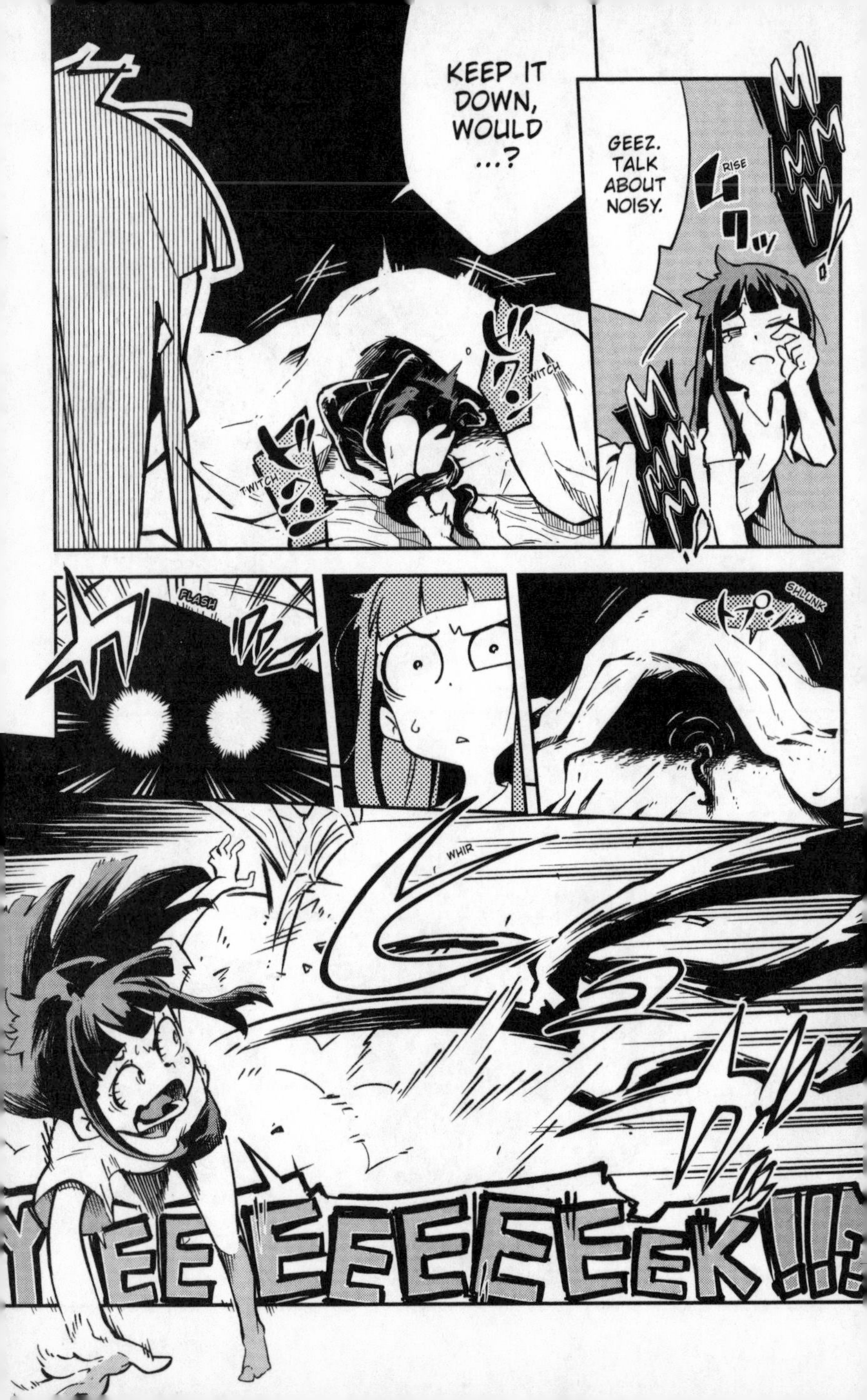
GEEZ. TALK ABOUT NOISY.
RISE
KEEP IT DOWN, WOULD ...?
TWITCH
TWITCH
SHLLINK
FLASH
WHIR
YEEEEEEEEEK!!

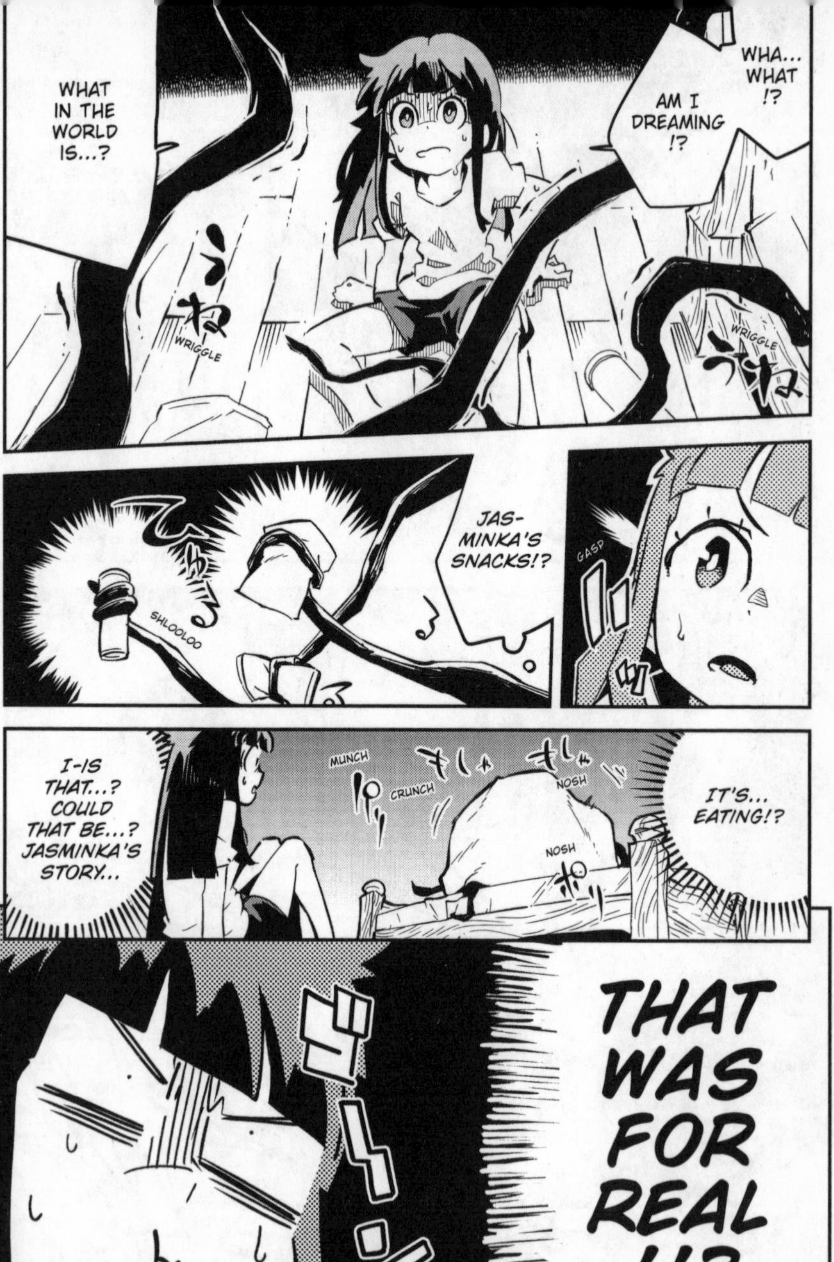
WHA... WHAT !?
AM I DREAMING !?
WHAT IN THE WORLD IS...?
WRIGGLE
WRIGGLE
GASP
JAS-MINKA'S SNACKS!?
SHLOOLOO
IT'S... EATING!?
NOSH
NOSH
CRUNCH
MUNCH
I-IS THAT...? COULD THAT BE...? JASMINKA'S STORY...
THAT WAS FOR REAL !!?
SHOCK

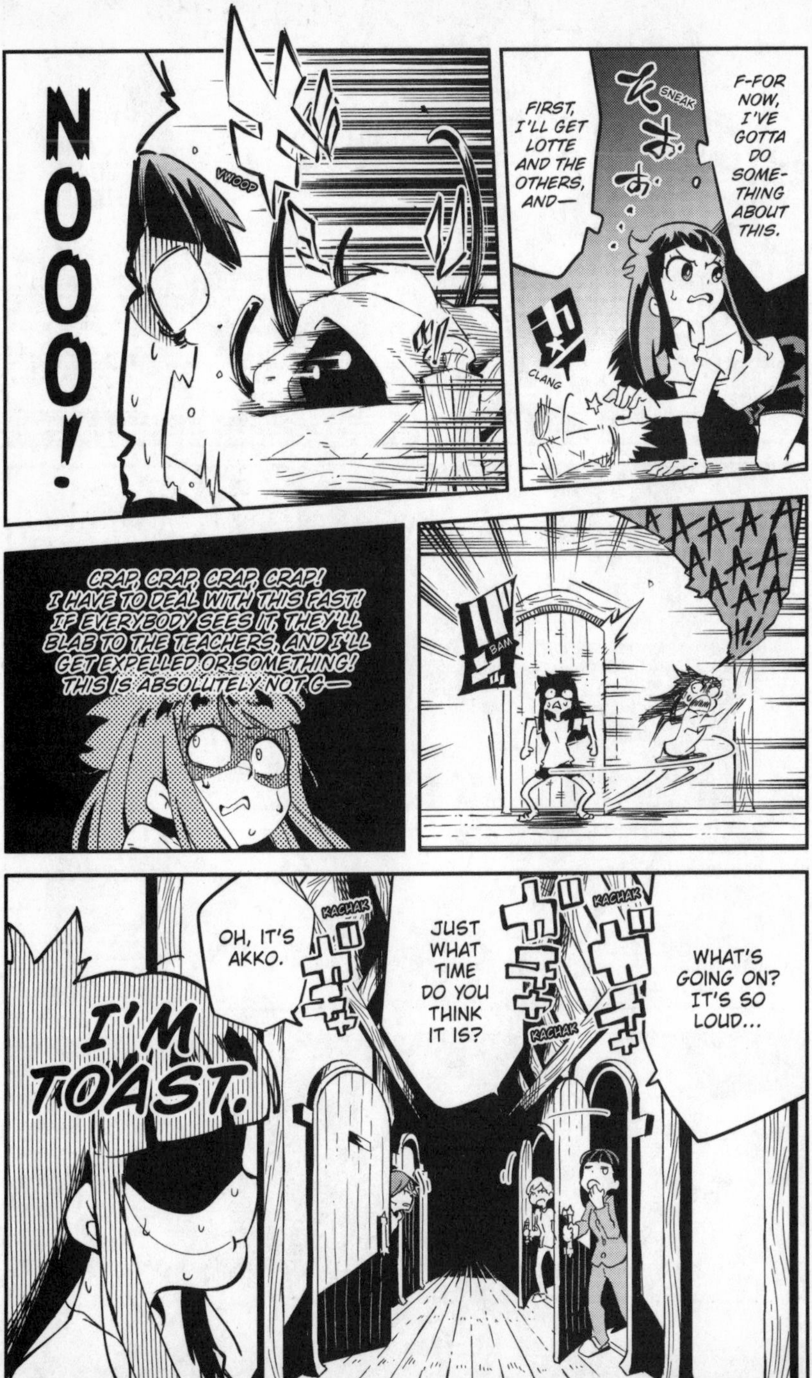
F-FOR NOW, I'VE GOTTA DO SOME-THING ABOUT THIS.
SNEAK
FIRST, I'LL GET LOTTE AND THE OTHERS, AND—
CLANG
VWOOP
NOOOO!
BAM
AAAAAAAAAH!
CRAP, CRAP, CRAP, CRAP! I HAVE TO DEAL WITH THIS FAST! IF EVERYBODY SEES IT, THEY'LL BLAB TO THE TEACHERS, AND I'LL GET EXPELLED OR SOMETHING! THIS IS ABSOLUTELY NOT G—
WHAT'S GOING ON? IT'S SO LOUD...
KACHAK
KACHAK
JUST WHAT TIME DO YOU THINK IT IS?
KACHAK
OH, IT'S AKKO.
I'M TOAST.

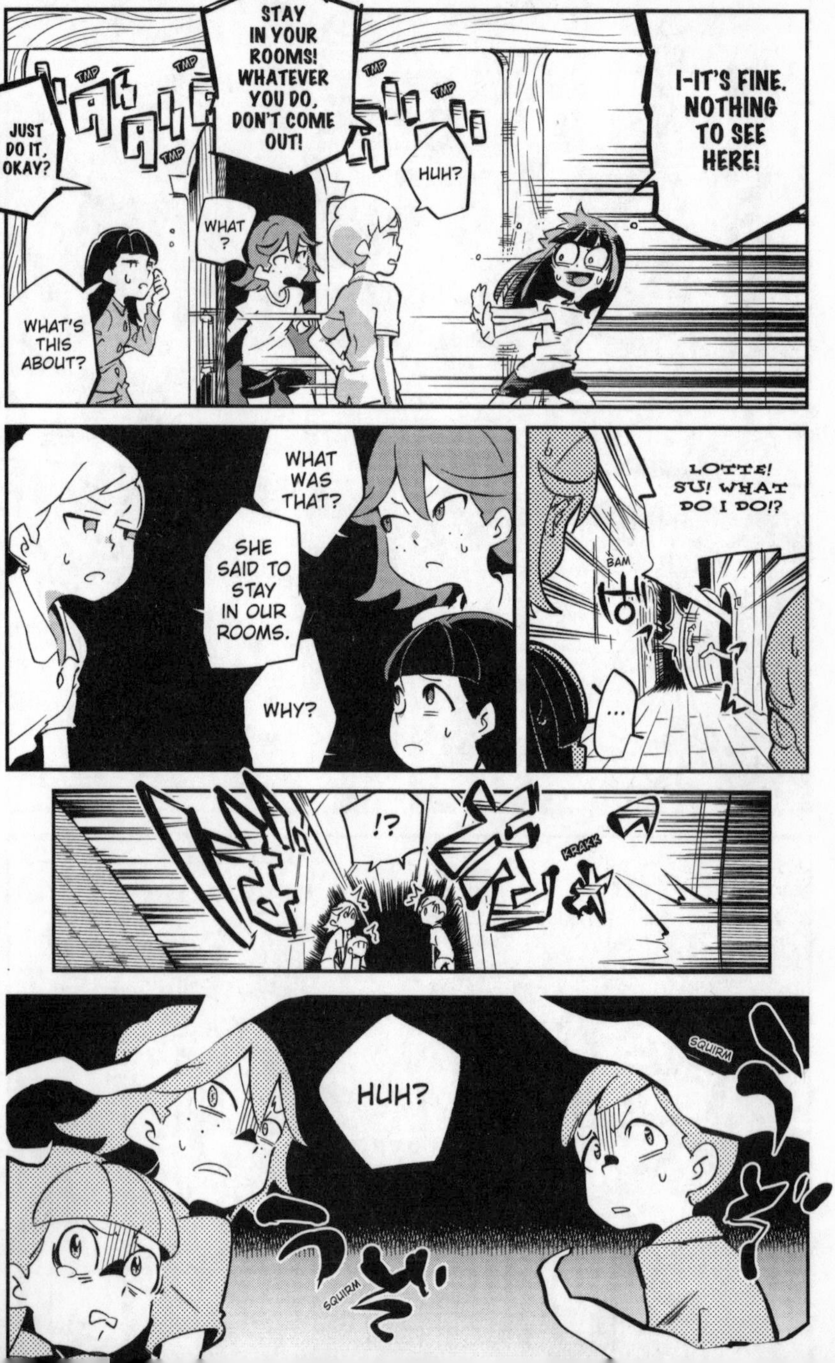
I-IT'S FINE. NOTHING TO SEE HERE!
TMP
HUH?
STAY IN YOUR ROOMS! WHATEVER YOU DO, DON'T COME OUT!
TMP
JUST DO IT, OKAY?
WHAT?
WHAT'S THIS ABOUT?
LOTTE! SU! WHAT DO I DO!?
BAM
...
WHAT WAS THAT?
SHE SAID TO STAY IN OUR ROOMS.
WHY?
KRAKK
!?
SQUIRM
HUH?
SQUIRM

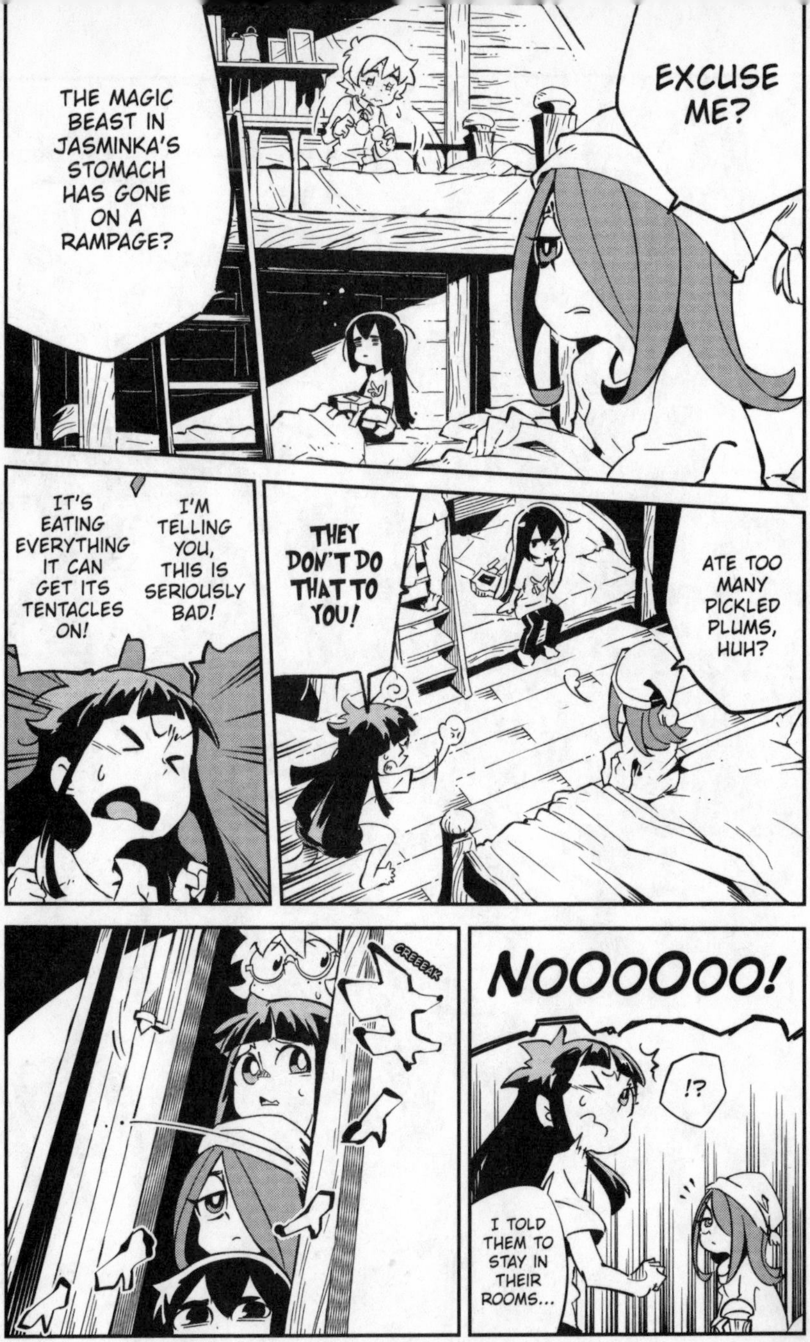
EXCUSE ME?
THE MAGIC BEAST IN JASMINKA'S STOMACH HAS GONE ON A RAMPAGE?
ATE TOO MANY PICKLED PLUMS, HUH?
THEY DON'T DO THAT TO YOU!
I'M TELLING YOU, THIS IS SERIOUSLY BAD!
IT'S EATING EVERYTHING IT CAN GET ITS TENTACLES ON!
NOOOOOO!
!?
I TOLD THEM TO STAY IN THEIR ROOMS...
CREEEAK

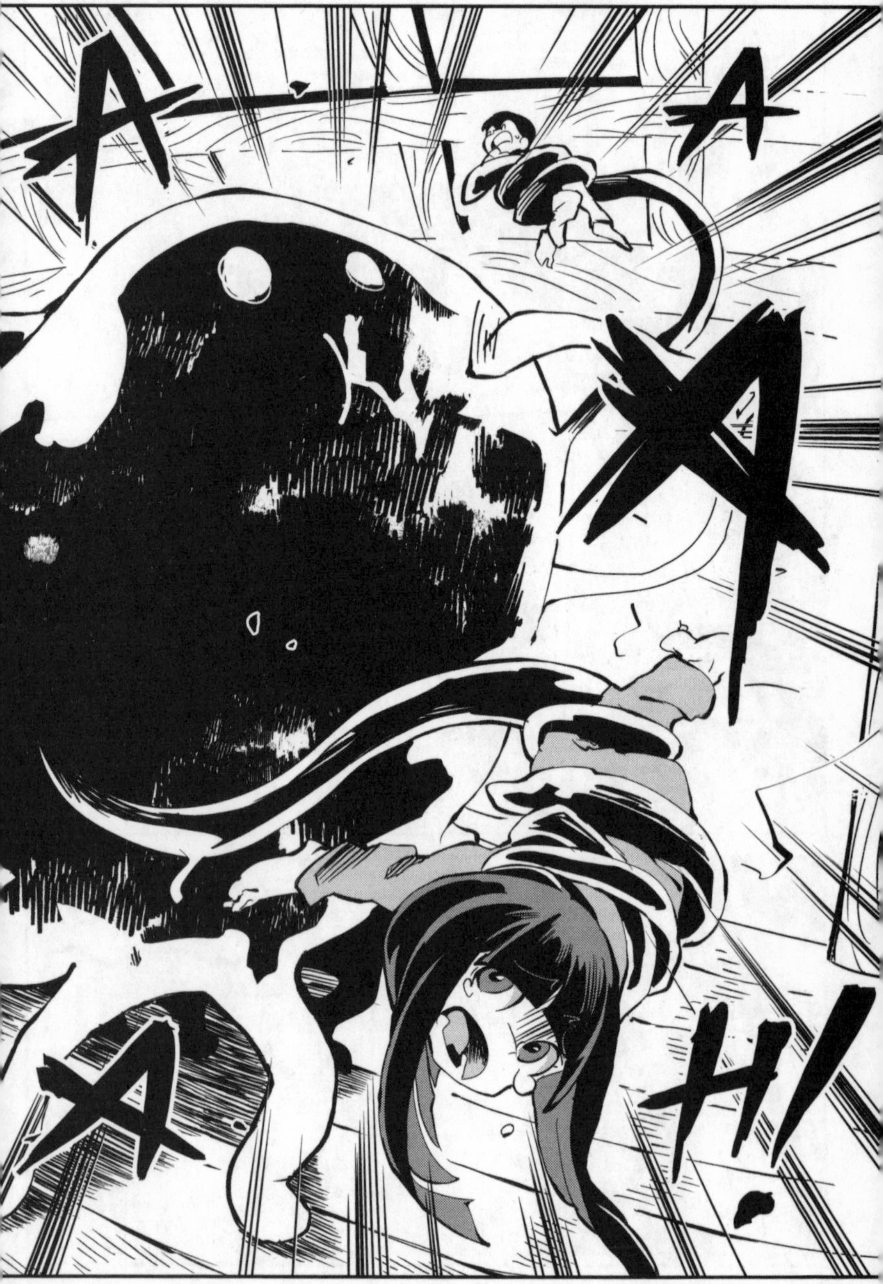
AAAAH!

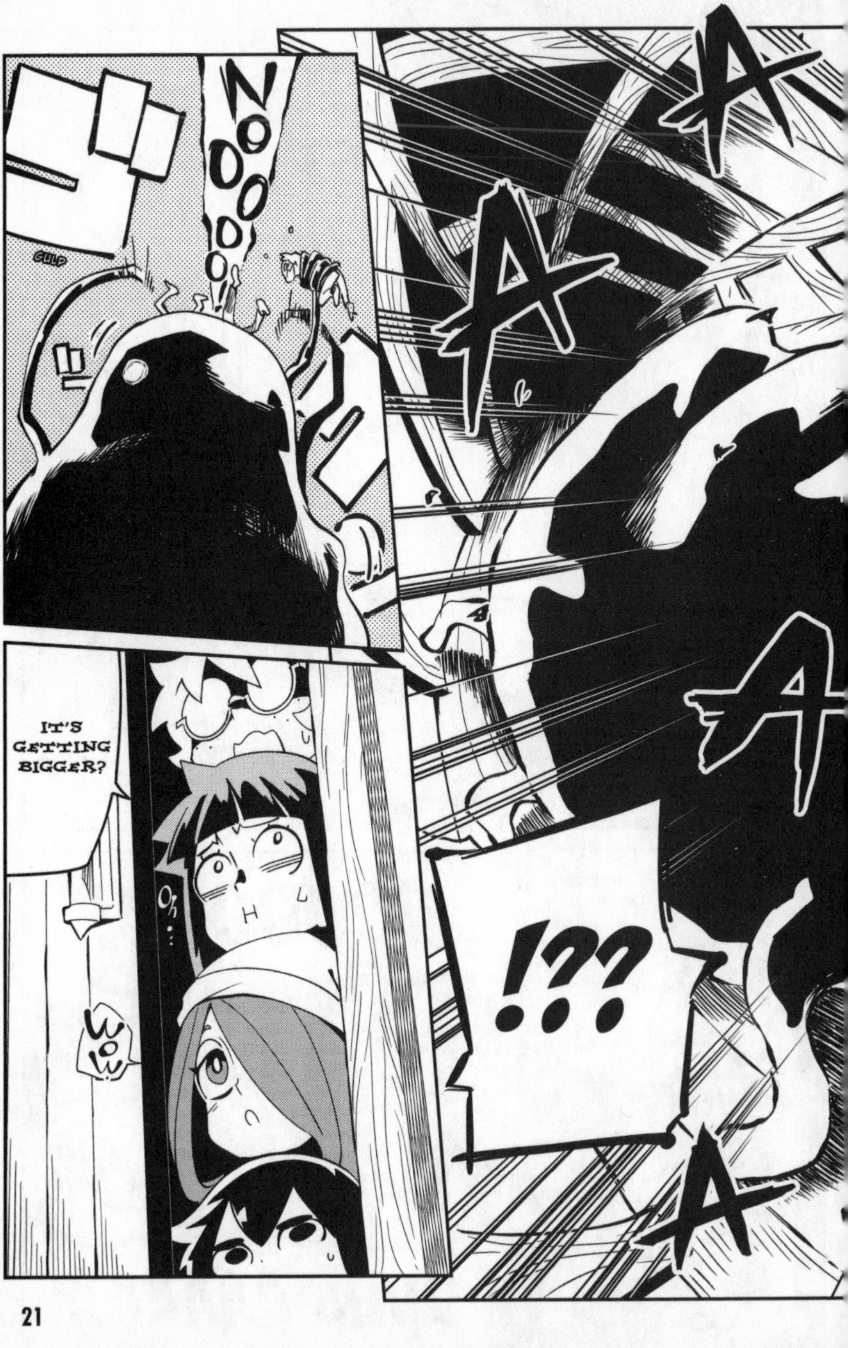
AAAA
!??
NOOOOOO!
GULP
IT'S GETTING BIGGER?
Oh...
WOW

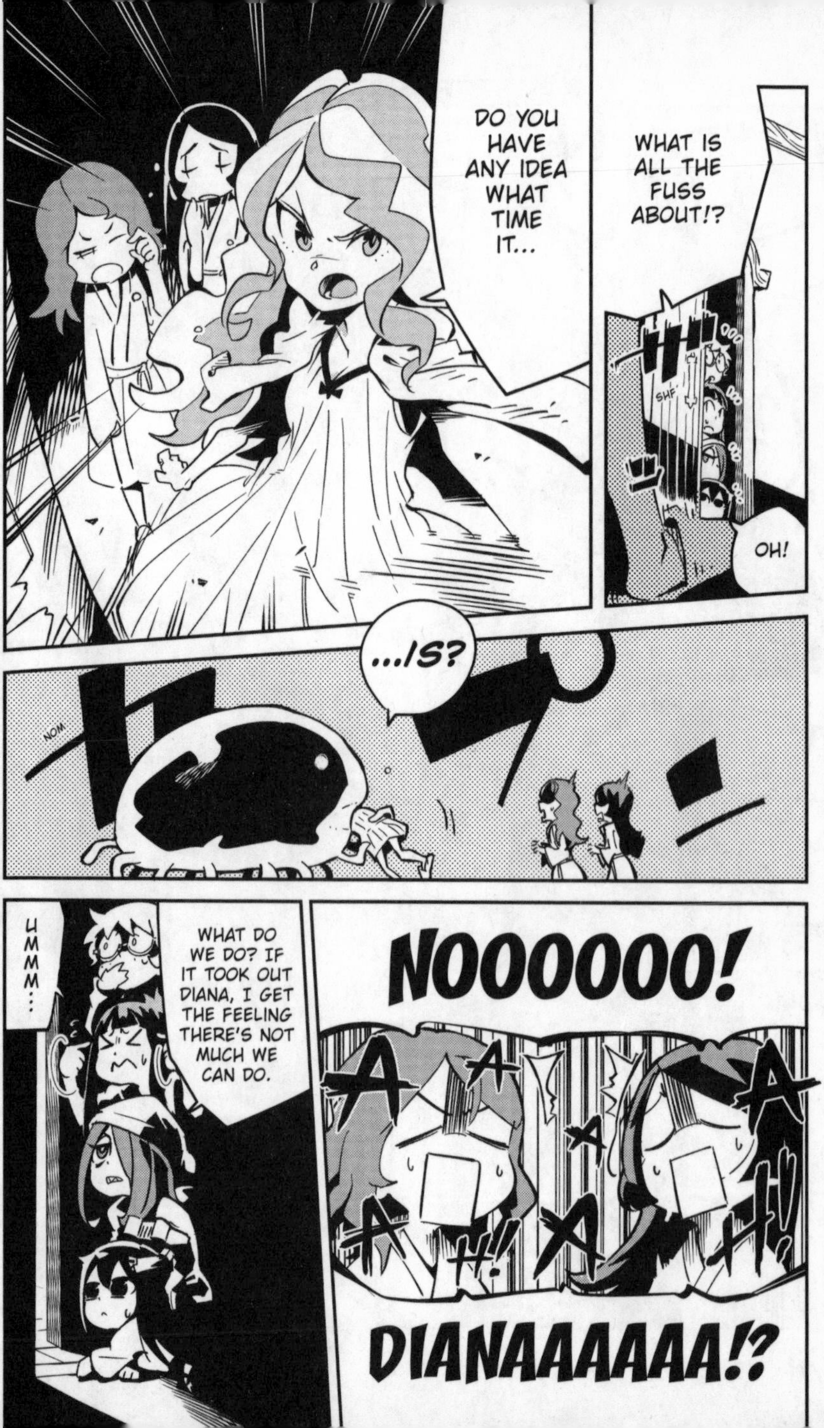
WHAT IS ALL THE FUSS ABOUT!?
SHF
OH!
DO YOU HAVE ANY IDEA WHAT TIME IT...
...IS?
NOM
NOOOOOO!
AAAAH!!
AAAAH!!
DIANAAAAAAA!?
WHAT DO WE DO? IF IT TOOK OUT DIANA, I GET THE FEELING THERE'S NOT MUCH WE CAN DO.
UMMM...

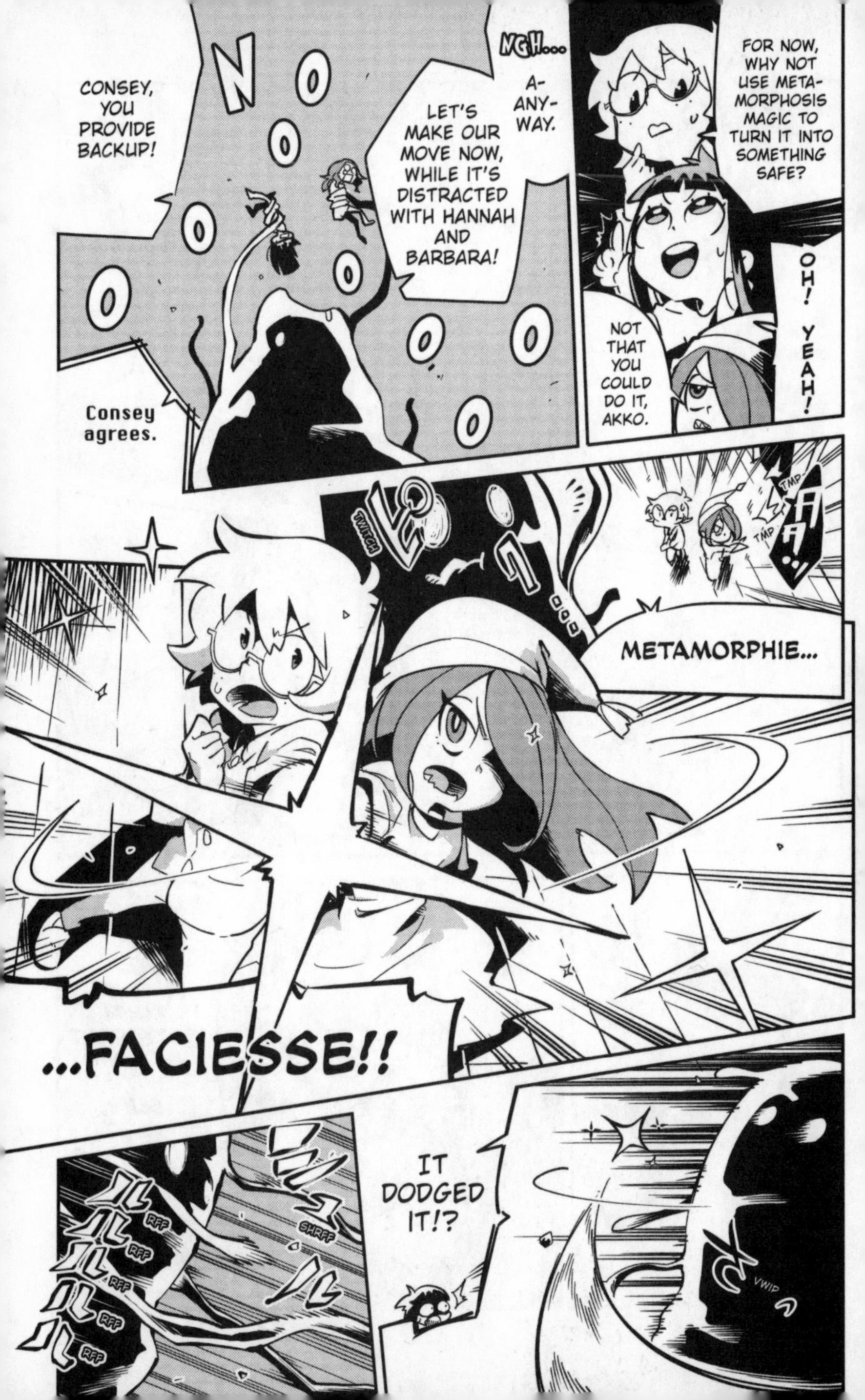

FOR NOW, WHY NOT USE METAMORPHOSIS MAGIC TO TURN IT INTO SOMETHING SAFE?
OH! YEAH!
NOT THAT YOU COULD DO IT, AKKO.
NGH...
A-ANYWAY.
LET'S MAKE OUR MOVE NOW, WHILE IT'S DISTRACTED WITH HANNAH AND BARBARA!
NOOOOOOOO
CONSEY, YOU PROVIDE BACKUP!
Consey agrees.
TMP TMP
AA..!
METAMORPHIE...
TWITCH
...FACIESSE!!
VWIP
IT DODGED IT!?
SHRFF
RFF RFF RFF RFF RFF

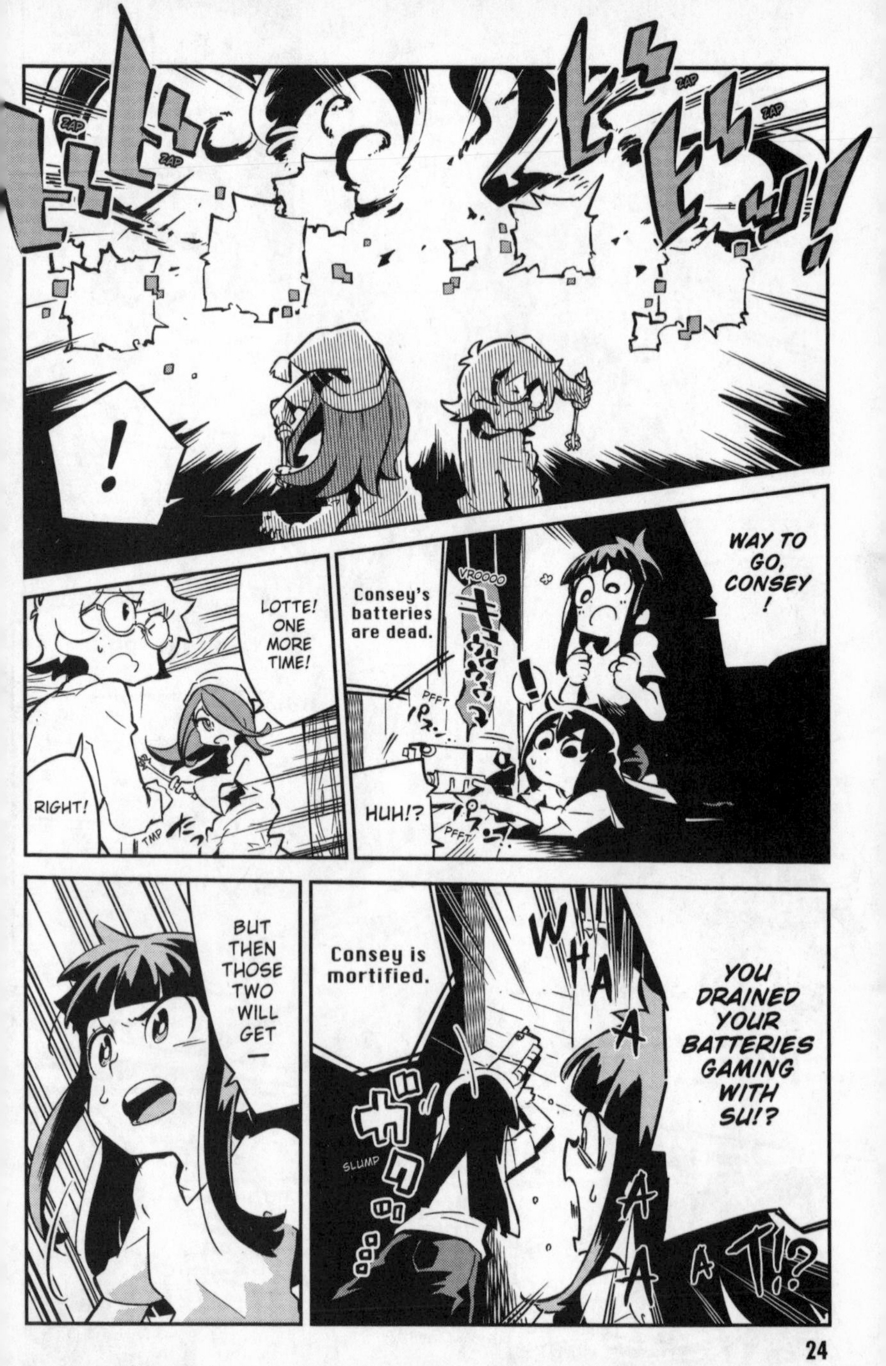
ZAP
ZAP
ZAP
ZAP
!
WAY TO GO, CONSEY!
VROOOO
Consey's batteries are dead.
PFFT
HUH!?
PFFT
LOTTE! ONE MORE TIME!
RIGHT!
TMP
YOU DRAINED YOUR BATTERIES GAMING WITH SU!?
WHAAAAAAT!?
Consey is mortified.
SLUMP
BUT THEN THOSE TWO WILL GET—

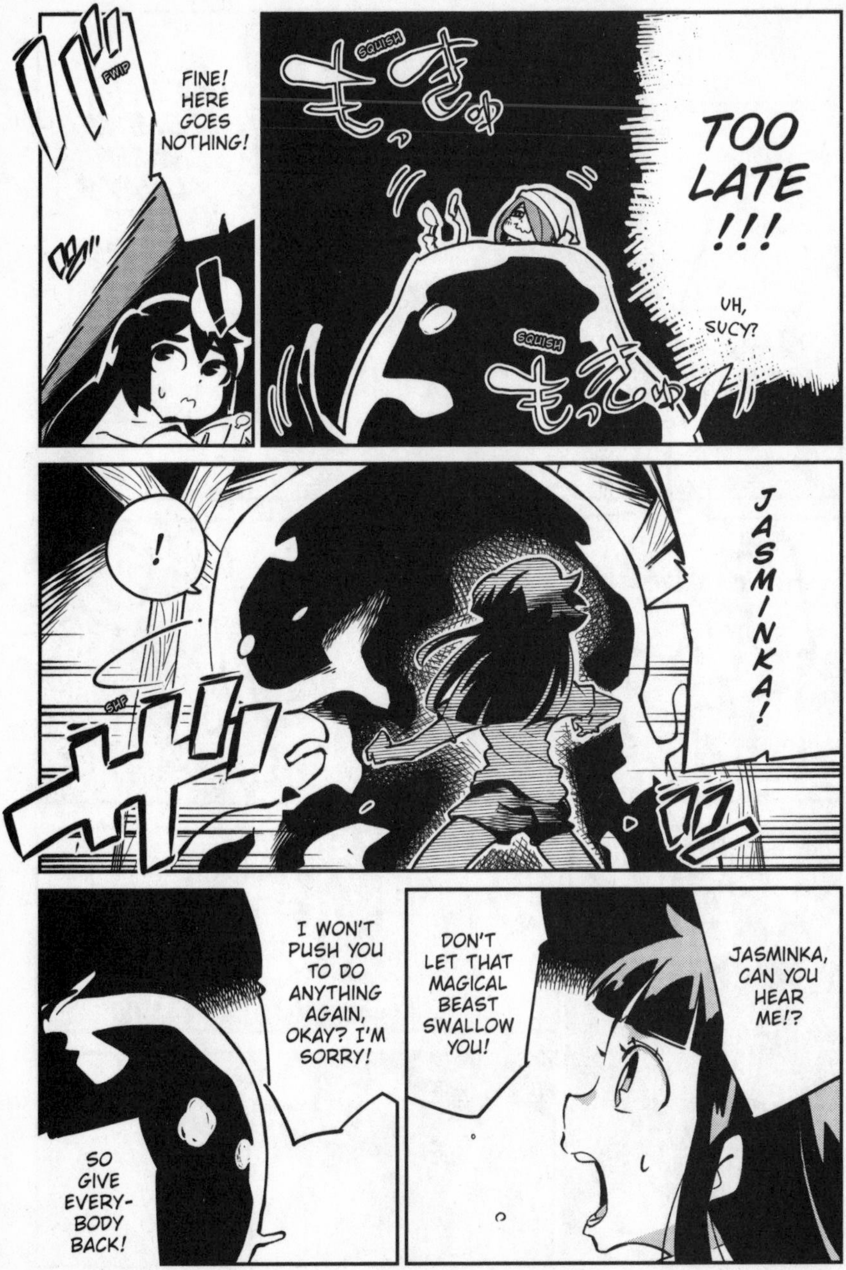
SQUISH
TOO LATE!!!
SQUISH
UH, SUCY?
FWIP
FINE! HERE GOES NOTHING!
JASMINKA!
!
SHF
JASMINKA, CAN YOU HEAR ME!?
DON'T LET THAT MAGICAL BEAST SWALLOW YOU!
I WON'T PUSH YOU TO DO ANYTHING AGAIN, OKAY? I'M SORRY!
SO GIVE EVERY-BODY BACK!

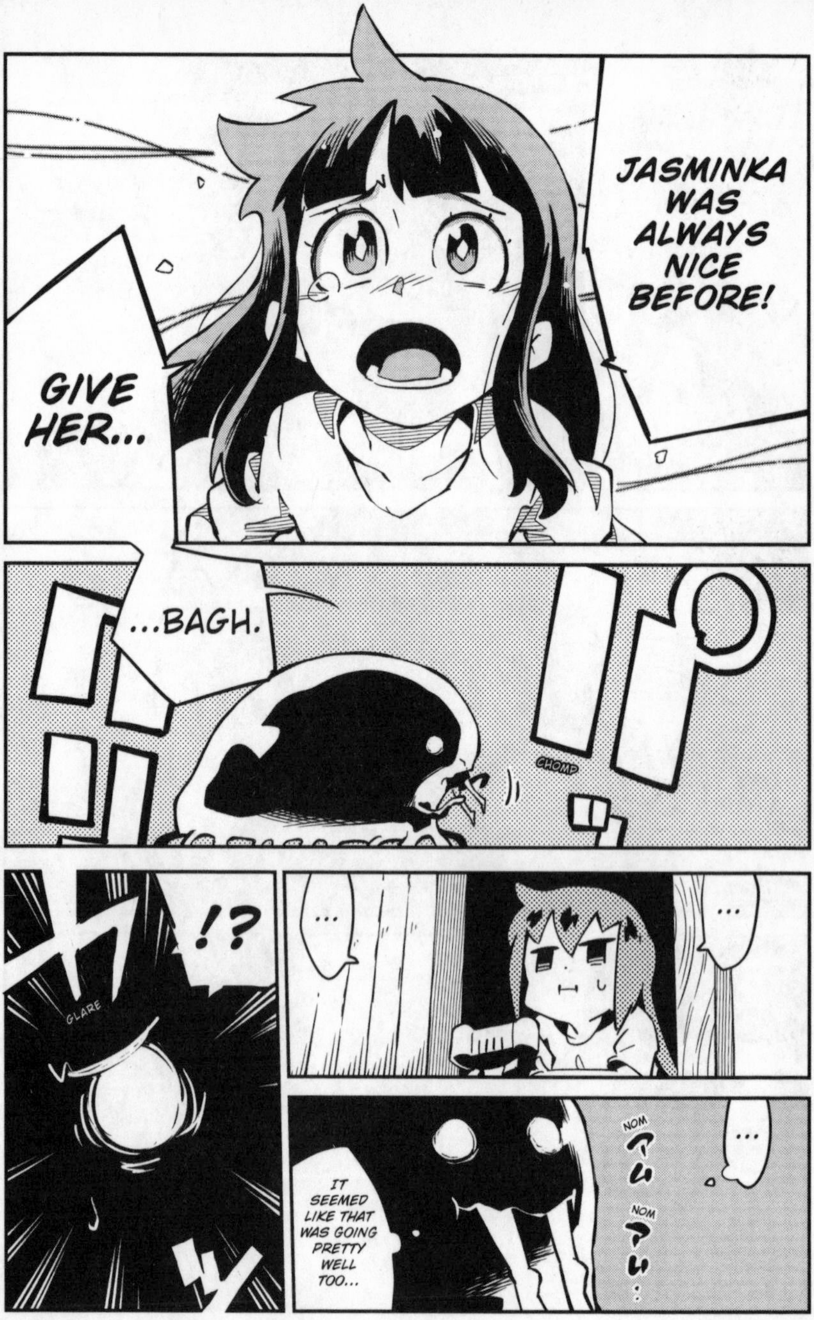
JASMINKA WAS ALWAYS NICE BEFORE!
GIVE HER...
...BAGH.
CHOMP
...
...
...
NOM
アム
NOM
アム..
IT SEEMED LIKE THAT WAS GOING PRETTY WELL TOO...
!?
GLARE

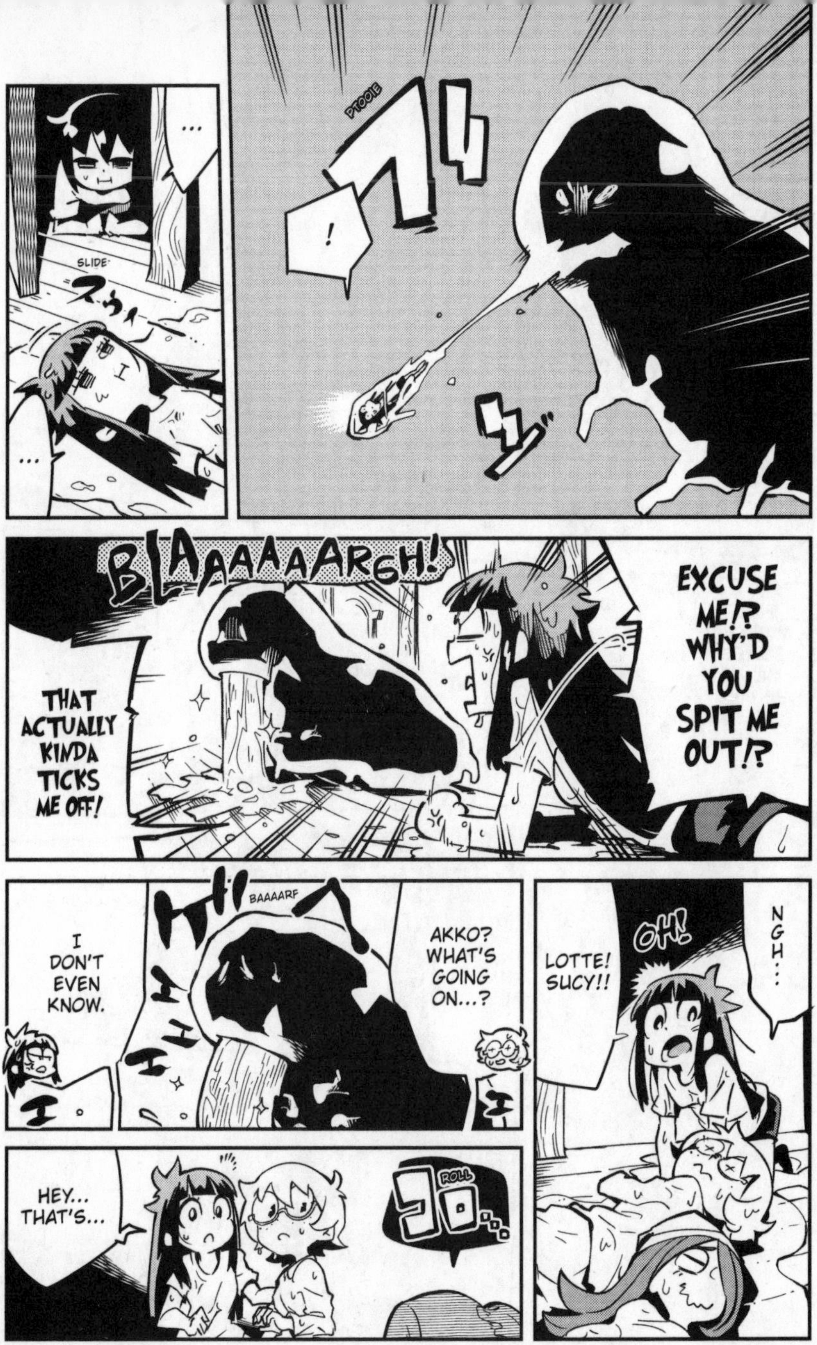
PTOOIE
!
...
SLIDE
...
EXCUSE ME!? WHY'D YOU SPIT ME OUT!?
BLAAAAAARGH!
THAT ACTUALLY KINDA TICKS ME OFF!
NGH...
OH!
LOTTE! SUCY!!
AKKO? WHAT'S GOING ON...?
BAAAARF
I DON'T EVEN KNOW.
ROLL
HEY... THAT'S...

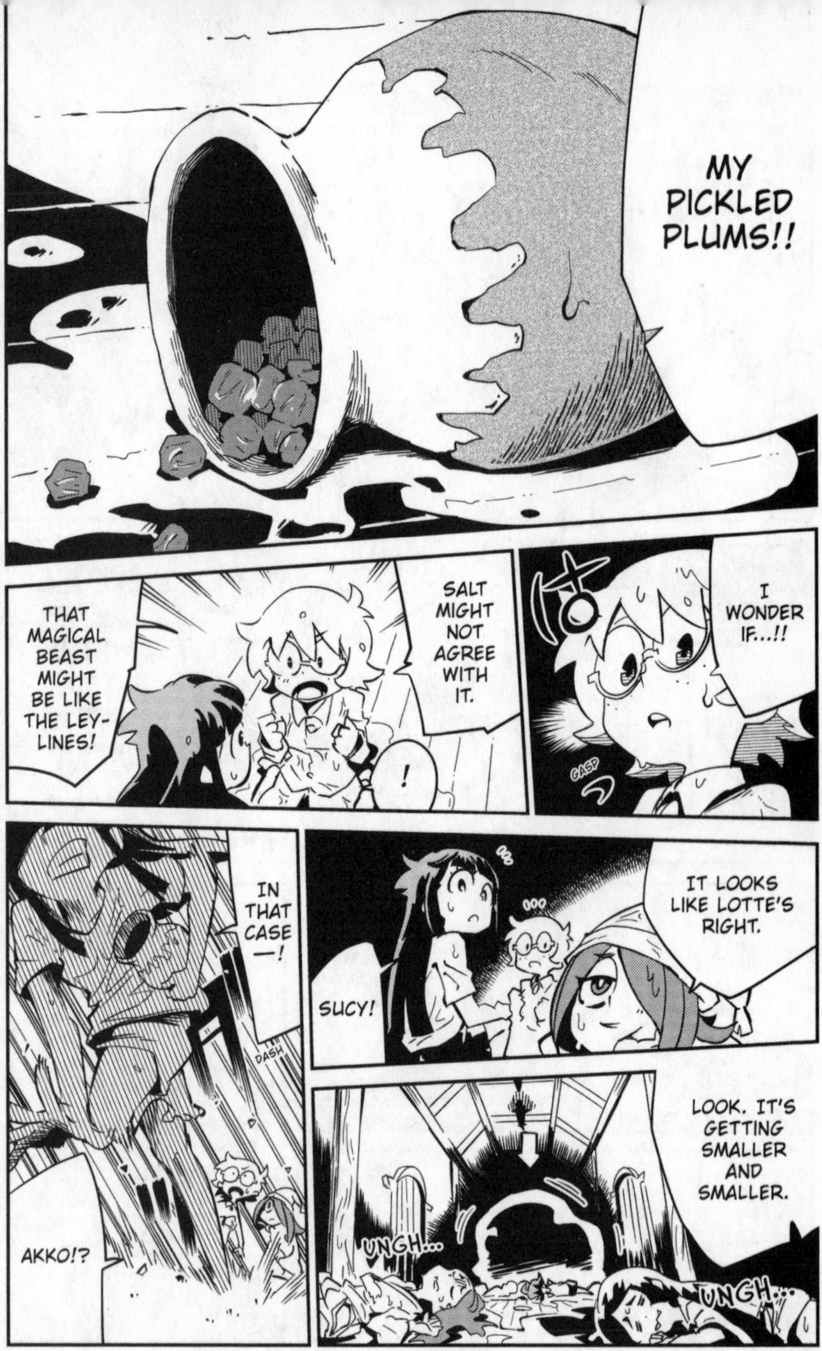
MY PICKLED PLUMS!!
I WONDER IF...!!
GASP
SALT MIGHT NOT AGREE WITH IT.
THAT MAGICAL BEAST MIGHT BE LIKE THE LEY-LINES!
!
IT LOOKS LIKE LOTTE'S RIGHT.
SUCY!
LOOK. IT'S GETTING SMALLER AND SMALLER.
UNGH...
UNGH...
IN THAT CASE—!
DASH
AKKO!?

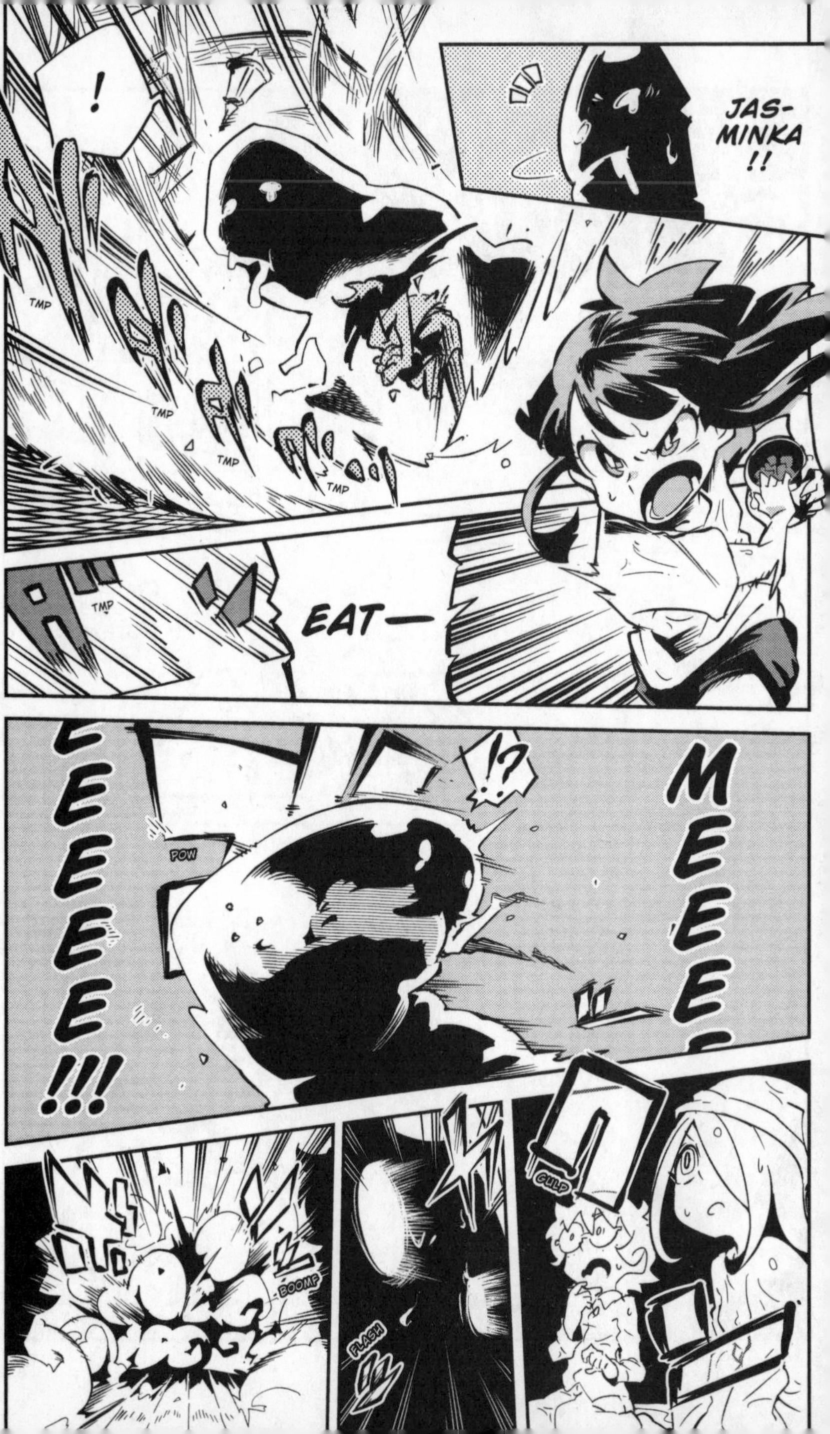
JAS-MINKA !!
!
TMP
TMP
TMP
TMP
TMP
EAT—
MEEEE
!?
POW
EEEEEE!!!
GULP
FLASH
BOOMF

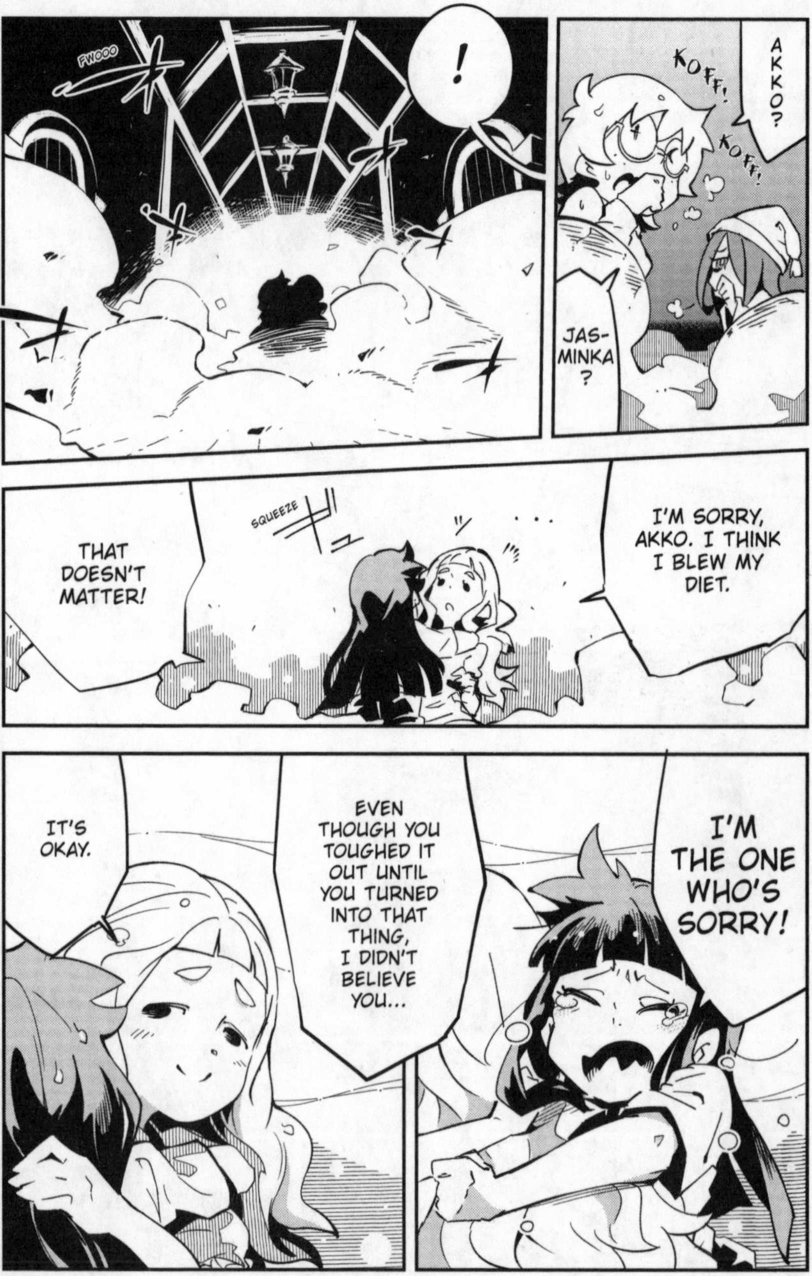
AKKO?
KOFF!
KOFF!
JAS-MINKA?
FWOOO
!
I'M SORRY, AKKO. I THINK I BLEW MY DIET.
...
SQUEEZE
THAT DOESN'T MATTER!
I'M THE ONE WHO'S SORRY!
EVEN THOUGH YOU TOUGHED IT OUT UNTIL YOU TURNED INTO THAT THING, I DIDN'T BELIEVE YOU...
IT'S OKAY.

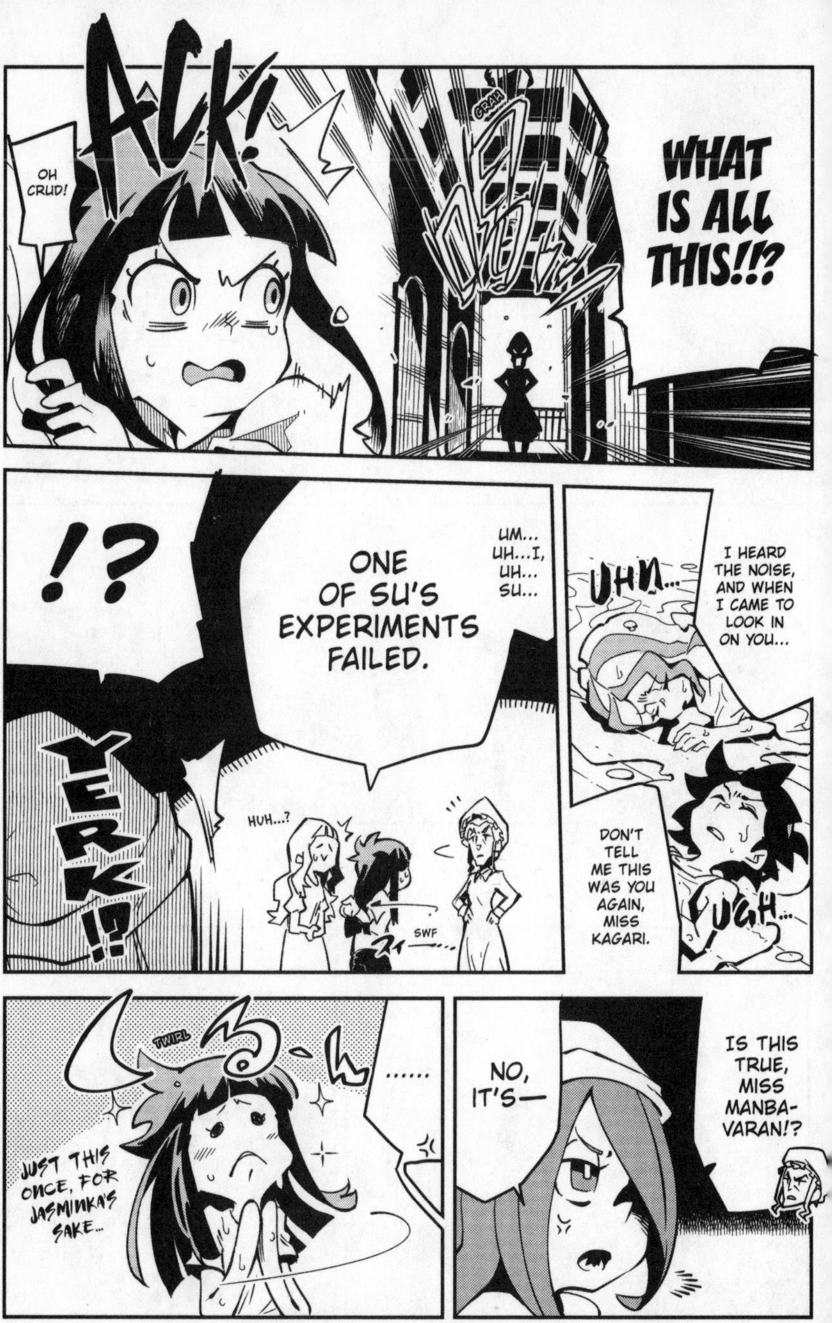
WHAT IS ALL THIS!!?
GRAH
ACK!
OH CRUD!
I HEARD THE NOISE, AND WHEN I CAME TO LOOK IN ON YOU...
UHN...
DON'T TELL ME THIS WAS YOU AGAIN, MISS KAGARI.
UGH...
UM... UH...I, UH... SU...
ONE OF SU'S EXPERIMENTS FAILED.
!?
HUH...?
YERK!!?
SWF
IS THIS TRUE, MISS MANBA-VARAN!?
NO, IT'S—
......
TWIRL
JUST THIS ONCE, FOR JASMINKA'S SAKE...

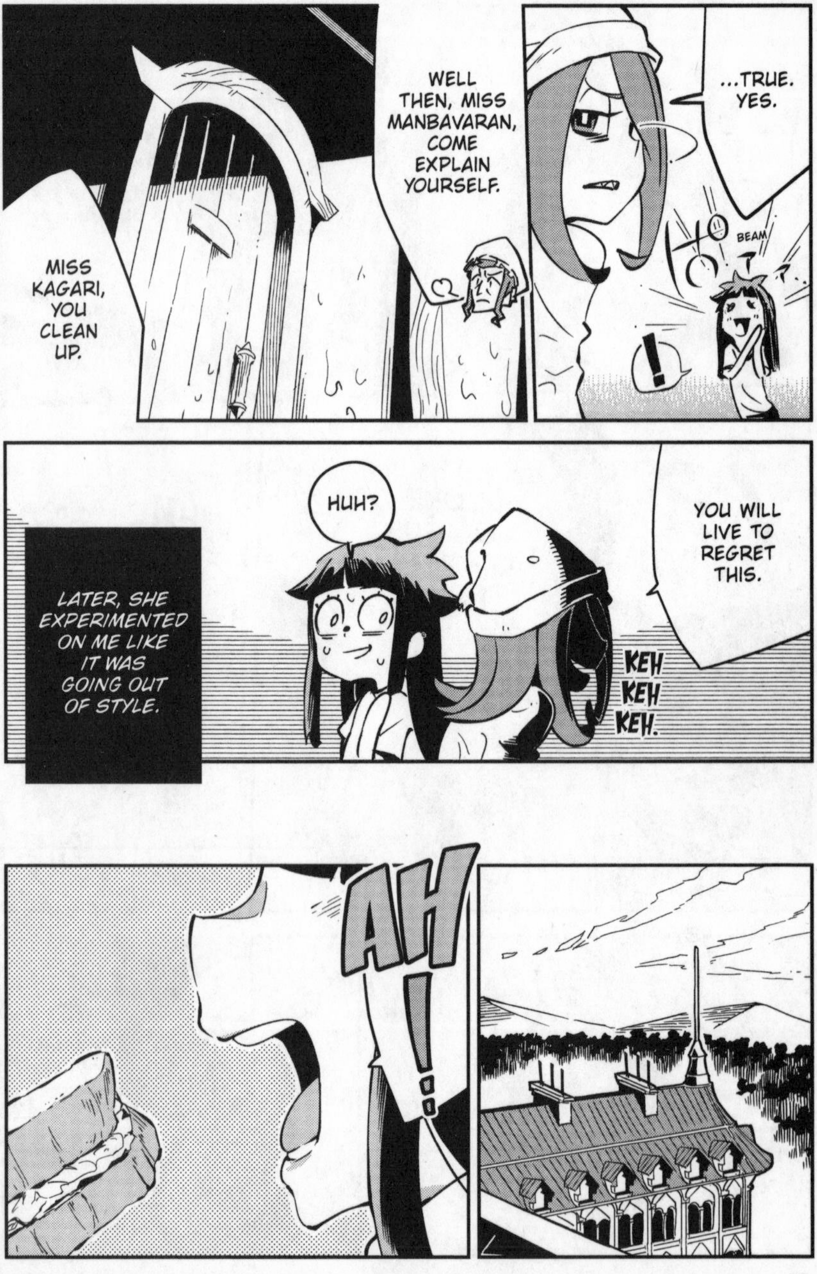
...TRUE. YES.
BEAM
!
WELL THEN, MISS MANBAVARAN, COME EXPLAIN YOURSELF.
MISS KAGARI, YOU CLEAN UP.
YOU WILL LIVE TO REGRET THIS.
KEH KEH KEH.
HUH?
LATER, SHE EXPERIMENTED ON ME LIKE IT WAS GOING OUT OF STYLE.
AH!

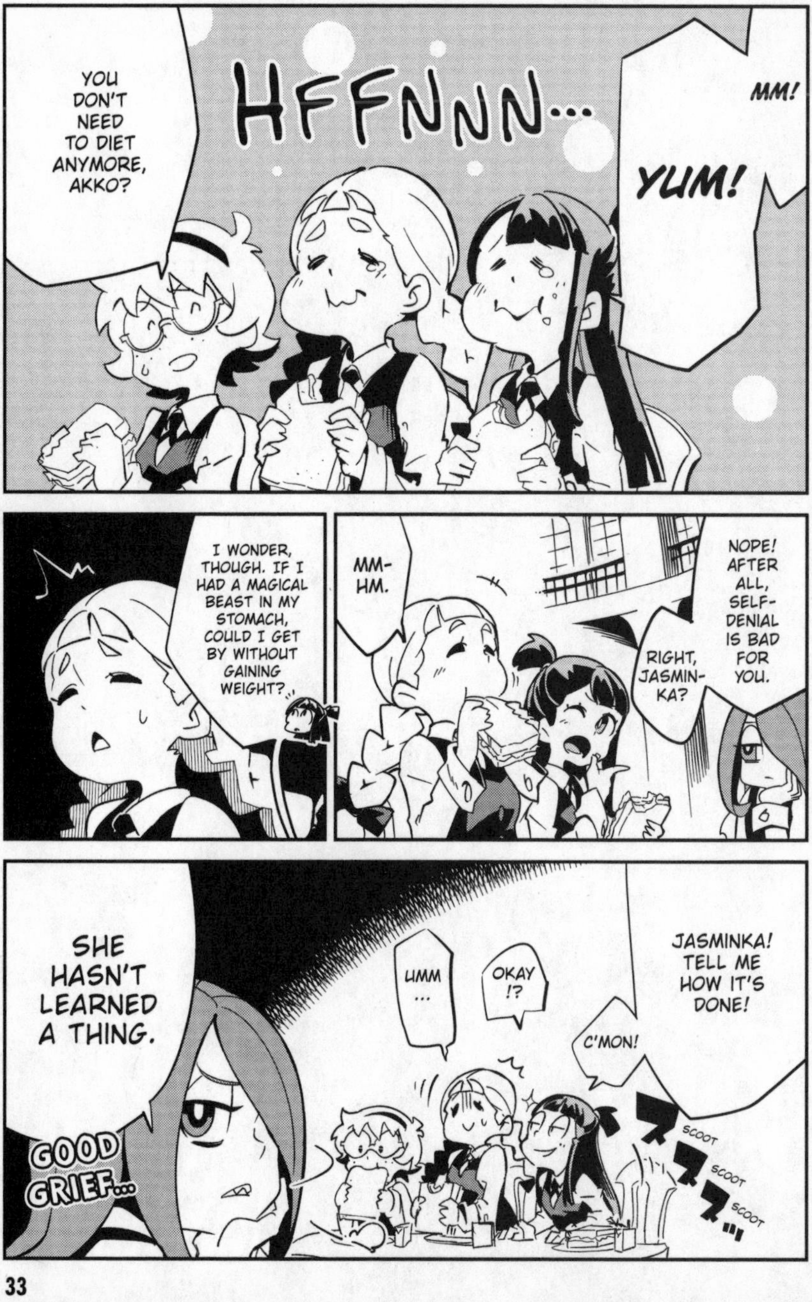
MM!
YUM!
HFFNNN...
YOU DON'T NEED TO DIET ANYMORE, AKKO?
NOPE! AFTER ALL, SELF-DENIAL IS BAD FOR YOU.
RIGHT, JASMINKA?
MM-HM.
I WONDER, THOUGH. IF I HAD A MAGICAL BEAST IN MY STOMACH, COULD I GET BY WITHOUT GAINING WEIGHT?
JASMINKA! TELL ME HOW IT'S DONE!
C'MON!
OKAY!?
UMM...
SHE HASN'T LEARNED A THING.
SCOOT
SCOOT
SCOOT
GOOD GRIEF...

Little Witch Academia

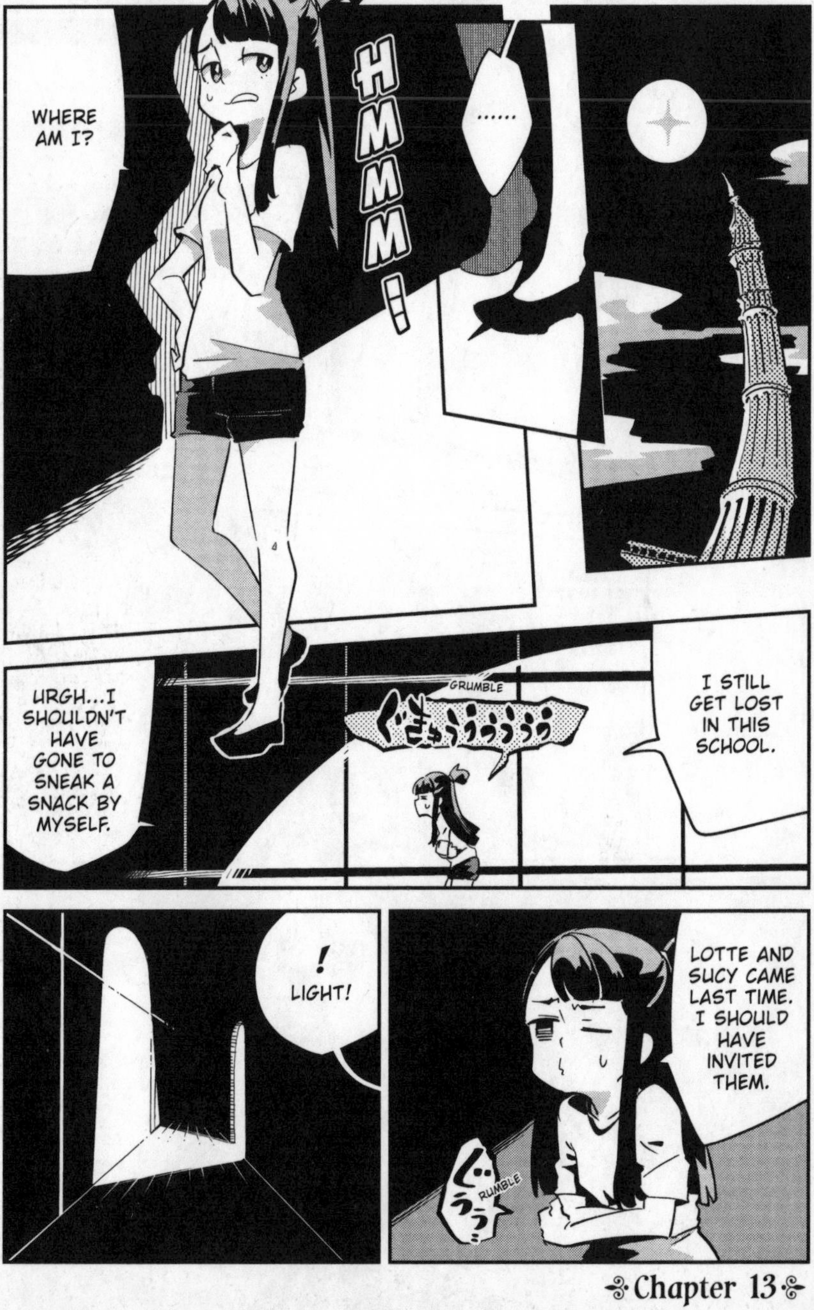
......
HMMM
WHERE AM I?
I STILL GET LOST IN THIS SCHOOL.
GRUMBLE
URGH...I SHOULDN'T HAVE GONE TO SNEAK A SNACK BY MYSELF.
LOTTE AND SUCY CAME LAST TIME. I SHOULD HAVE INVITED THEM.
RUMBLE
!
LIGHT!

Chapter 13

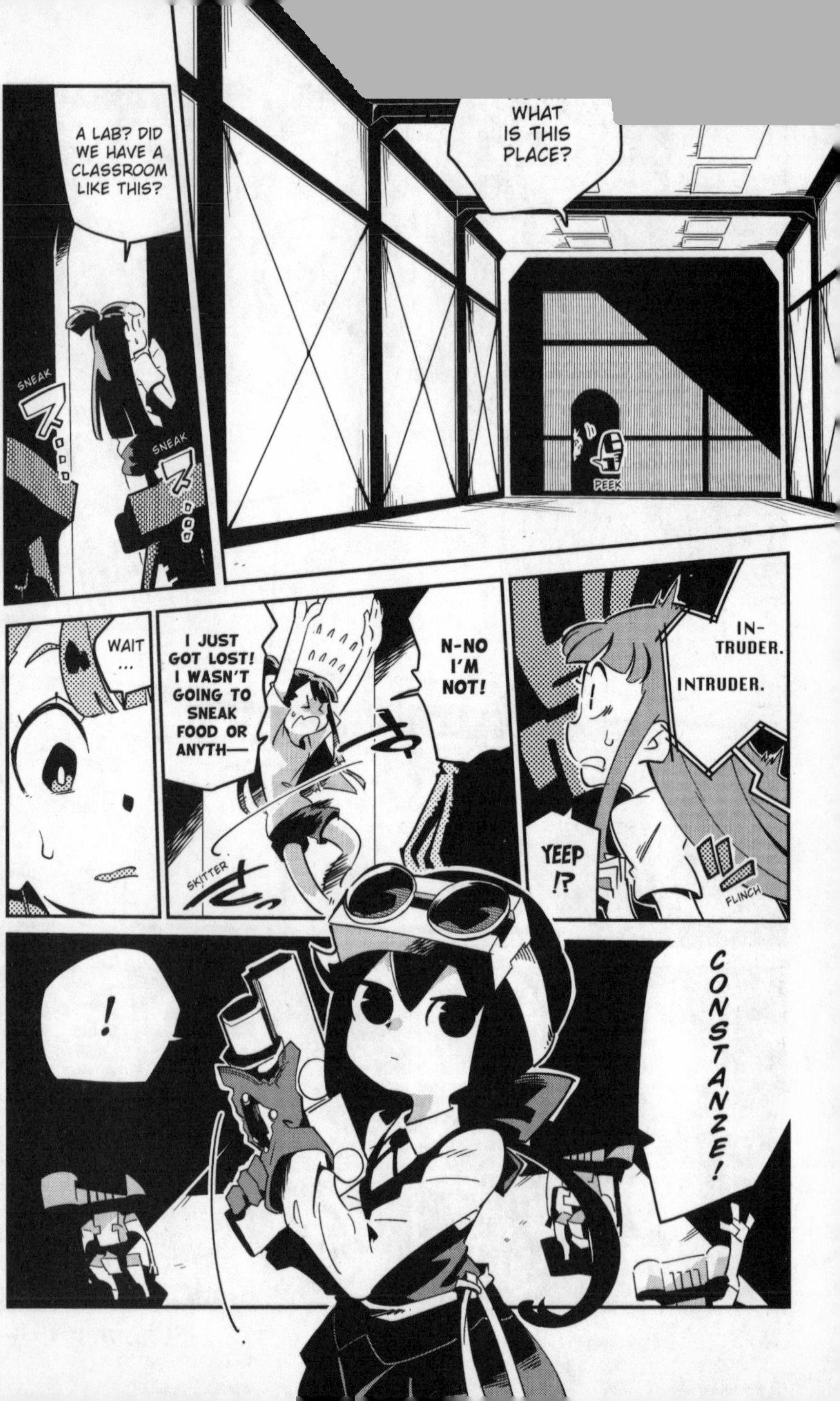
WHAT IS THIS PLACE?
PEEK
A LAB? DID WE HAVE A CLASSROOM LIKE THIS?
SNEAK
SNEAK
IN-TRUDER.
INTRUDER.
YEEP !?
FLINCH
N-NO I'M NOT!
I JUST GOT LOST! I WASN'T GOING TO SNEAK FOOD OR ANYTH—
SKITTER
WAIT ...
CONSTANZE!
!

Chapter 13 TRICK OR TREAT

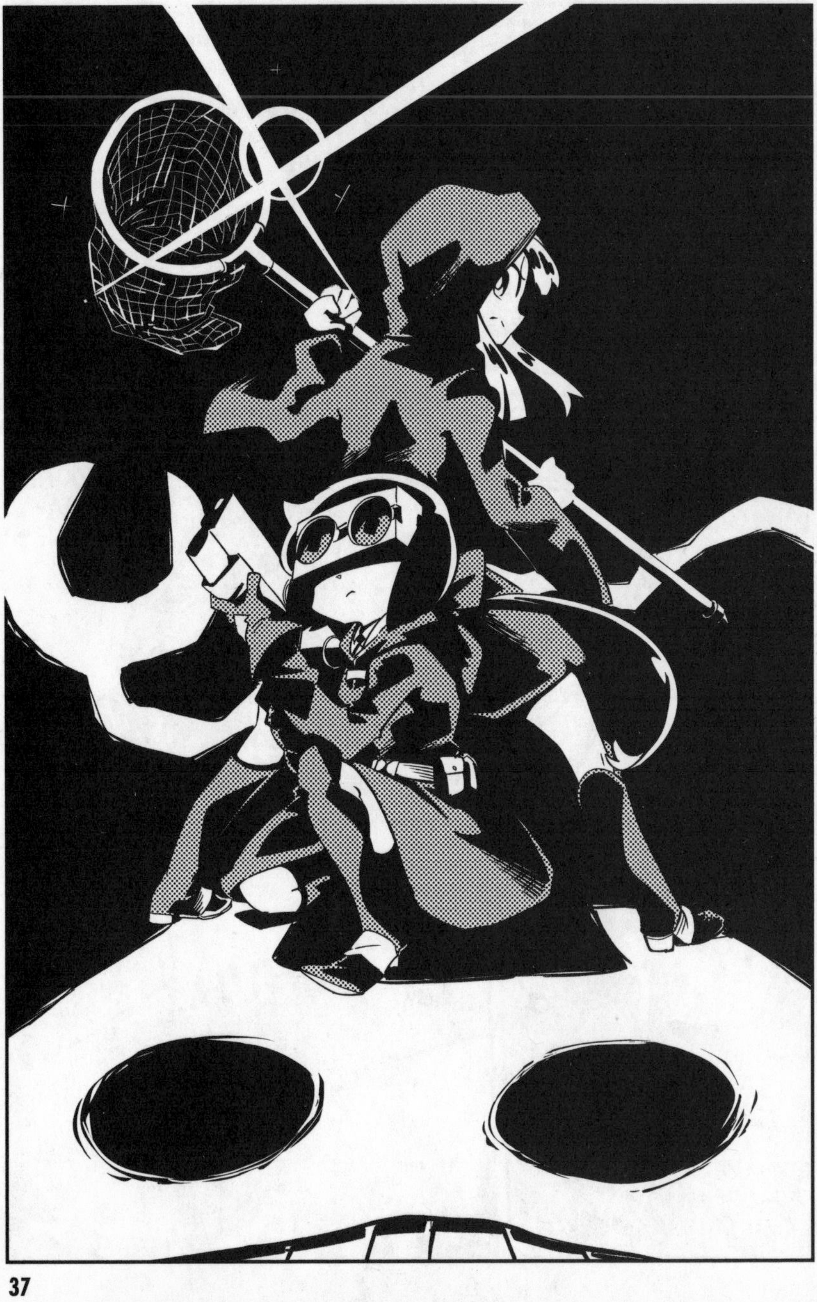

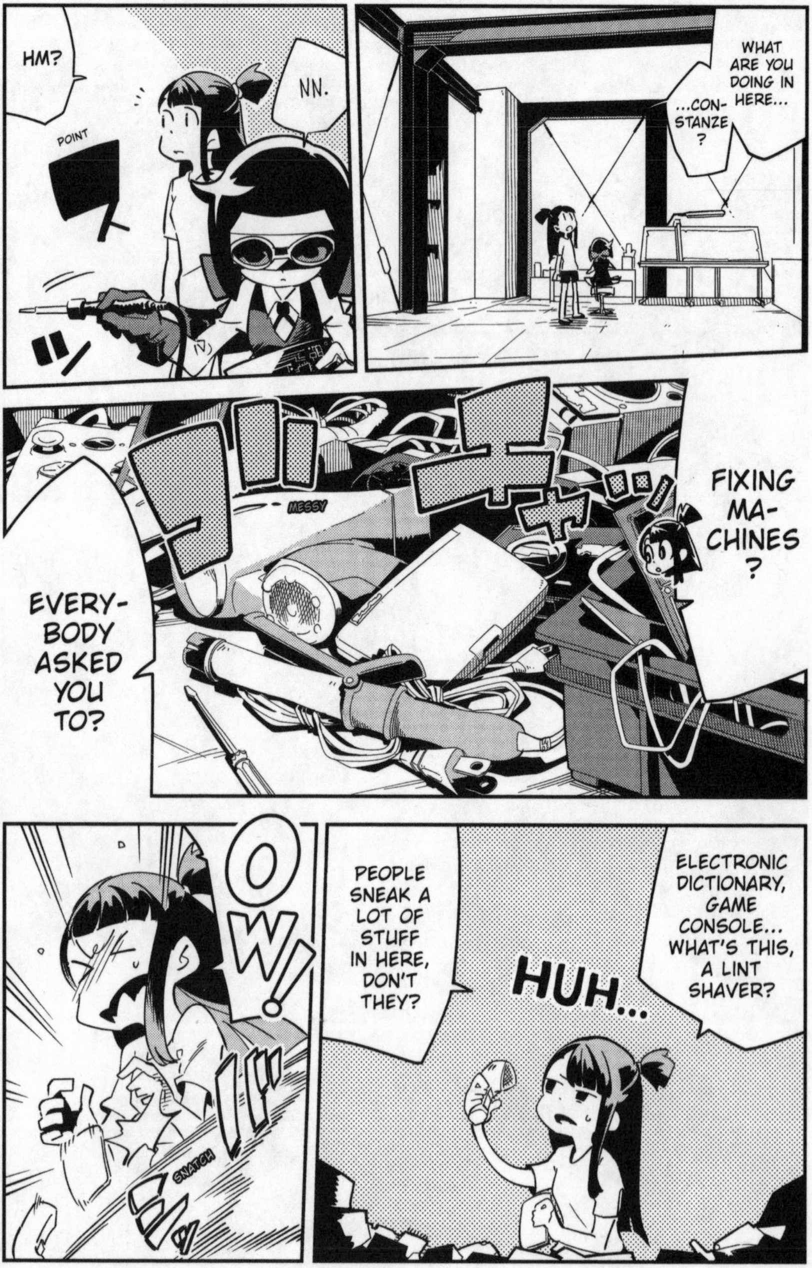
WHAT ARE YOU DOING IN HERE...
...CONSTANZE?
NN.
HM?
POINT
FIXING MA-CHINES?
MESSY
EVERY-BODY ASKED YOU TO?
ELECTRONIC DICTIONARY, GAME CONSOLE... WHAT'S THIS, A LINT SHAVER?
HUH...
PEOPLE SNEAK A LOT OF STUFF IN HERE, DON'T THEY?
OW!
SNATCH

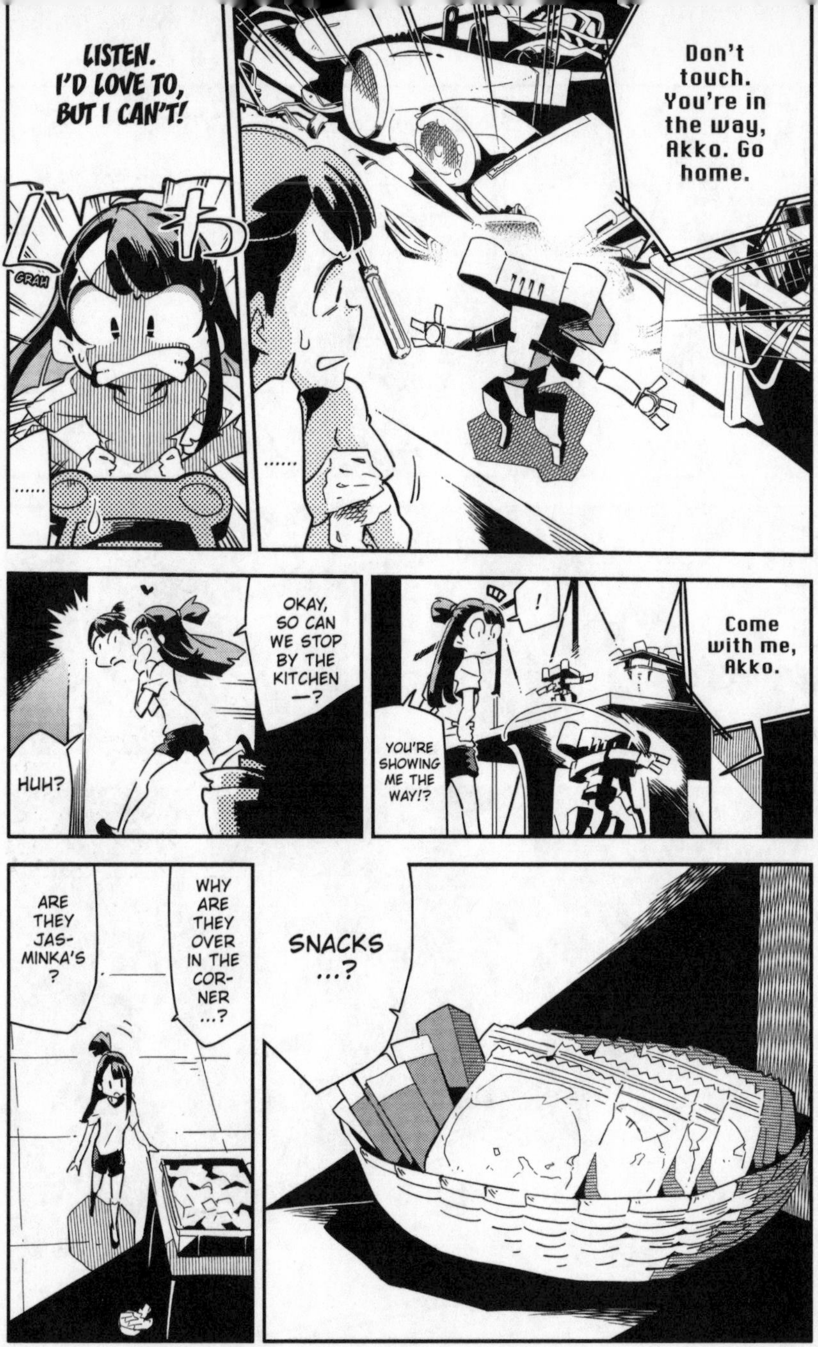
Don't touch. You're in the way, Akko. Go home.
......
LISTEN. I'D LOVE TO, BUT I CAN'T!
GRAH
......
Come with me, Akko.
!
YOU'RE SHOWING ME THE WAY!?
OKAY, SO CAN WE STOP BY THE KITCHEN—?
HUH?
SNACKS ...?
WHY ARE THEY OVER IN THE CORNER ...?
ARE THEY JASMINKA'S?

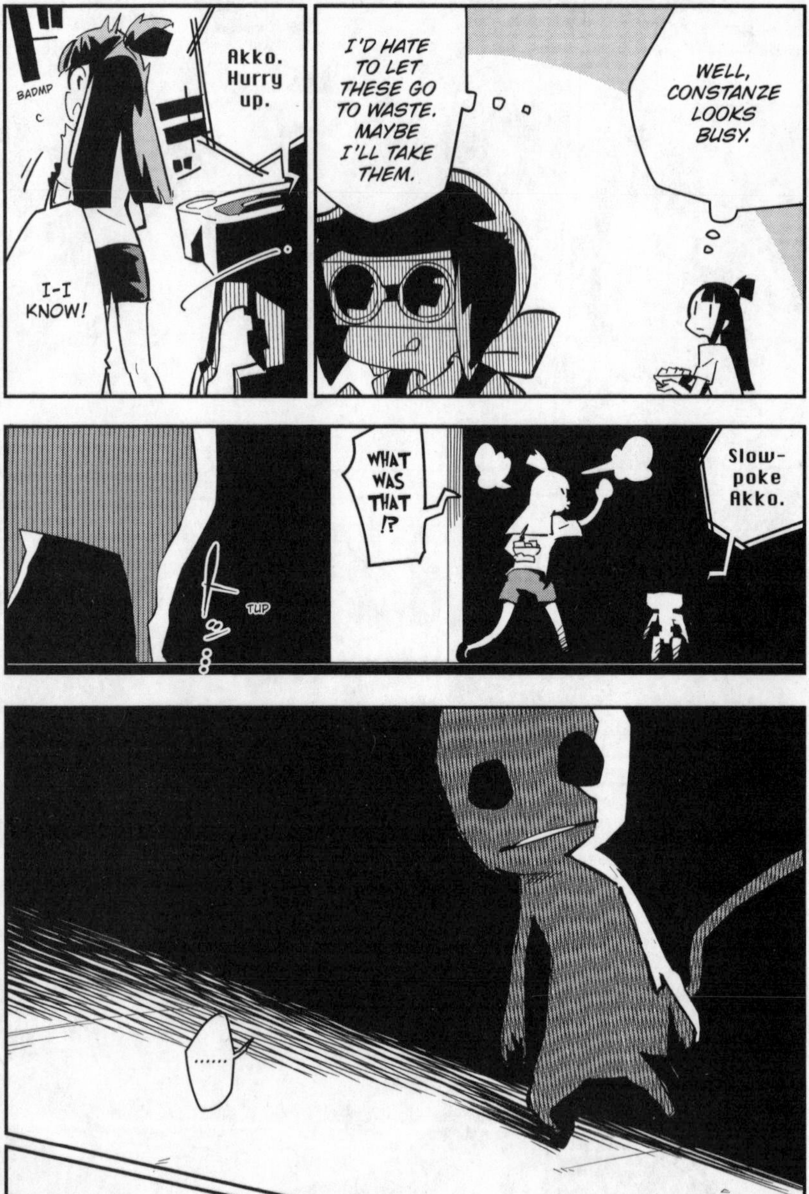
WELL, CONSTANZE LOOKS BUSY.
I'D HATE TO LET THESE GO TO WASTE. MAYBE I'LL TAKE THEM.
Akko. Hurry up.
BADMP
I-I KNOW!
Slow-poke Akko.
WHAT WAS THAT!?
TUP
......

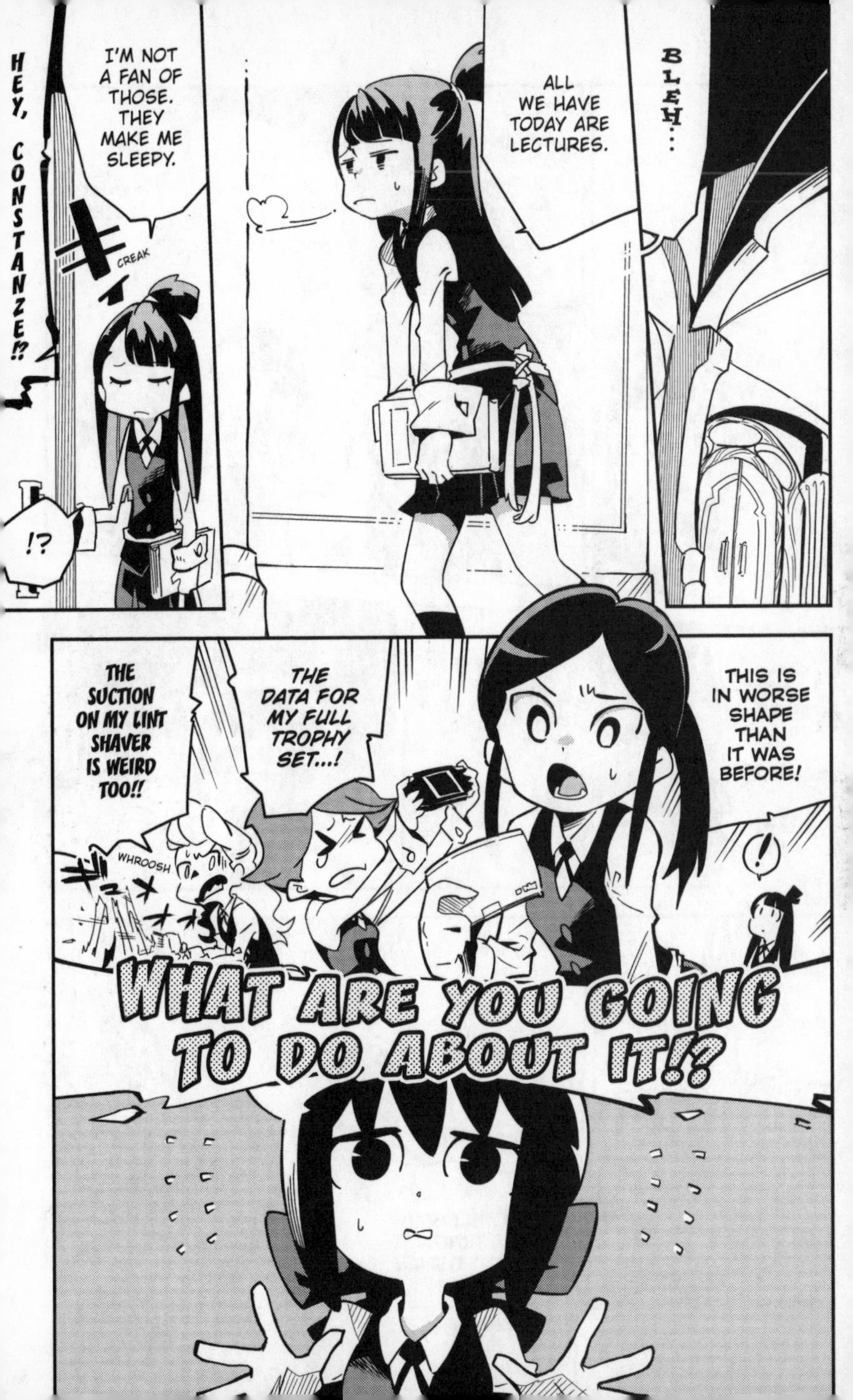
BLEH...
ALL WE HAVE TODAY ARE LECTURES.
I'M NOT A FAN OF THOSE. THEY MAKE ME SLEEPY.
HEY, CONSTANZE!?
CREAK
!?
THIS IS IN WORSE SHAPE THAN IT WAS BEFORE!
!
THE DATA FOR MY FULL TROPHY SET...!
THE SUCTION ON MY LINT SHAVER IS WEIRD TOO!!
WHROOSH
WHAT ARE YOU GOING TO DO ABOUT IT!?

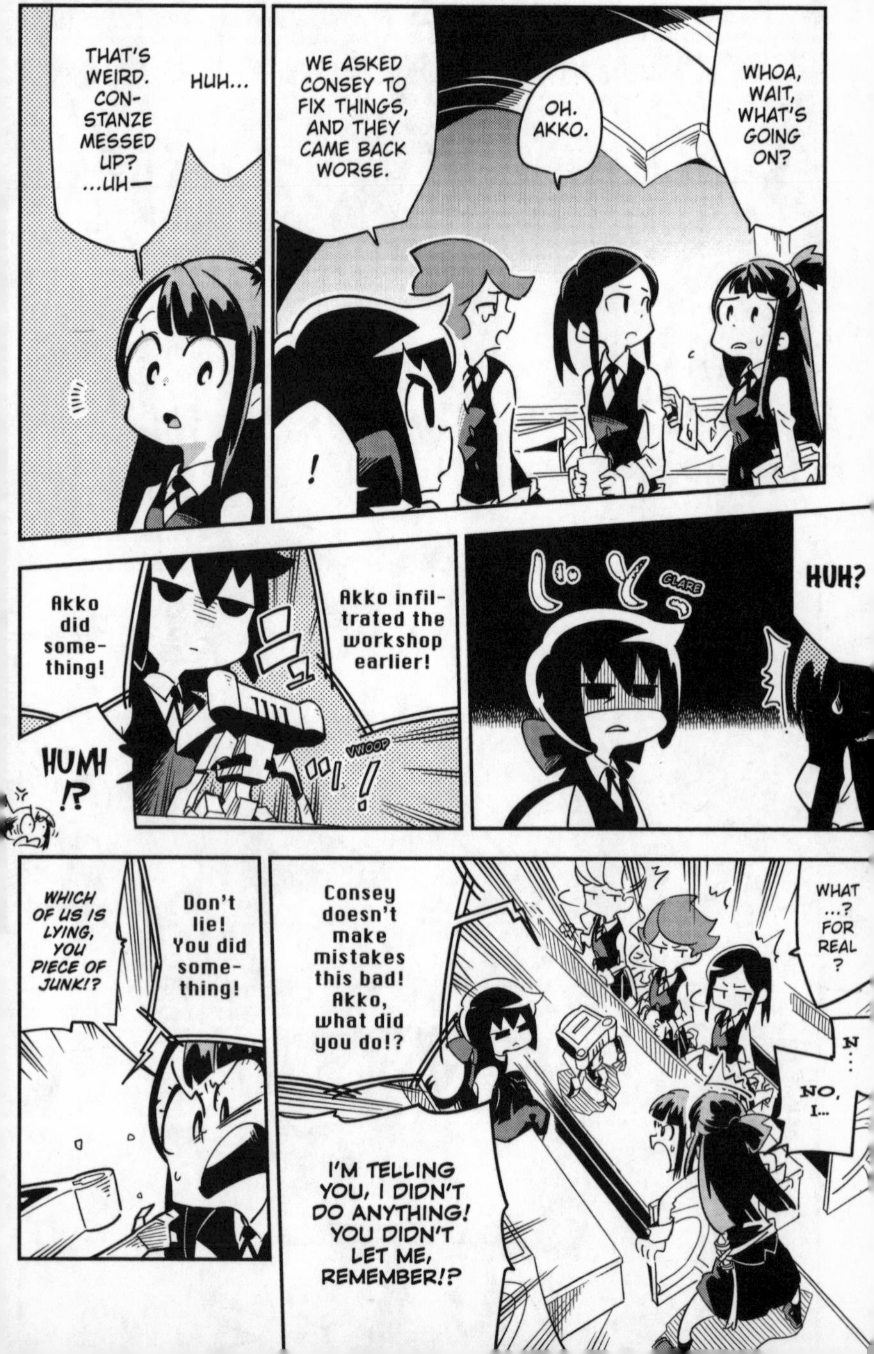
WHOA, WAIT, WHAT'S GOING ON?
OH. AKKO.
WE ASKED CONSEY TO FIX THINGS, AND THEY CAME BACK WORSE.
HUH...
THAT'S WEIRD. CON-STANZE MESSED UP? ...UH—
HUH?
GLARE
Akko infil-trated the workshop earlier!
Akko did some-thing!
VWOOP
HUMH !?
WHAT ...? FOR REAL ?
Consey doesn't make mistakes this bad! Akko, what did you do!?
N...
NO, I...
I'M TELLING YOU, I DIDN'T DO ANYTHING! YOU DIDN'T LET ME, REMEMBER!?
Don't lie! You did some-thing!
WHICH OF US IS LYING, YOU PIECE OF JUNK!?

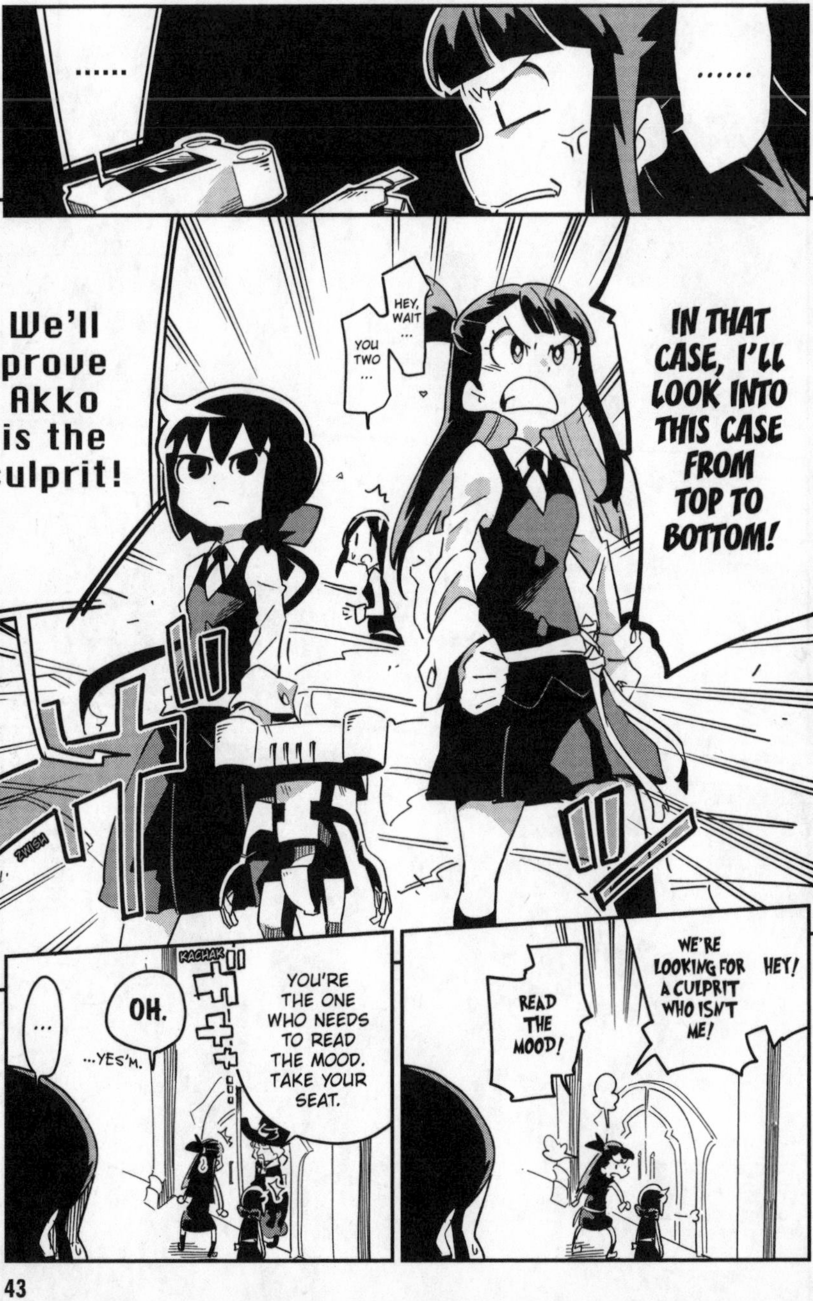
......
......
IN THAT CASE, I'LL LOOK INTO THIS CASE FROM TOP TO BOTTOM!
HEY, WAIT ... YOU TWO ...
We'll prove Akko is the culprit!
ZWISH
HEY!
WE'RE LOOKING FOR A CULPRIT WHO ISN'T ME!
READ THE MOOD!
YOU'RE THE ONE WHO NEEDS TO READ THE MOOD. TAKE YOUR SEAT.
KACHAK
OH.
...YES'M.
...

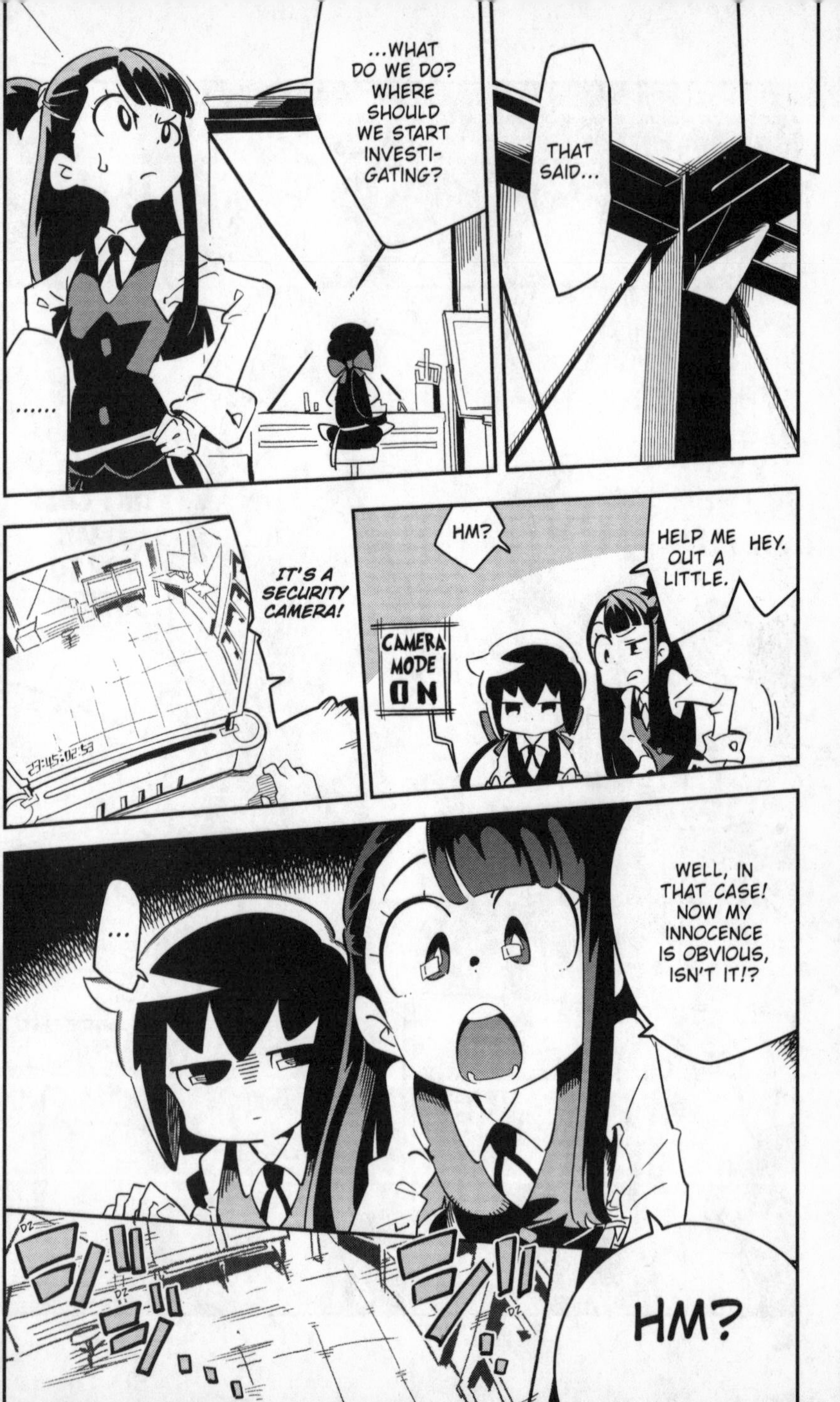
THAT SAID...
...WHAT DO WE DO? WHERE SHOULD WE START INVESTIGATING?
......
HEY.
HELP ME OUT A LITTLE.
HM?
CAMERA MODE ON
IT'S A SECURITY CAMERA!
23:45:02:53
WELL, IN THAT CASE! NOW MY INNOCENCE IS OBVIOUS, ISN'T IT!?
...
DZ
DZ
DZ
HM?

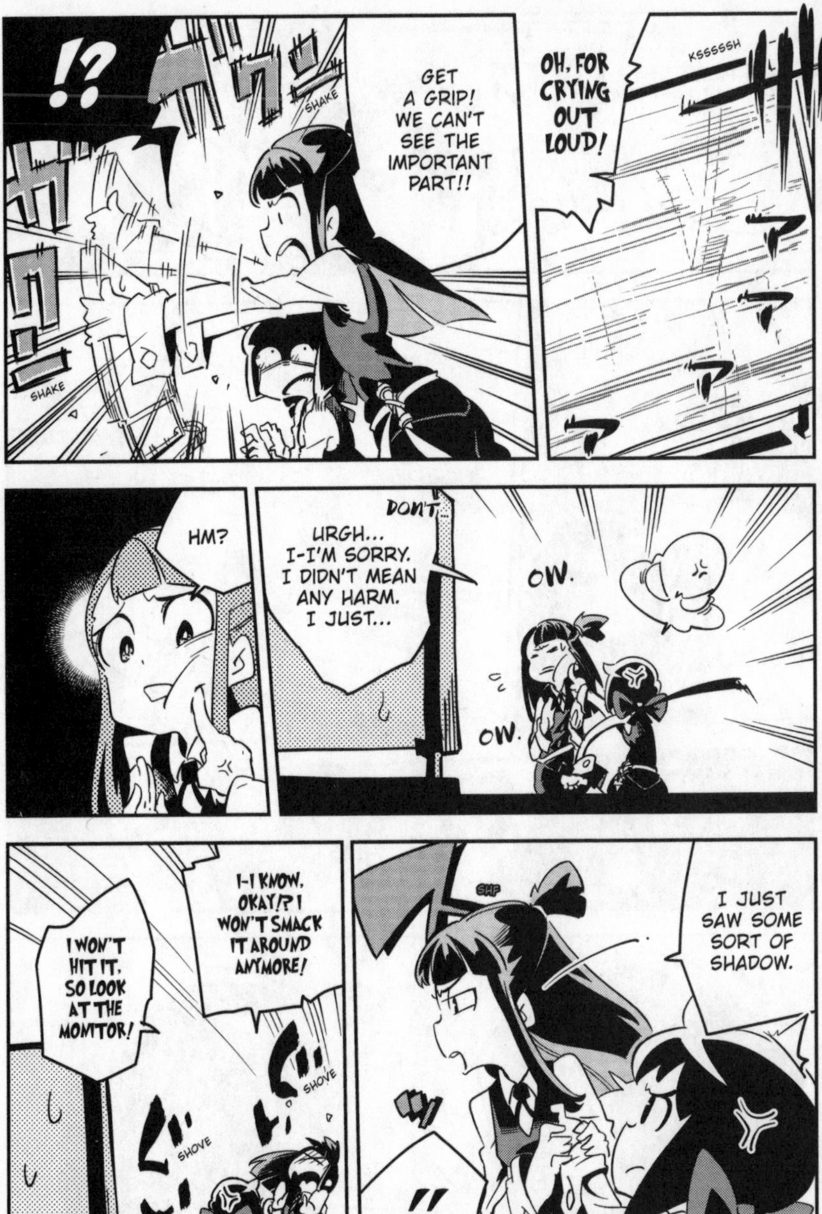
KSSSSSH
OH, FOR CRYING OUT LOUD!
GET A GRIP! WE CAN'T SEE THE IMPORTANT PART!!
SHAKE
!?
SHAKE
OW.
OW.
DON'T...
URGH... I-I'M SORRY. I DIDN'T MEAN ANY HARM. I JUST...
HM?
SHF
I JUST SAW SOME SORT OF SHADOW.
!!
I-I KNOW, OKAY!? I WON'T SMACK IT AROUND ANYMORE!
I WON'T HIT IT, SO LOOK AT THE MONITOR!
SHOVE
SHOVE

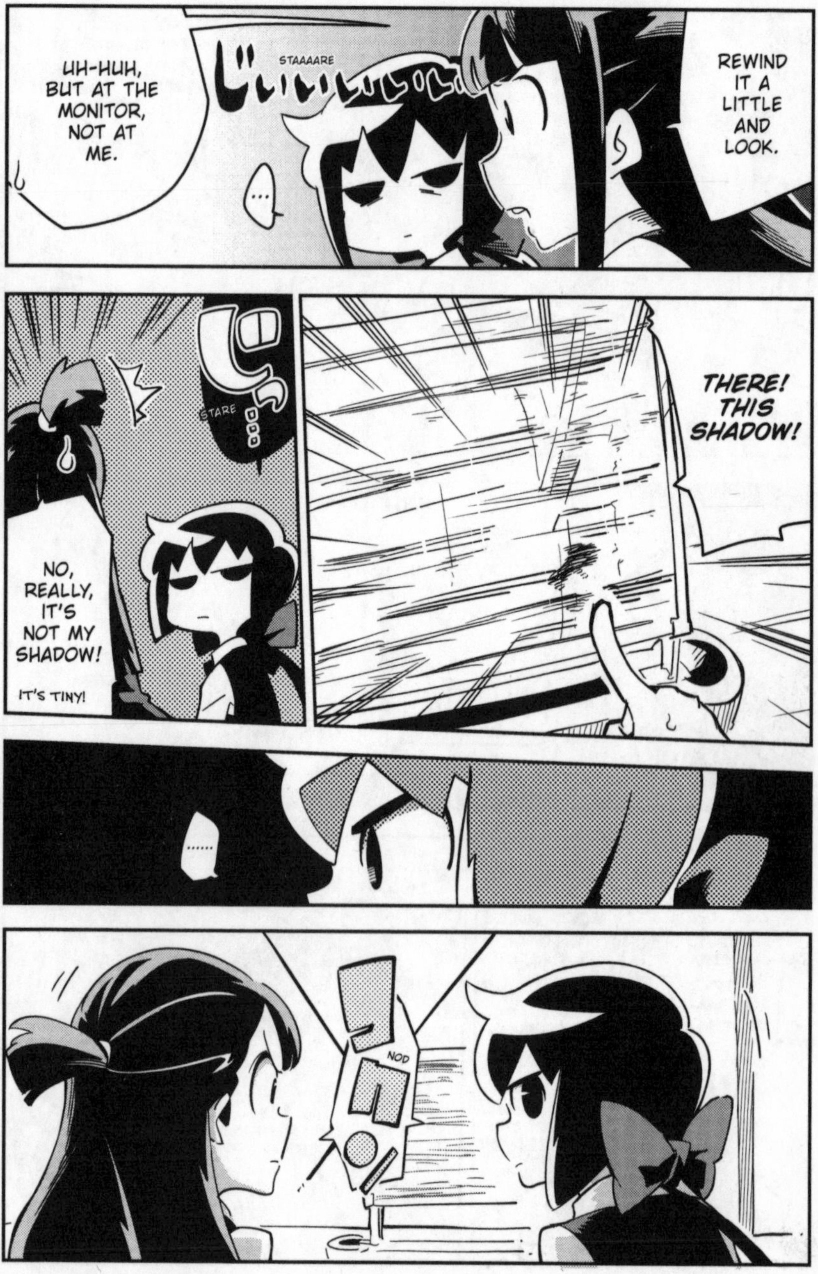
REWIND IT A LITTLE AND LOOK.
STAAAARE
...
UH-HUH, BUT AT THE MONITOR, NOT AT ME.
THERE! THIS SHADOW!
STARE
NO, REALLY, IT'S NOT MY SHADOW!
IT'S TINY!
......
NOD

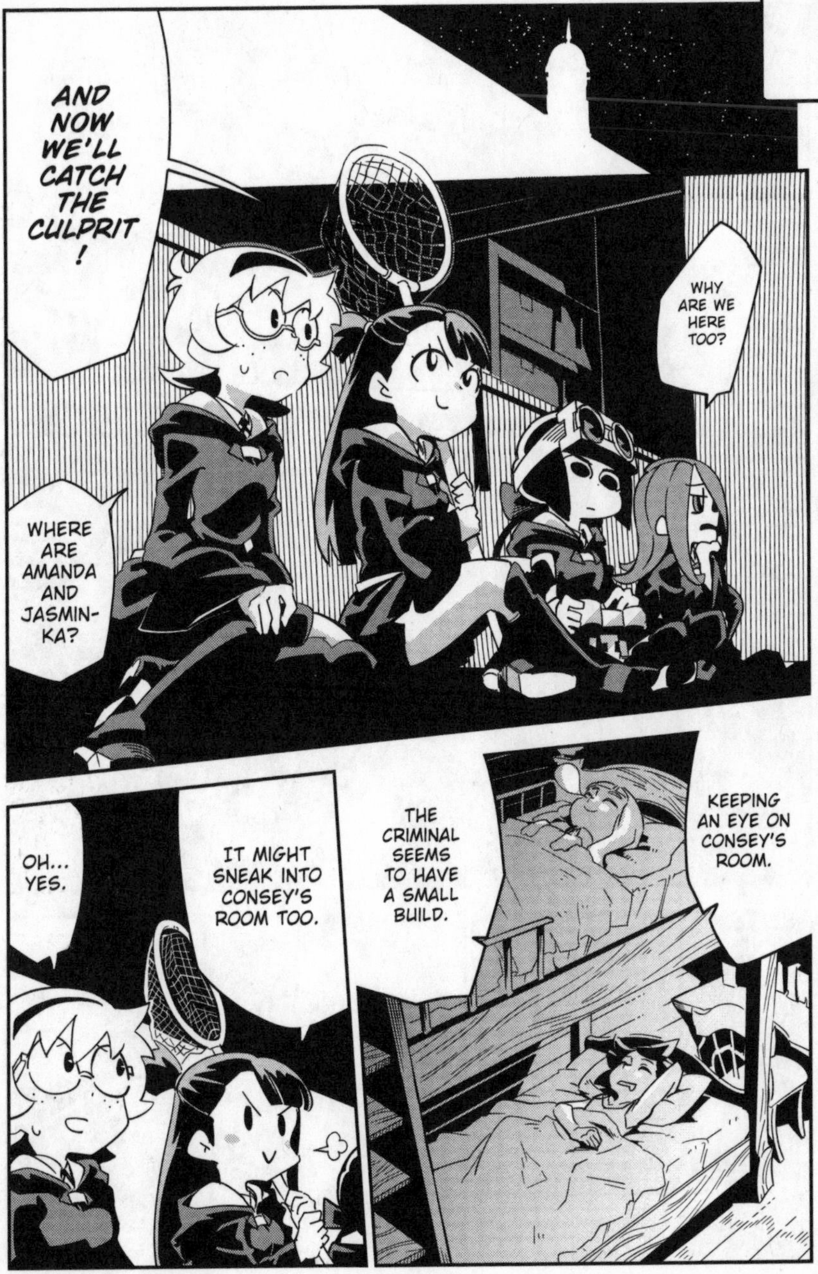
AND NOW WE'LL CATCH THE CULPRIT!
WHY ARE WE HERE TOO?
WHERE ARE AMANDA AND JASMIN-KA?
KEEPING AN EYE ON CONSEY'S ROOM.
THE CRIMINAL SEEMS TO HAVE A SMALL BUILD.
IT MIGHT SNEAK INTO CONSEY'S ROOM TOO.
OH... YES.

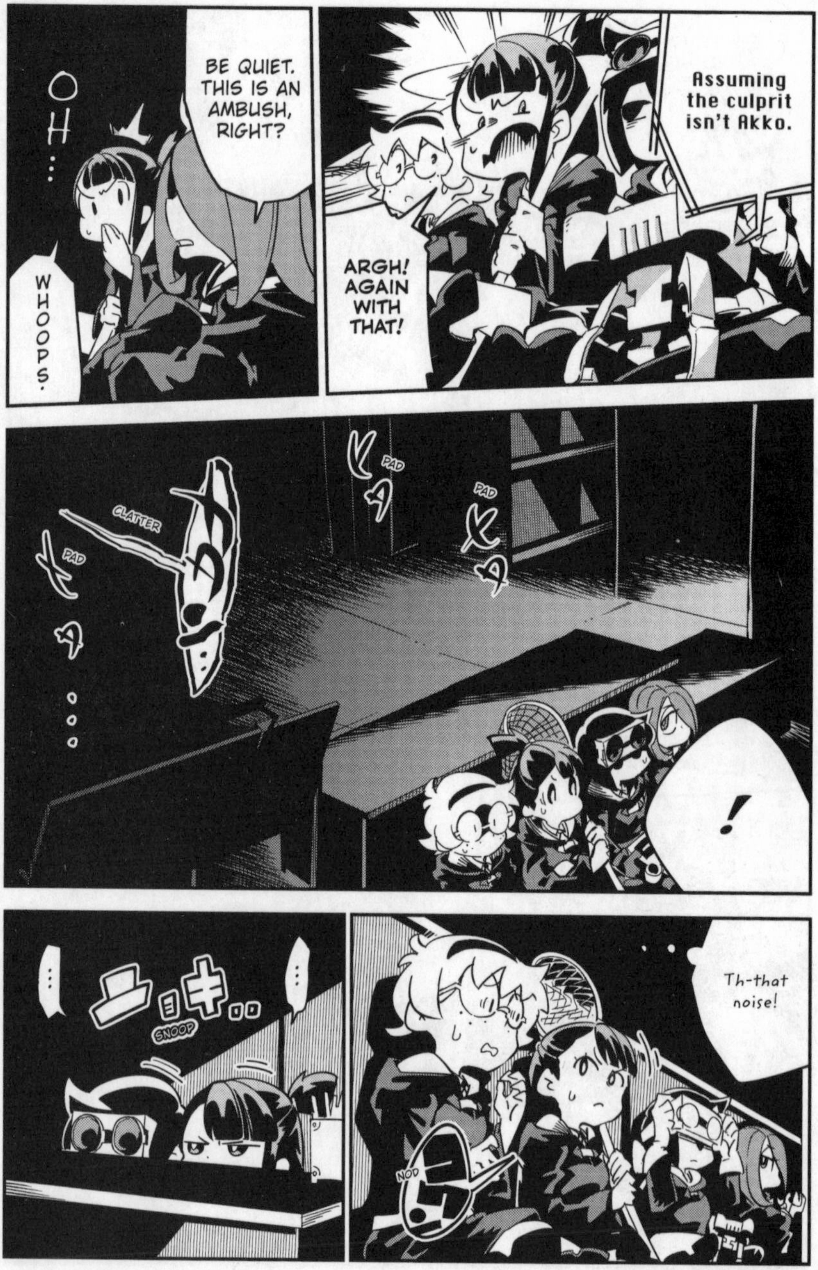
Assuming the culprit isn't Akko.
ARGH! AGAIN WITH THAT!
BE QUIET. THIS IS AN AMBUSH, RIGHT?
OH...
WHOOPS.
!
PAD
PAD
CLATTER
PAD
...
...
Th-that noise!
NOD
...
...
SNOOP

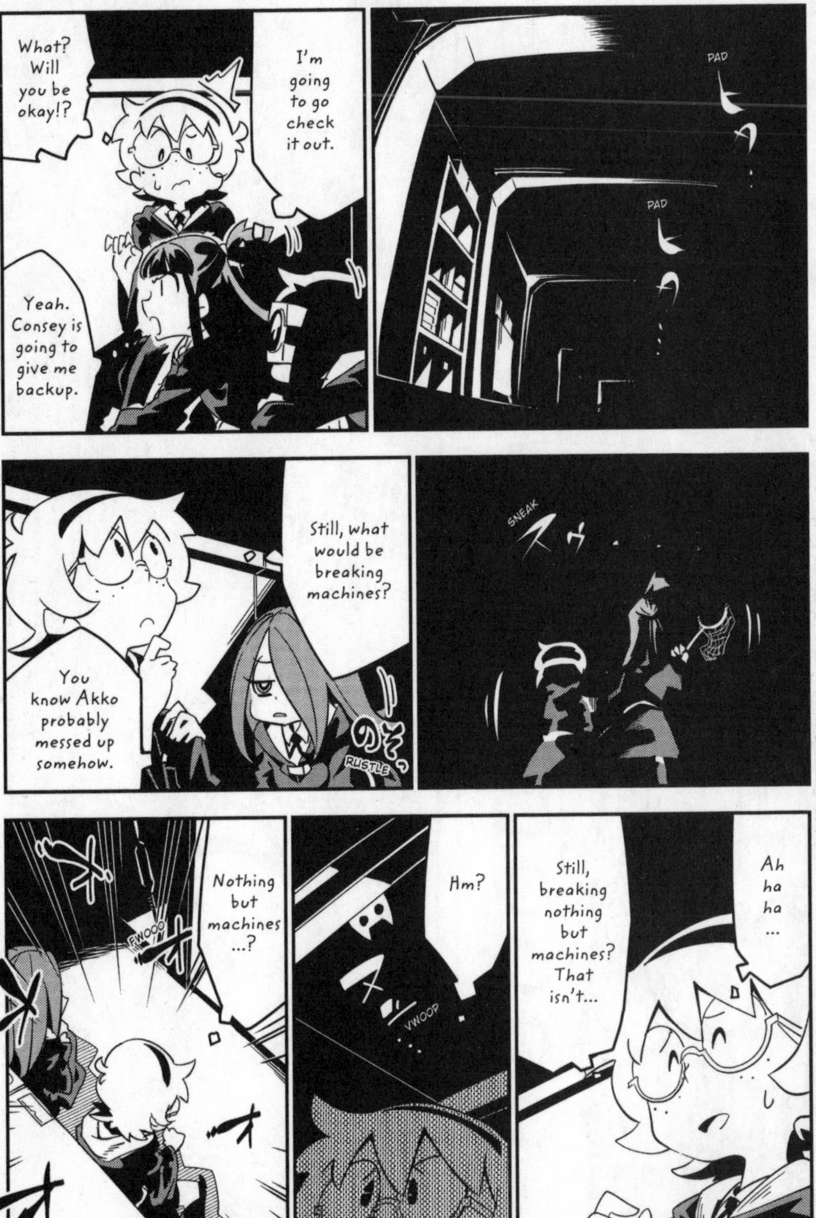
PAD
PAD
I'm going to go check it out.
What? Will you be okay!?
Yeah. Consey is going to give me backup.
SNEAK
Still, what would be breaking machines?
You know Akko probably messed up somehow.
RUSTLE
Ah ha ha ...
Still, breaking nothing but machines? That isn't...
Hm?
VWOOP
Nothing but machines ...?
FWOOO

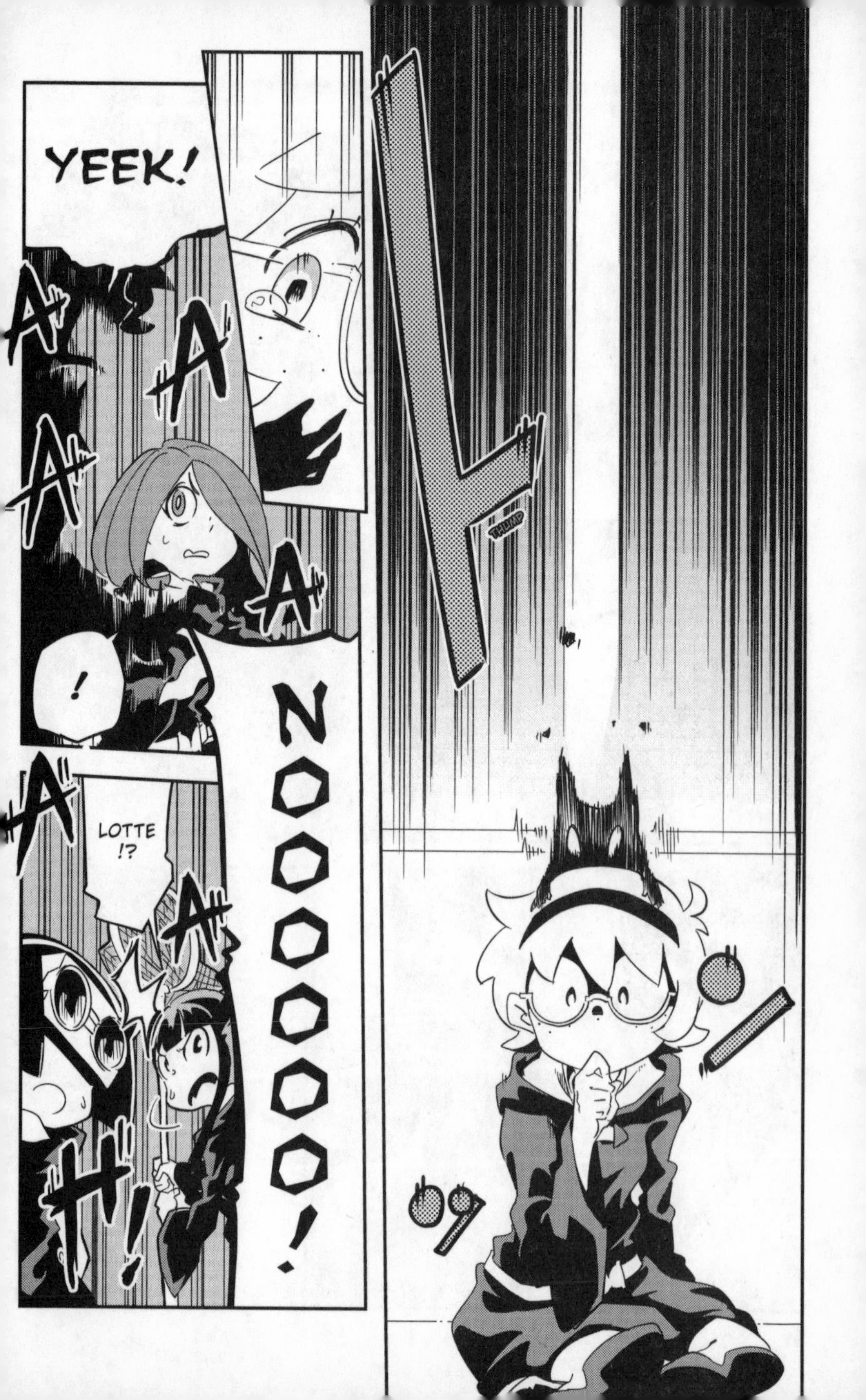
THUMP
YEEK!
A A A A
!
LOTTE !?
A A H!
NOOOOOO!

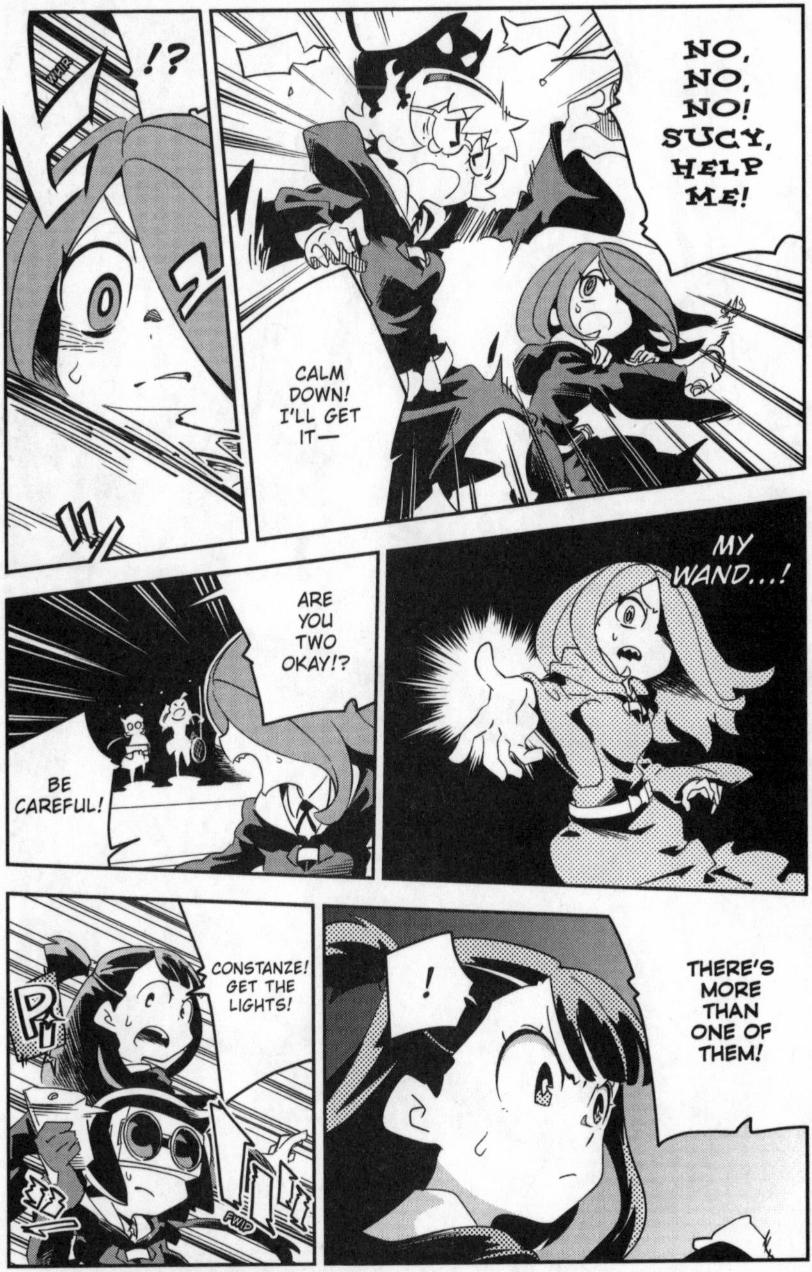
NO, NO, NO! SUCY, HELP ME!
CALM DOWN! I'LL GET IT—
WHIR
!?
MY WAND...!
ARE YOU TWO OKAY!?
BE CAREFUL!
!
THERE'S MORE THAN ONE OF THEM!
CONSTANZE! GET THE LIGHTS!
PWIP

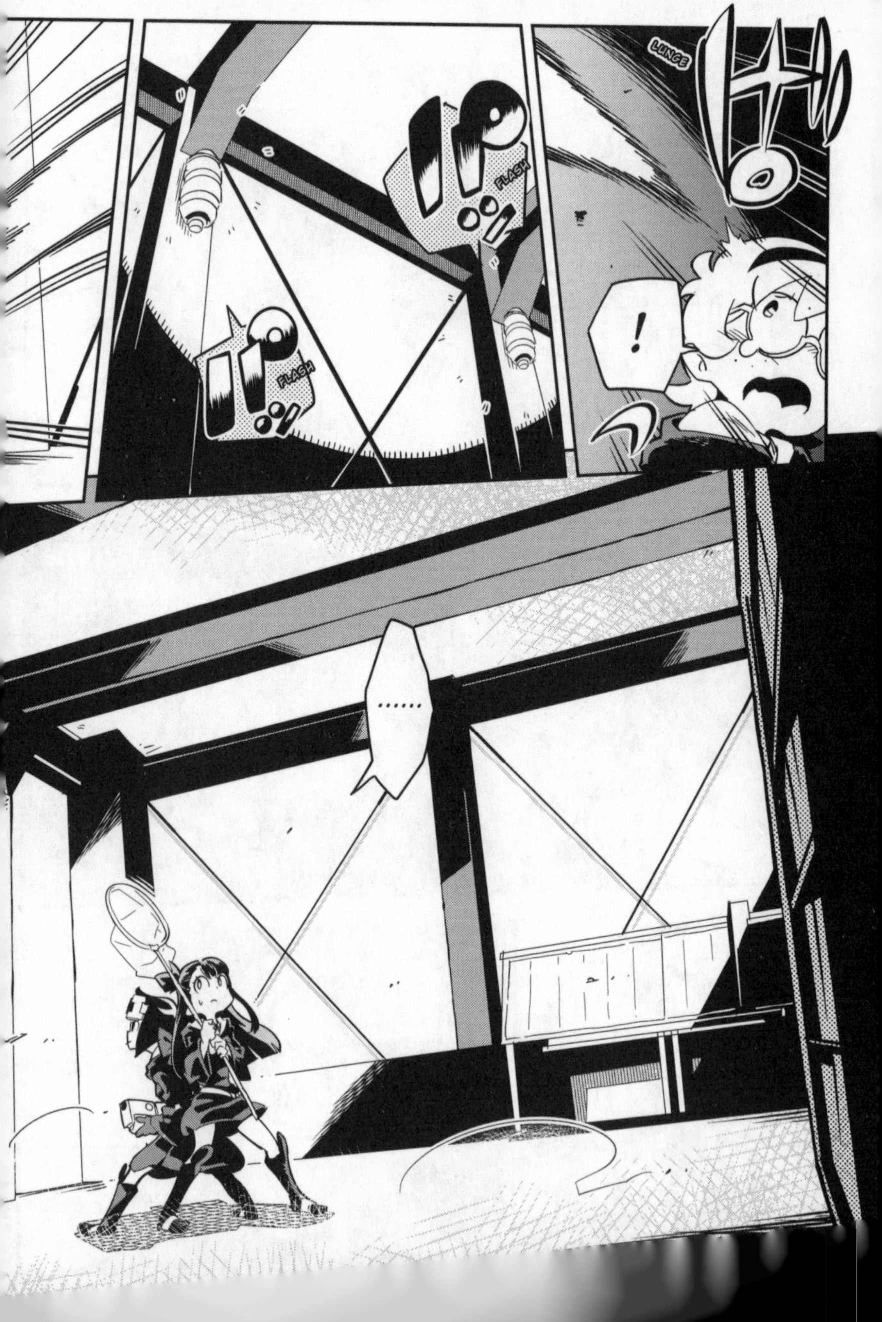
LUNGE
!
FLASH
FLASH
......

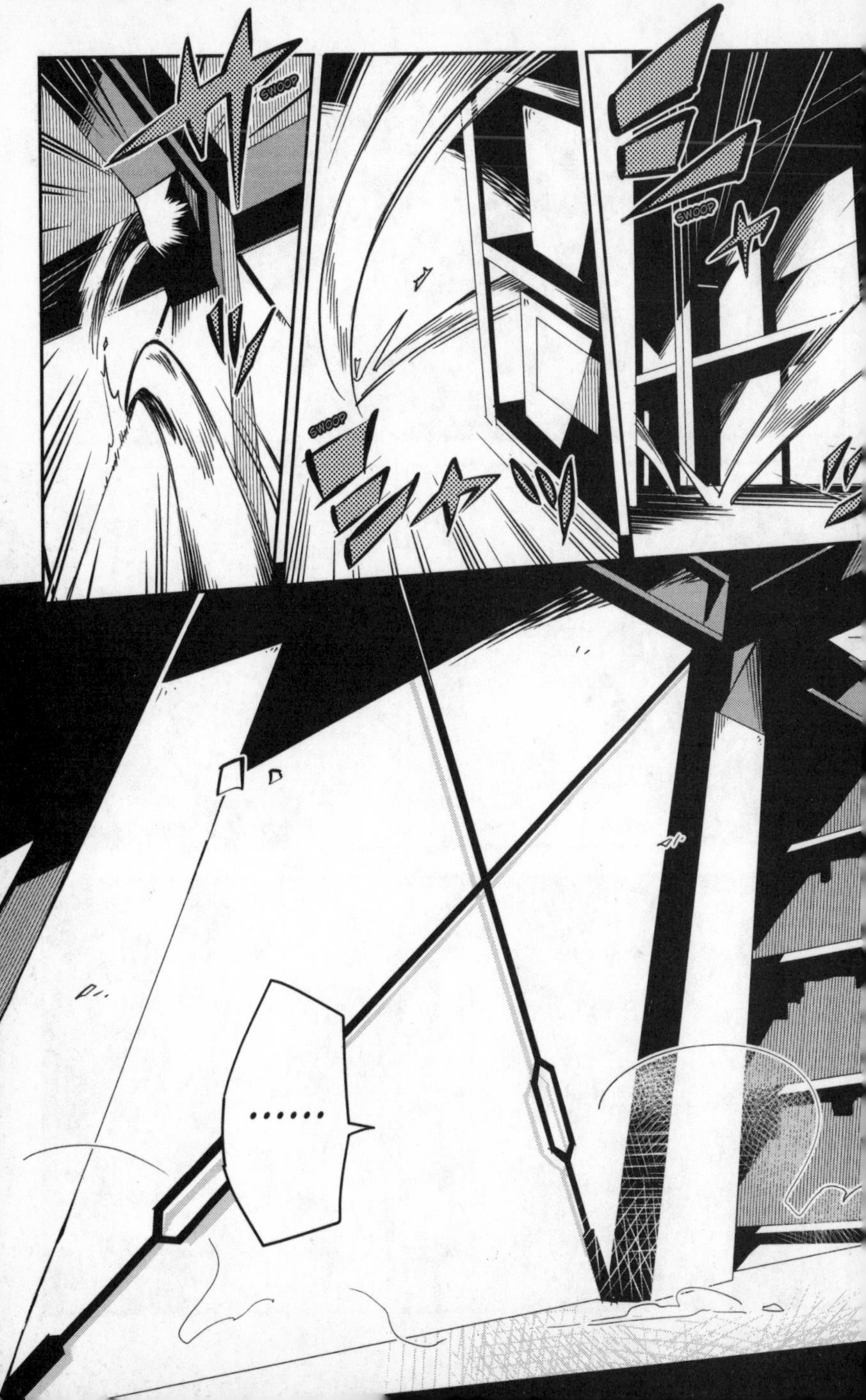
SWOOP
SWOOP
SWOOP
......

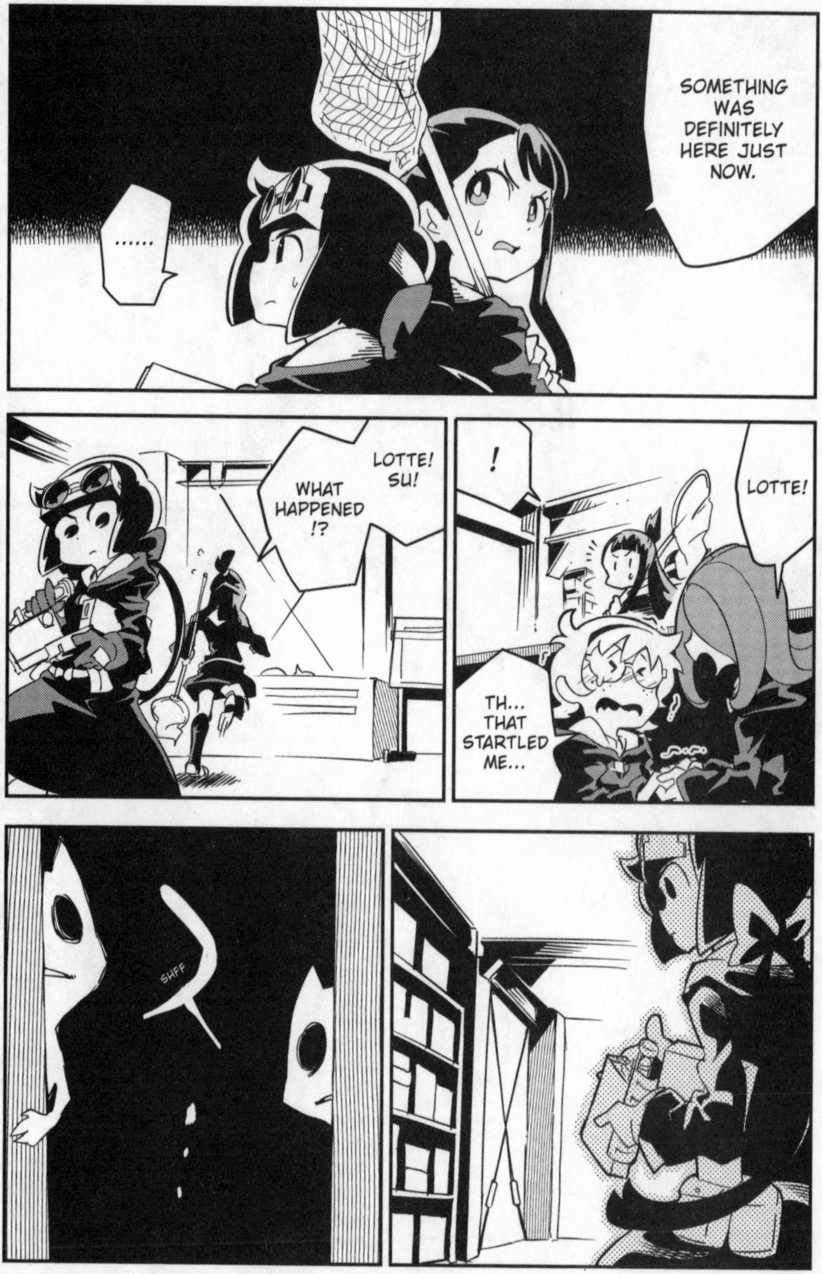
SOMETHING WAS DEFINITELY HERE JUST NOW.
......
LOTTE!
!
TH... THAT STARTLED ME...
LOTTE! SU!
WHAT HAPPENED!?
SHFF

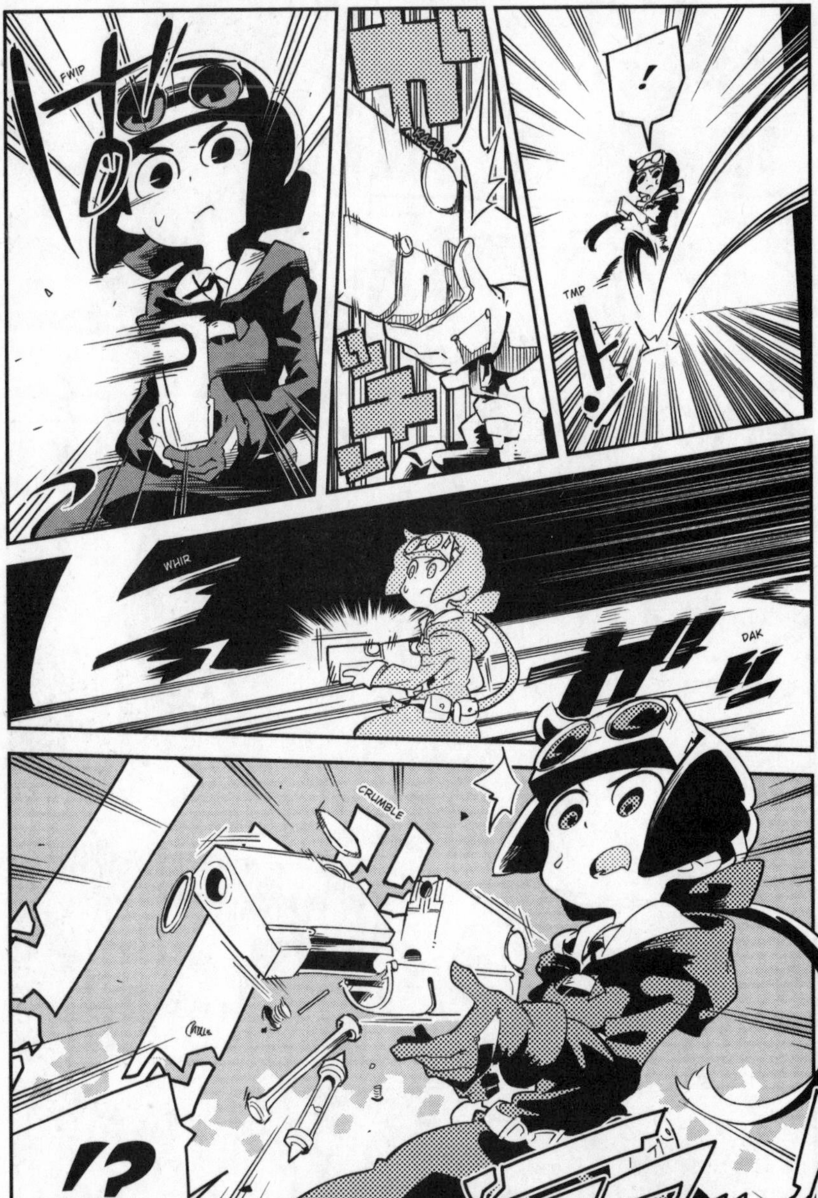
!
TMP
KACHAK
FWIP
DAK
WHIR
CRUMBLE
!?

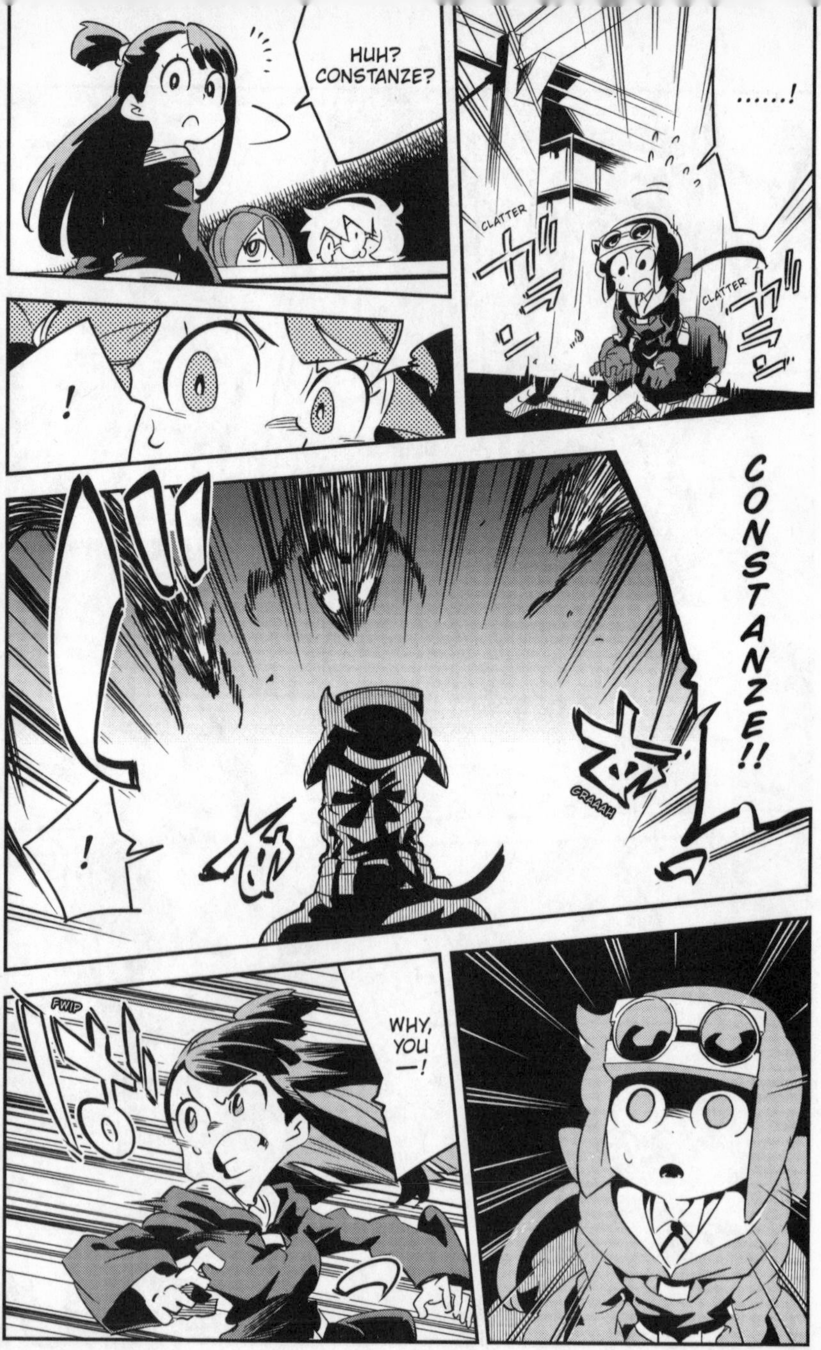
......!
CLATTER
CLATTER
HUH? CONSTANZE?
!
CONSTANZE!!
GRAAAH
!
FWIP
WHY, YOU—!

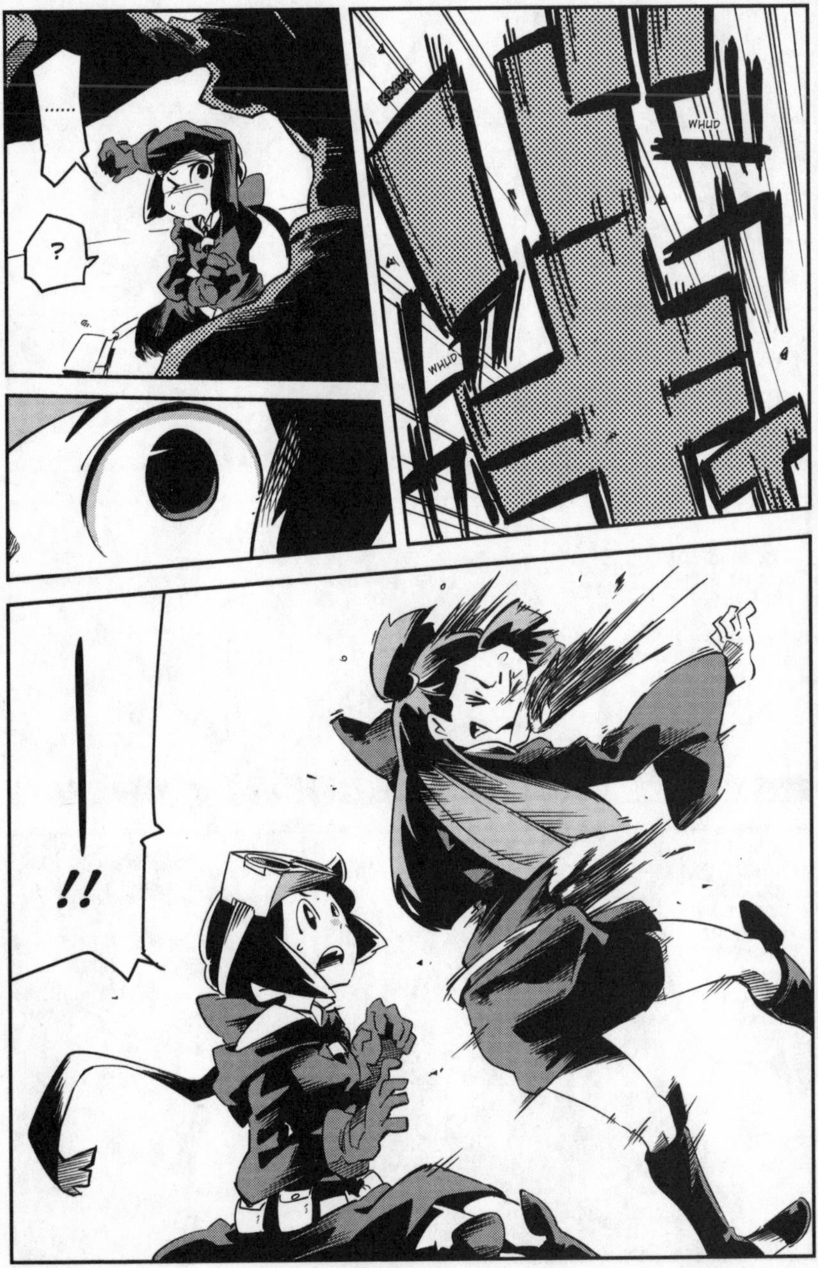

KRAKK
WHUD
WHUD
......
?
—!!

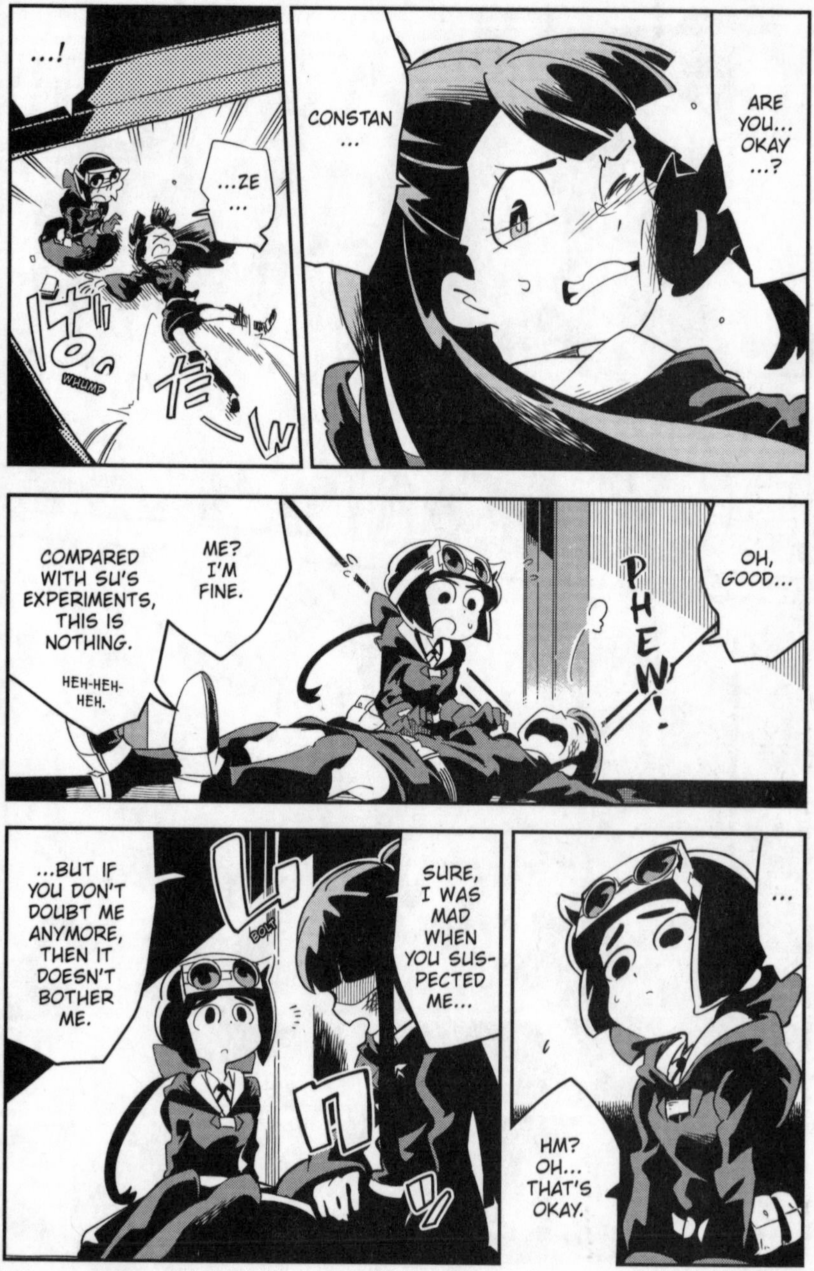
ARE YOU... OKAY ...?
CONSTAN ...
...!
...ZE ...
WHUMP
OH, GOOD...
PHEW!
ME? I'M FINE.
COMPARED WITH SU'S EXPERIMENTS, THIS IS NOTHING.
HEH-HEH-HEH.
...
HM? OH... THAT'S OKAY.
SURE, I WAS MAD WHEN YOU SUS-PECTED ME...
BOLT
...BUT IF YOU DON'T DOUBT ME ANYMORE, THEN IT DOESN'T BOTHER ME.

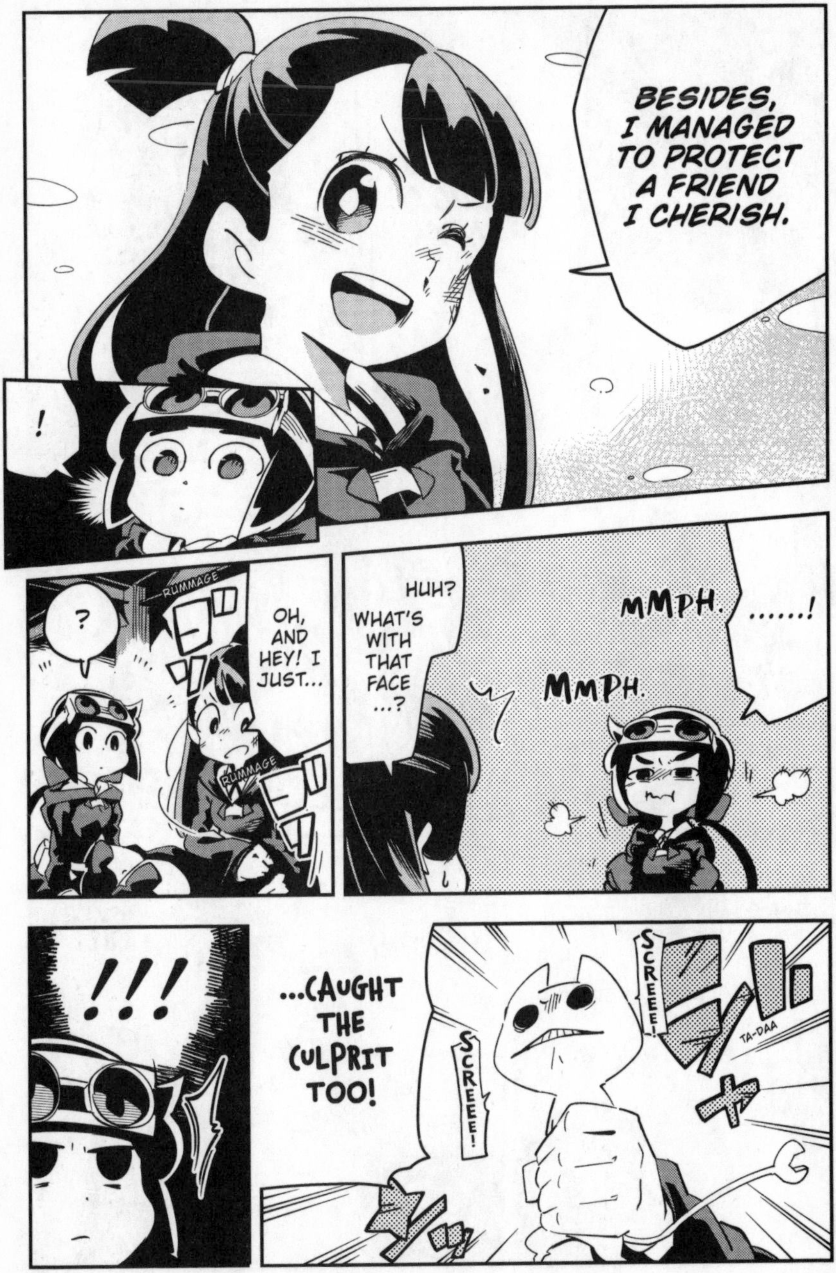
BESIDES, I MANAGED TO PROTECT A FRIEND I CHERISH.
!
......!
MMPH.
HUH? WHAT'S WITH THAT FACE ...?
MMPH.
RUMMAGE
OH, AND HEY! I JUST...
?
RUMMAGE
SCREEE!
TA-DAA
SCREEE!
...CAUGHT THE CULPRIT TOO!
!!!

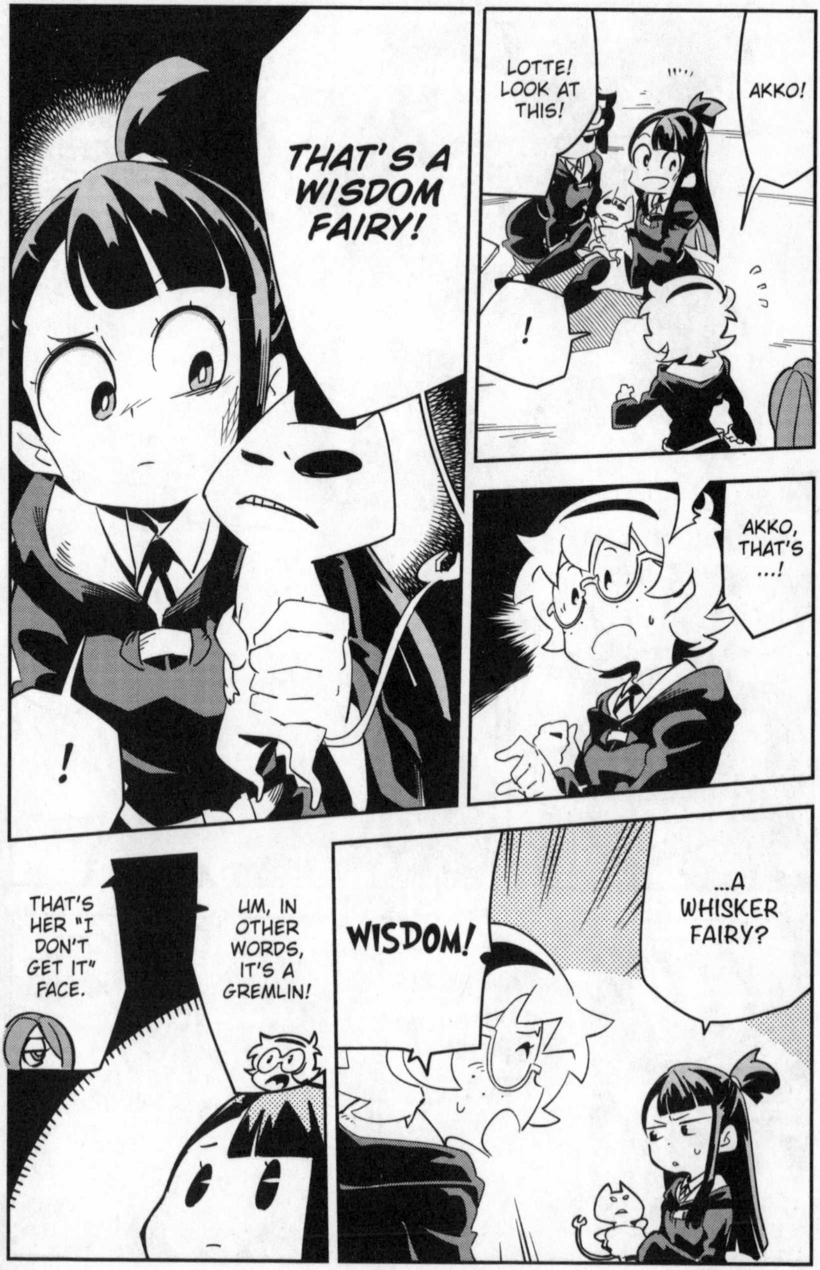
AKKO!
LOTTE! LOOK AT THIS!
!
AKKO, THAT'S ...!
THAT'S A WISDOM FAIRY!
!
...A WHISKER FAIRY?
WISDOM!
UM, IN OTHER WORDS, IT'S A GREMLIN!
THAT'S HER "I DON'T GET IT" FACE.

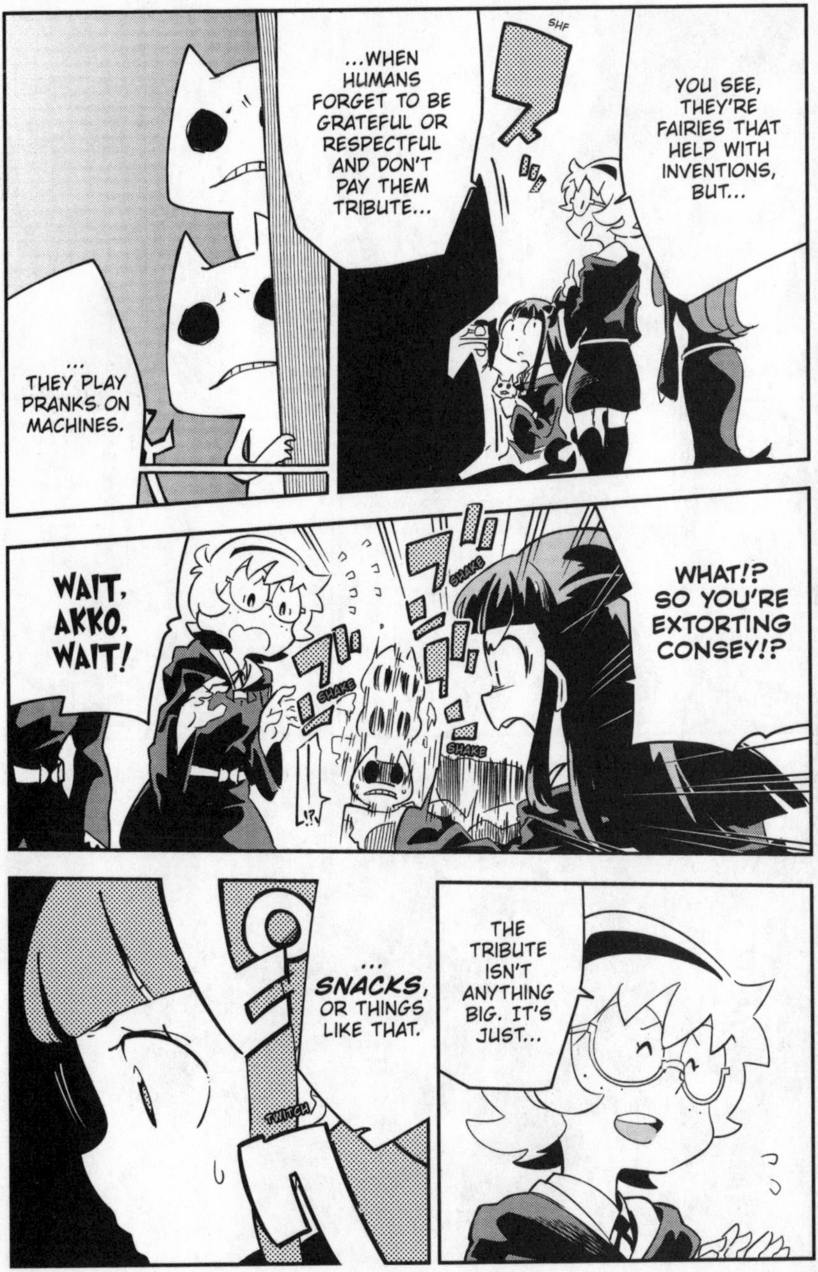
SHF
YOU SEE, THEY'RE FAIRIES THAT HELP WITH INVENTIONS, BUT...
...WHEN HUMANS FORGET TO BE GRATEFUL OR RESPECTFUL AND DON'T PAY THEM TRIBUTE...
...THEY PLAY PRANKS ON MACHINES.
WHAT!? SO YOU'RE EXTORTING CONSEY!?
SHAKE
SHAKE
SHAKE
WAIT, AKKO, WAIT!
!?
THE TRIBUTE ISN'T ANYTHING BIG. IT'S JUST...
...SNACKS, OR THINGS LIKE THAT.
TWITCH

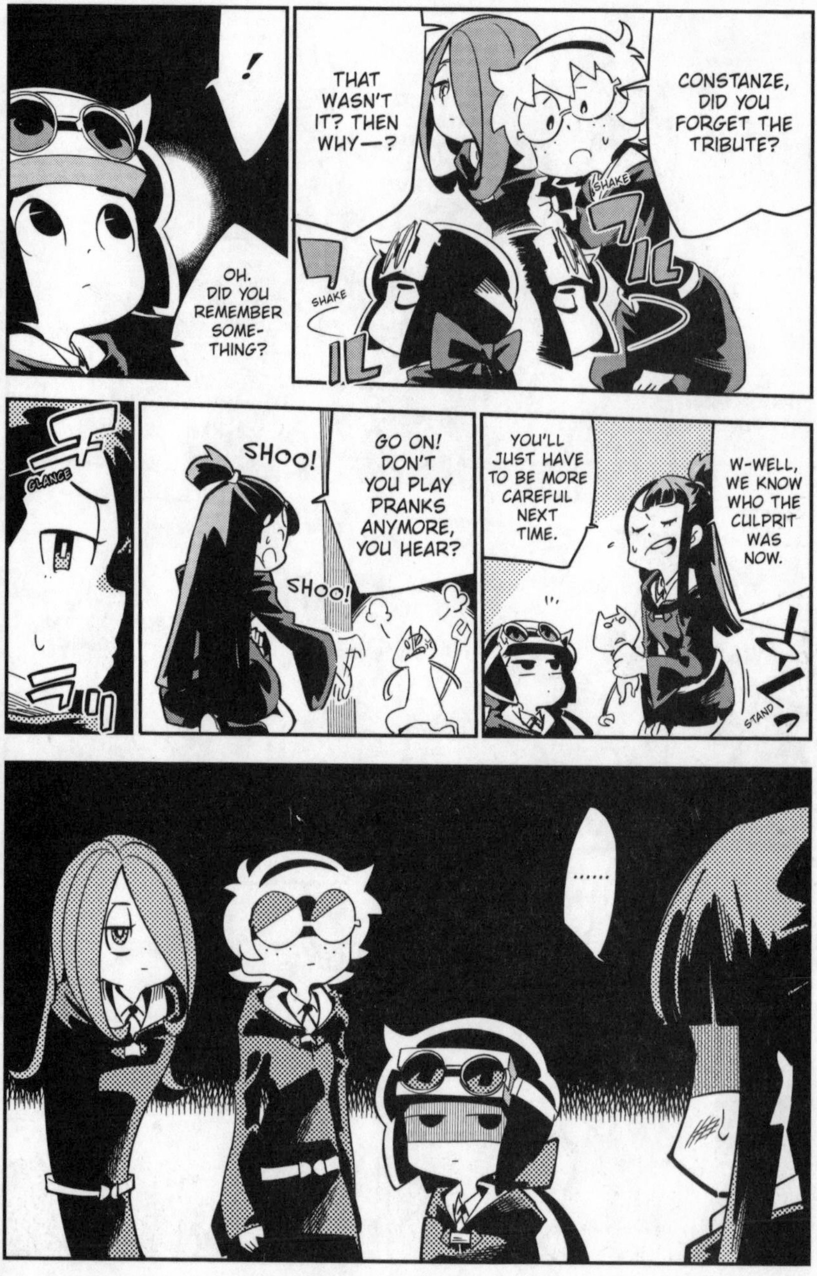
CONSTANZE, DID YOU FORGET THE TRIBUTE?
SHAKE
THAT WASN'T IT? THEN WHY—?
SHAKE
!
OH. DID YOU REMEMBER SOME-THING?
W-WELL, WE KNOW WHO THE CULPRIT WAS NOW.
YOU'LL JUST HAVE TO BE MORE CAREFUL NEXT TIME.
STAND
GO ON! DON'T YOU PLAY PRANKS ANYMORE, YOU HEAR?
SHOO!
SHOO!
GLANCE
......

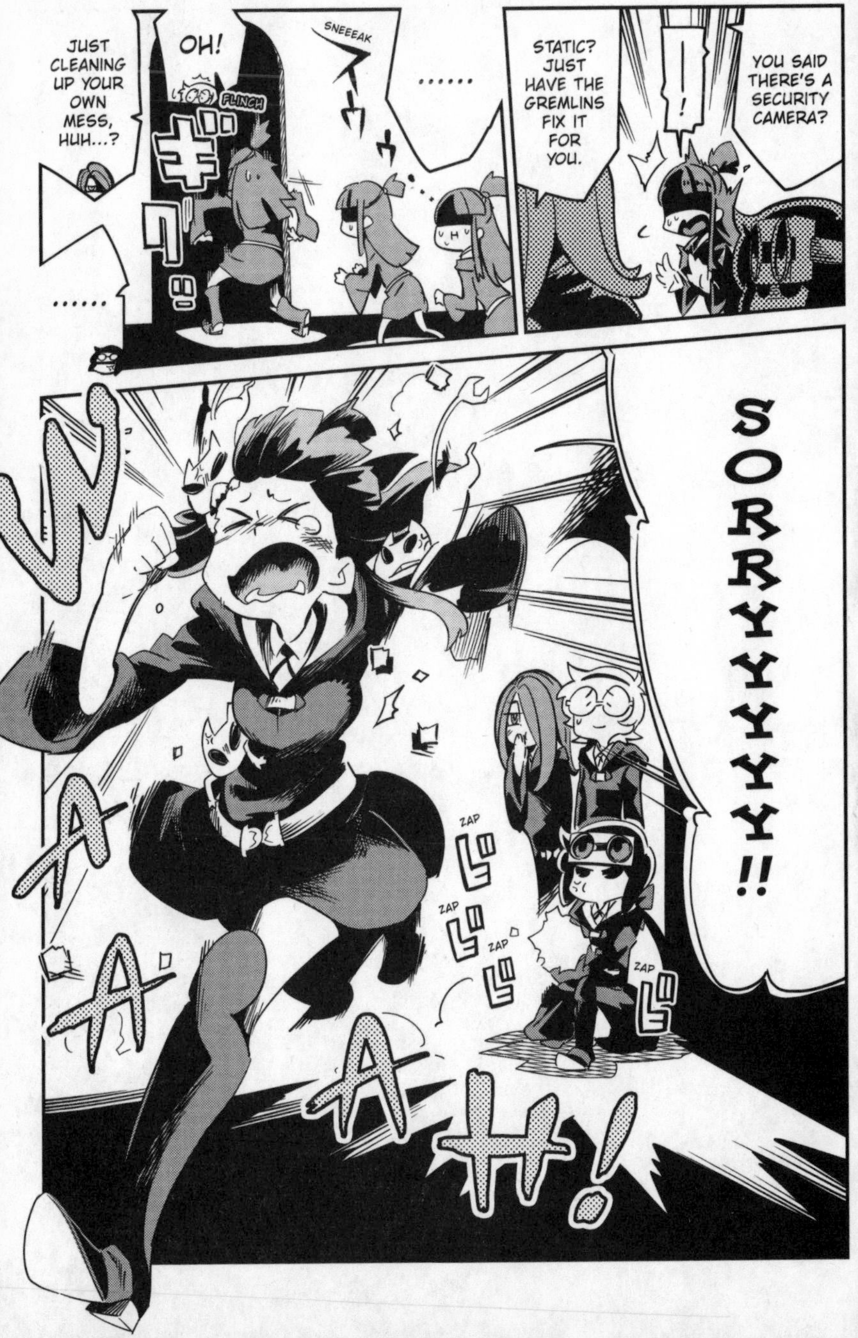
YOU SAID THERE'S A SECURITY CAMERA?
!
STATIC? JUST HAVE THE GREMLINS FIX IT FOR YOU.
......
SNEEEAK
OH!
FLINCH
JUST CLEANING UP YOUR OWN MESS, HUH...?
......
SORRYYYY!!
ZAP
ZAP
ZAP
ZAP
WAAAAH!

Little Witch Academia

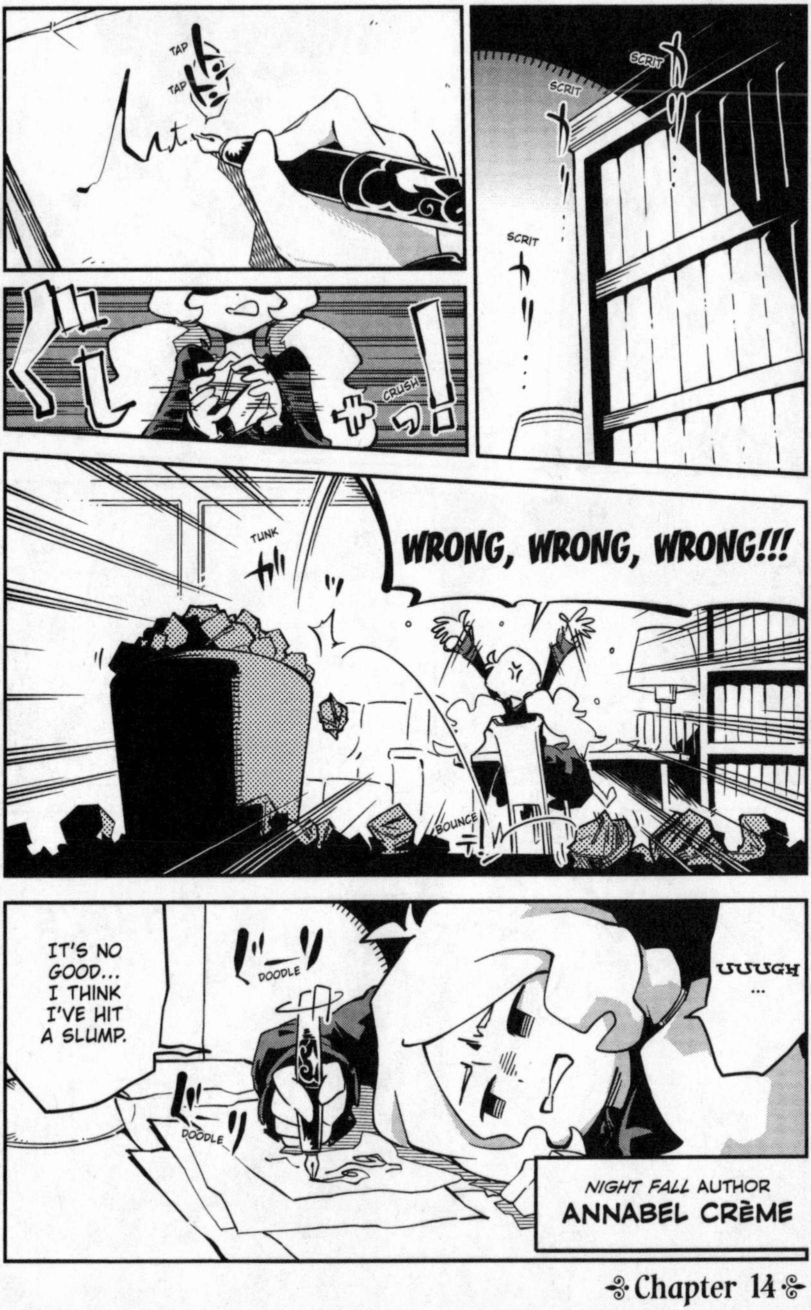
SCRIT
SCRIT
SCRIT
TAP
TAP
CRUSH
WRONG, WRONG, WRONG!!!
TUNK
BOUNCE
UUUGH...
IT'S NO GOOD... I THINK I'VE HIT A SLUMP.
DOODLE
DOODLE
NIGHT FALL AUTHOR
ANNABEL CRÈME

Chapter 14

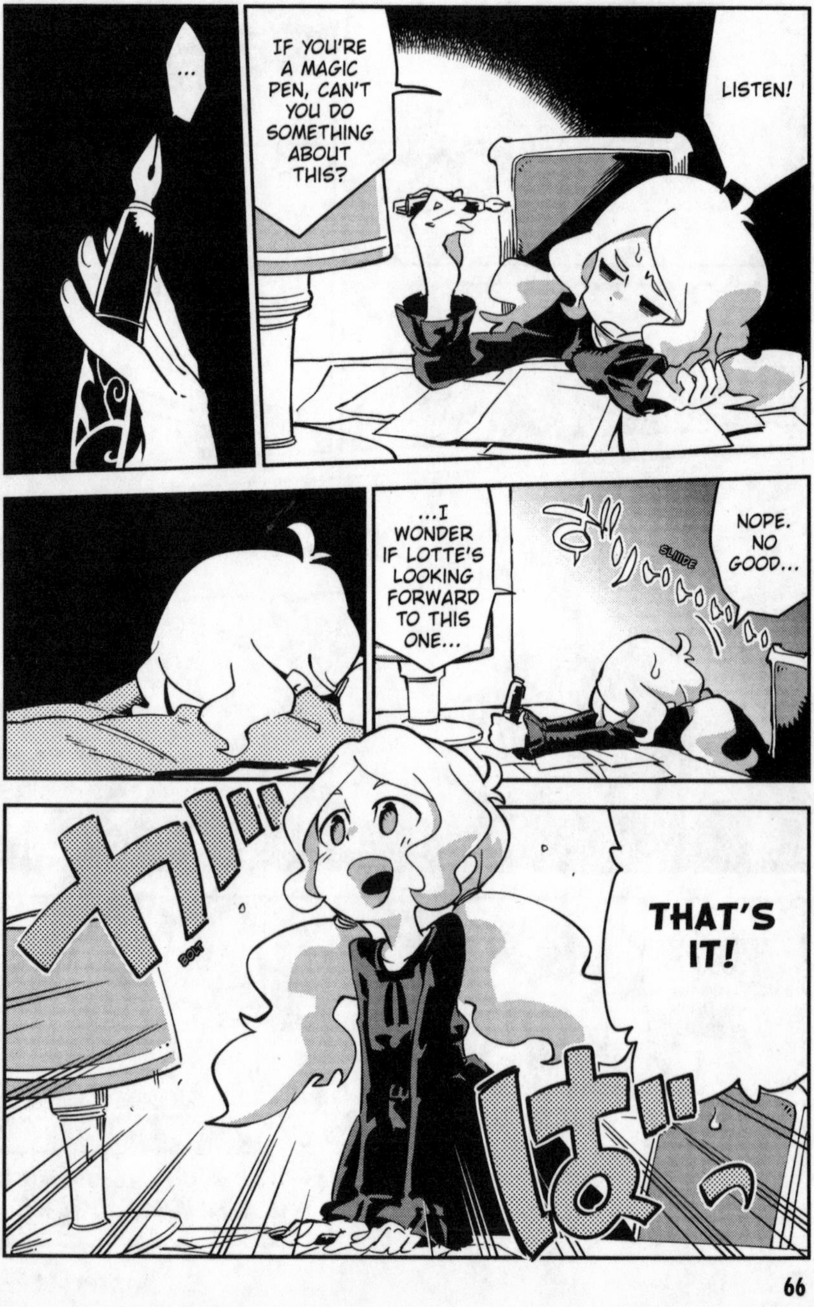
LISTEN!
IF YOU'RE A MAGIC PEN, CAN'T YOU DO SOMETHING ABOUT THIS?
...
NOPE. NO GOOD...
SLIIIDE
...I WONDER IF LOTTE'S LOOKING FORWARD TO THIS ONE...
THAT'S IT!
BOLT

Chapter 14 LET'S VISIT LUNA NOVA!

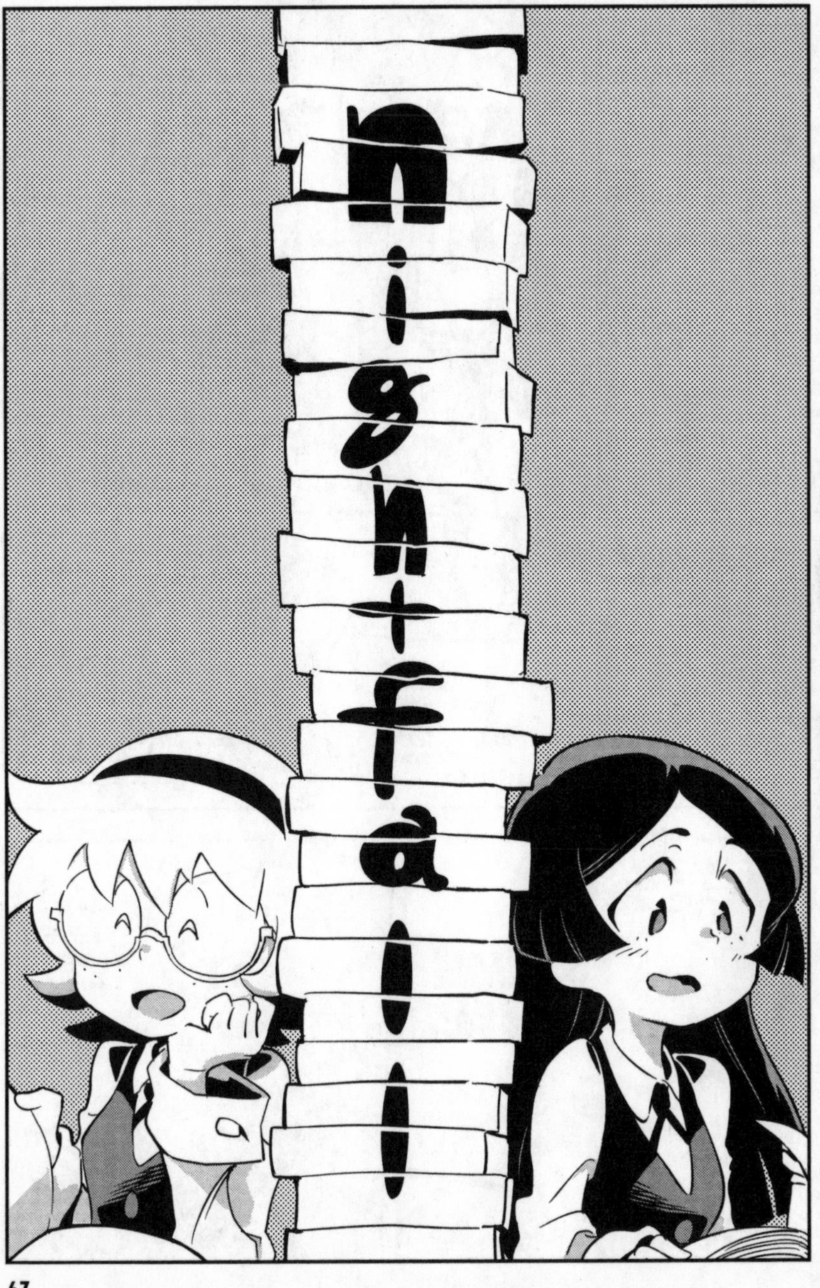
nightfall

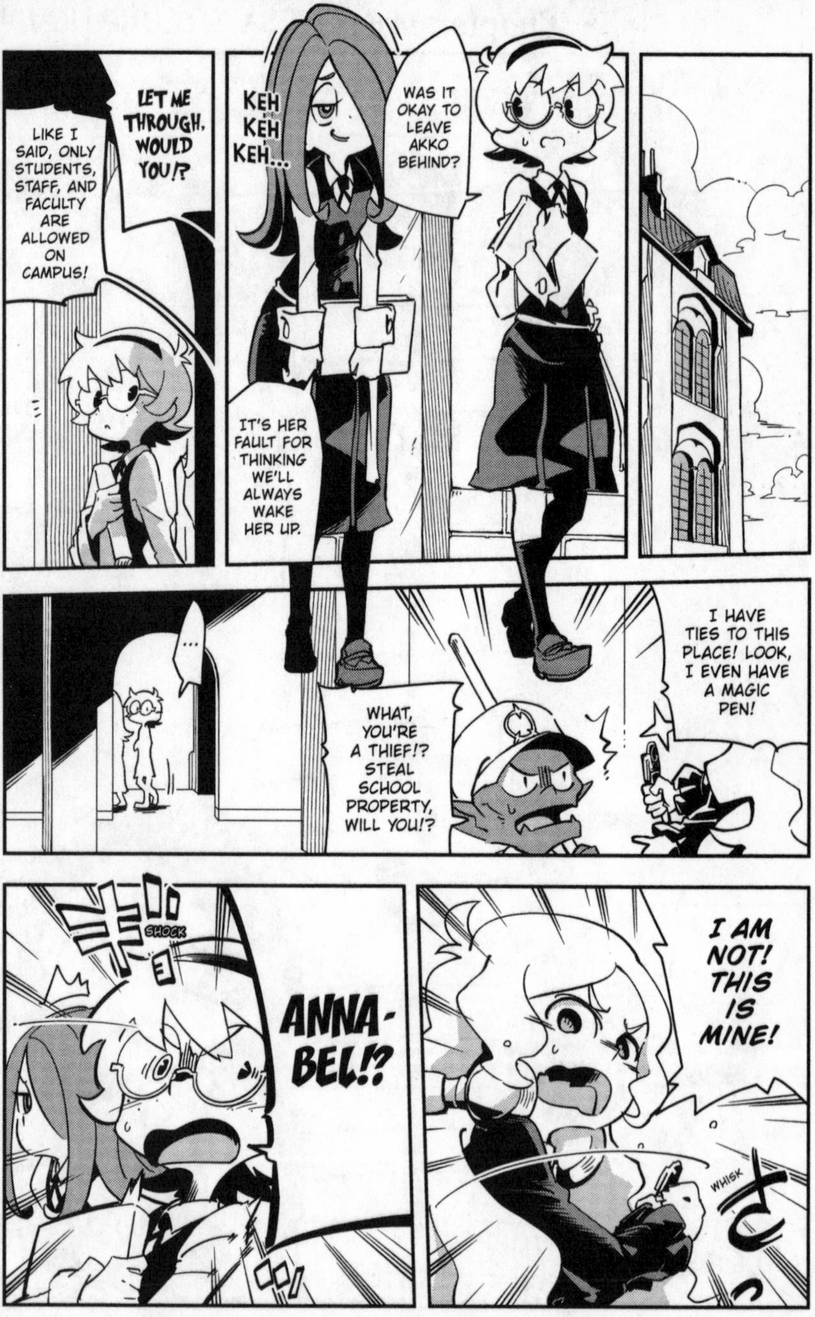
WAS IT OKAY TO LEAVE AKKO BEHIND?
KEH KEH KEH...
IT'S HER FAULT FOR THINKING WE'LL ALWAYS WAKE HER UP.
LET ME THROUGH, WOULD YOU!?
LIKE I SAID, ONLY STUDENTS, STAFF, AND FACULTY ARE ALLOWED ON CAMPUS!
I HAVE TIES TO THIS PLACE! LOOK, I EVEN HAVE A MAGIC PEN!
WHAT, YOU'RE A THIEF!? STEAL SCHOOL PROPERTY, WILL YOU!?
...
I AM NOT! THIS IS MINE!
WHISK
SHOCK
ANNA-BEL!?

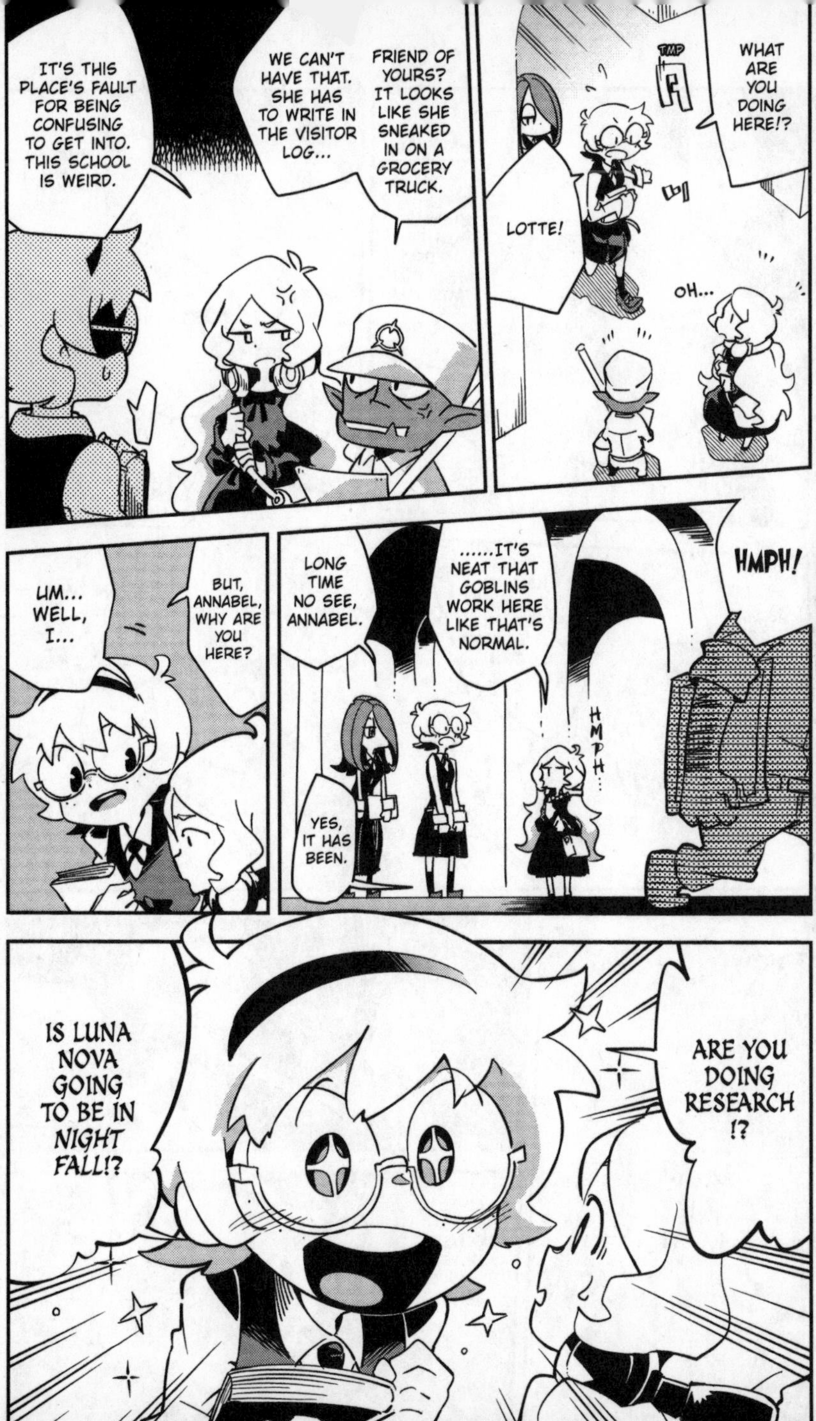
WHAT ARE YOU DOING HERE!?
TMP
LOTTE!
OH...
FRIEND OF YOURS? IT LOOKS LIKE SHE SNEAKED IN ON A GROCERY TRUCK.
WE CAN'T HAVE THAT. SHE HAS TO WRITE IN THE VISITOR LOG...
IT'S THIS PLACE'S FAULT FOR BEING CONFUSING TO GET INTO. THIS SCHOOL IS WEIRD.
HMPH!
......IT'S NEAT THAT GOBLINS WORK HERE LIKE THAT'S NORMAL.
LONG TIME NO SEE, ANNABEL.
HMPH...
YES, IT HAS BEEN.
BUT, ANNABEL, WHY ARE YOU HERE?
UM... WELL, I...
ARE YOU DOING RESEARCH!?
IS LUNA NOVA GOING TO BE IN NIGHT FALL!?

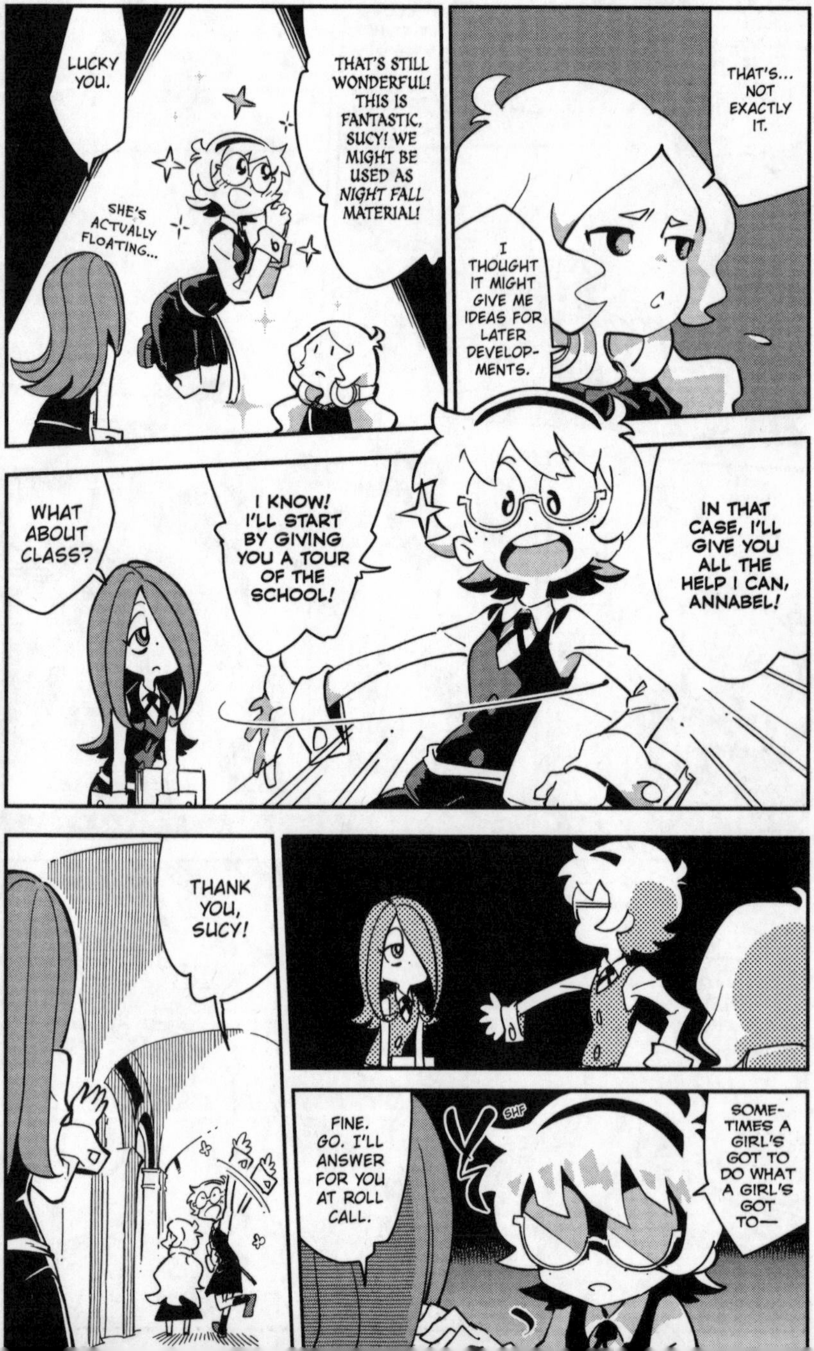
THAT'S... NOT EXACTLY IT.
I THOUGHT IT MIGHT GIVE ME IDEAS FOR LATER DEVELOPMENTS.
THAT'S STILL WONDERFUL! THIS IS FANTASTIC, SUCY! WE MIGHT BE USED AS *NIGHT FALL* MATERIAL!
LUCKY YOU.
SHE'S ACTUALLY FLOATING...
IN THAT CASE, I'LL GIVE YOU ALL THE HELP I CAN, ANNABEL!
I KNOW! I'LL START BY GIVING YOU A TOUR OF THE SCHOOL!
WHAT ABOUT CLASS?
SOMETIMES A GIRL'S GOT TO DO WHAT A GIRL'S GOT TO—
SHF
FINE. GO. I'LL ANSWER FOR YOU AT ROLL CALL.
THANK YOU, SUCY!

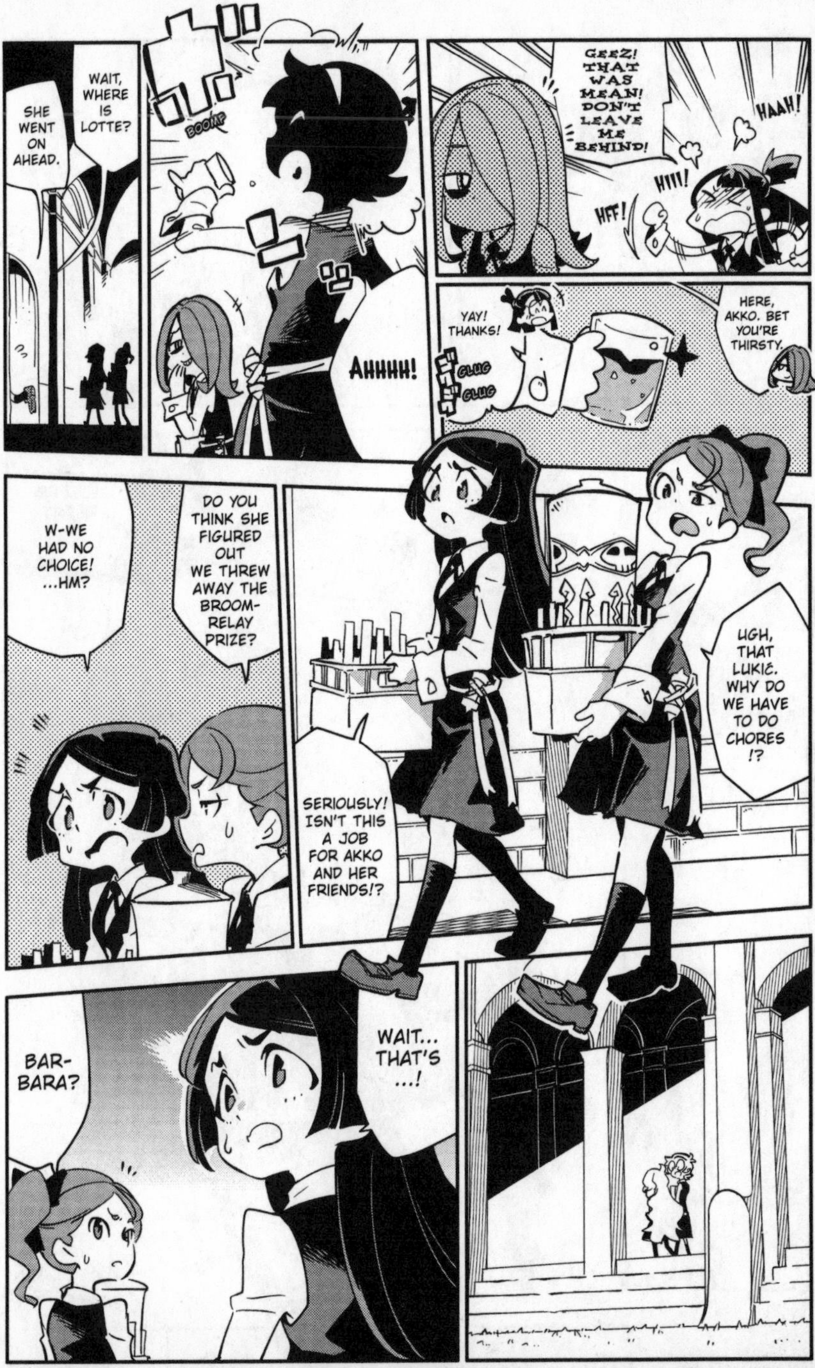
GEEZ! THAT WAS MEAN! DON'T LEAVE ME BEHIND!
HAAH!
HIII!
HFF!
HERE, AKKO. BET YOU'RE THIRSTY.
YAY! THANKS!
GLUG GLUG
BOOMP
AHHHH!
WAIT, WHERE IS LOTTE?
SHE WENT ON AHEAD.
UGH, THAT LUKIĆ. WHY DO WE HAVE TO DO CHORES!?
SERIOUSLY! ISN'T THIS A JOB FOR AKKO AND HER FRIENDS!?
DO YOU THINK SHE FIGURED OUT WE THREW AWAY THE BROOM-RELAY PRIZE?
W-WE HAD NO CHOICE! ...HM?
WAIT... THAT'S ...!
BAR-BARA?

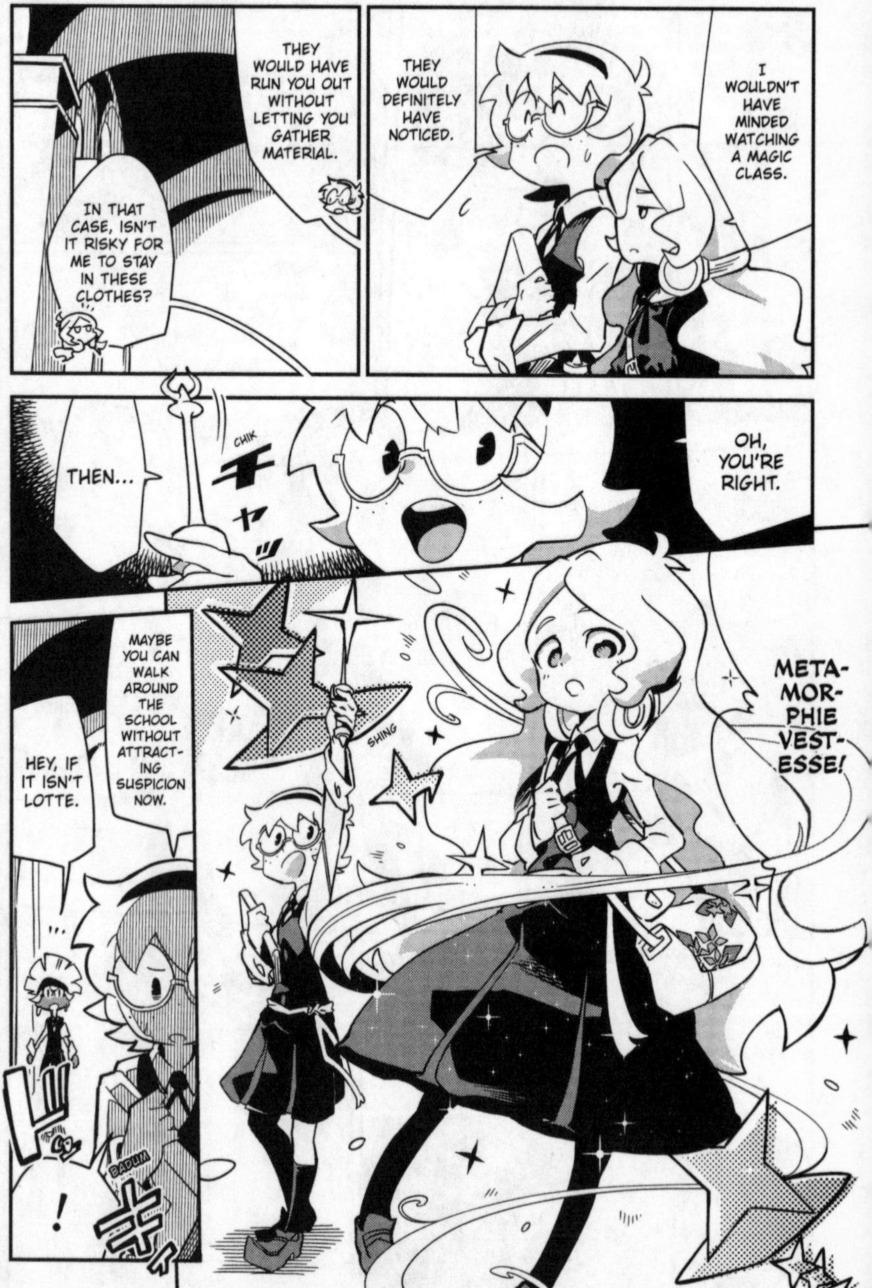
I WOULDN'T HAVE MINDED WATCHING A MAGIC CLASS.
THEY WOULD DEFINITELY HAVE NOTICED.
THEY WOULD HAVE RUN YOU OUT WITHOUT LETTING YOU GATHER MATERIAL.
IN THAT CASE, ISN'T IT RISKY FOR ME TO STAY IN THESE CLOTHES?
OH, YOU'RE RIGHT.
THEN...
CHIK
METAMORPHIE VESTESSE!
SHING
MAYBE YOU CAN WALK AROUND THE SCHOOL WITHOUT ATTRACTING SUSPICION NOW.
HEY, IF IT ISN'T LOTTE.
...
BADUM
!

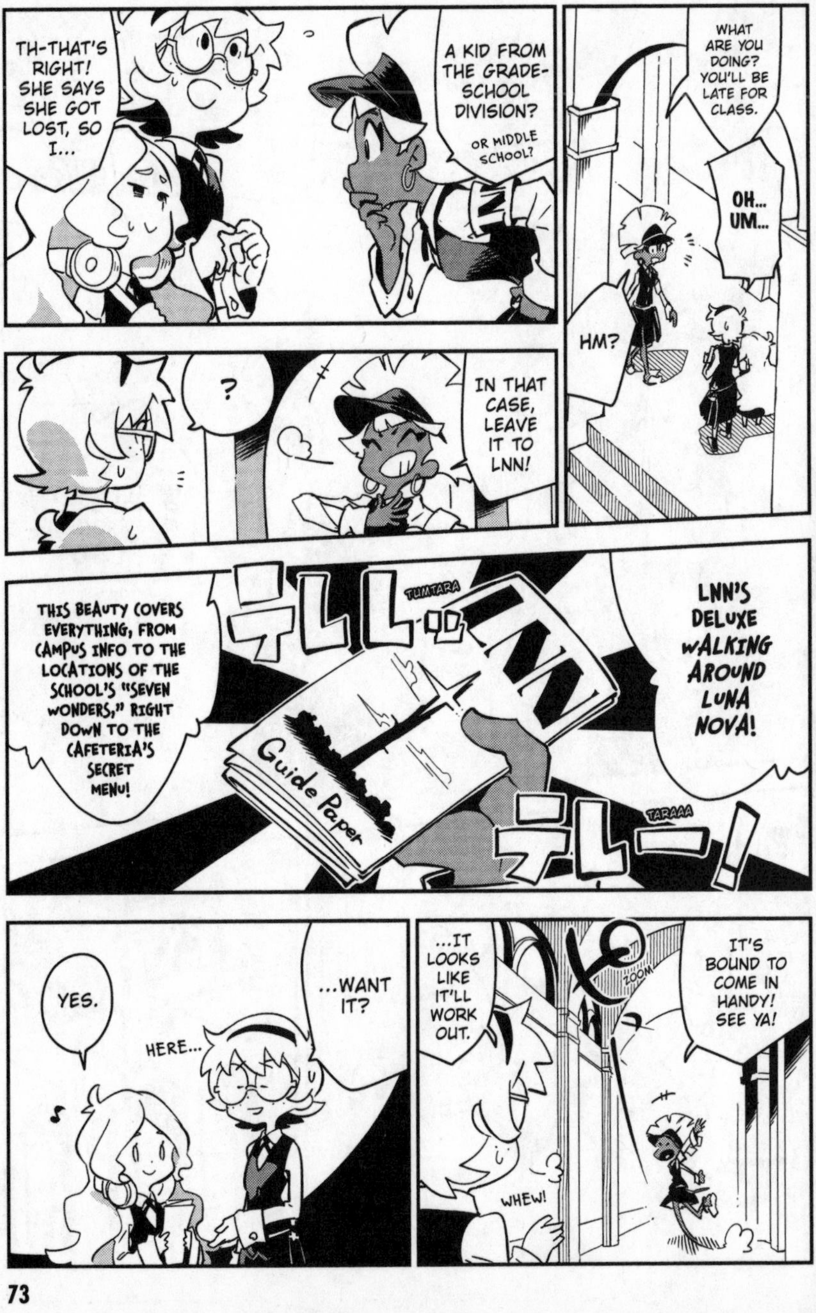
WHAT ARE YOU DOING? YOU'LL BE LATE FOR CLASS.
OH... UM...
HM?
A KID FROM THE GRADE-SCHOOL DIVISION?
OR MIDDLE SCHOOL?
TH-THAT'S RIGHT! SHE SAYS SHE GOT LOST, SO I...
IN THAT CASE, LEAVE IT TO LNN!
?
LNN'S DELUXE WALKING AROUND LUNA NOVA!
TUMTARA
THIS BEAUTY COVERS EVERYTHING, FROM CAMPUS INFO TO THE LOCATIONS OF THE SCHOOL'S "SEVEN WONDERS," RIGHT DOWN TO THE CAFETERIA'S SECRET MENU!
Guide Paper
TARAAA
IT'S BOUND TO COME IN HANDY! SEE YA!
ZOOM
...IT LOOKS LIKE IT'LL WORK OUT.
WHEW!
...WANT IT?
HERE...
YES.

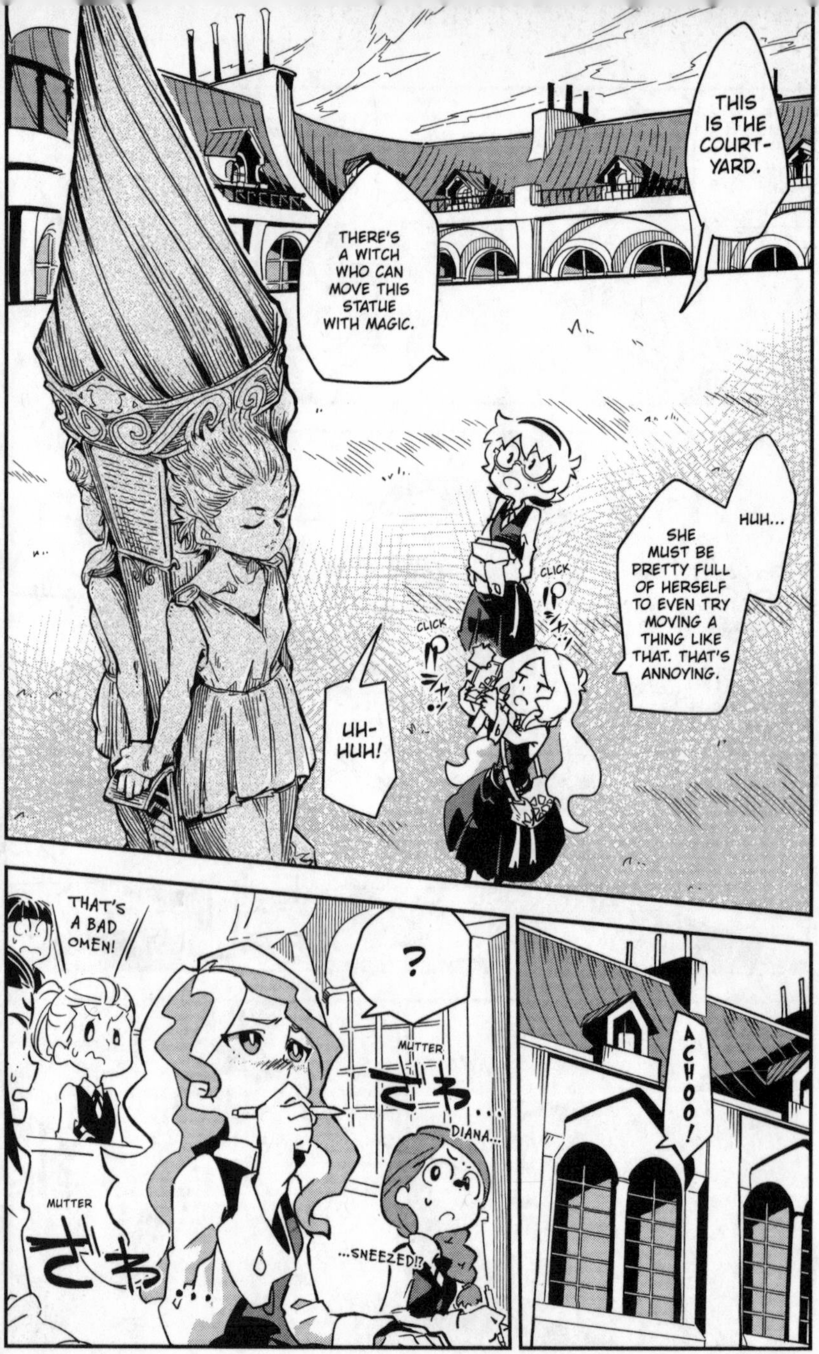
THIS IS THE COURTYARD.
THERE'S A WITCH WHO CAN MOVE THIS STATUE WITH MAGIC.
HUH...
SHE MUST BE PRETTY FULL OF HERSELF TO EVEN TRY MOVING A THING LIKE THAT. THAT'S ANNOYING.
CLICK
CLICK
UH-HUH!
ACHOO!
?
MUTTER
DIANA...
THAT'S A BAD OMEN!
MUTTER
...SNEEZED!?

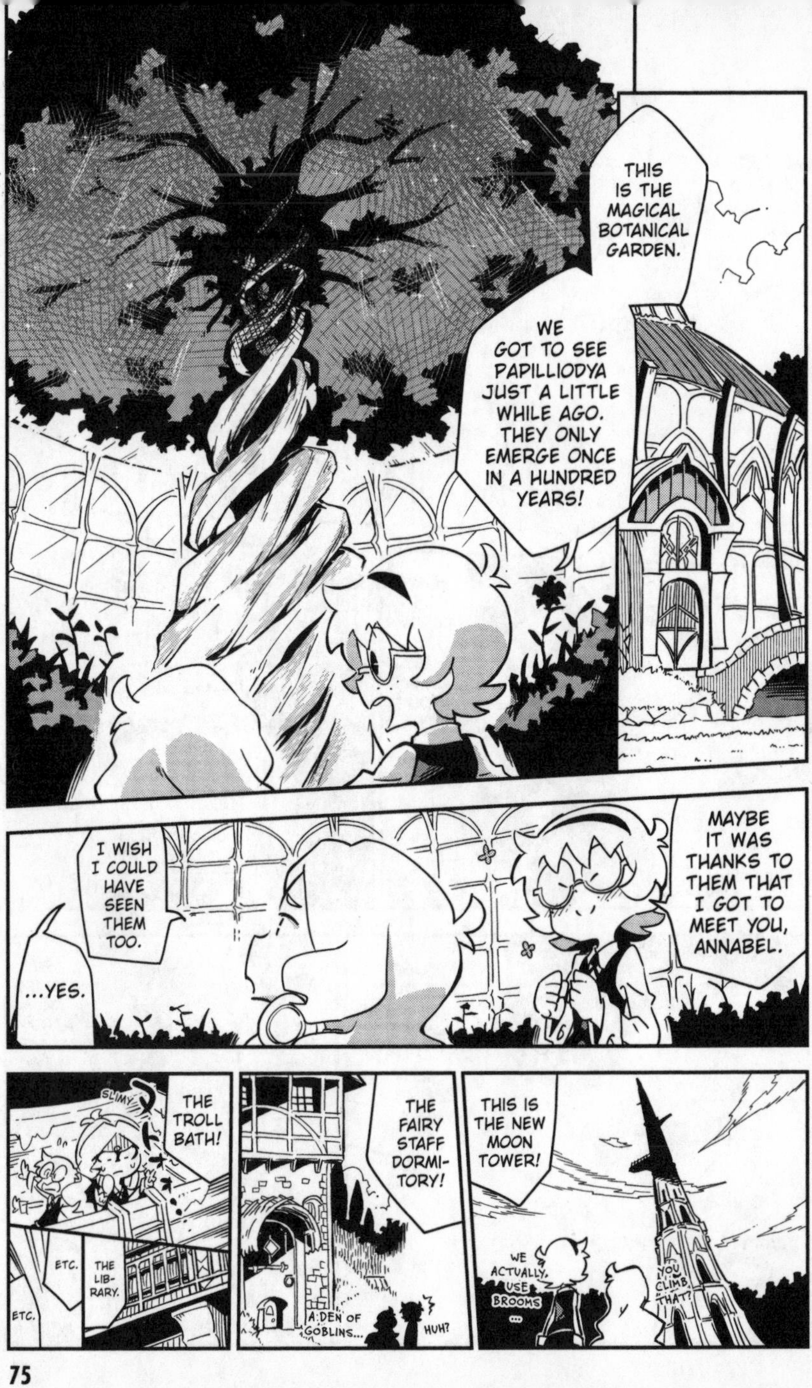
THIS IS THE MAGICAL BOTANICAL GARDEN.
WE GOT TO SEE PAPILLIODYA JUST A LITTLE WHILE AGO. THEY ONLY EMERGE ONCE IN A HUNDRED YEARS!
MAYBE IT WAS THANKS TO THEM THAT I GOT TO MEET YOU, ANNABEL.
I WISH I COULD HAVE SEEN THEM TOO.
...YES.
THIS IS THE NEW MOON TOWER!
YOU CLIMB THAT?
WE ACTUALLY USE BROOMS ...
THE FAIRY STAFF DORMITORY!
A DEN OF GOBLINS...
HUH?
THE TROLL BATH!
SLIMY
THE LIBRARY.
ETC.
ETC.

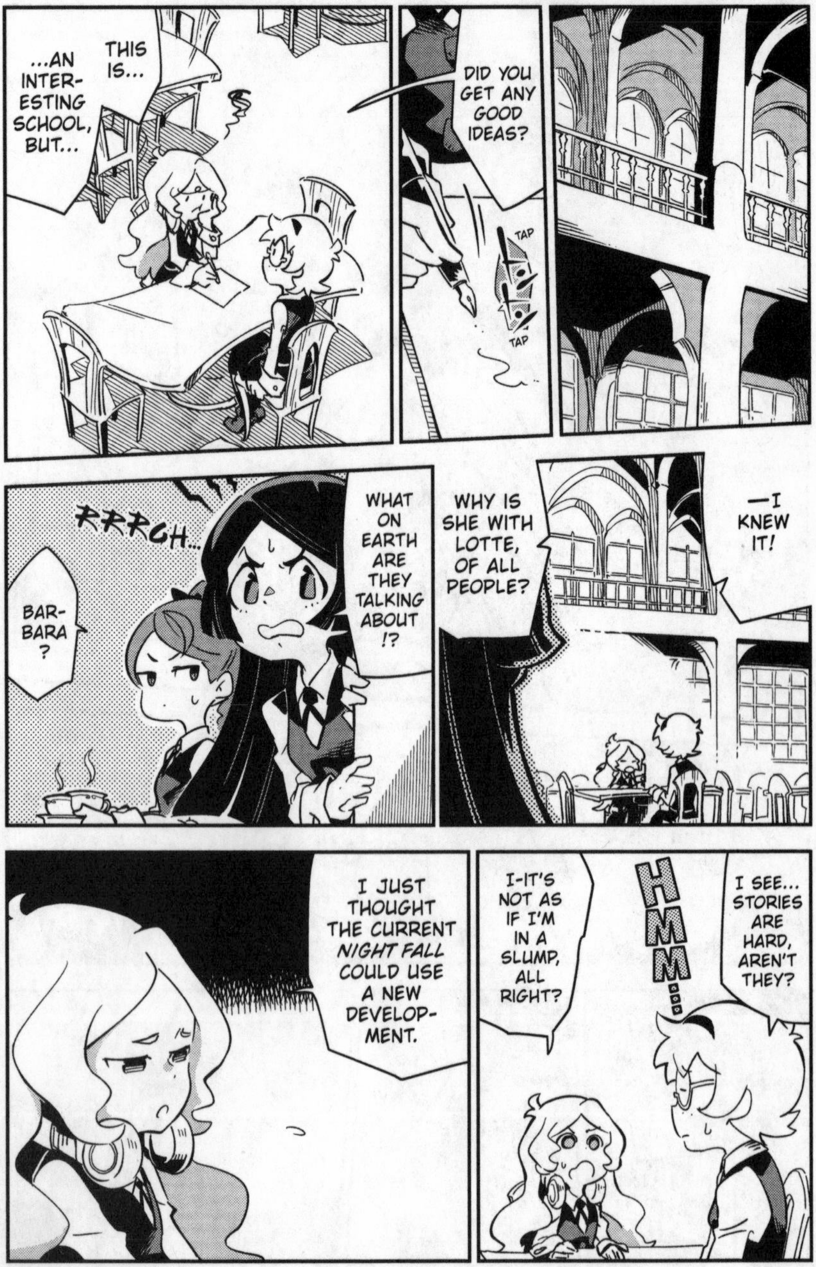
DID YOU GET ANY GOOD IDEAS?
TAP
TAP
THIS IS...
...AN INTERESTING SCHOOL, BUT...
—I KNEW IT!
WHY IS SHE WITH LOTTE, OF ALL PEOPLE?
WHAT ON EARTH ARE THEY TALKING ABOUT!?
RRRGH...
BARBARA?
I SEE... STORIES ARE HARD, AREN'T THEY?
HMM...
I-IT'S NOT AS IF I'M IN A SLUMP, ALL RIGHT?
I JUST THOUGHT THE CURRENT *NIGHT FALL* COULD USE A NEW DEVELOPMENT.

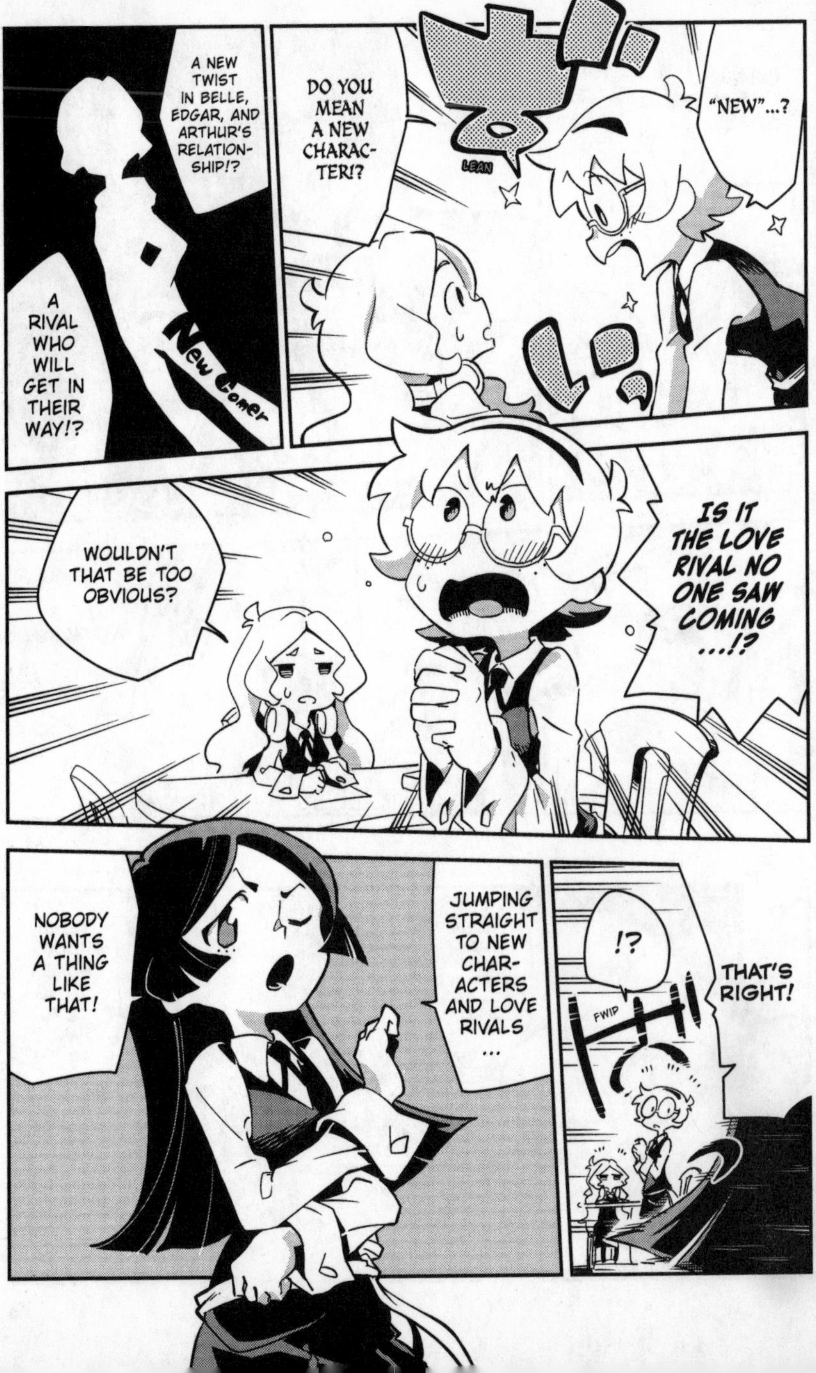
"NEW"...?
LEAN
DO YOU MEAN A NEW CHARACTER!?
A NEW TWIST IN BELLE, EDGAR, AND ARTHUR'S RELATIONSHIP!?
A RIVAL WHO WILL GET IN THEIR WAY!?
New Comer
IS IT THE LOVE RIVAL NO ONE SAW COMING ...!?
WOULDN'T THAT BE TOO OBVIOUS?
THAT'S RIGHT!
!?
FWIP
JUMPING STRAIGHT TO NEW CHARACTERS AND LOVE RIVALS ...
NOBODY WANTS A THING LIKE THAT!

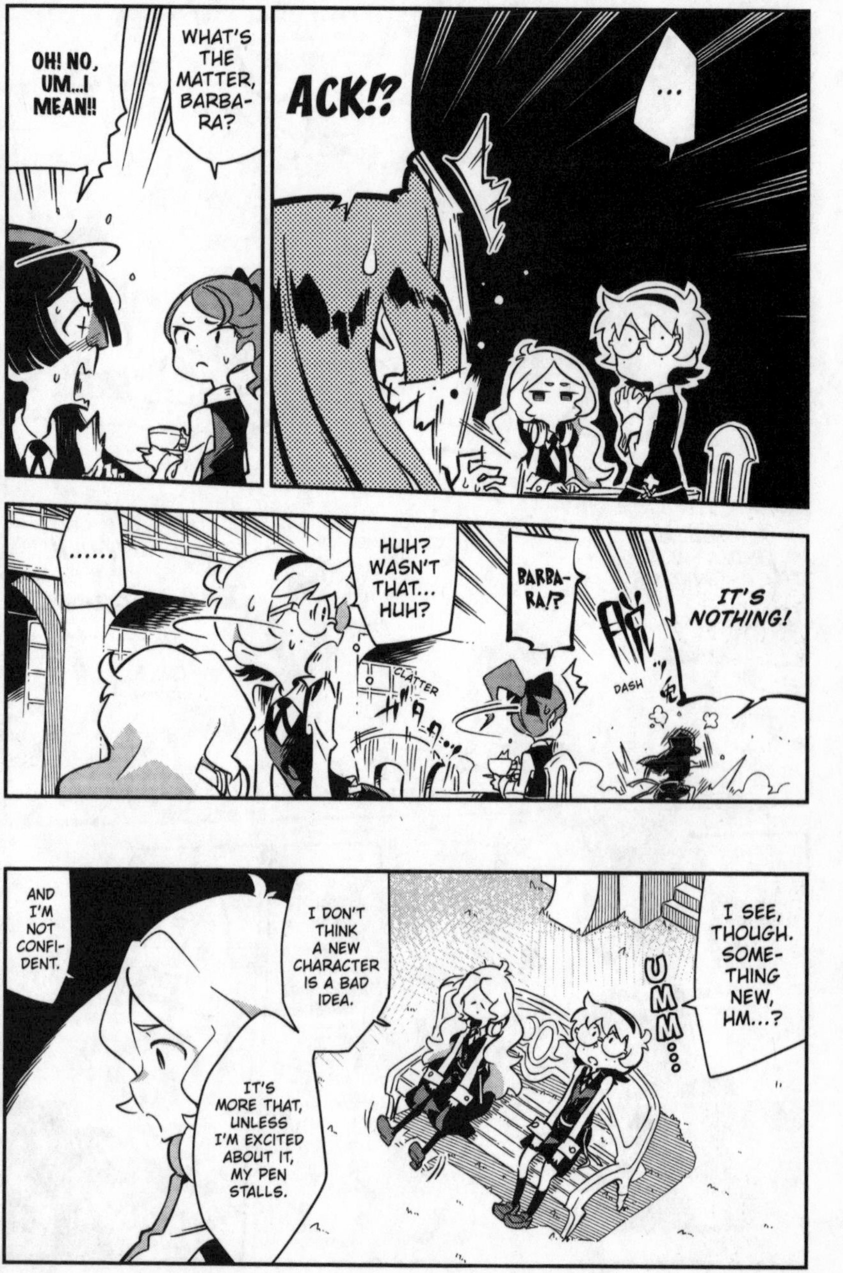
...
ACK!?
WHAT'S THE MATTER, BARBA-RA?
OH! NO, UM...I MEAN!!
IT'S NOTHING!
DASH
BARBA-RA!?
CLATTER
HUH? WASN'T THAT... HUH?
......
I SEE, THOUGH. SOME-THING NEW, HM...?
UMM...
I DON'T THINK A NEW CHARACTER IS A BAD IDEA.
AND I'M NOT CONFI-DENT.
IT'S MORE THAT, UNLESS I'M EXCITED ABOUT IT, MY PEN STALLS.

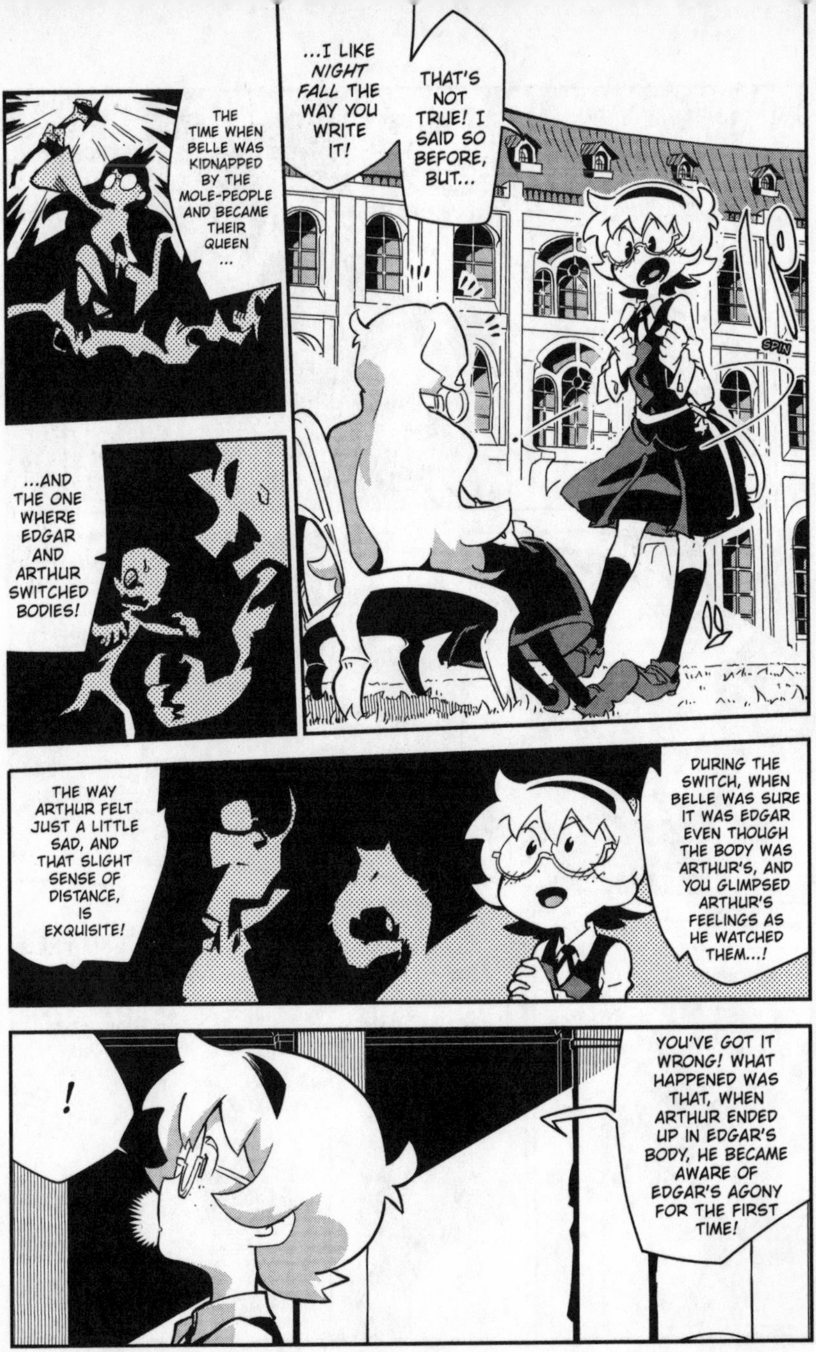
THAT'S NOT TRUE! I SAID SO BEFORE, BUT...
...I LIKE *NIGHT FALL* THE WAY YOU WRITE IT!
SPIN
THE TIME WHEN BELLE WAS KIDNAPPED BY THE MOLE-PEOPLE AND BECAME THEIR QUEEN ...
...AND THE ONE WHERE EDGAR AND ARTHUR SWITCHED BODIES!
DURING THE SWITCH, WHEN BELLE WAS SURE IT WAS EDGAR EVEN THOUGH THE BODY WAS ARTHUR'S, AND YOU GLIMPSED ARTHUR'S FEELINGS AS HE WATCHED THEM...!
THE WAY ARTHUR FELT JUST A LITTLE SAD, AND THAT SLIGHT SENSE OF DISTANCE, IS EXQUISITE!
YOU'VE GOT IT WRONG! WHAT HAPPENED WAS THAT, WHEN ARTHUR ENDED UP IN EDGAR'S BODY, HE BECAME AWARE OF EDGAR'S AGONY FOR THE FIRST TIME!
!

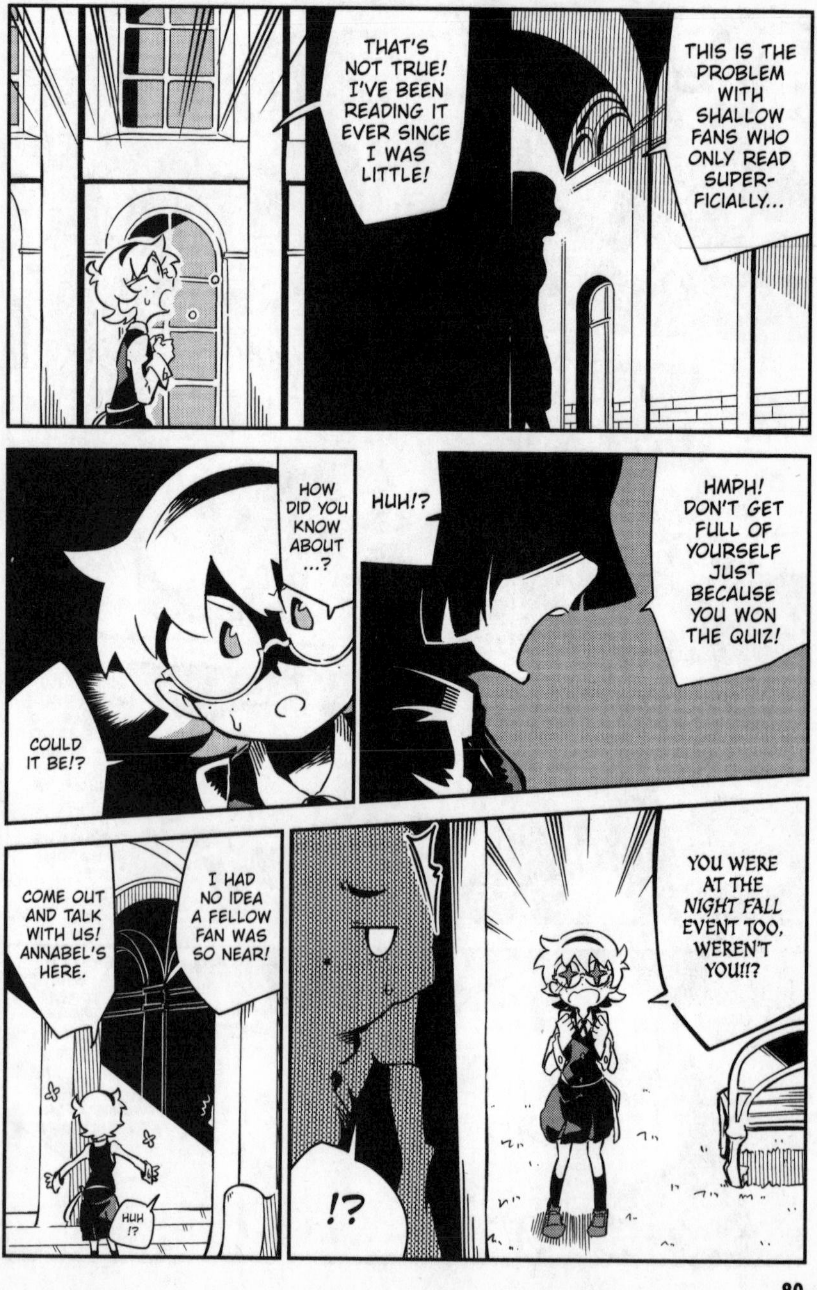
THIS IS THE PROBLEM WITH SHALLOW FANS WHO ONLY READ SUPER-FICIALLY...
THAT'S NOT TRUE! I'VE BEEN READING IT EVER SINCE I WAS LITTLE!
HMPH! DON'T GET FULL OF YOURSELF JUST BECAUSE YOU WON THE QUIZ!
HUH!?
HOW DID YOU KNOW ABOUT ...?
COULD IT BE!?
YOU WERE AT THE *NIGHT FALL* EVENT TOO, WEREN'T YOU!!?
!?
I HAD NO IDEA A FELLOW FAN WAS SO NEAR!
COME OUT AND TALK WITH US! ANNABEL'S HERE.
HUH !?

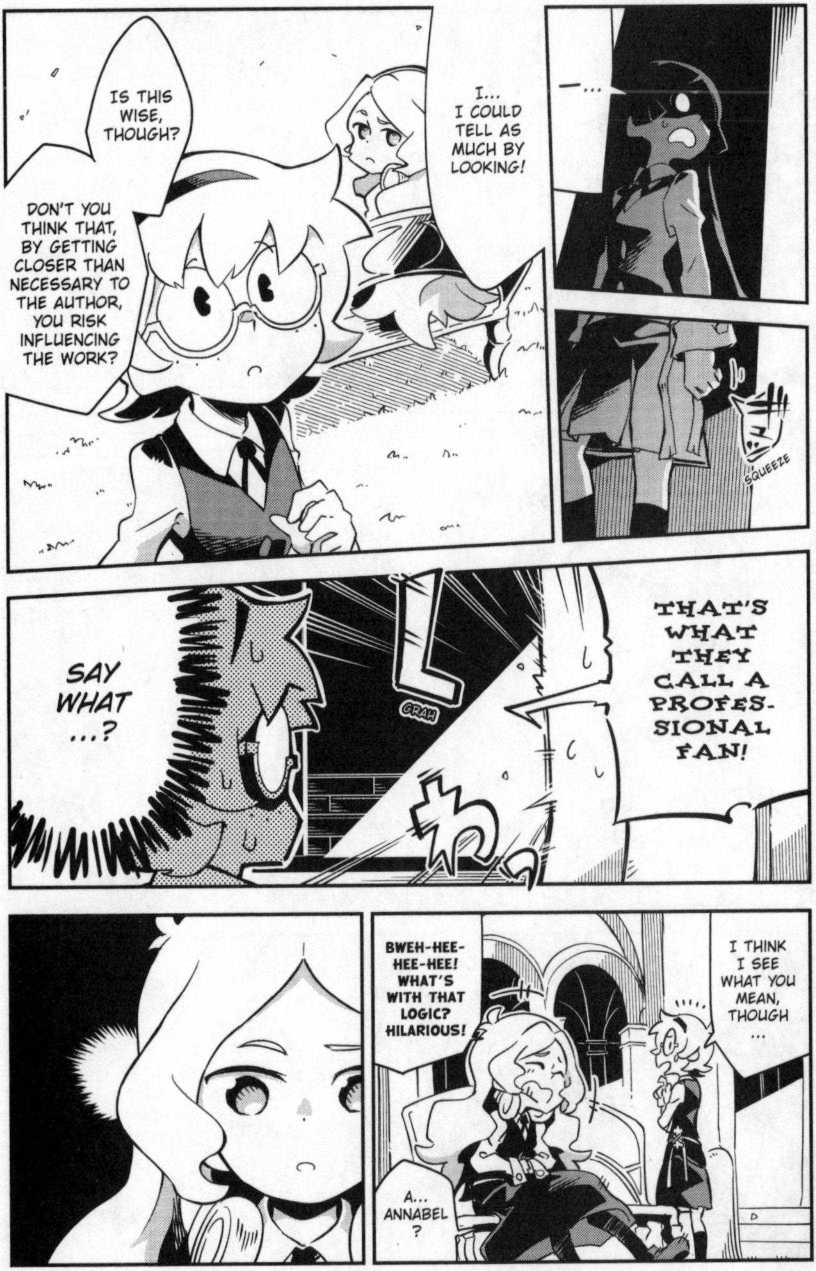
—...
SQUEEZE
I... I COULD TELL AS MUCH BY LOOKING!
IS THIS WISE, THOUGH?
DON'T YOU THINK THAT, BY GETTING CLOSER THAN NECESSARY TO THE AUTHOR, YOU RISK INFLUENCING THE WORK?
THAT'S WHAT THEY CALL A PROFES-SIONAL FAN!
GRAH
SAY WHAT ...?
I THINK I SEE WHAT YOU MEAN, THOUGH ...
BWEH-HEE-HEE-HEE! WHAT'S WITH THAT LOGIC? HILARIOUS!
A... ANNABEL ?

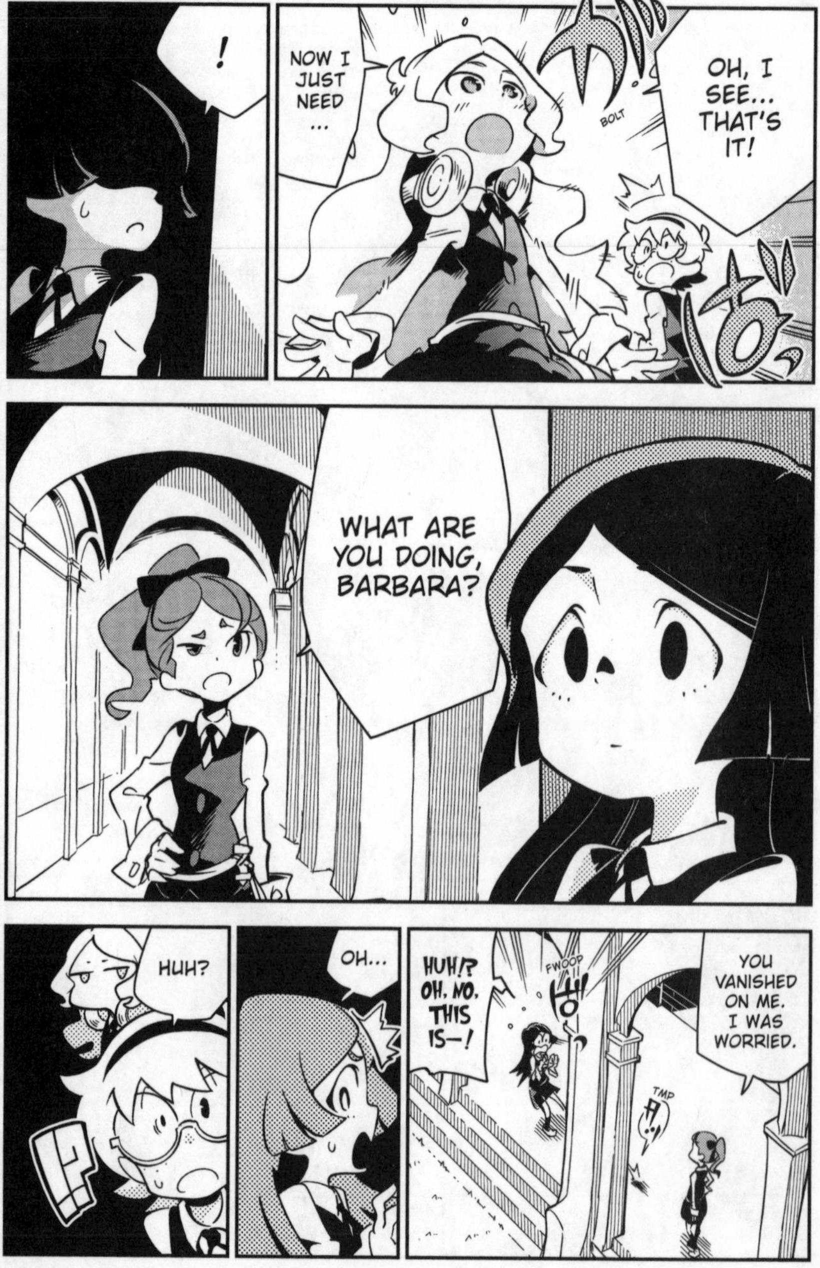
OH, I SEE... THAT'S IT!
BOLT
NOW I JUST NEED ...
!
WHAT ARE YOU DOING, BARBARA?
YOU VANISHED ON ME. I WAS WORRIED.
FWOOP
HUH!? OH, NO, THIS IS—!
TMP
OH...
HUH?

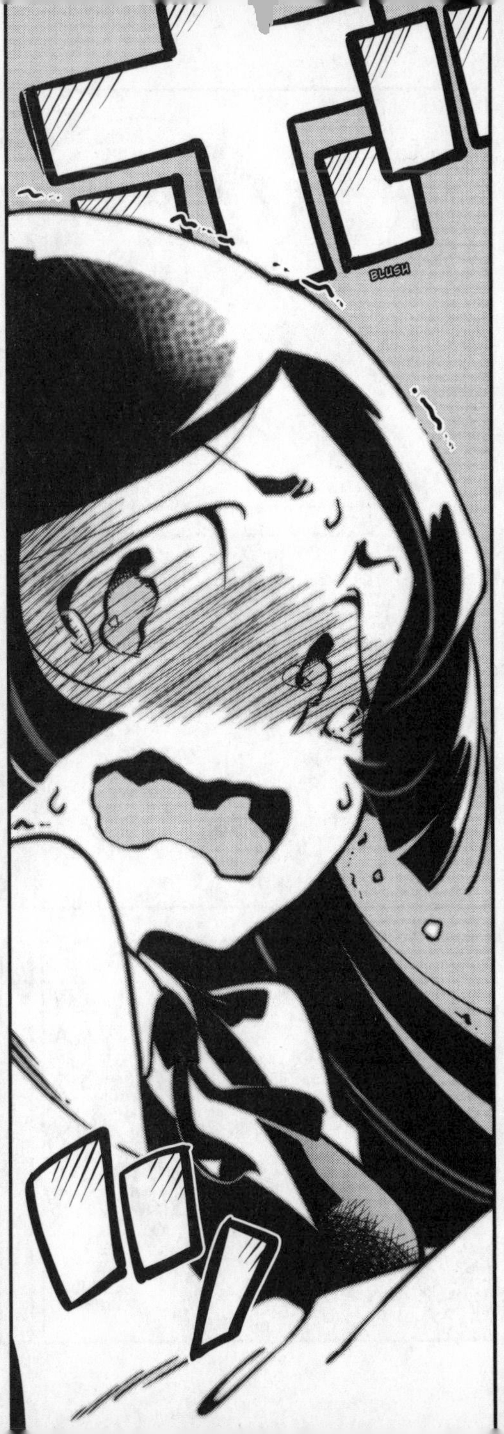
BLUSH

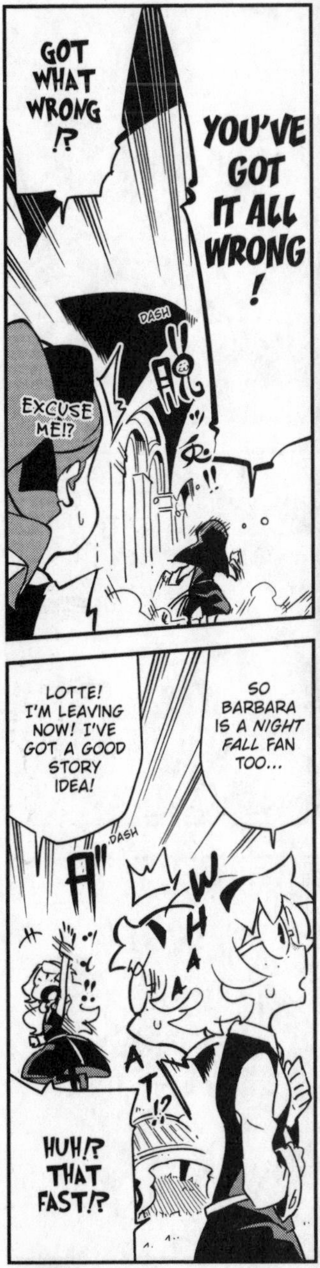
YOU'VE GOT IT ALL WRONG!
GOT WHAT WRONG!?
DASH
EXCUSE ME!?
SO BARBARA IS A NIGHT FALL FAN TOO...
LOTTE! I'M LEAVING NOW! I'VE GOT A GOOD STORY IDEA!
DASH
WHAAAAT!?
HUH!? THAT FAST!?

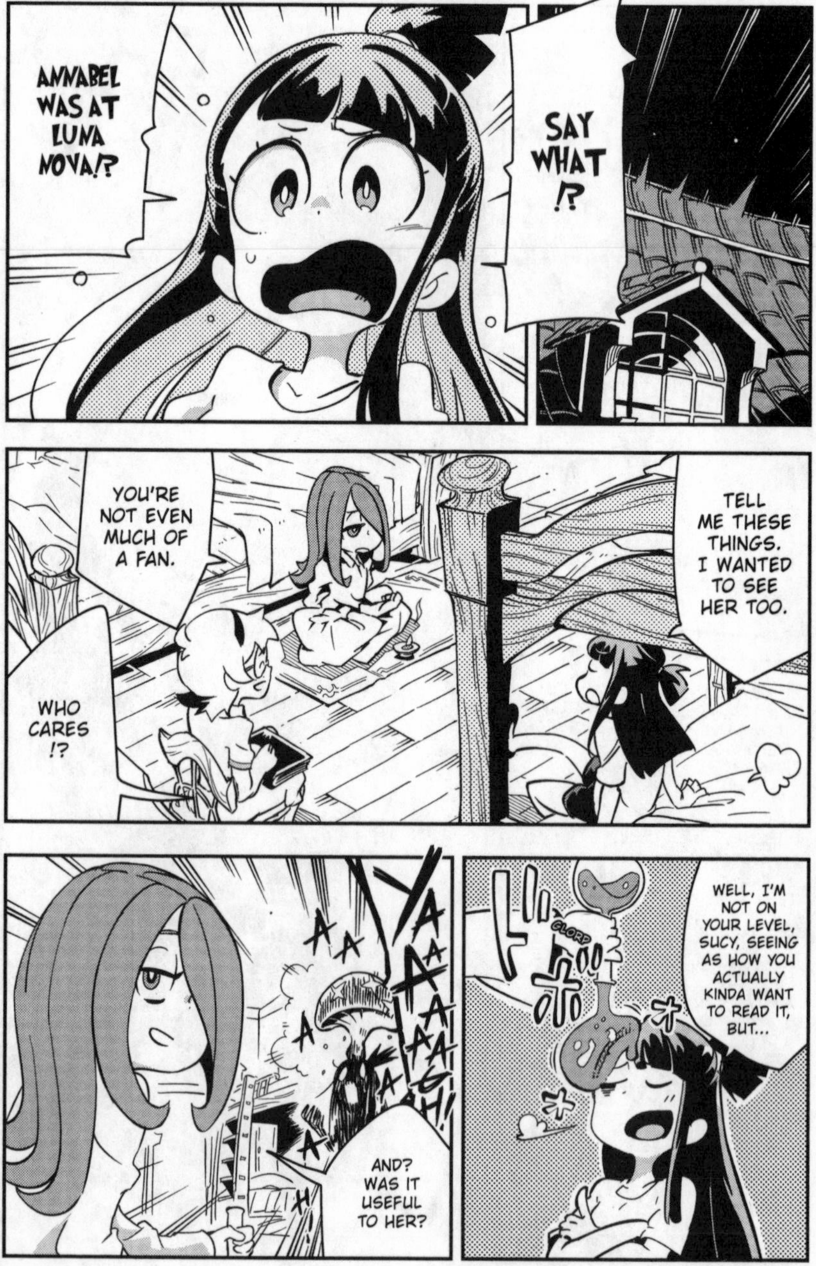
SAY WHAT !?
ANNABEL WAS AT LUNA NOVA!?
TELL ME THESE THINGS. I WANTED TO SEE HER TOO.
YOU'RE NOT EVEN MUCH OF A FAN.
WHO CARES !?
GLORP
WELL, I'M NOT ON YOUR LEVEL, SUCY, SEEING AS HOW YOU ACTUALLY KINDA WANT TO READ IT, BUT...
YAAAAAAAAAGH!
AND? WAS IT USEFUL TO HER?

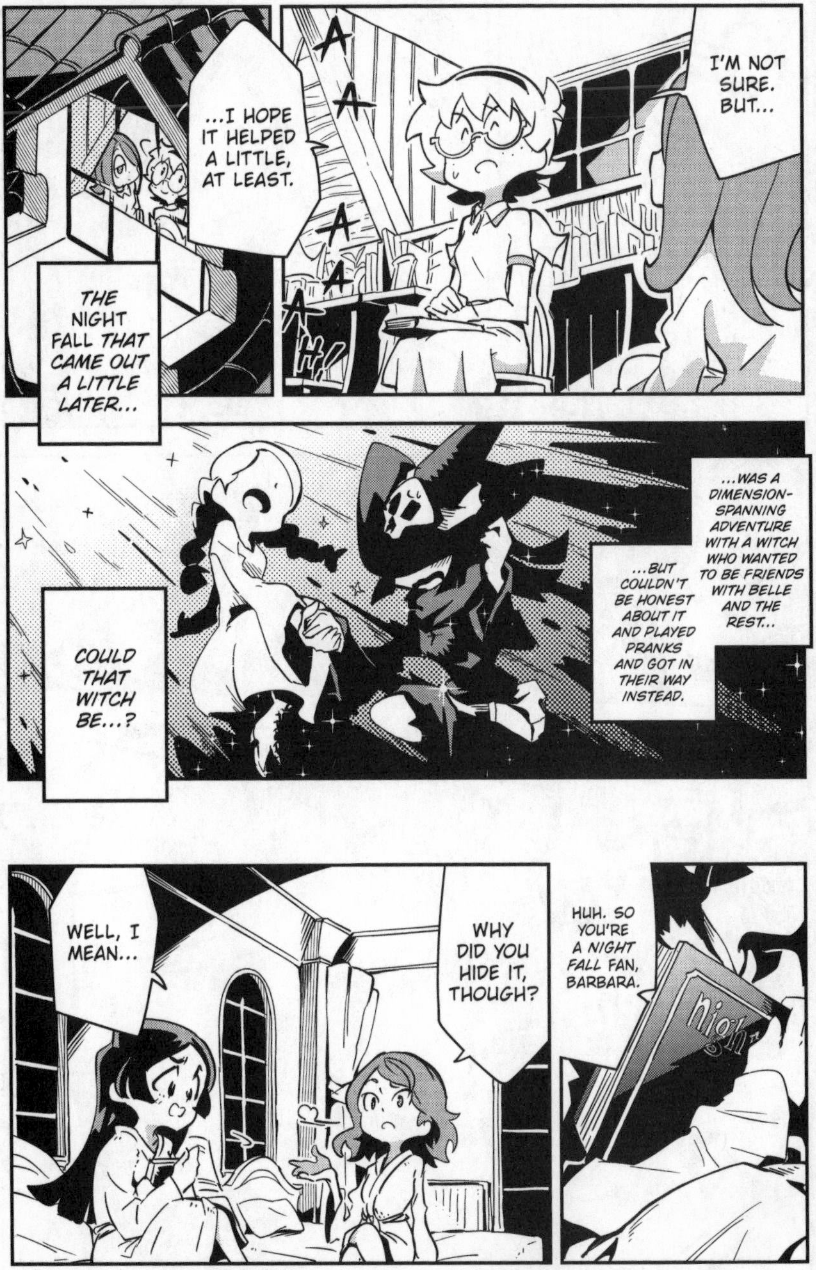
I'M NOT SURE. BUT...
...I HOPE IT HELPED A LITTLE, AT LEAST.
AAAAAH!
THE NIGHT FALL THAT CAME OUT A LITTLE LATER...
...WAS A DIMENSION-SPANNING ADVENTURE WITH A WITCH WHO WANTED TO BE FRIENDS WITH BELLE AND THE REST...
...BUT COULDN'T BE HONEST ABOUT IT AND PLAYED PRANKS AND GOT IN THEIR WAY INSTEAD.
COULD THAT WITCH BE...?
HUH. SO YOU'RE A NIGHT FALL FAN, BARBARA.
night
WHY DID YOU HIDE IT, THOUGH?
WELL, I MEAN...

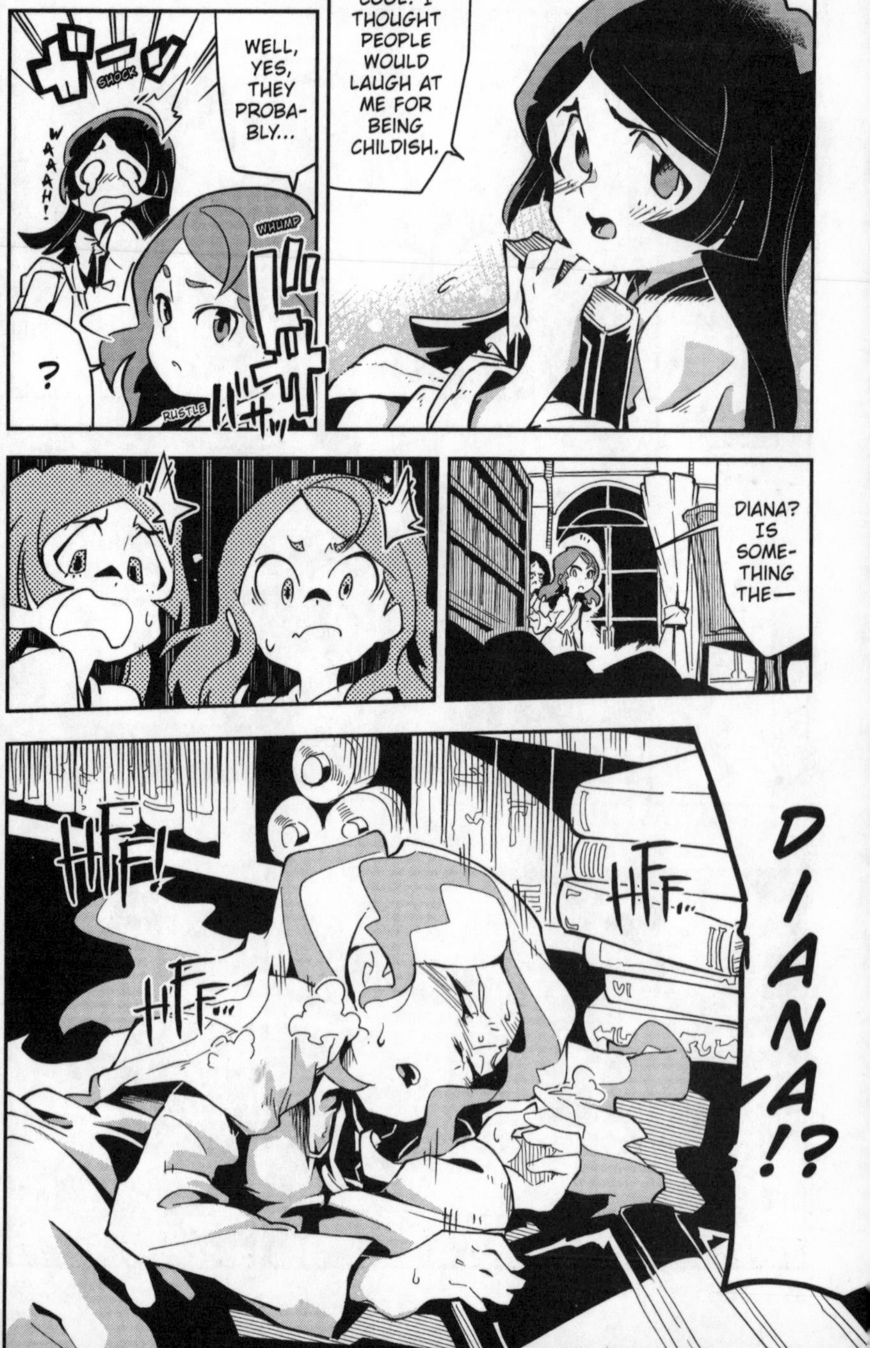
IT ISN'T COOL. I THOUGHT PEOPLE WOULD LAUGH AT ME FOR BEING CHILDISH.
WELL, YES, THEY PROBABLY...
SHOCK
WAAAAH!
WHUMP
RUSTLE
?
DIANA? IS SOMETHING THE—
HFF...
HFF!
HFF...
DIANA!?

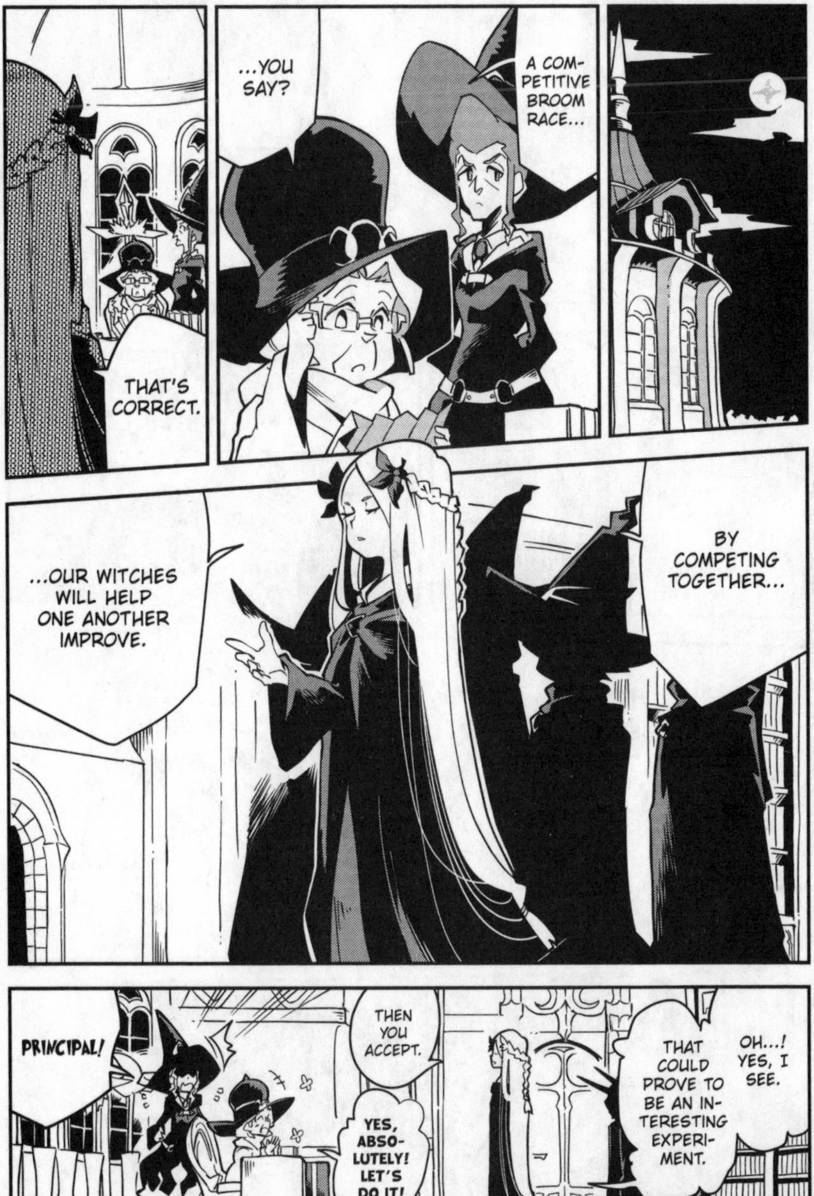
A COMPETITIVE BROOM RACE...
...YOU SAY?
THAT'S CORRECT.
BY COMPETING TOGETHER...
...OUR WITCHES WILL HELP ONE ANOTHER IMPROVE.
OH...! YES, I SEE.
THAT COULD PROVE TO BE AN INTERESTING EXPERIMENT.
THEN YOU ACCEPT.
YES, ABSOLUTELY! LET'S DO IT!
PRINCIPAL!

Chapter 15

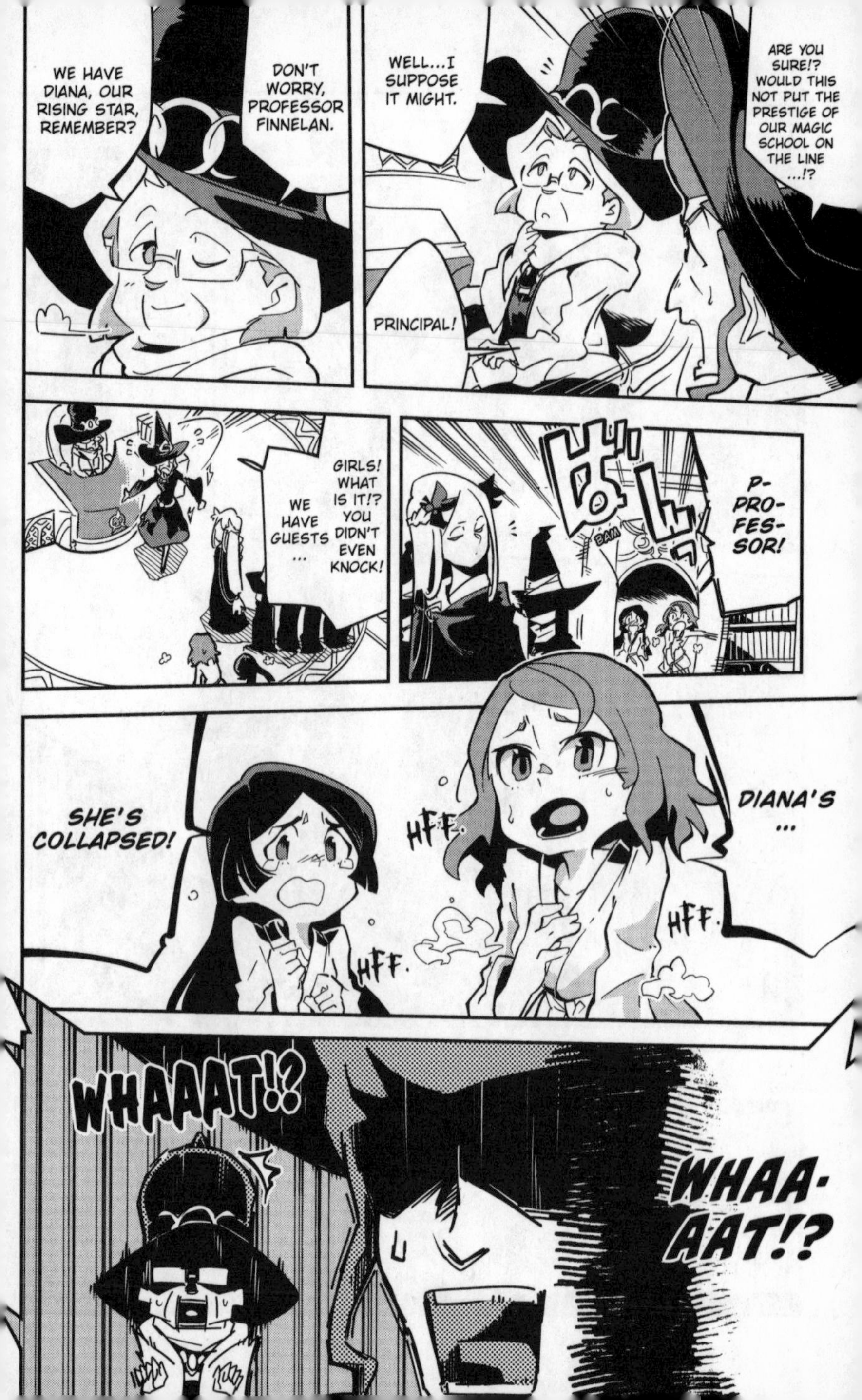

ARE YOU SURE!? WOULD THIS NOT PUT THE PRESTIGE OF OUR MAGIC SCHOOL ON THE LINE ...!?
WELL...I SUPPOSE IT MIGHT.
PRINCIPAL!
DON'T WORRY, PROFESSOR FINNELAN.
WE HAVE DIANA, OUR RISING STAR, REMEMBER?
P-PRO-FES-SOR!
BAM
GIRLS! WHAT IS IT!? YOU DIDN'T EVEN KNOCK!
WE HAVE GUESTS ...
DIANA'S ...
HFF.
HFF.
SHE'S COLLAPSED!
HFF.
WHAA-AAT!?
WHAAAT!?

Chapter 15 WITCHES FROM ELSEWHERE

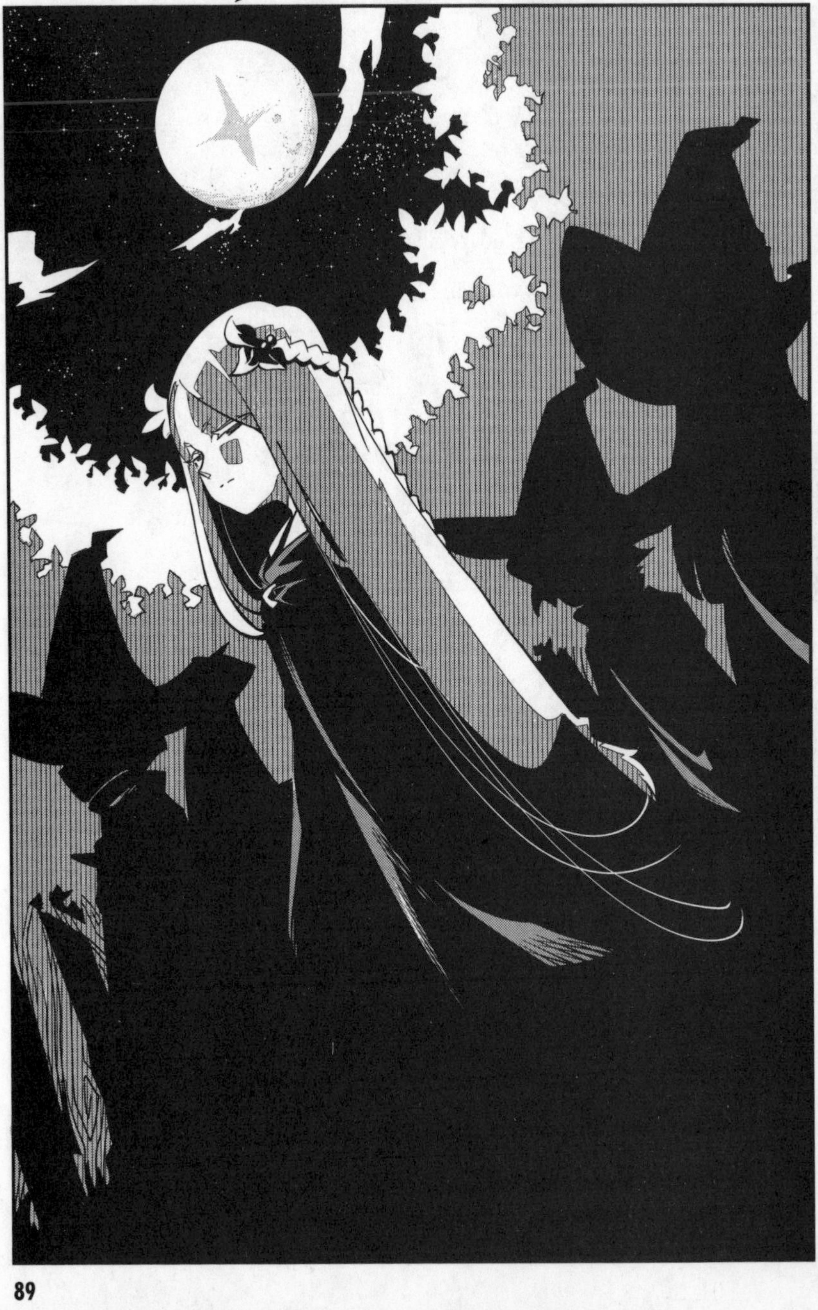

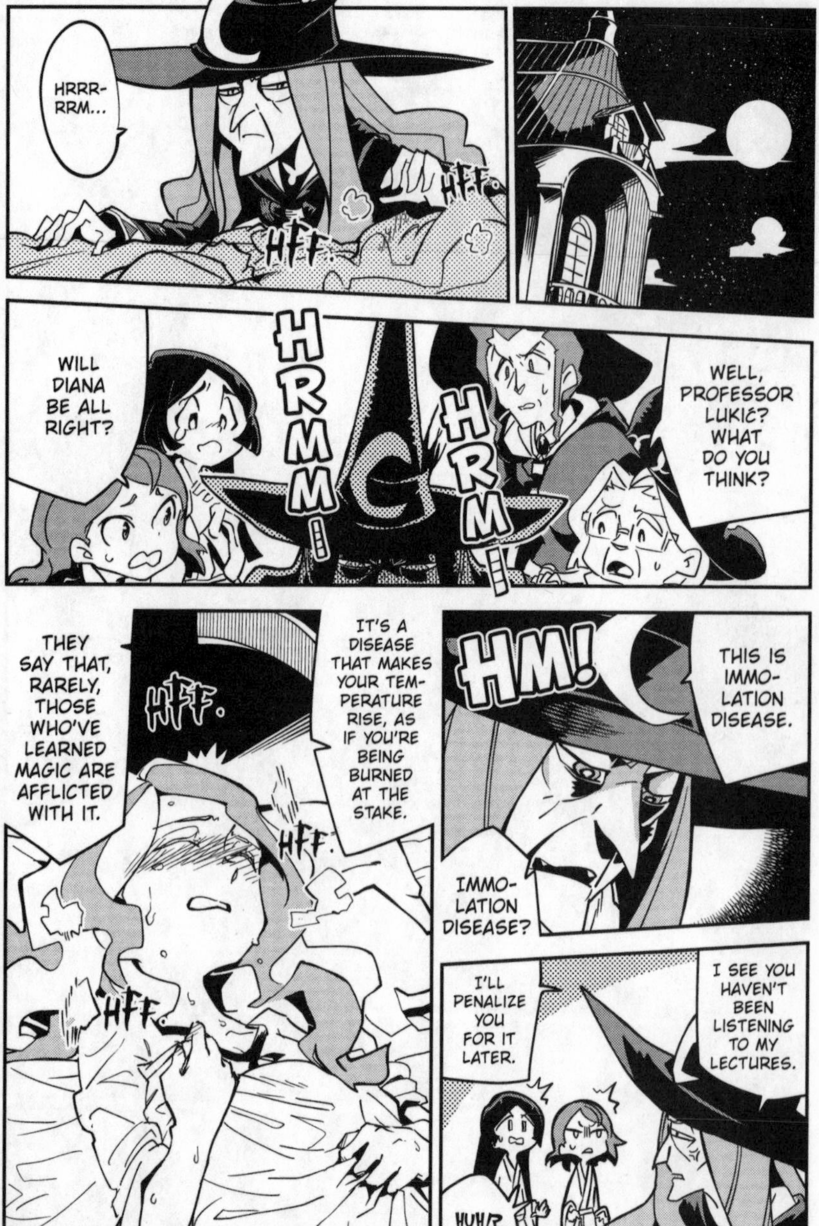
HRRR-RRM...
HFF.
HFF.
WELL, PROFESSOR LUKIĆ? WHAT DO YOU THINK?
HRM!
HRMM!
WILL DIANA BE ALL RIGHT?
HM!
THIS IS IMMO-LATION DISEASE.
IMMO-LATION DISEASE?
I SEE YOU HAVEN'T BEEN LISTENING TO MY LECTURES.
I'LL PENALIZE YOU FOR IT LATER.
HUH!?
IT'S A DISEASE THAT MAKES YOUR TEM-PERATURE RISE, AS IF YOU'RE BEING BURNED AT THE STAKE.
THEY SAY THAT, RARELY, THOSE WHO'VE LEARNED MAGIC ARE AFFLICTED WITH IT.
HFF.
HFF.
HFF.

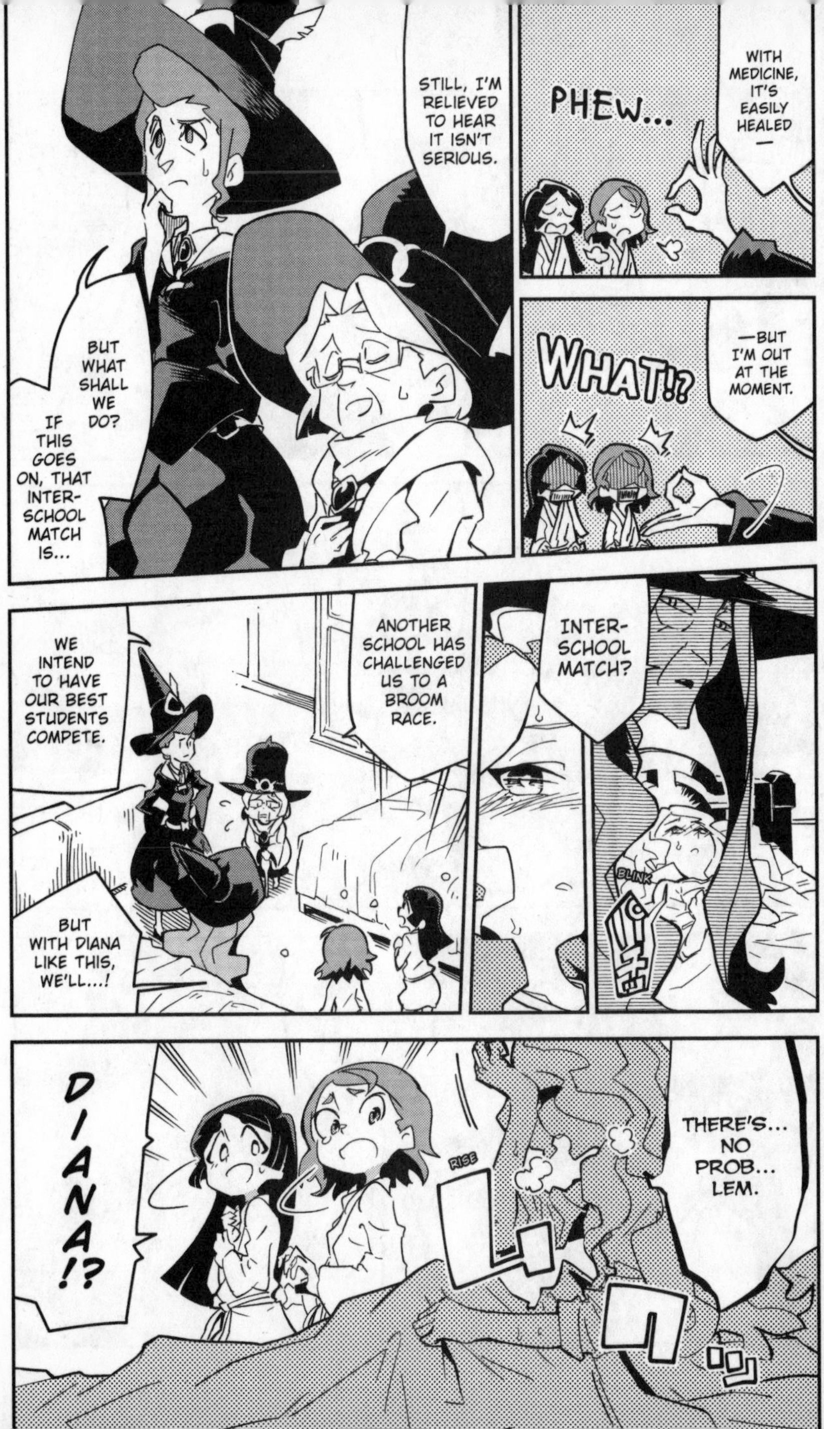
WITH MEDICINE, IT'S EASILY HEALED—
PHEW...
—BUT I'M OUT AT THE MOMENT.
WHAT!?
STILL, I'M RELIEVED TO HEAR IT ISN'T SERIOUS.
BUT WHAT SHALL WE DO?
IF THIS GOES ON, THAT INTER-SCHOOL MATCH IS...
INTER-SCHOOL MATCH?
BLINK
ANOTHER SCHOOL HAS CHALLENGED US TO A BROOM RACE.
WE INTEND TO HAVE OUR BEST STUDENTS COMPETE.
BUT WITH DIANA LIKE THIS, WE'LL...!
THERE'S... NO PROB... LEM.
RISE
DIANA!?

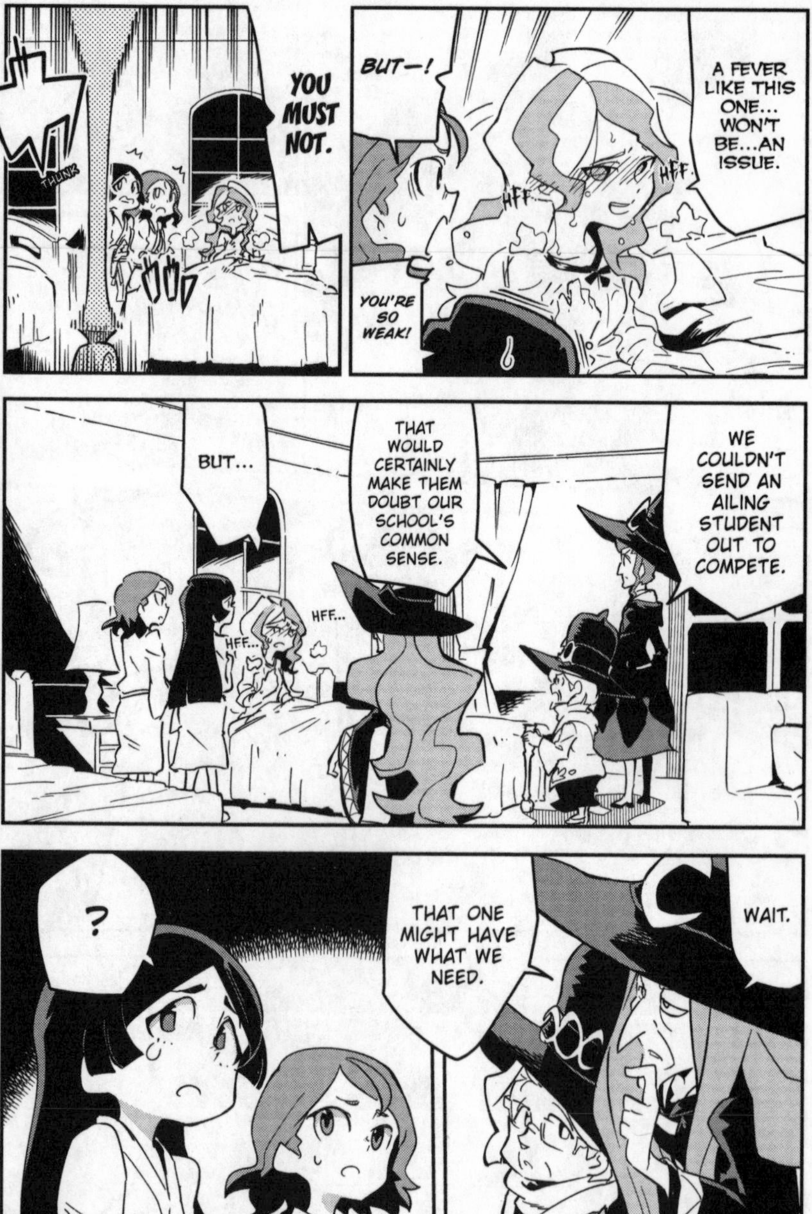
A FEVER LIKE THIS ONE... WON'T BE...AN ISSUE.
HFF.
HFF...
BUT—!
YOU'RE SO WEAK!
YOU MUST NOT.
THUNK
WE COULDN'T SEND AN AILING STUDENT OUT TO COMPETE.
THAT WOULD CERTAINLY MAKE THEM DOUBT OUR SCHOOL'S COMMON SENSE.
BUT...
HFF...
HFF...
WAIT.
THAT ONE MIGHT HAVE WHAT WE NEED.
?

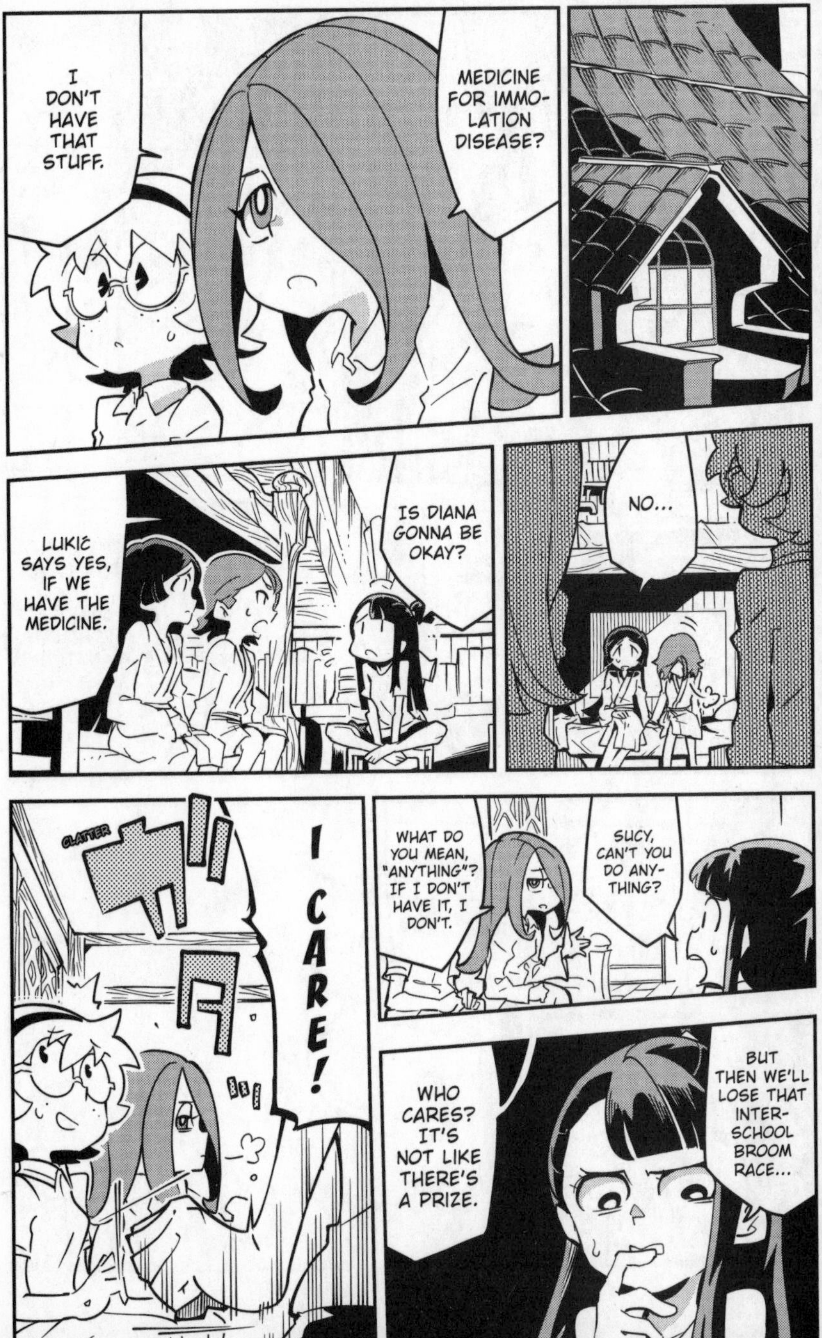
MEDICINE FOR IMMOLATION DISEASE?
I DON'T HAVE THAT STUFF.
NO...
IS DIANA GONNA BE OKAY?
LUKIC SAYS YES, IF WE HAVE THE MEDICINE.
SUCY, CAN'T YOU DO ANYTHING?
WHAT DO YOU MEAN, "ANYTHING"? IF I DON'T HAVE IT, I DON'T.
BUT THEN WE'LL LOSE THAT INTER-SCHOOL BROOM RACE...
WHO CARES? IT'S NOT LIKE THERE'S A PRIZE.
I CARE!
CLATTER

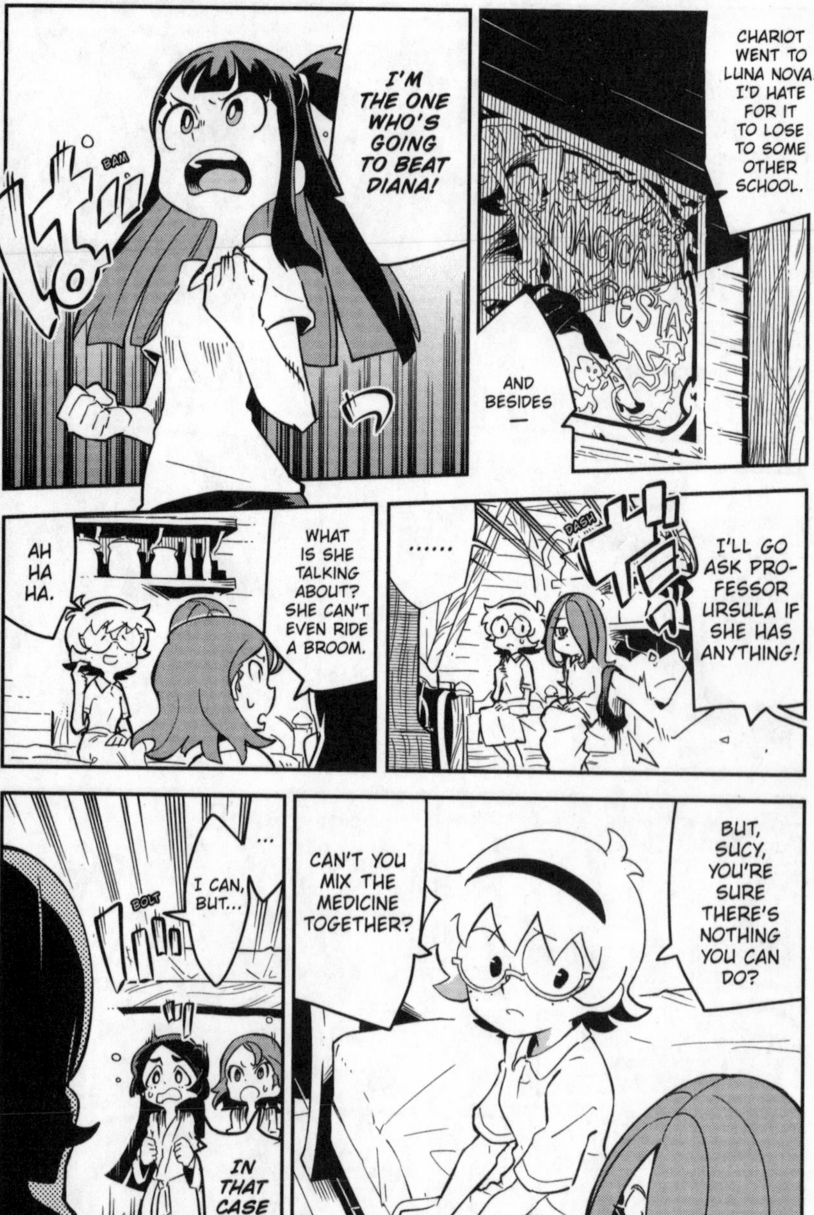
CHARIOT WENT TO LUNA NOVA. I'D HATE FOR IT TO LOSE TO SOME OTHER SCHOOL.
AND BESIDES —
I'M THE ONE WHO'S GOING TO BEAT DIANA!
BAM
I'LL GO ASK PROFESSOR URSULA IF SHE HAS ANYTHING!
DASH
......
WHAT IS SHE TALKING ABOUT? SHE CAN'T EVEN RIDE A BROOM.
AH HA HA.
BUT, SUCY, YOU'RE SURE THERE'S NOTHING YOU CAN DO?
CAN'T YOU MIX THE MEDICINE TOGETHER?
...
I CAN, BUT...
BOLT
IN THAT CASE —!

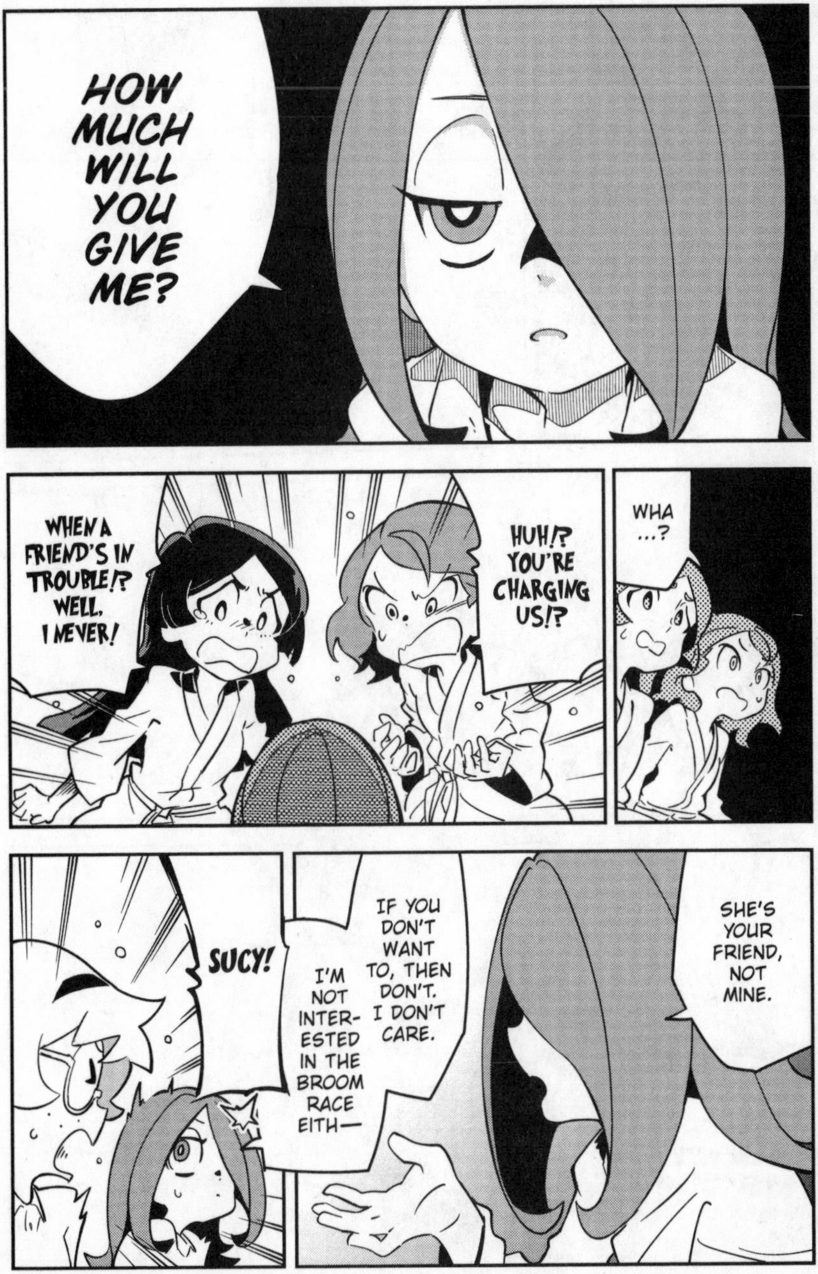
HOW MUCH WILL YOU GIVE ME?
WHA ...?
HUH!? YOU'RE CHARGING US!?
WHEN A FRIEND'S IN TROUBLE!? WELL, I NEVER!
SHE'S YOUR FRIEND, NOT MINE.
IF YOU DON'T WANT TO, THEN DON'T. I DON'T CARE.
I'M NOT INTER-ESTED IN THE BROOM RACE EITH—
SUCY!

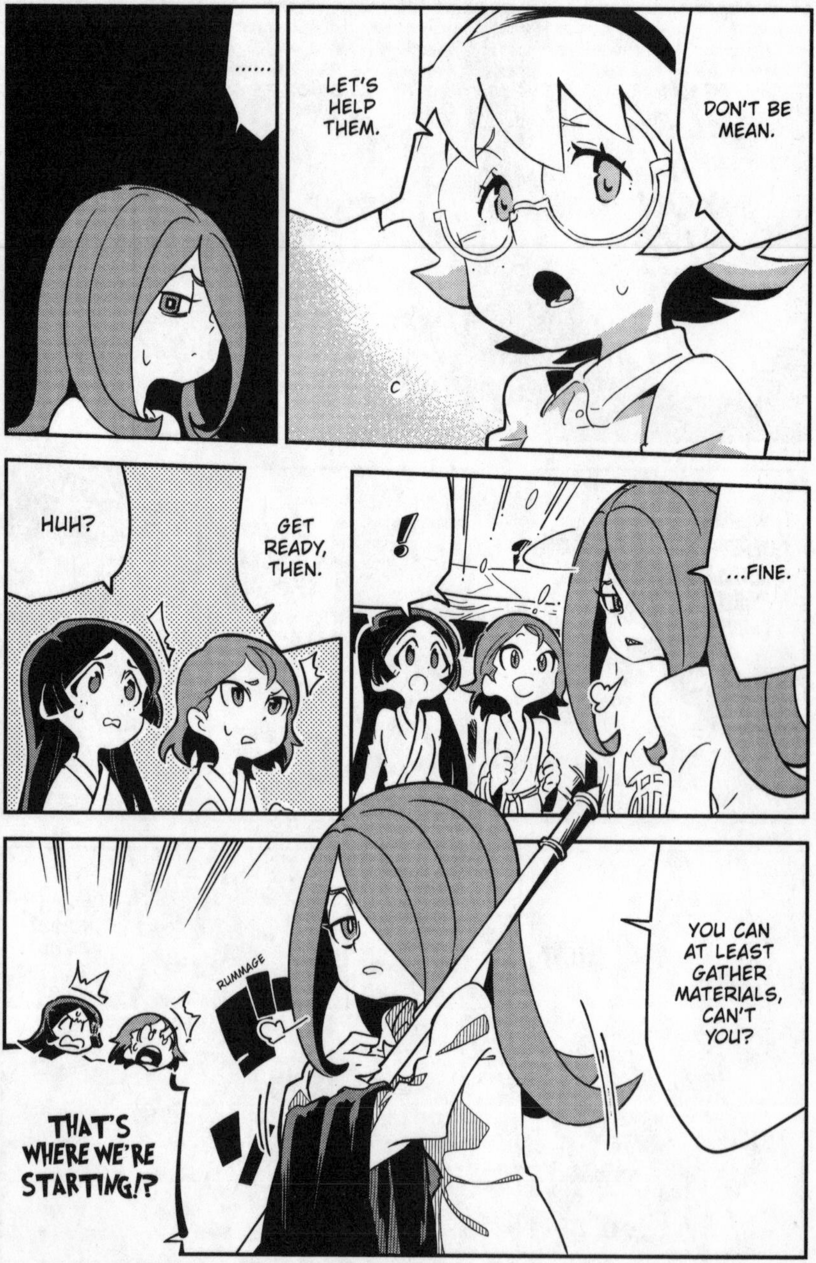
DON'T BE MEAN.
LET'S HELP THEM.
......
...FINE.
!
GET READY, THEN.
HUH?
YOU CAN AT LEAST GATHER MATERIALS, CAN'T YOU?
RUMMAGE
THAT'S WHERE WE'RE STARTING!?

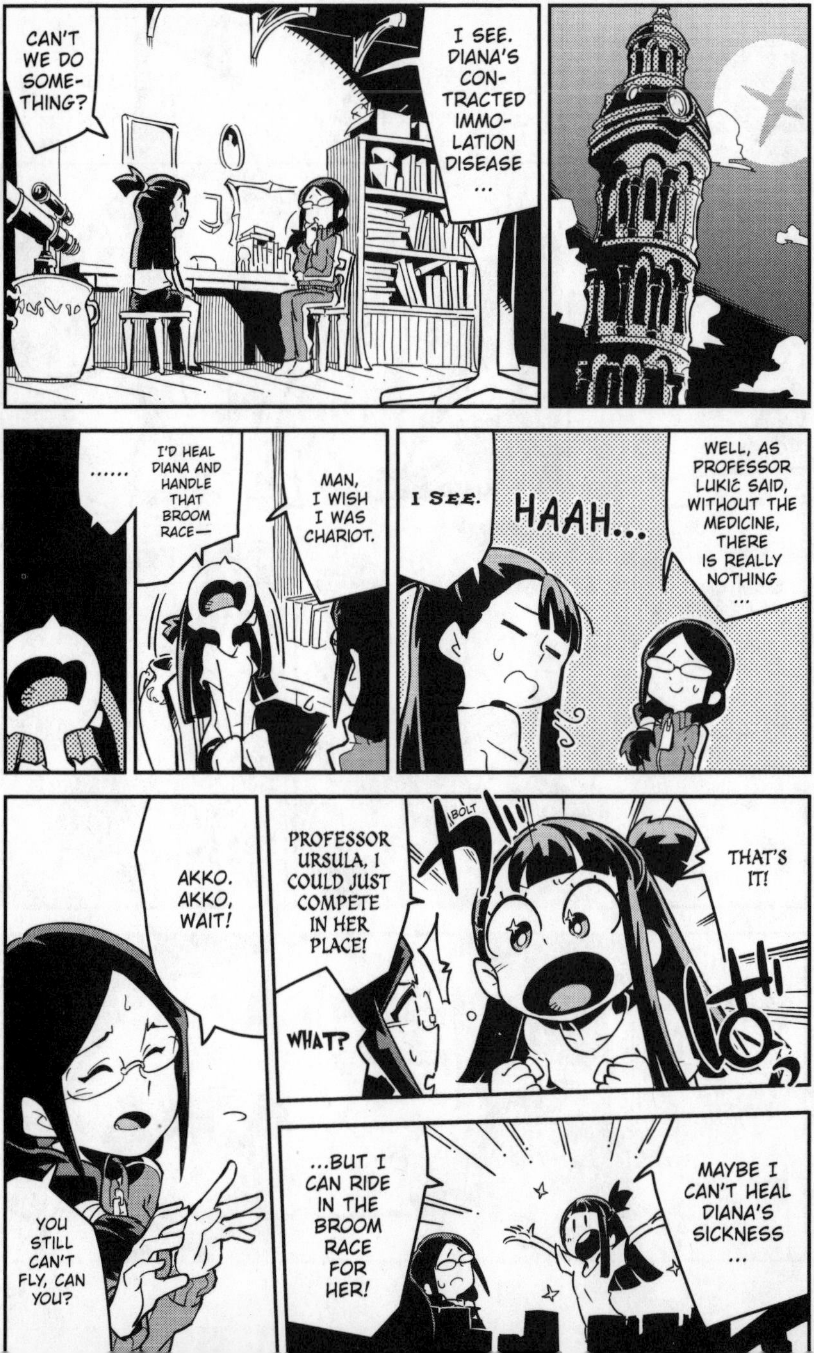
I SEE. DIANA'S CONTRACTED IMMOLATION DISEASE ...
CAN'T WE DO SOMETHING?
WELL, AS PROFESSOR LUKIĆ SAID, WITHOUT THE MEDICINE, THERE IS REALLY NOTHING ...
HAAH...
I SEE.
MAN, I WISH I WAS CHARIOT.
I'D HEAL DIANA AND HANDLE THAT BROOM RACE—
......
THAT'S IT!
BOLT
PROFESSOR URSULA, I COULD JUST COMPETE IN HER PLACE!
WHAT?
MAYBE I CAN'T HEAL DIANA'S SICKNESS ...
...BUT I CAN RIDE IN THE BROOM RACE FOR HER!
AKKO. AKKO, WAIT!
YOU STILL CAN'T FLY, CAN YOU?

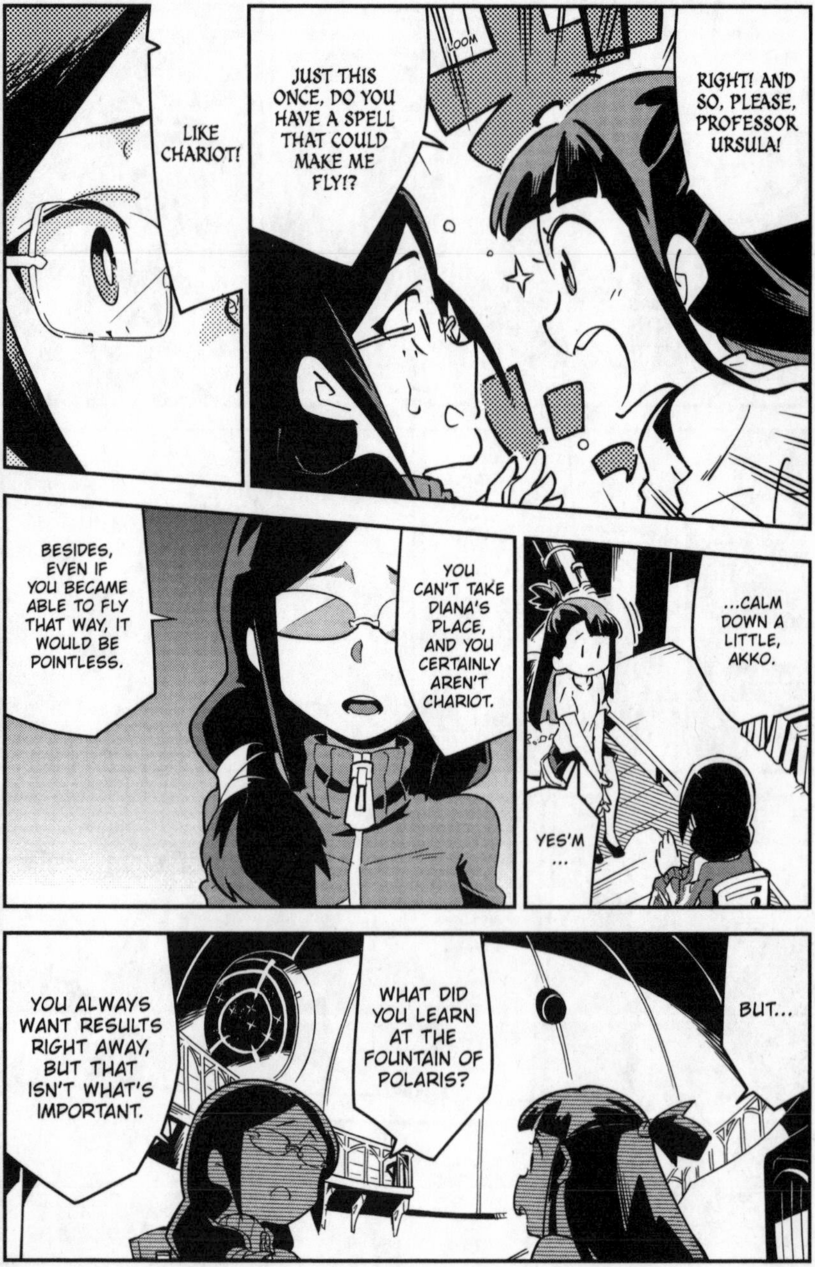
RIGHT! AND SO, PLEASE, PROFESSOR URSULA!
LOOM
JUST THIS ONCE, DO YOU HAVE A SPELL THAT COULD MAKE ME FLY!?
LIKE CHARIOT!
...CALM DOWN A LITTLE, AKKO.
YES'M ...
YOU CAN'T TAKE DIANA'S PLACE, AND YOU CERTAINLY AREN'T CHARIOT.
BESIDES, EVEN IF YOU BECAME ABLE TO FLY THAT WAY, IT WOULD BE POINTLESS.
BUT...
WHAT DID YOU LEARN AT THE FOUNTAIN OF POLARIS?
YOU ALWAYS WANT RESULTS RIGHT AWAY, BUT THAT ISN'T WHAT'S IMPORTANT.

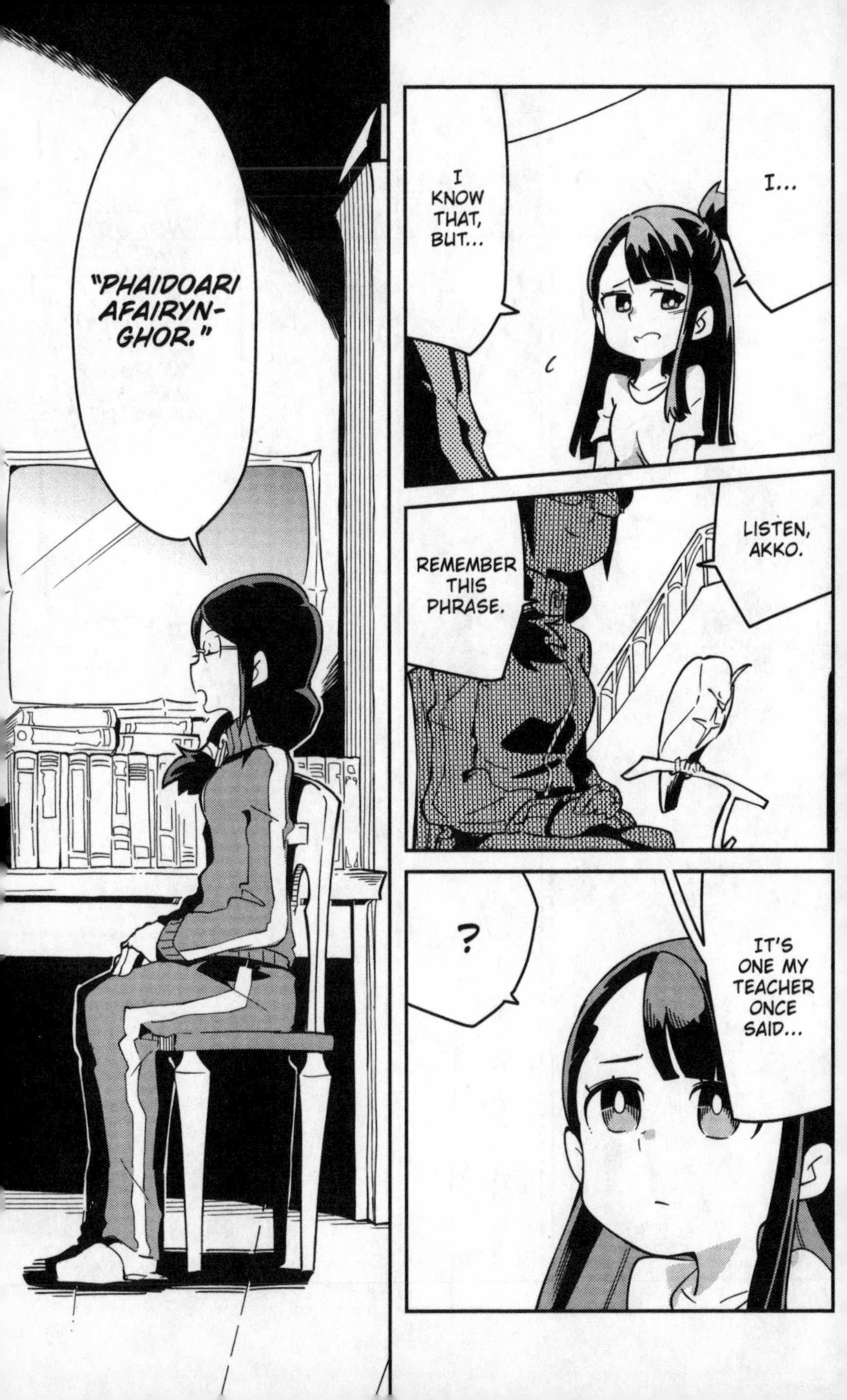
I...
I KNOW THAT, BUT...
LISTEN, AKKO.
REMEMBER THIS PHRASE.
IT'S ONE MY TEACHER ONCE SAID...
?
"PHAIDOARI AFAIRYN-GHOR."

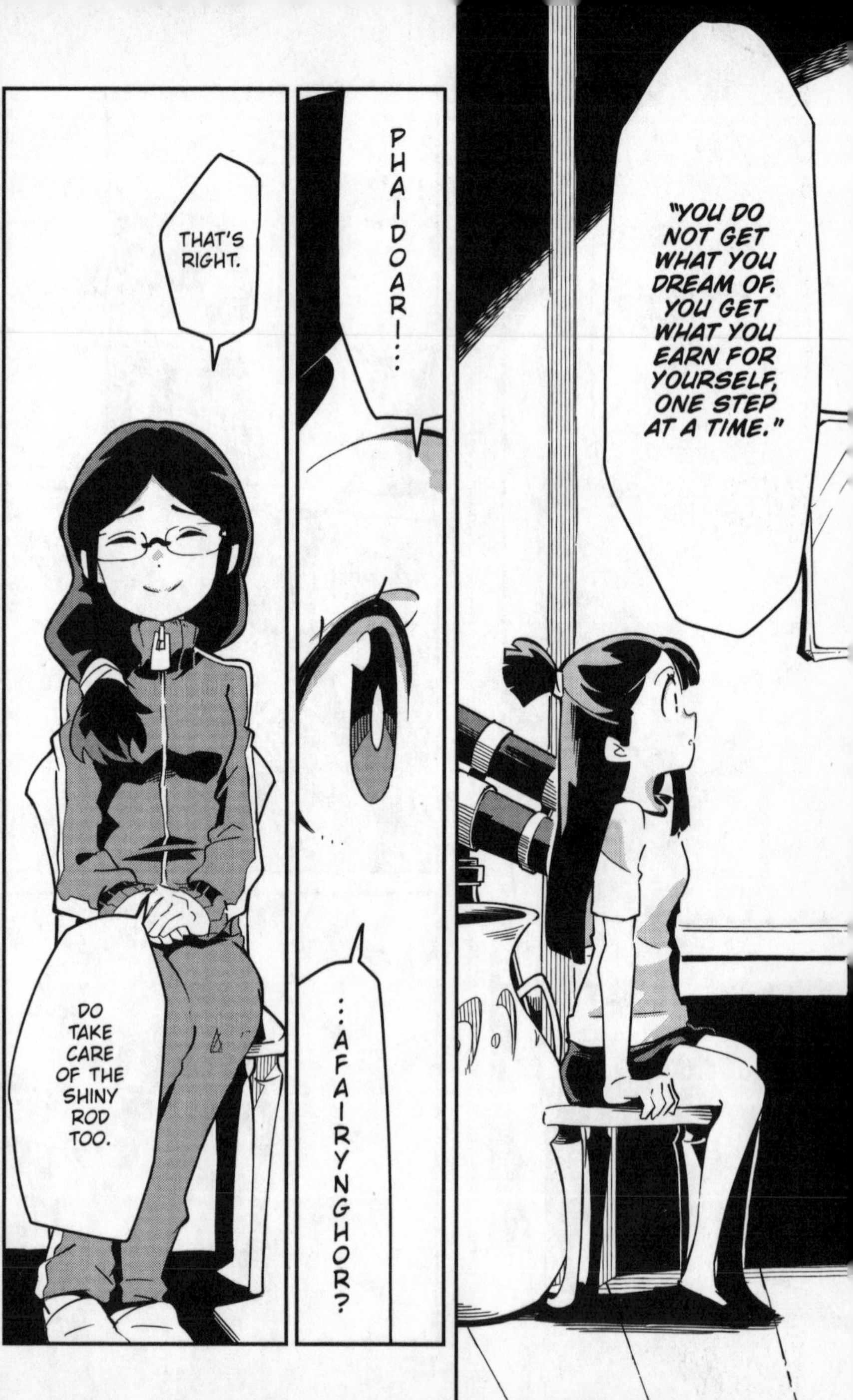
"YOU DO NOT GET WHAT YOU DREAM OF. YOU GET WHAT YOU EARN FOR YOURSELF, ONE STEP AT A TIME."
PHAIDOAR!...
...AFAIRYNGHOR?
THAT'S RIGHT.
DO TAKE CARE OF THE SHINY ROD TOO.

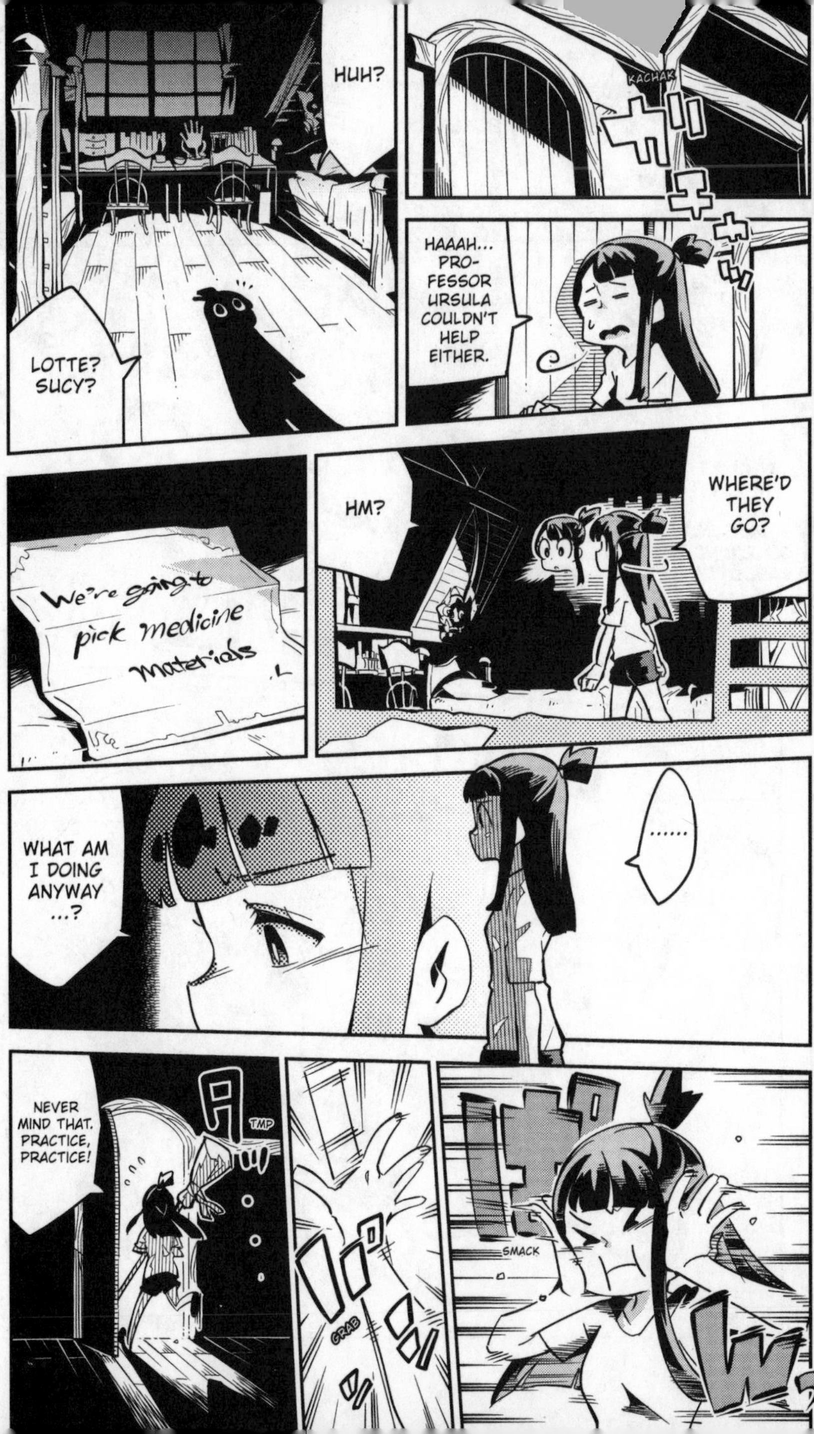
KACHAK
HAAAH... PRO-FESSOR URSULA COULDN'T HELP EITHER.
HUH?
LOTTE? SUCY?
WHERE'D THEY GO?
HM?
We're going to pick medicine materials
.L
......
WHAT AM I DOING ANYWAY ...?
SMACK
GRAB
NEVER MIND THAT. PRACTICE, PRACTICE!
TMP

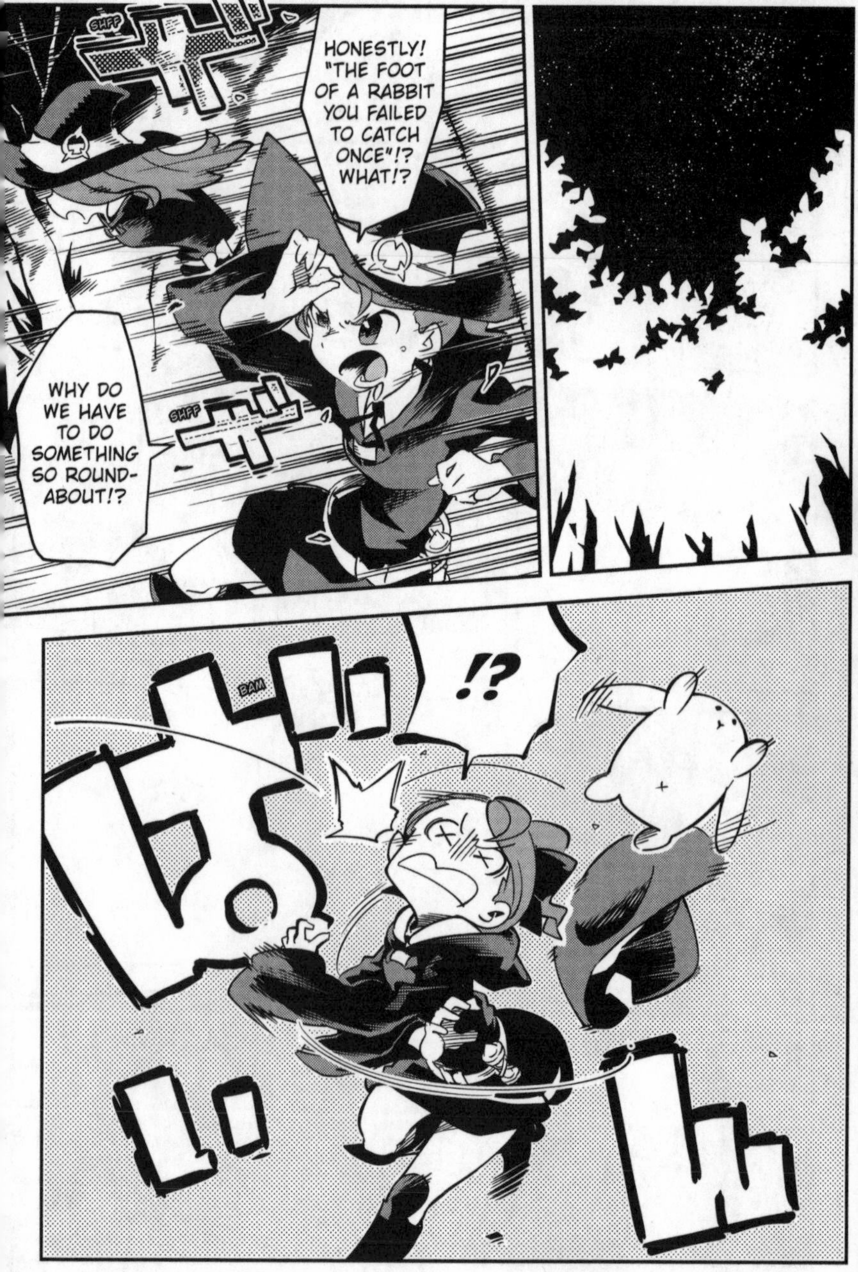
SHFF
HONESTLY! "THE FOOT OF A RABBIT YOU FAILED TO CATCH ONCE"!? WHAT!?
SHFF
WHY DO WE HAVE TO DO SOMETHING SO ROUND-ABOUT!?
!?
BAM

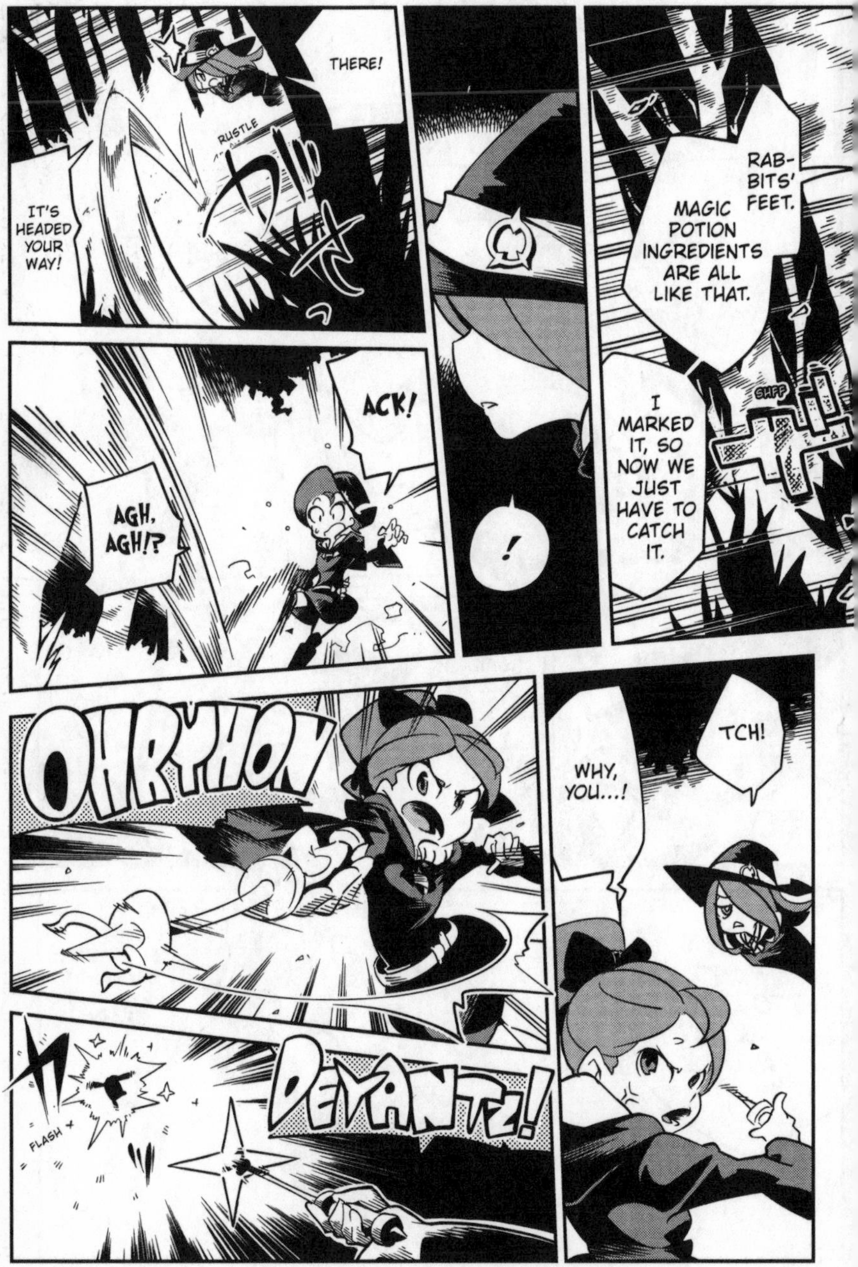
RAB-BITS' FEET.
MAGIC POTION INGREDIENTS ARE ALL LIKE THAT.
SHFF
I MARKED IT, SO NOW WE JUST HAVE TO CATCH IT.
!
THERE!
RUSTLE
IT'S HEADED YOUR WAY!
ACK!
AGH, AGH!?
TCH!
WHY, YOU...!
OHRYHON
DEYANTZ!
FLASH

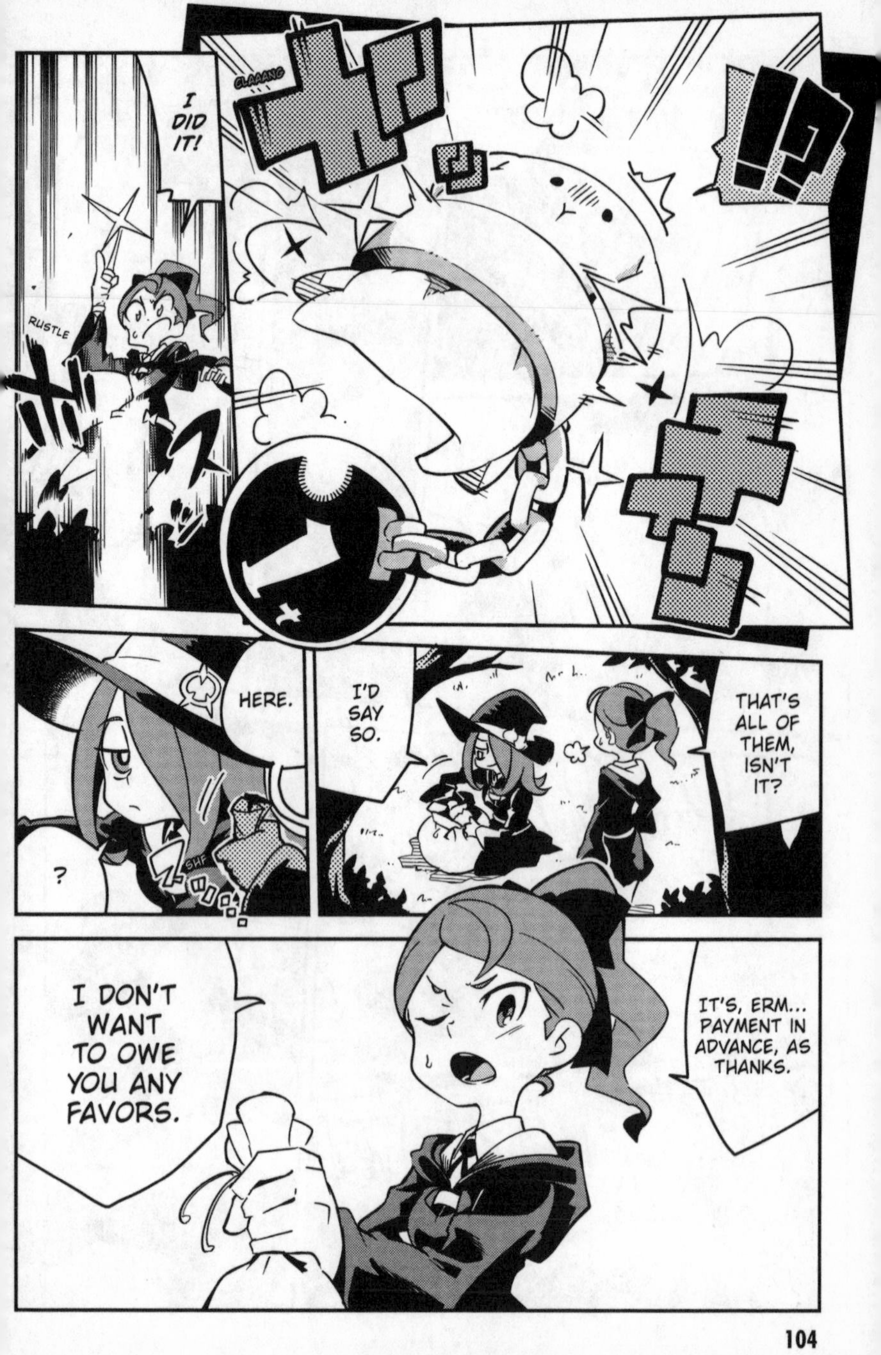
CLAAANG
!?
I DID IT!
RUSTLE
THAT'S ALL OF THEM, ISN'T IT?
I'D SAY SO.
HERE.
SHF
?
IT'S, ERM... PAYMENT IN ADVANCE, AS THANKS.
I DON'T WANT TO OWE YOU ANY FAVORS.

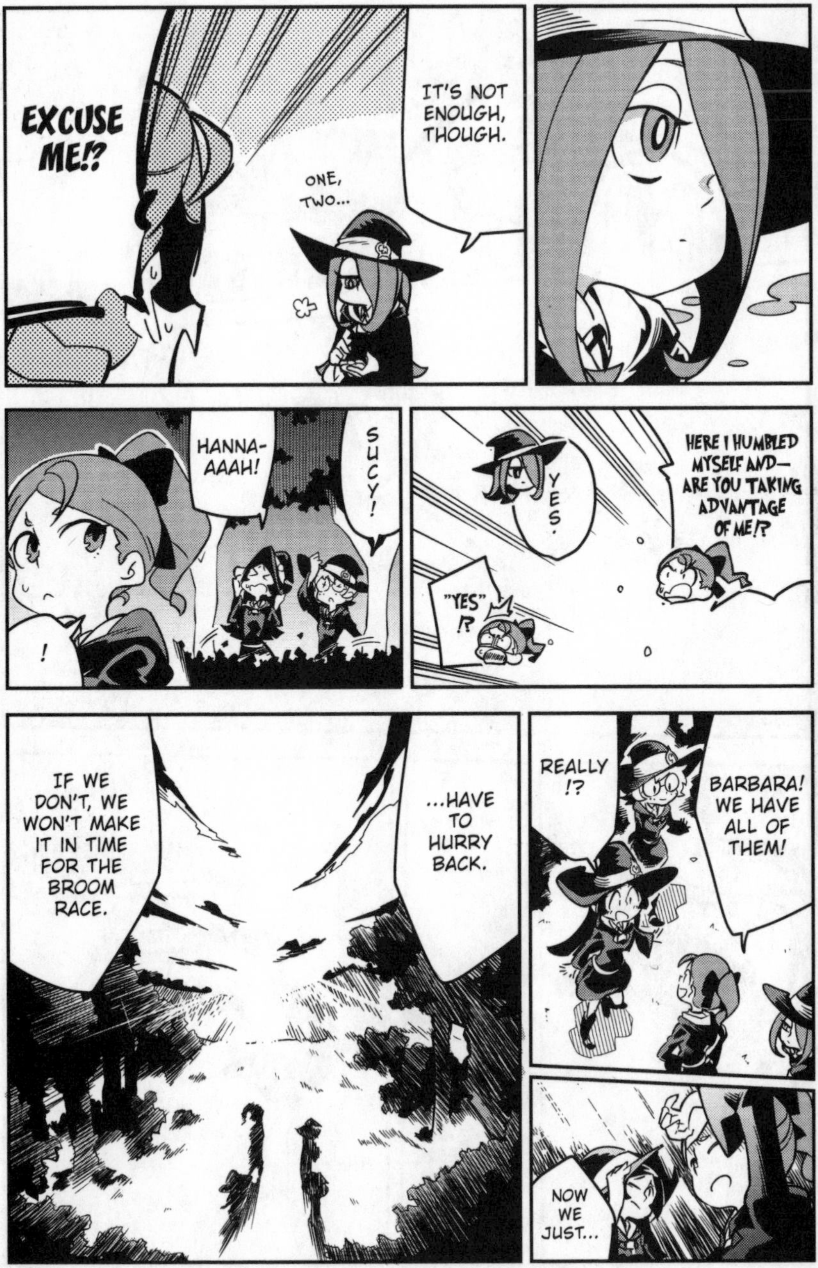
IT'S NOT ENOUGH, THOUGH.
EXCUSE ME!?
ONE, TWO...
HERE I HUMBLED MYSELF AND— ARE YOU TAKING ADVANTAGE OF ME!?
YES.
"YES" !?
SUCY!
HANNA-AAAH!
!
BARBARA! WE HAVE ALL OF THEM!
REALLY !?
NOW WE JUST...
...HAVE TO HURRY BACK.
IF WE DON'T, WE WON'T MAKE IT IN TIME FOR THE BROOM RACE.

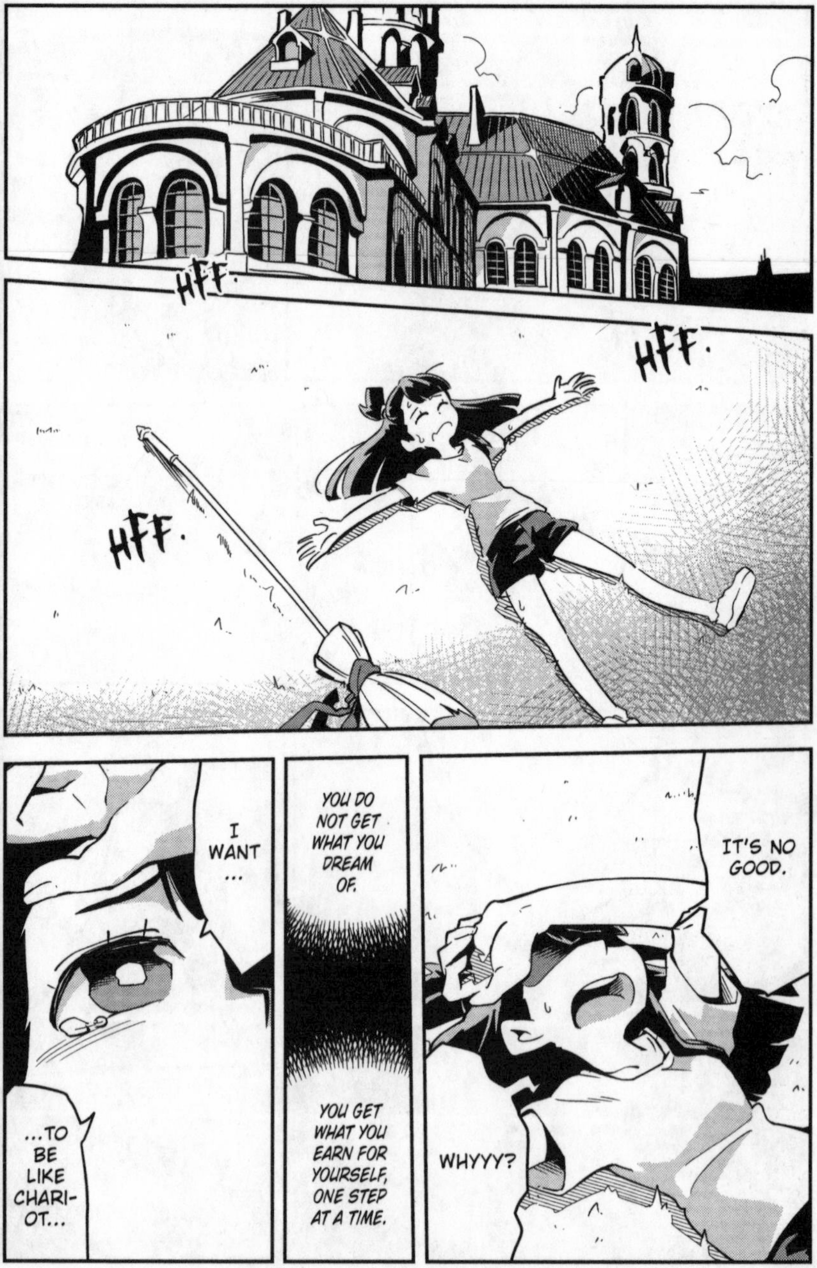
HFF.
HFF.
HFF.
IT'S NO GOOD.
WHYYY?
YOU DO NOT GET WHAT YOU DREAM OF.
YOU GET WHAT YOU EARN FOR YOURSELF, ONE STEP AT A TIME.
I WANT...
...TO BE LIKE CHARIOT...

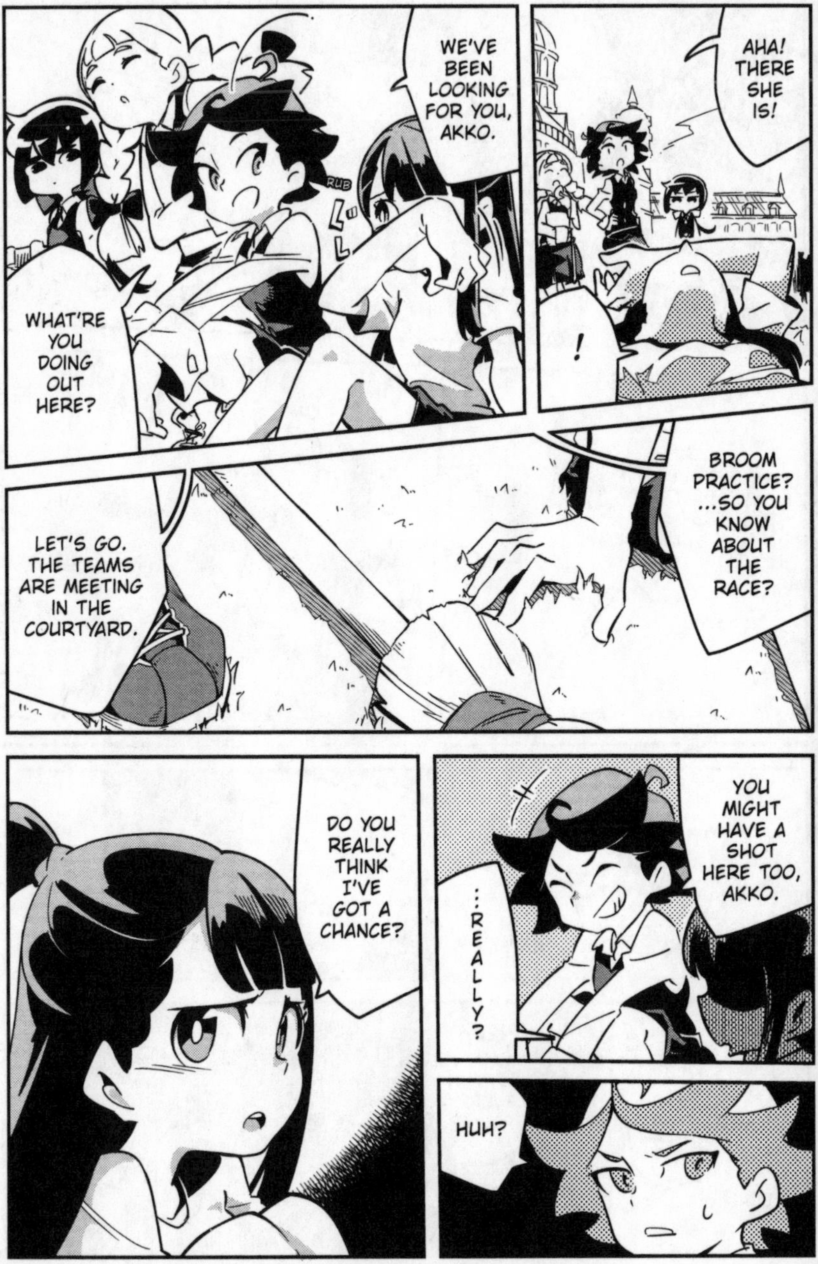
AHA! THERE SHE IS!
!
WE'VE BEEN LOOKING FOR YOU, AKKO.
RUB
WHAT'RE YOU DOING OUT HERE?
BROOM PRACTICE? ...SO YOU KNOW ABOUT THE RACE?
LET'S GO. THE TEAMS ARE MEETING IN THE COURTYARD.
YOU MIGHT HAVE A SHOT HERE TOO, AKKO.
...REALLY?
HUH?
DO YOU REALLY THINK I'VE GOT A CHANCE?

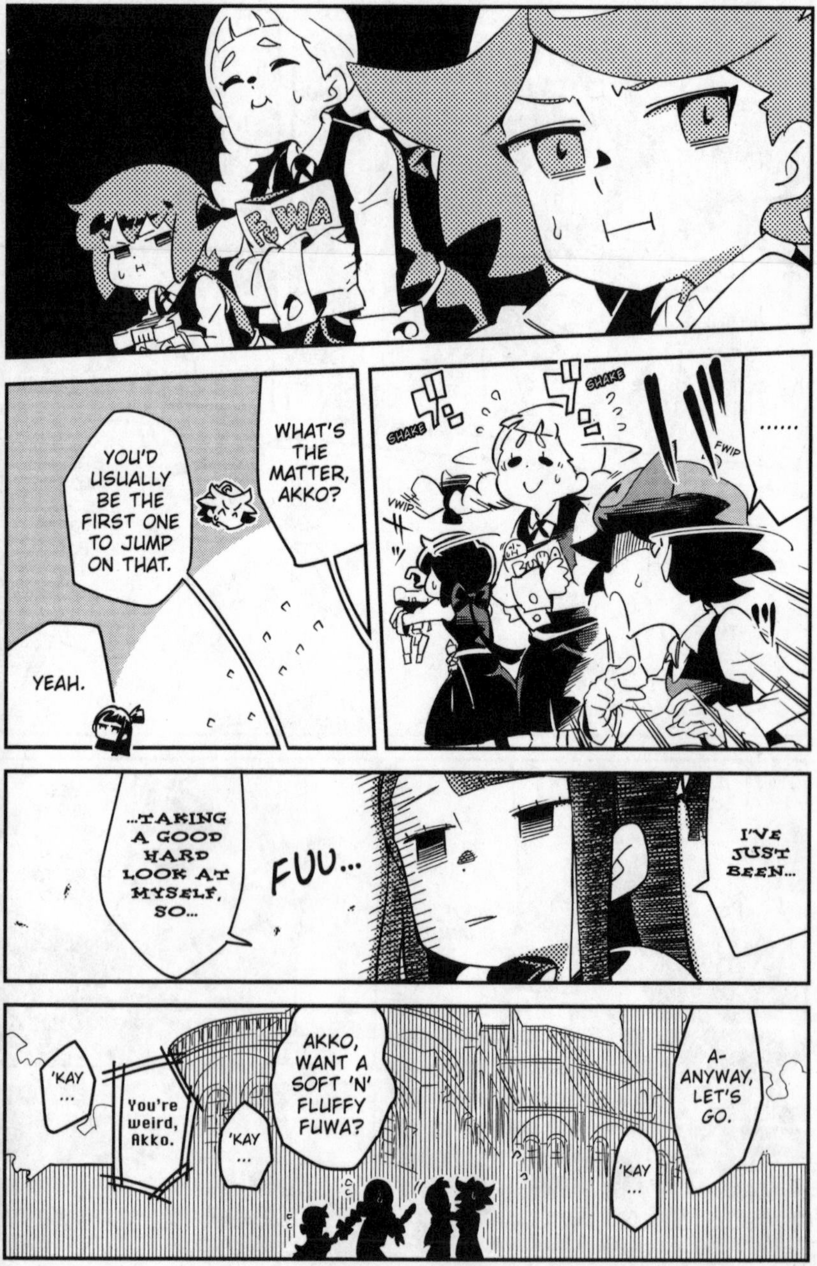

......
SHAKE
SHAKE
FWIP
VWIP
WHAT'S THE MATTER, AKKO?
YOU'D USUALLY BE THE FIRST ONE TO JUMP ON THAT.
YEAH.
I'VE JUST BEEN...
FUU...
...TAKING A GOOD HARD LOOK AT MYSELF, SO...
A- ANYWAY, LET'S GO.
'KAY...
AKKO, WANT A SOFT 'N' FLUFFY FUWA?
'KAY...
You're weird, Akko.
'KAY...

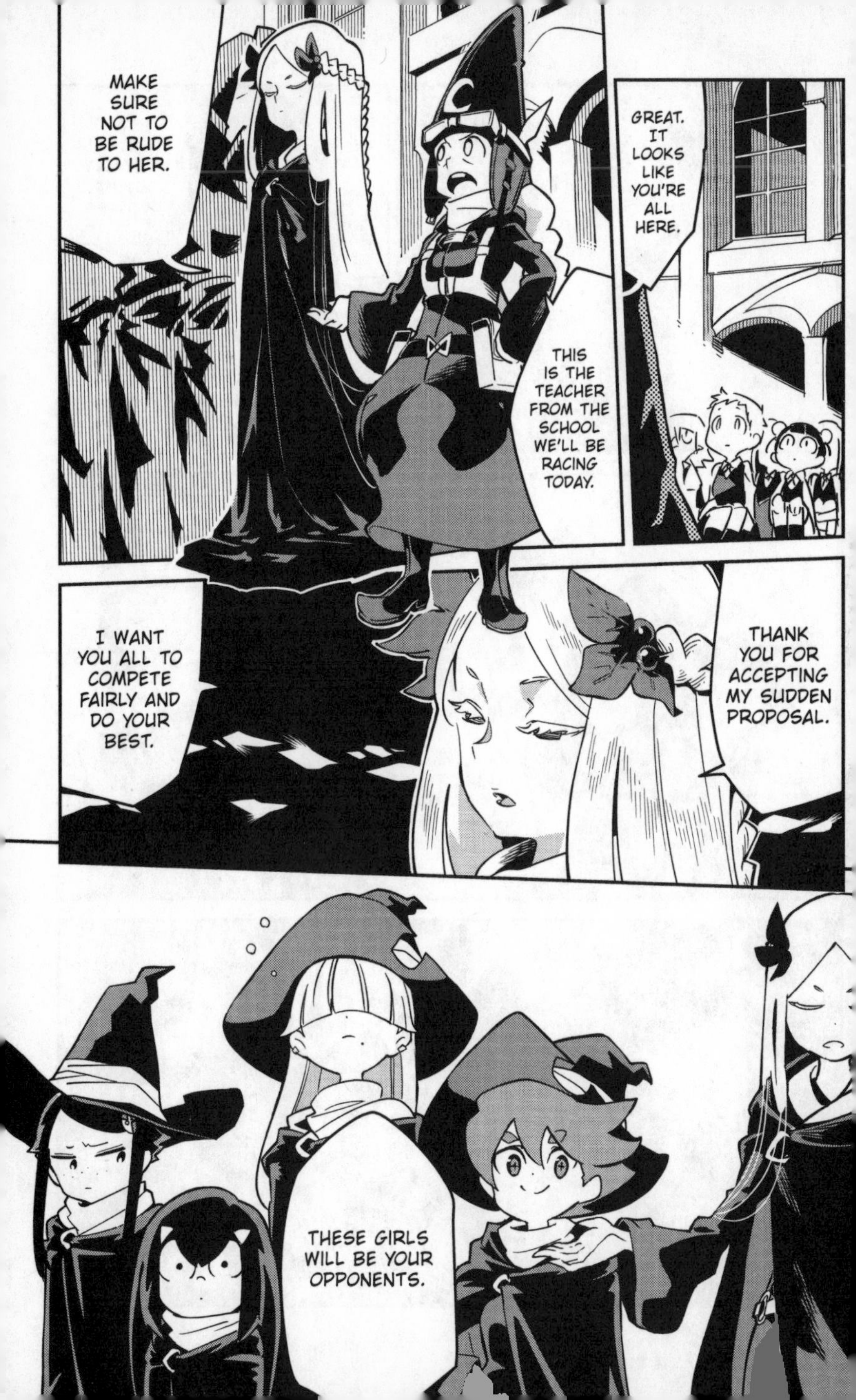
GREAT. IT LOOKS LIKE YOU'RE ALL HERE.
THIS IS THE TEACHER FROM THE SCHOOL WE'LL BE RACING TODAY.
MAKE SURE NOT TO BE RUDE TO HER.
THANK YOU FOR ACCEPTING MY SUDDEN PROPOSAL.
I WANT YOU ALL TO COMPETE FAIRLY AND DO YOUR BEST.
THESE GIRLS WILL BE YOUR OPPONENTS.

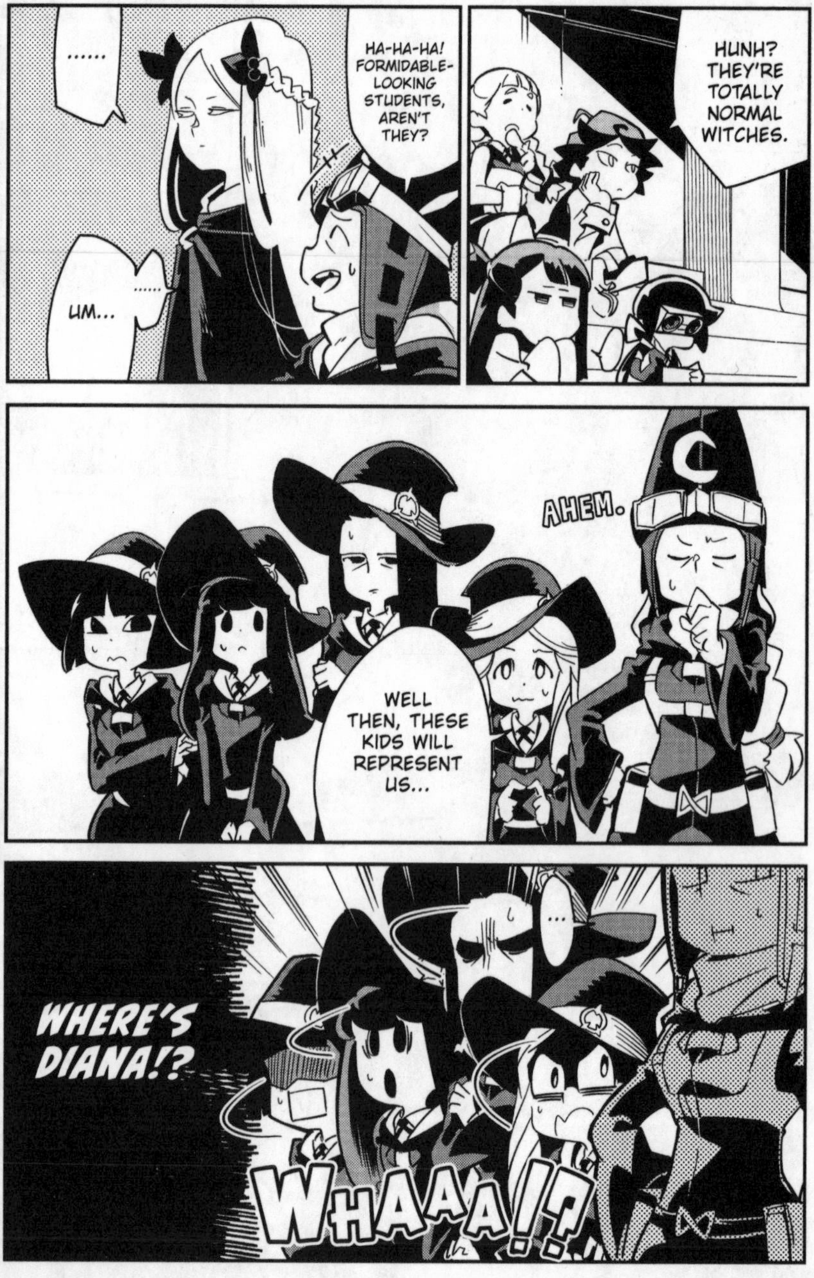
HUNH? THEY'RE TOTALLY NORMAL WITCHES.
HA-HA-HA! FORMIDABLE-LOOKING STUDENTS, AREN'T THEY?
......
......
UM...
AHEM.
WELL THEN, THESE KIDS WILL REPRESENT US...
...
WHERE'S DIANA!?
WHAAAA!?

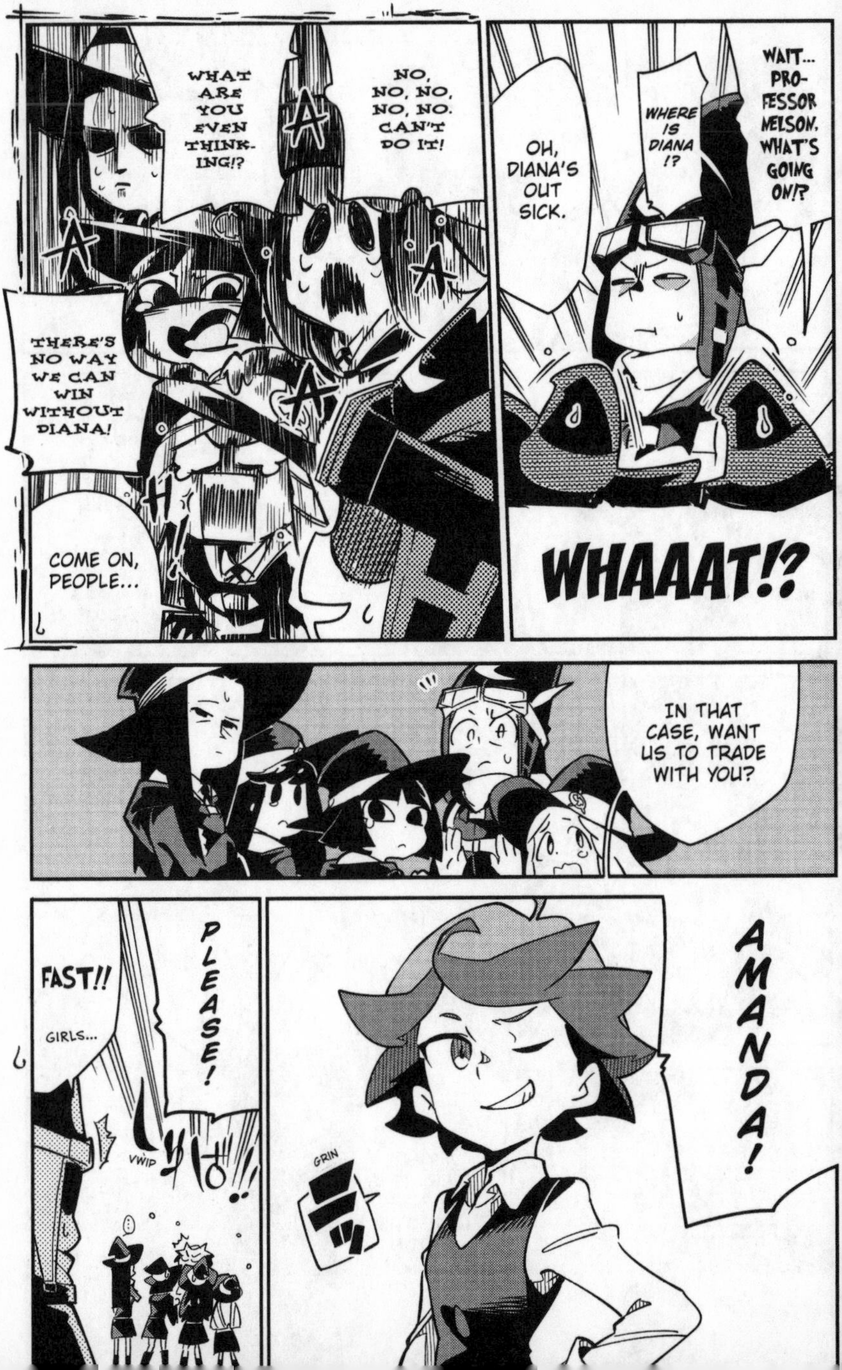
WAIT... PRO-FESSOR NELSON. WHAT'S GOING ON!?
WHERE IS DIANA!?
OH, DIANA'S OUT SICK.
WHAAAT!?
NO, NO, NO, NO, NO. CAN'T DO IT!
WHAT ARE YOU EVEN THINK-ING!?
THERE'S NO WAY WE CAN WIN WITHOUT DIANA!
COME ON, PEOPLE...
IN THAT CASE, WANT US TO TRADE WITH YOU?
AMANDA!
GRIN
PLEASE!
FAST!!
GIRLS...
VWIP

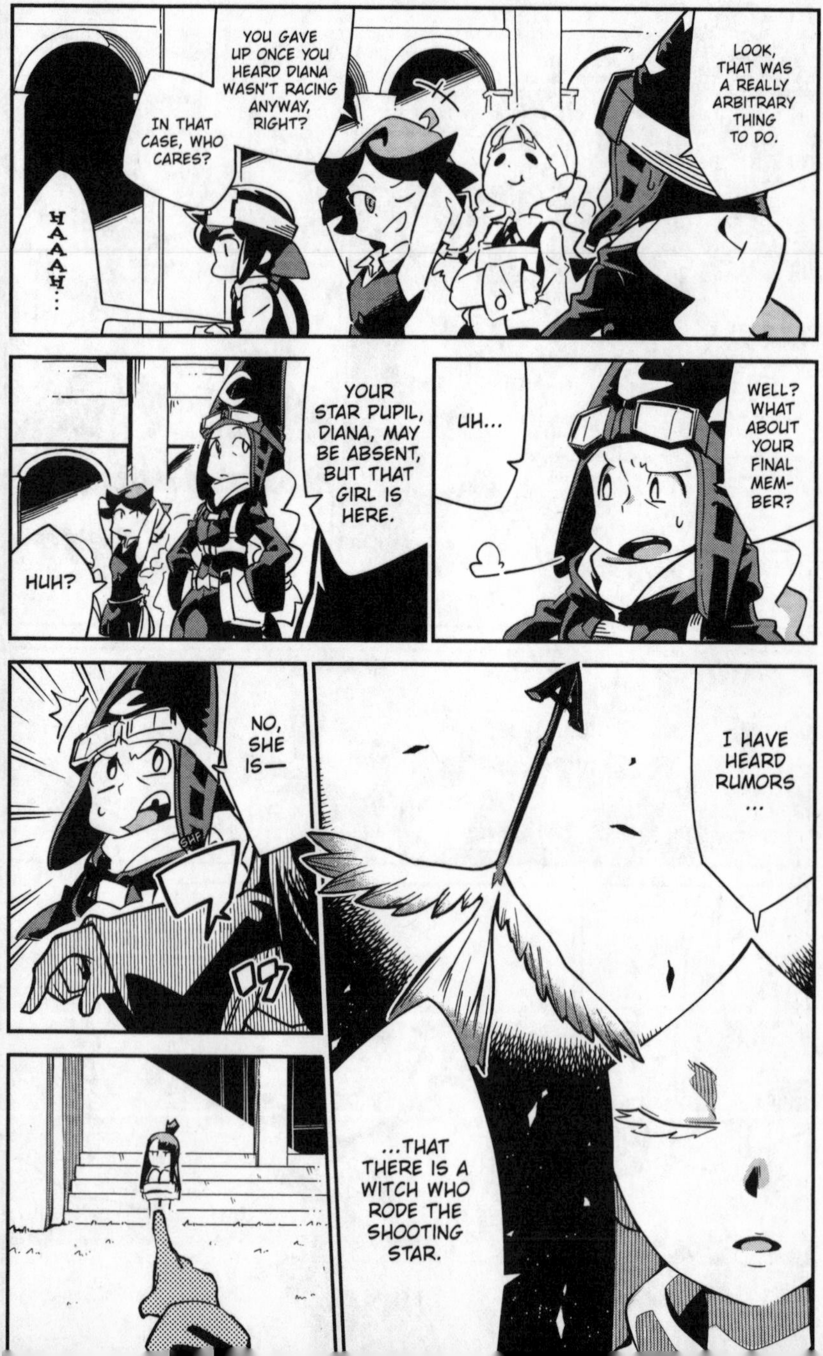
LOOK, THAT WAS A REALLY ARBITRARY THING TO DO.
YOU GAVE UP ONCE YOU HEARD DIANA WASN'T RACING ANYWAY, RIGHT?
IN THAT CASE, WHO CARES?
HAAAAH...
WELL? WHAT ABOUT YOUR FINAL MEM-BER?
UH...
YOUR STAR PUPIL, DIANA, MAY BE ABSENT, BUT THAT GIRL IS HERE.
HUH?
I HAVE HEARD RUMORS...
...THAT THERE IS A WITCH WHO RODE THE SHOOTING STAR.
NO, SHE IS—

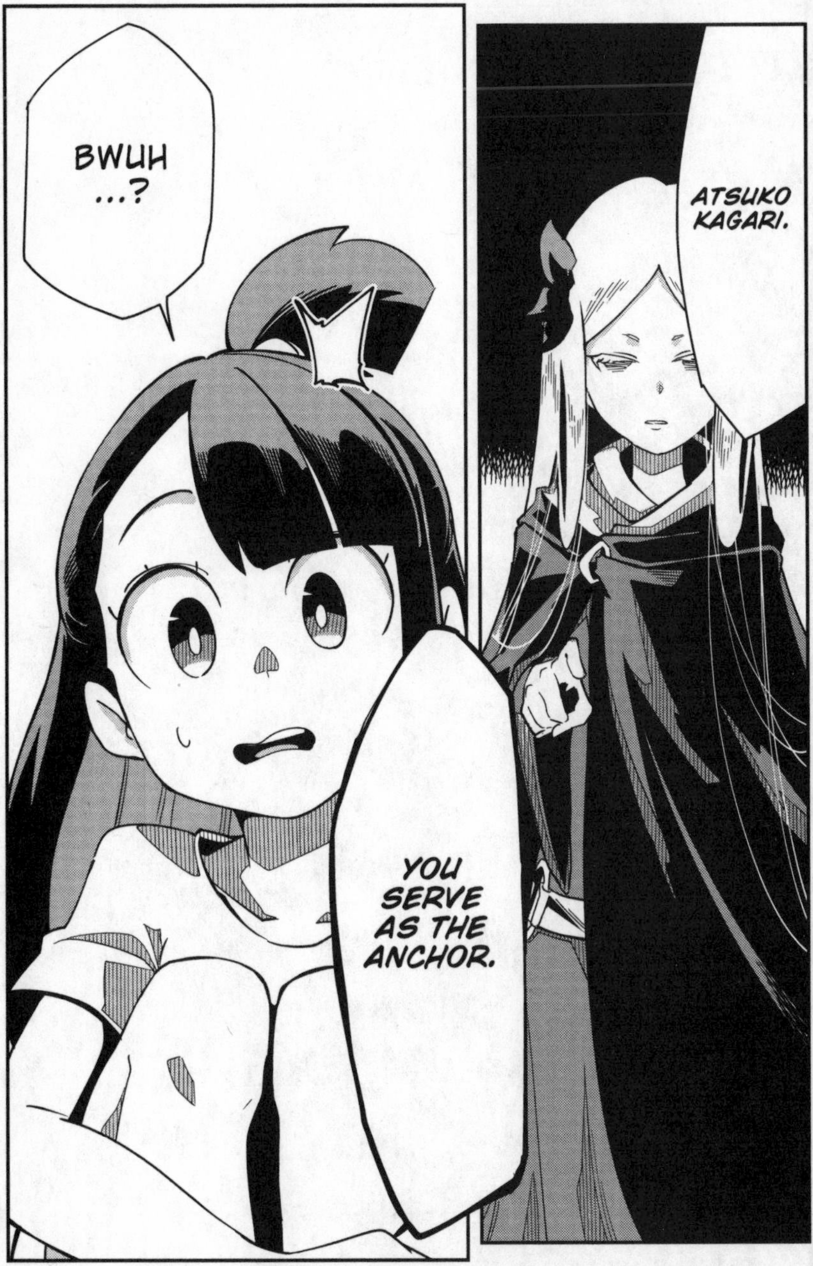
ATSUKO KAGARI.
YOU SERVE AS THE ANCHOR.
BWUH ...?

Little
Witch
Academia

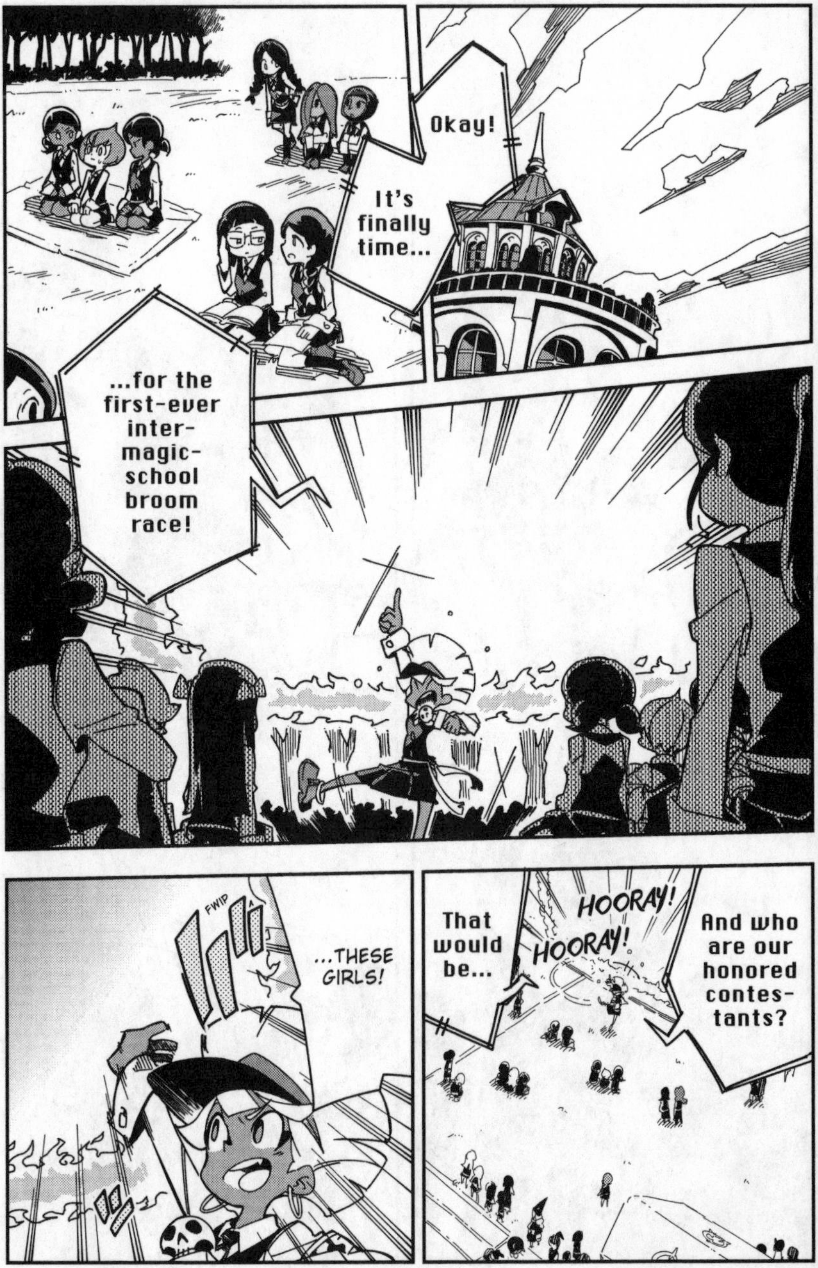
Okay!
It's finally time...
...for the first-ever inter-magic-school broom race!
And who are our honored contestants?
HOORAY!
HOORAY!
That would be...
FWIP
...THESE GIRLS!

Chapter 16

Chapter 16 THE OUTSTRETCHED HAND

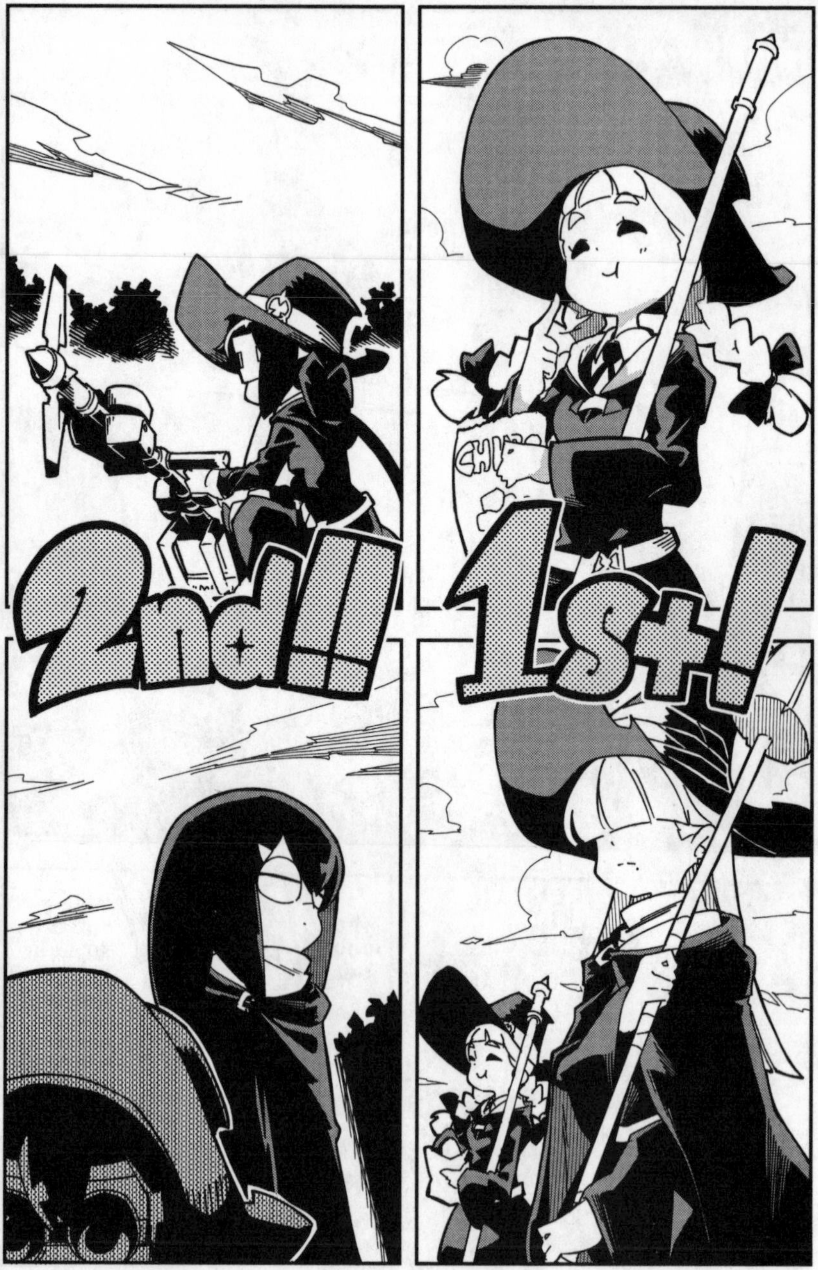
1st!
2nd!!

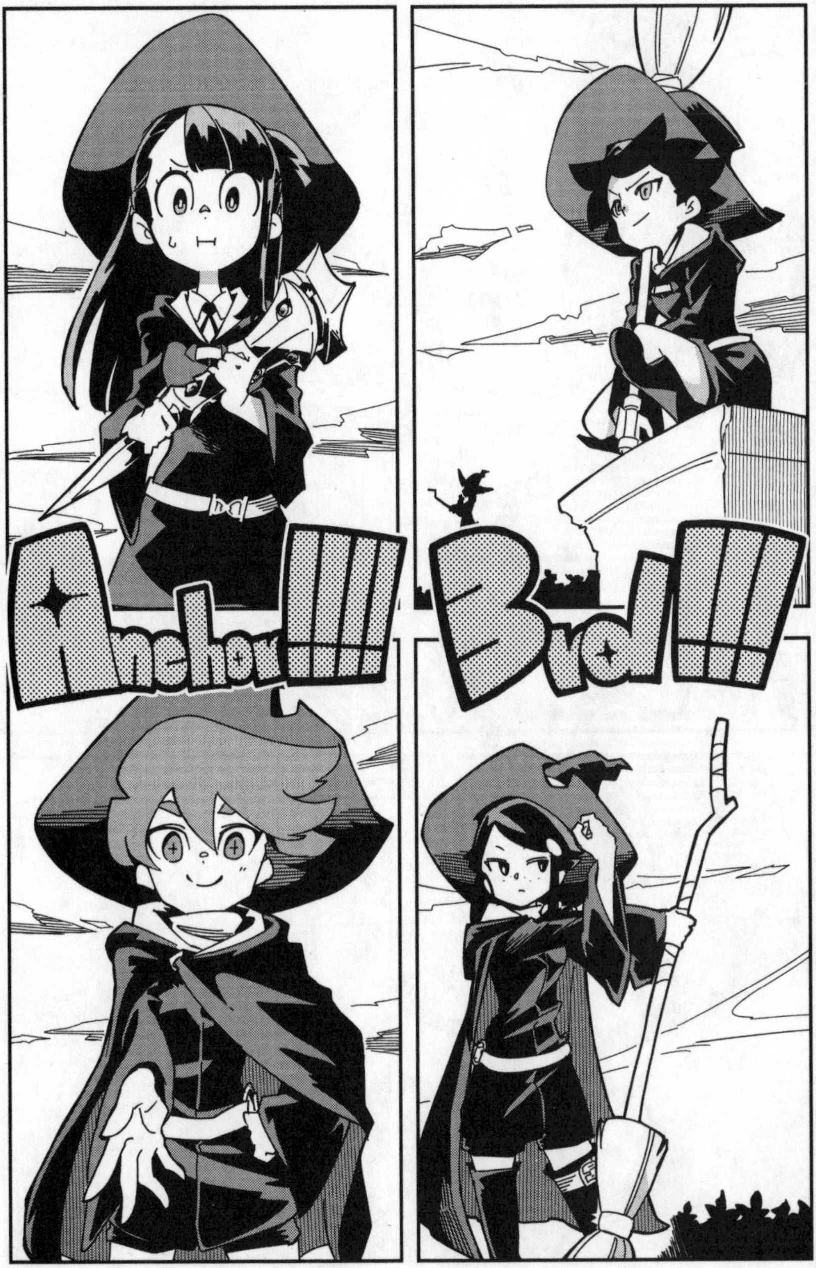
Bird!!!
Anchor!!!

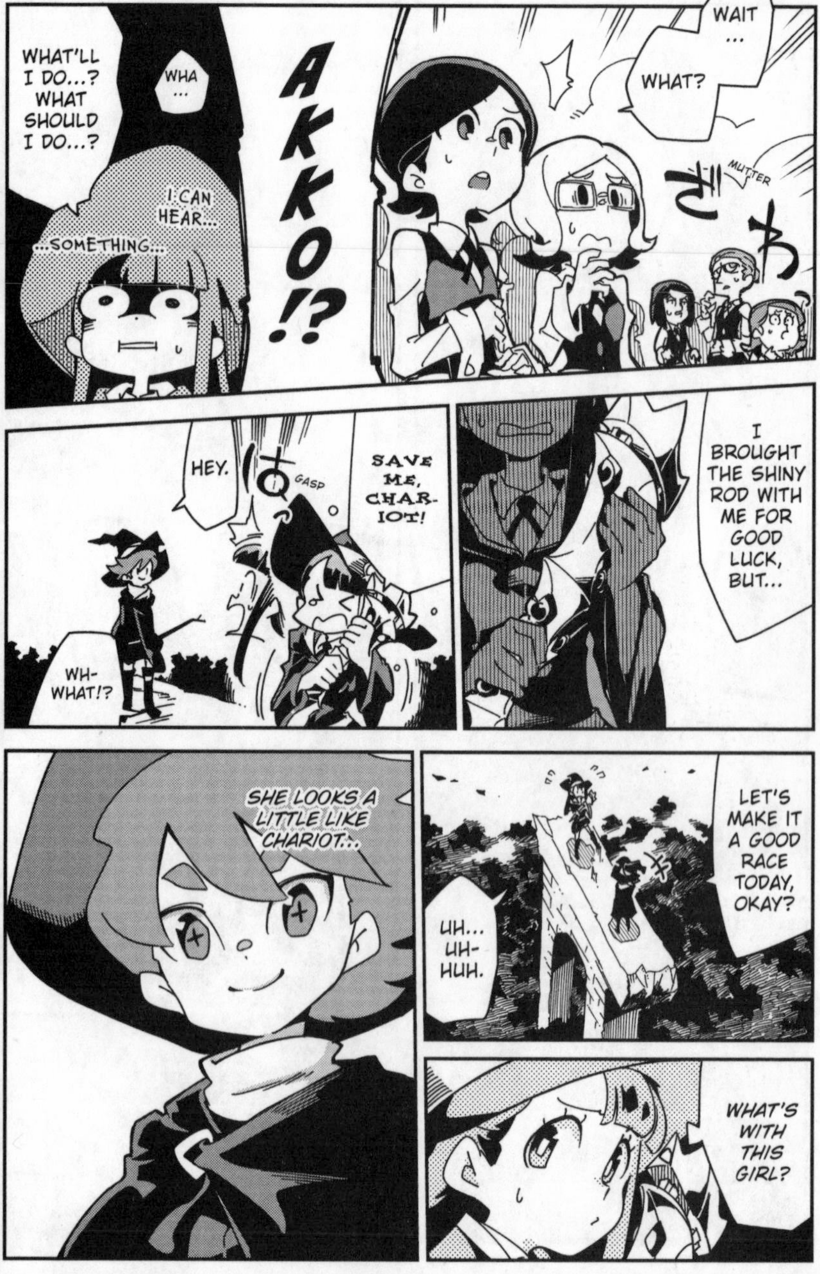
WAIT ... WHAT?
MUTTER
AKKO!?
WHA ...
WHAT'LL I DO...? WHAT SHOULD I DO...?
I CAN HEAR... ...SOMETHING...
I BROUGHT THE SHINY ROD WITH ME FOR GOOD LUCK, BUT...
SAVE ME, CHARIOT!
GASP
HEY.
WH-WHAT!?
LET'S MAKE IT A GOOD RACE TODAY, OKAY?
UH... UH-HUH.
WHAT'S WITH THIS GIRL?
SHE LOOKS A LITTLE LIKE CHARIOT...

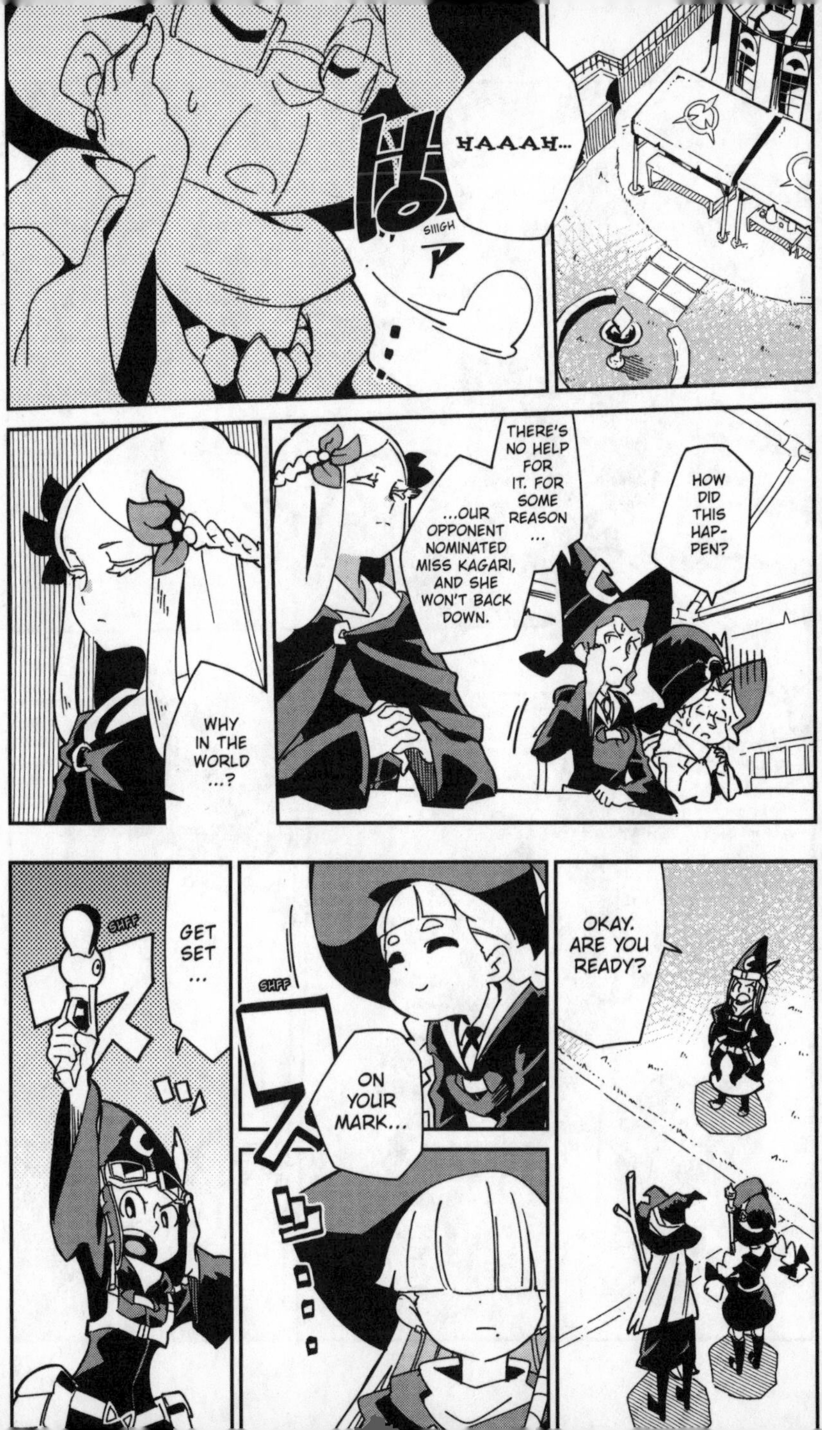
HAAAH...
SIIIGH
HOW DID THIS HAP-PEN?
THERE'S NO HELP FOR IT. FOR SOME REASON ...
...OUR OPPONENT NOMINATED MISS KAGARI, AND SHE WON'T BACK DOWN.
WHY IN THE WORLD ...?
OKAY. ARE YOU READY?
SHFF
ON YOUR MARK...
SHFF
GET SET ...

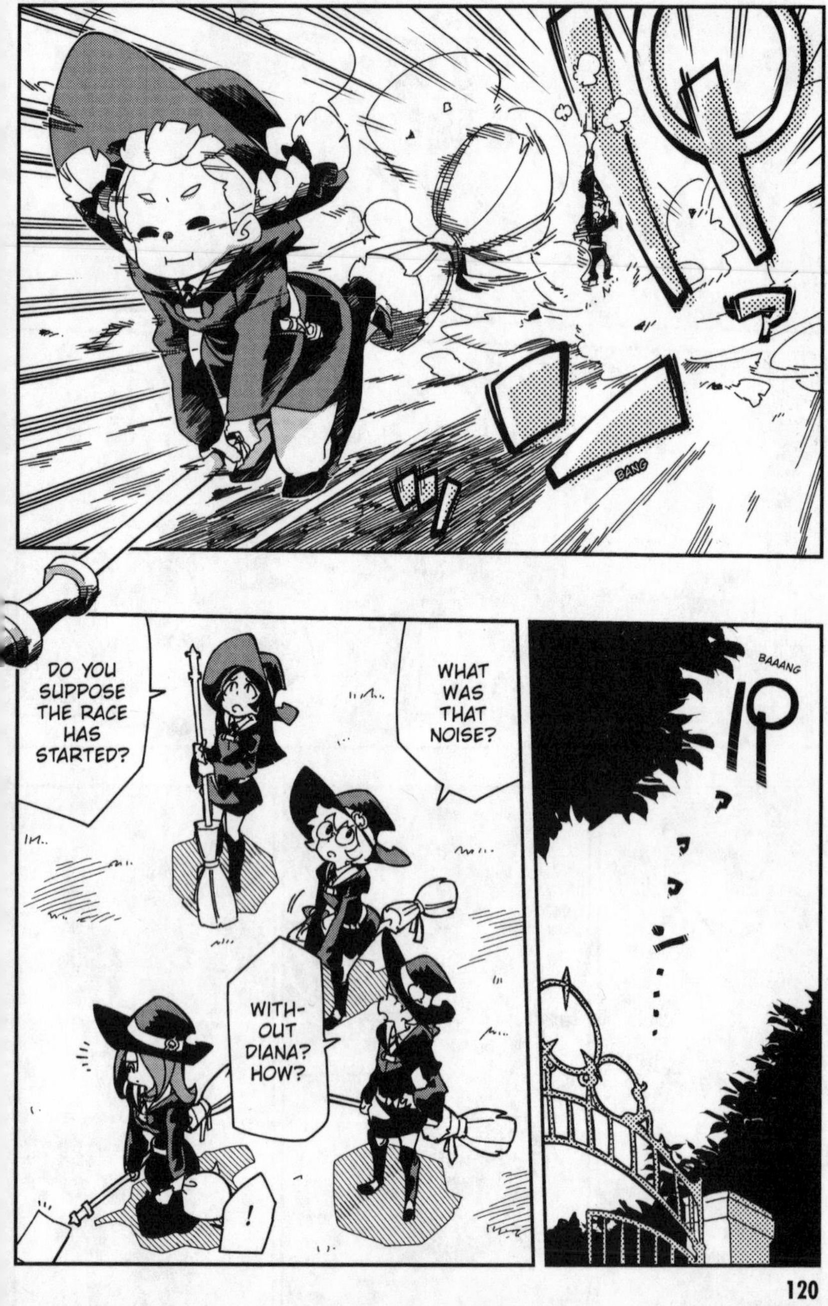
BANG
BAAANG
!?
WHAT WAS THAT NOISE?
DO YOU SUPPOSE THE RACE HAS STARTED?
WITH-OUT DIANA? HOW?
!

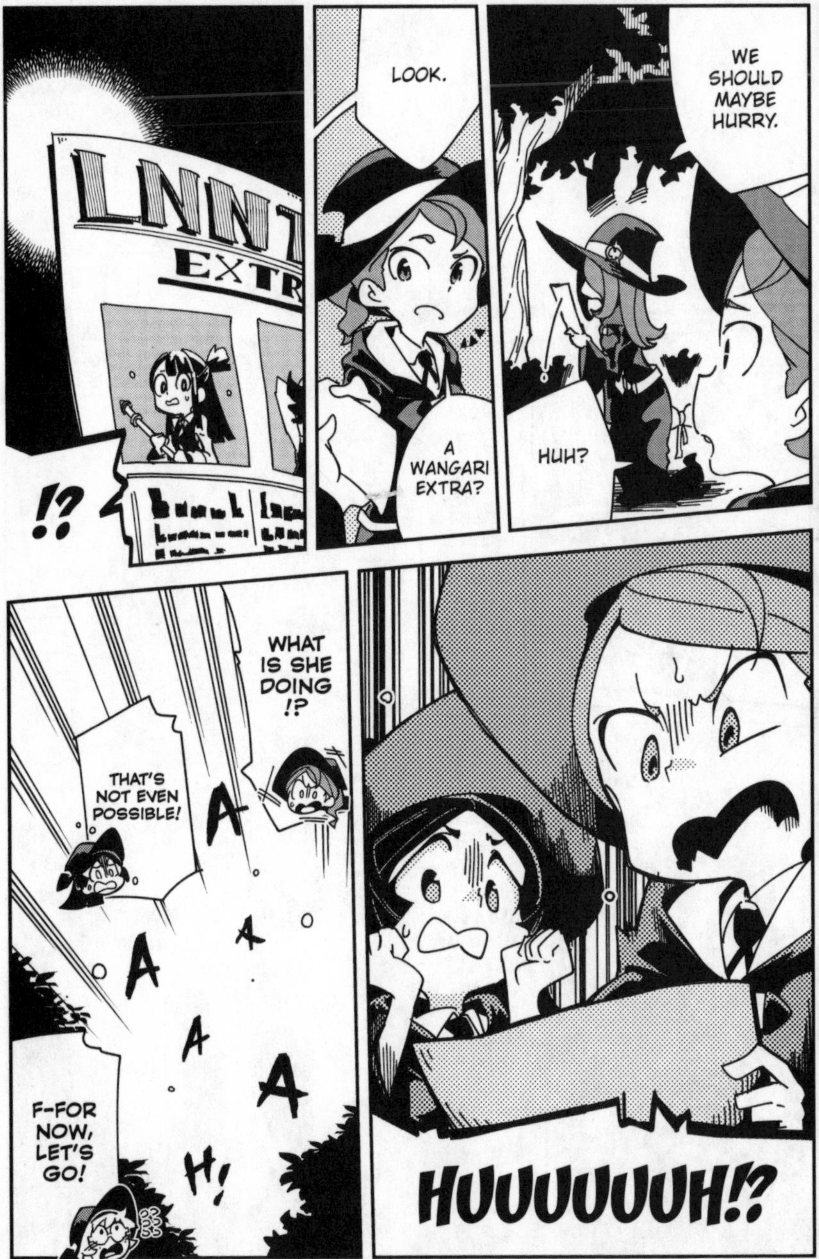

WE SHOULD MAYBE HURRY.
HUH?
LOOK.
A WANGARI EXTRA?
!?
HUUUUUUUH!?
WHAT IS SHE DOING !?
THAT'S NOT EVEN POSSIBLE!
AAAAAH!
F-FOR NOW, LET'S GO!

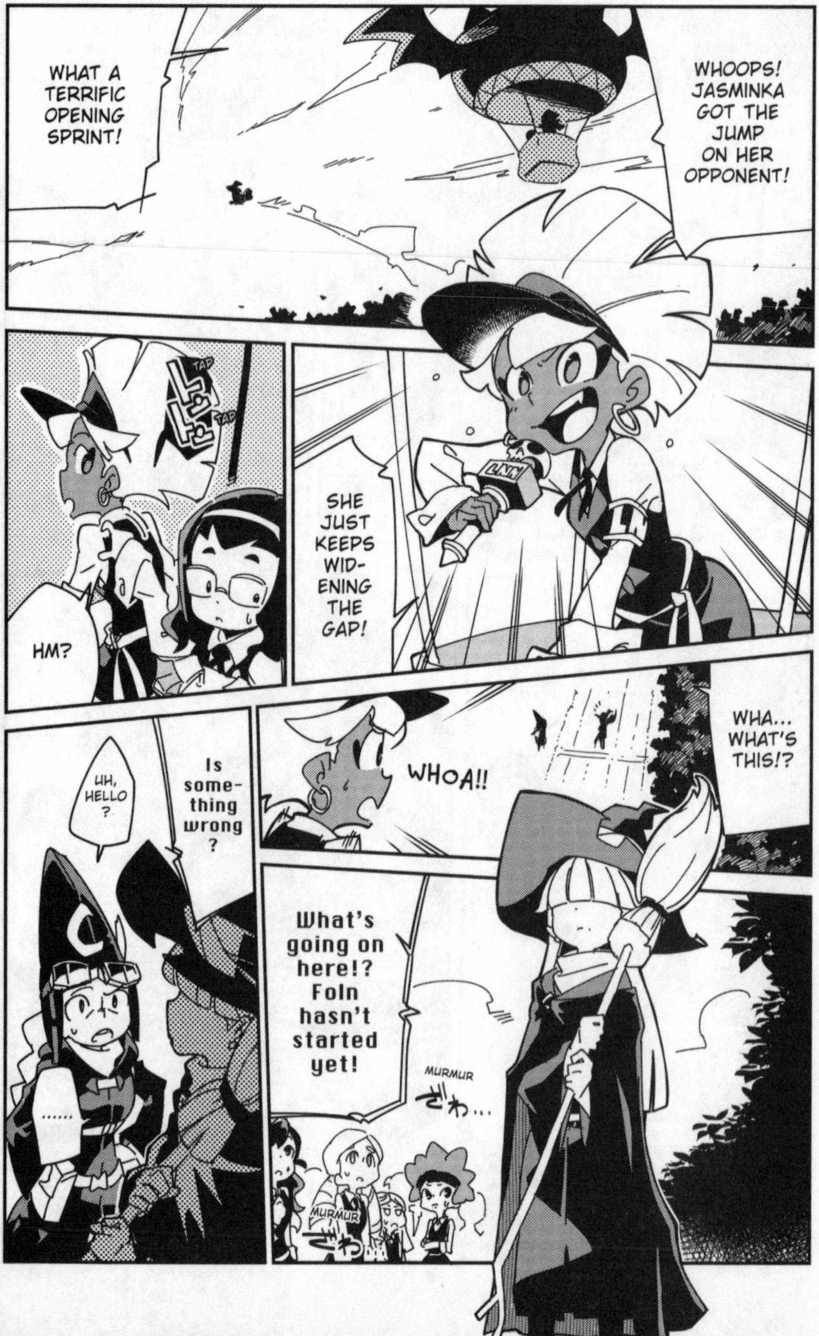
WHOOPS! JASMINKA GOT THE JUMP ON HER OPPONENT!
WHAT A TERRIFIC OPENING SPRINT!
SHE JUST KEEPS WID-ENING THE GAP!
TAP TAP
HM?
WHA... WHAT'S THIS!?
WHOA!!
What's going on here!? Foln hasn't started yet!
MURMUR
MURMUR
Is some-thing wrong?
UH, HELLO?
......

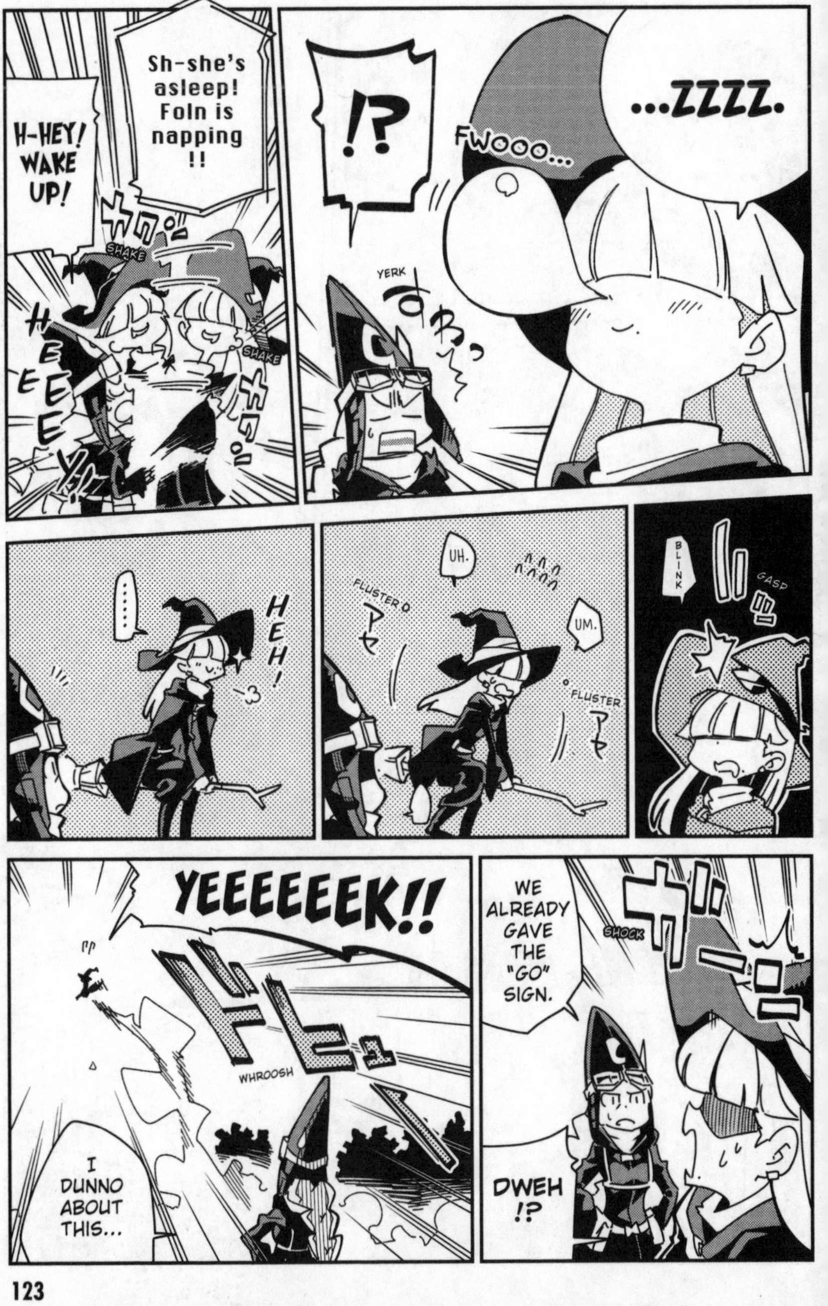
...ZZZZ.
FWOOO...
!?
YERK
Sh-she's asleep! Foln is napping !!
H-HEY! WAKE UP!
SHAKE
SHAKE
HEEEEEY!!
BLINK
GASP
UH.
UM.
FLUSTER
FLUSTER
...
HEH!
WE ALREADY GAVE THE "GO" SIGN.
SHOCK
DWEH !?
YEEEEEEK!!
WHROOSH
I DUNNO ABOUT THIS...

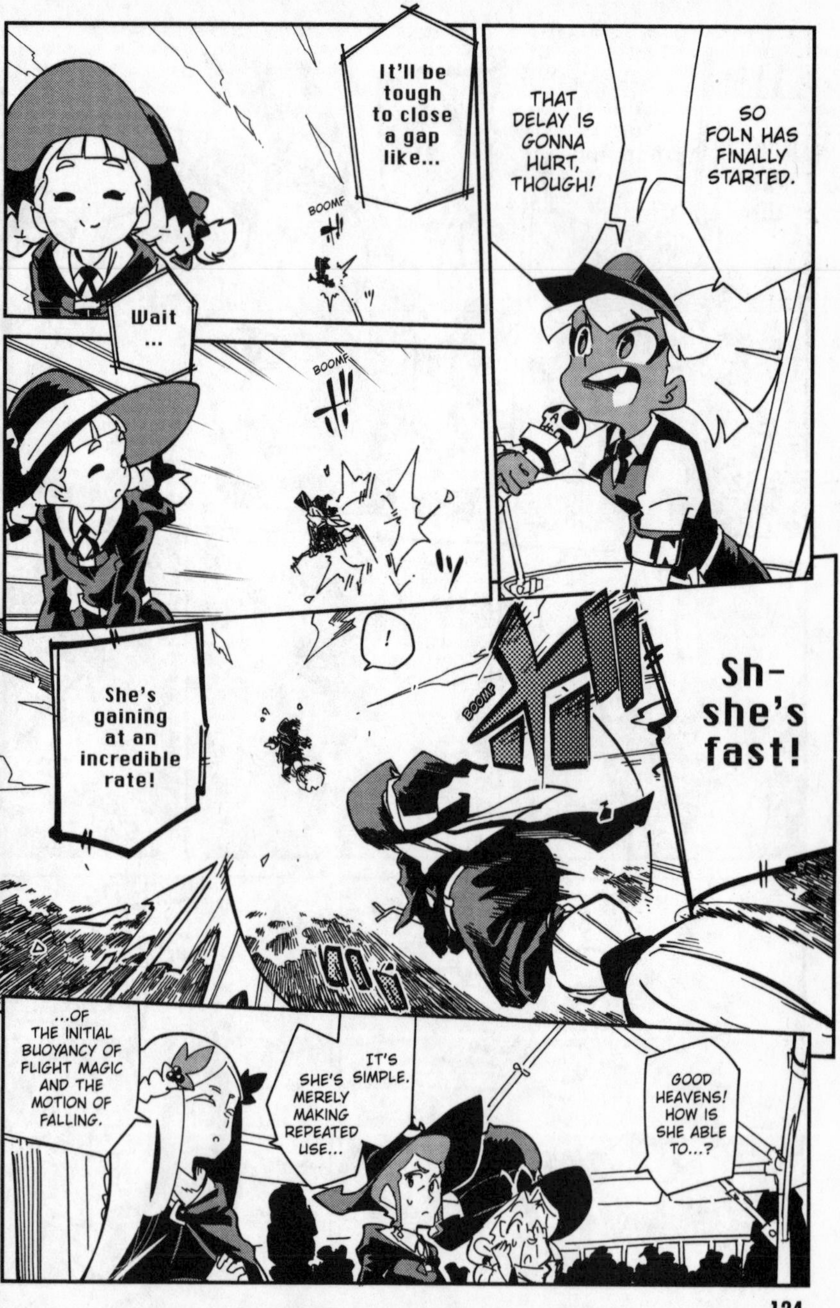
SO FOLN HAS FINALLY STARTED.
THAT DELAY IS GONNA HURT, THOUGH!
It'll be tough to close a gap like...
BOOMF
Wait ...
BOOMF
Sh-she's fast!
BOOMF
!
She's gaining at an incredible rate!
GOOD HEAVENS! HOW IS SHE ABLE TO...?
IT'S SIMPLE.
SHE'S MERELY MAKING REPEATED USE...
...OF THE INITIAL BUOYANCY OF FLIGHT MAGIC AND THE MOTION OF FALLING.

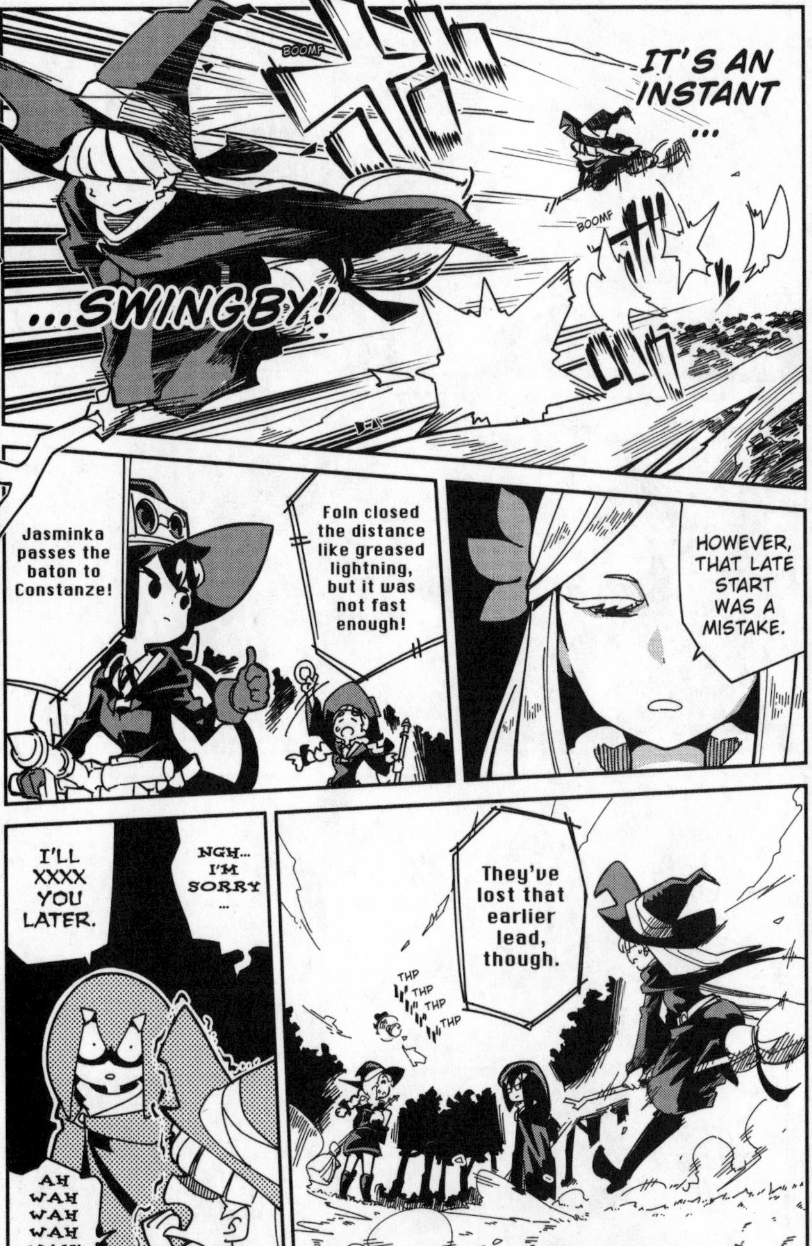
IT'S AN INSTANT ...
BOOMF
BOOMF
...SWINGBY!
HOWEVER, THAT LATE START WAS A MISTAKE.
Foln closed the distance like greased lightning, but it was not fast enough!
Jasminka passes the baton to Constanze!
They've lost that earlier lead, though.
THP THP THP THP
NGH... I'M SORRY ...
I'LL XXXX YOU LATER.
AH WAH WAH WAH WAH!

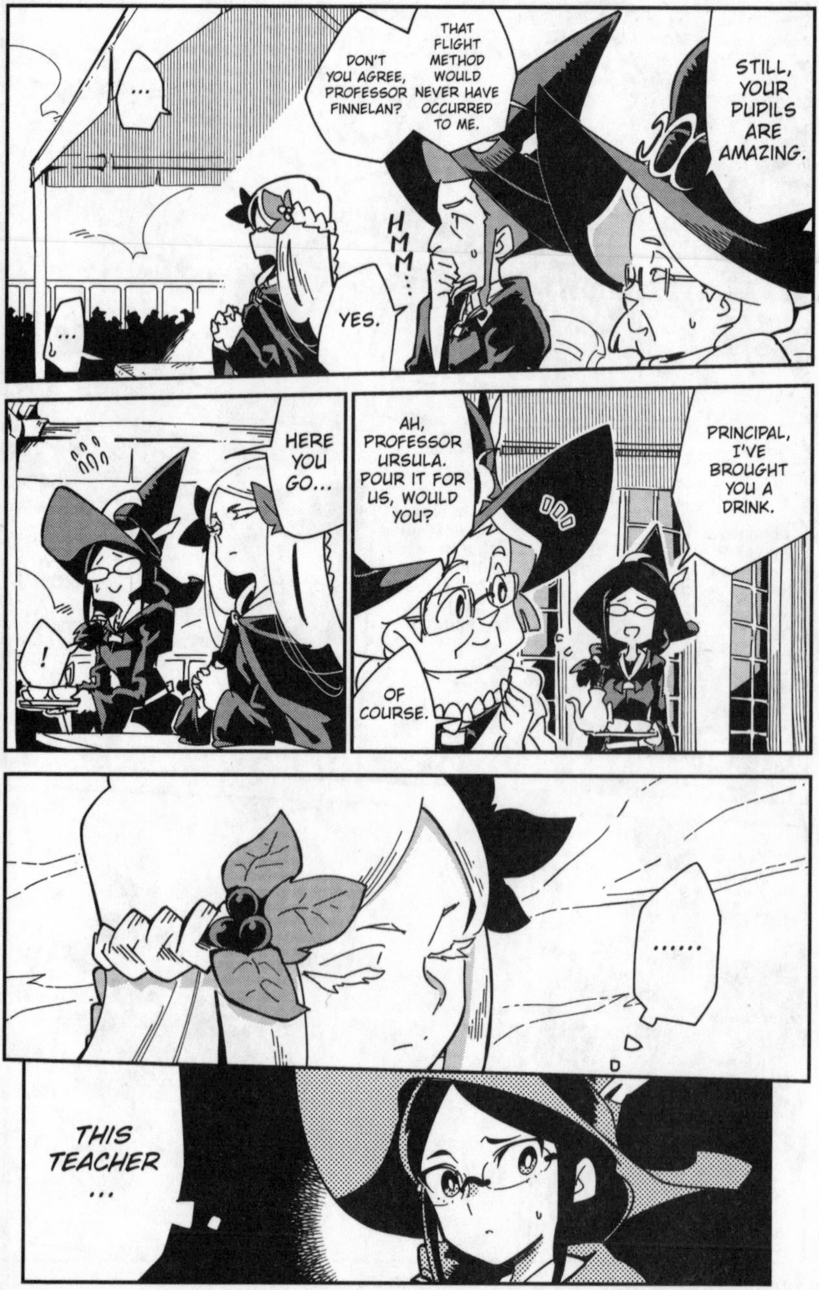
STILL, YOUR PUPILS ARE AMAZING.
THAT FLIGHT METHOD WOULD NEVER HAVE OCCURRED TO ME.
DON'T YOU AGREE, PROFESSOR FINNELAN?
...
HMM...
YES.
...
PRINCIPAL, I'VE BROUGHT YOU A DRINK.
AH, PROFESSOR URSULA. POUR IT FOR US, WOULD YOU?
OF COURSE.
HERE YOU GO...
!
......
THIS TEACHER ...

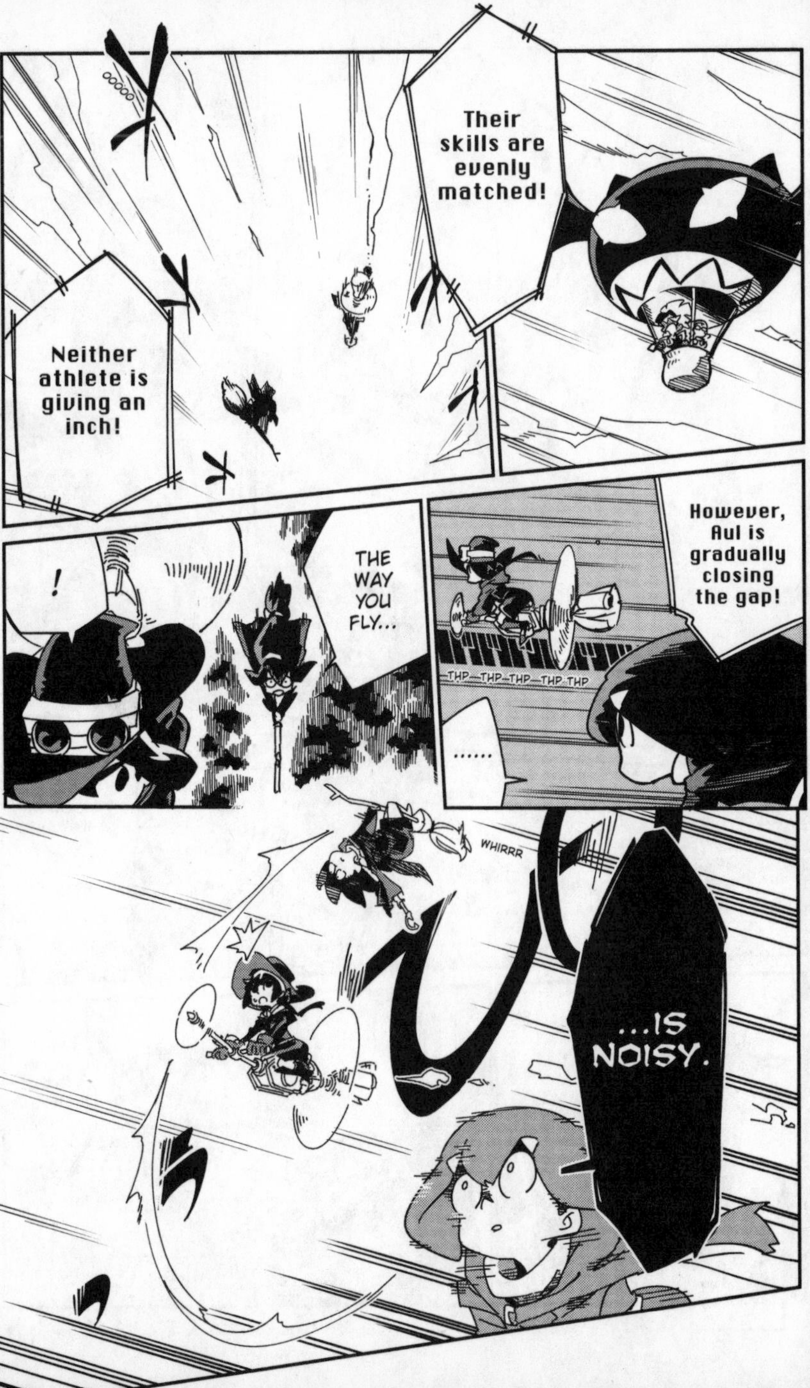
Their skills are evenly matched!
Neither athlete is giving an inch!
However, Aul is gradually closing the gap!
THP THP THP THP THP
......
THE WAY YOU FLY...
!
WHIRRR
...IS NOISY.

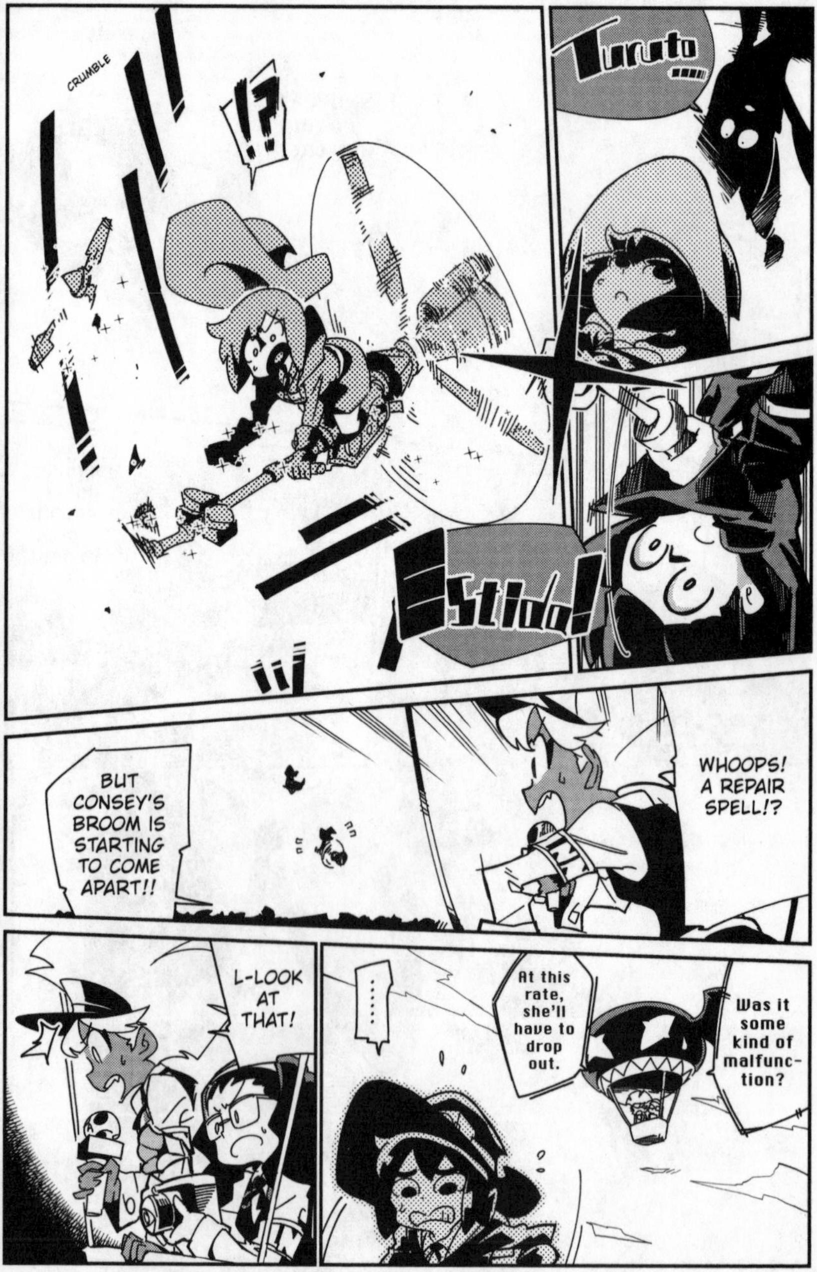
Turuto.....
Estido!
CRUMBLE
!?
WHOOPS! A REPAIR SPELL!?
BUT CONSEY'S BROOM IS STARTING TO COME APART!!
Was it some kind of malfunction?
At this rate, she'll have to drop out.
......
L-LOOK AT THAT!

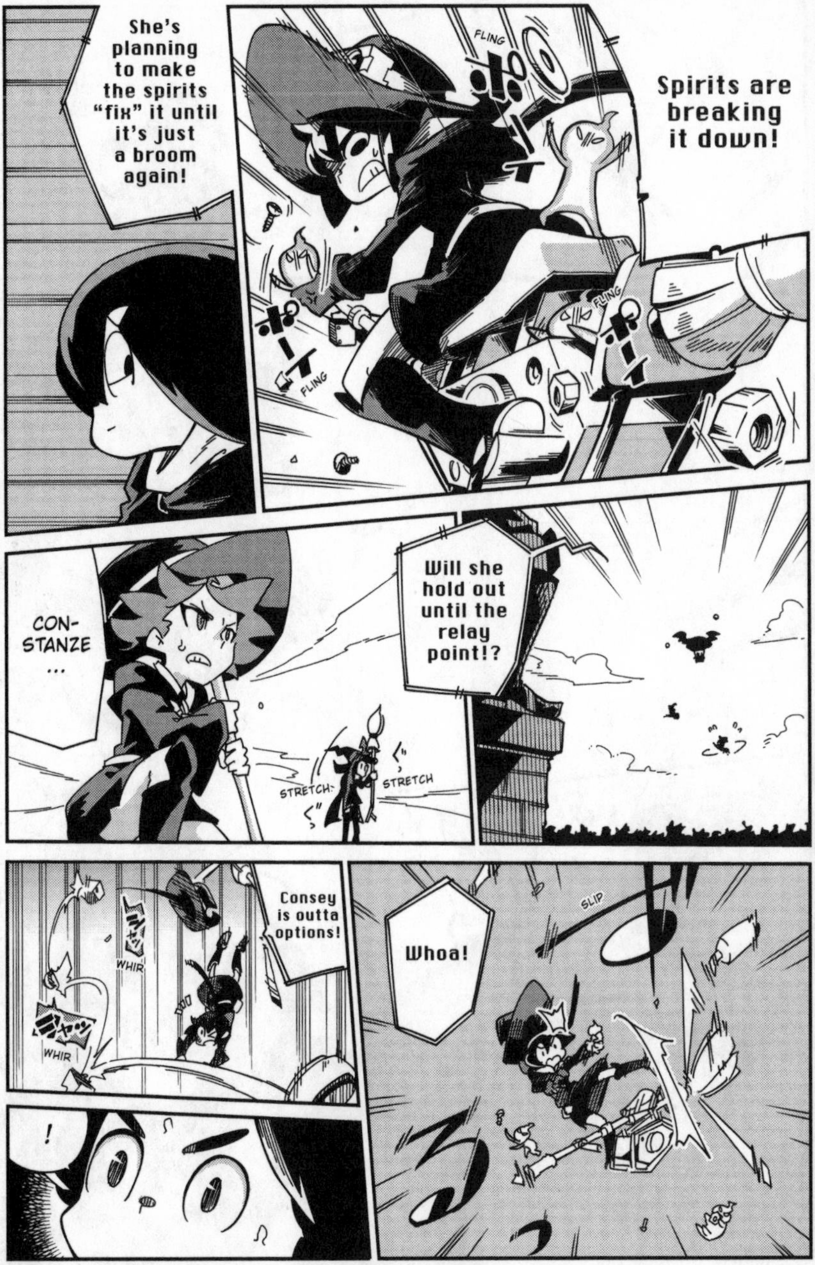
Spirits are breaking it down!
FLING
FLING
FLING
She's planning to make the spirits "fix" it until it's just a broom again!
Will she hold out until the relay point!?
STRETCH
STRETCH
CON-STANZE ...
SLIP
Whoa!
Consey is outta options!
WHIR
WHIR
!

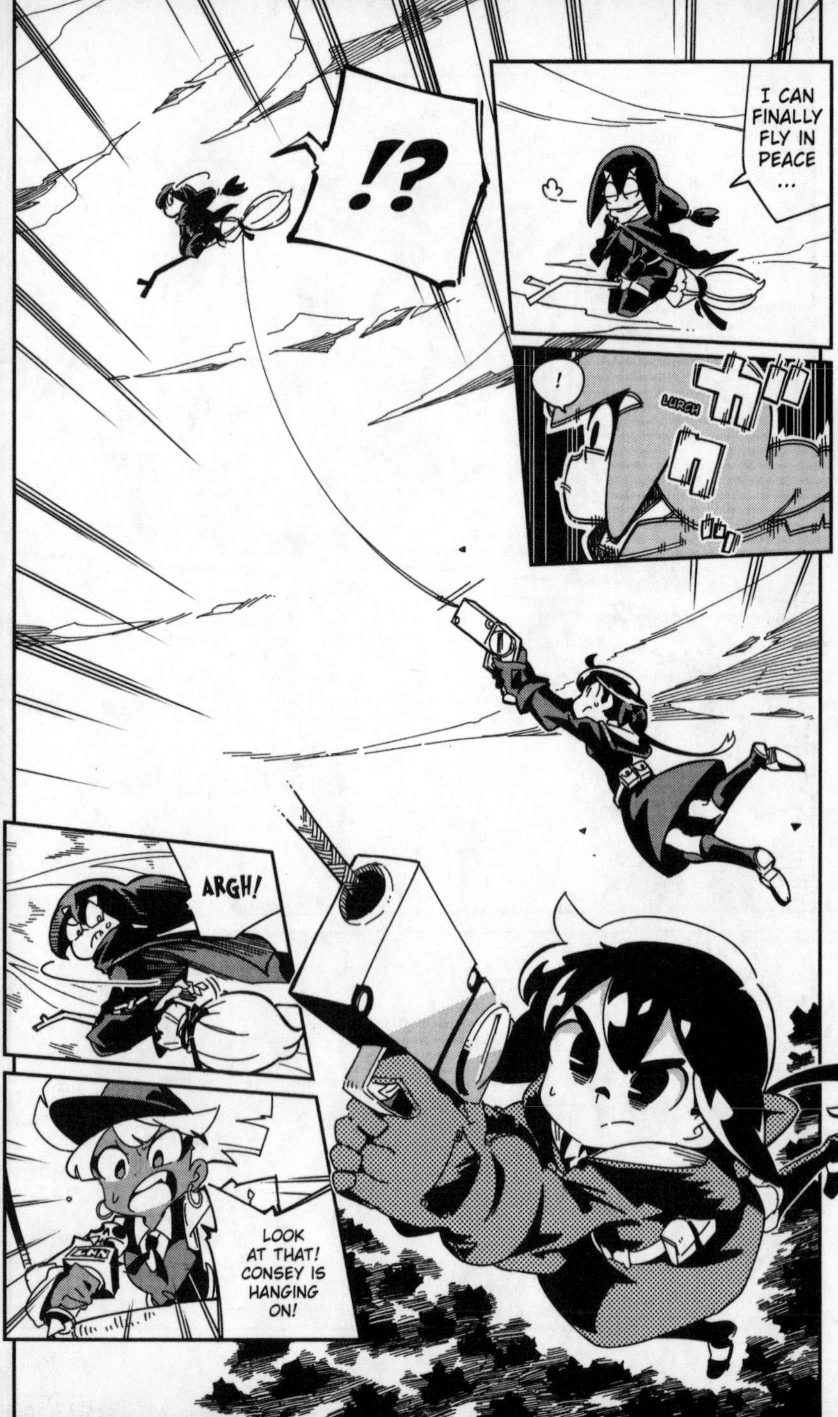
I CAN FINALLY FLY IN PEACE ...
!?
!
LURCH
ARGH!
LOOK AT THAT! CONSEY IS HANGING ON!

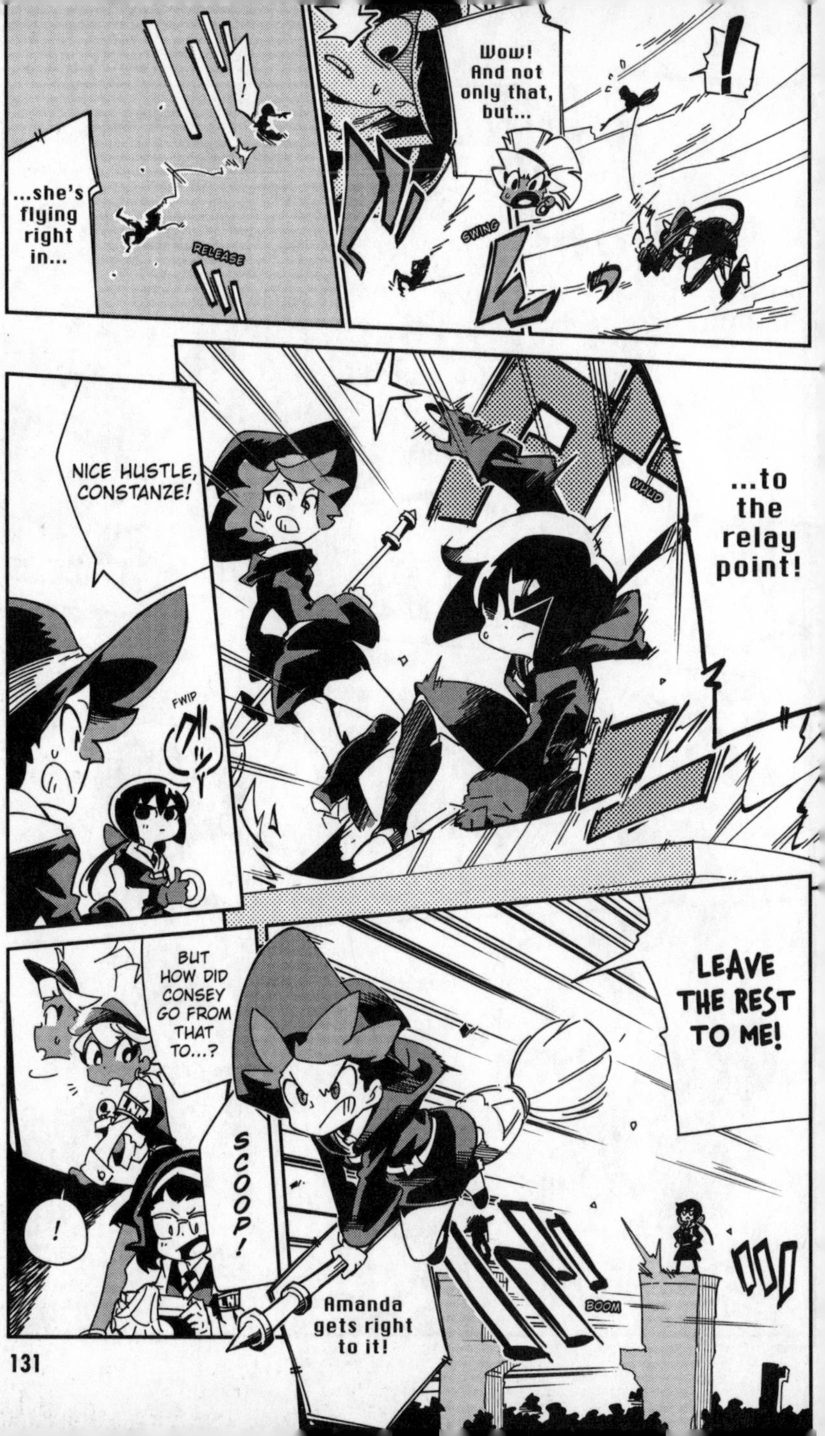
Wow! And not only that, but...
SWING
...she's flying right in...
RELEASE
...to the relay point!
WHUD
NICE HUSTLE, CONSTANZE!
FWIP
LEAVE THE REST TO ME!
SCOOP!
Amanda gets right to it!
BOOM
BUT HOW DID CONSEY GO FROM THAT TO...?
!

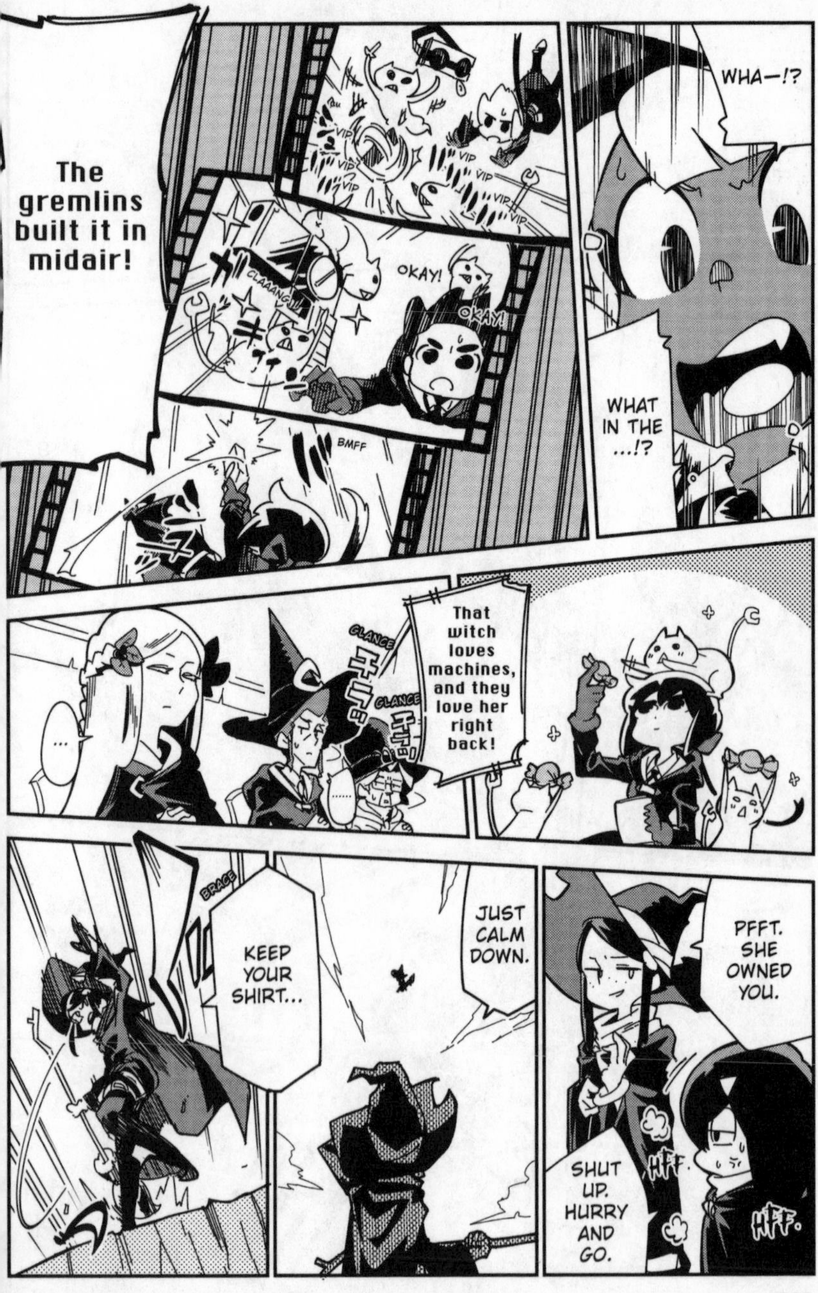
WHA—!?
WHAT IN THE ...!?
VIP VIP VIP VIP VIP VIP
CLAAAANG
OKAY!
OKAY!
BMFF
The gremlins built it in midair!
That witch loves machines, and they love her right back!
GLANCE
GLANCE
......
...
PFFT. SHE OWNED YOU.
SHUT UP. HURRY AND GO.
HFF.
HFF.
JUST CALM DOWN.
KEEP YOUR SHIRT...
BRACE

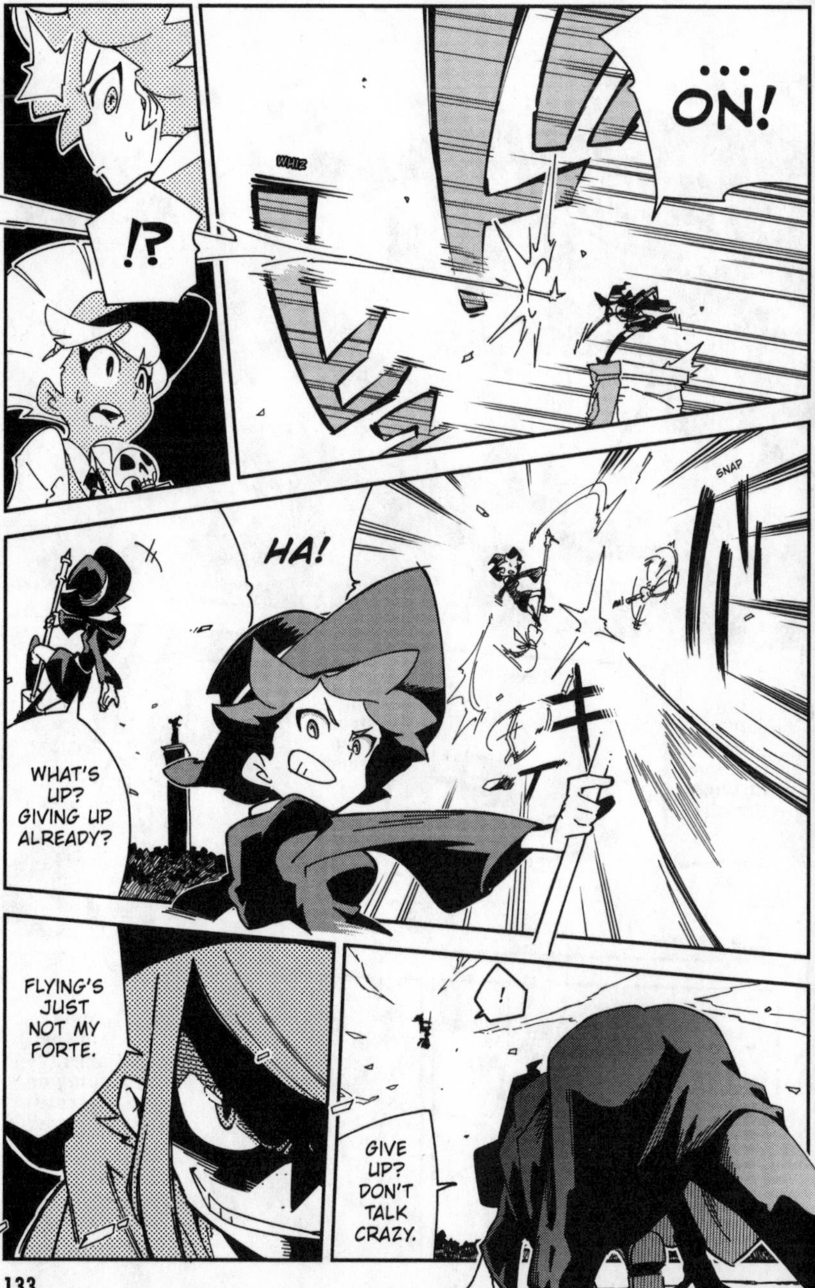

...ON!
WHIZ
!?
SNAP
HA!
WHAT'S UP? GIVING UP ALREADY?
!
GIVE UP? DON'T TALK CRAZY.
FLYING'S JUST NOT MY FORTE.

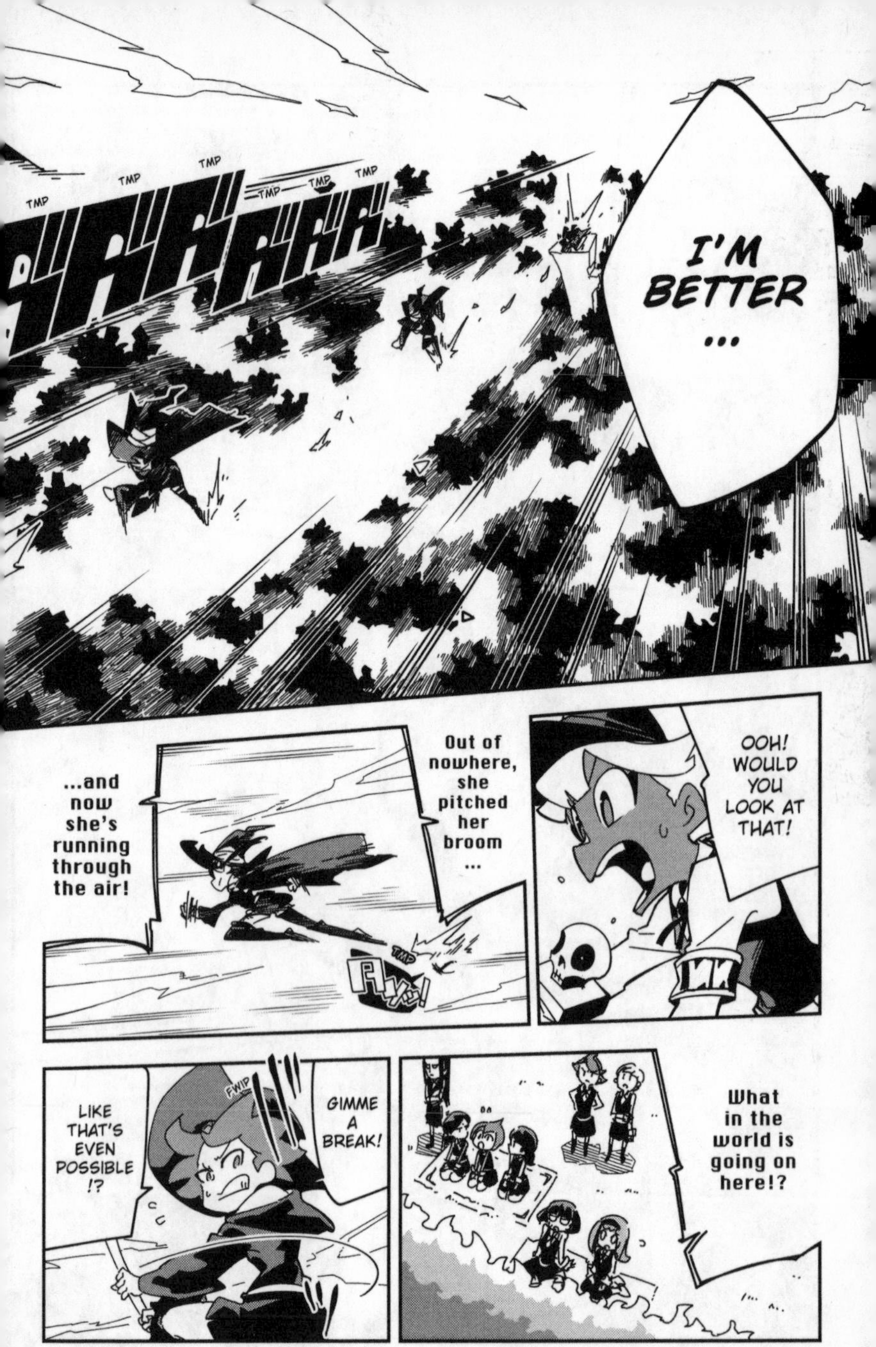
I'M BETTER ...
TMP
TMP
TMP
TMP
TMP
TMP
OOH! WOULD YOU LOOK AT THAT!
Out of nowhere, she pitched her broom ...
...and now she's running through the air!
TMP
What in the world is going on here!?
GIMME A BREAK!
FWIP
LIKE THAT'S EVEN POSSIBLE!?

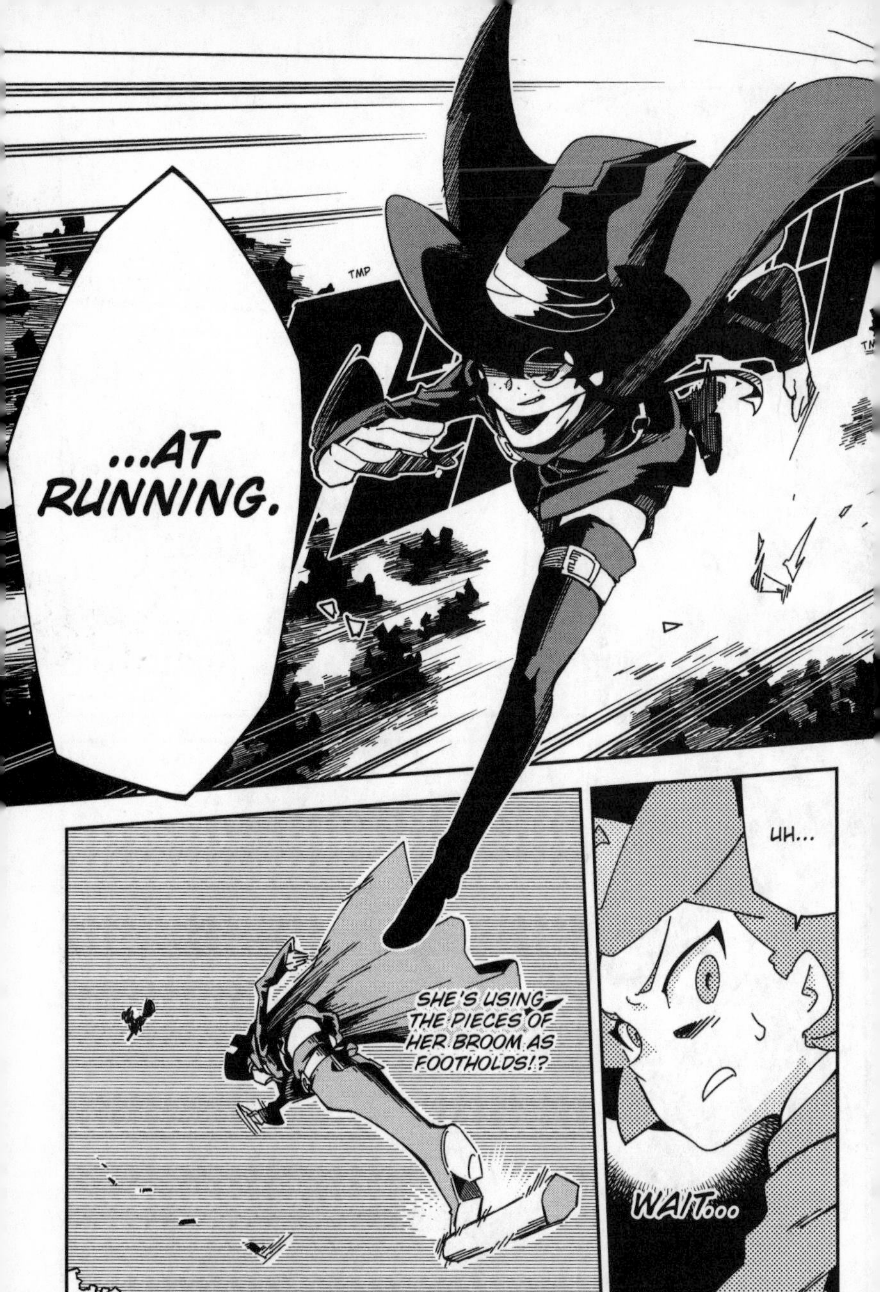
...AT RUNNING.
TMP
UH...
WAIT...
SHE'S USING THE PIECES OF HER BROOM AS FOOTHOLDS!?

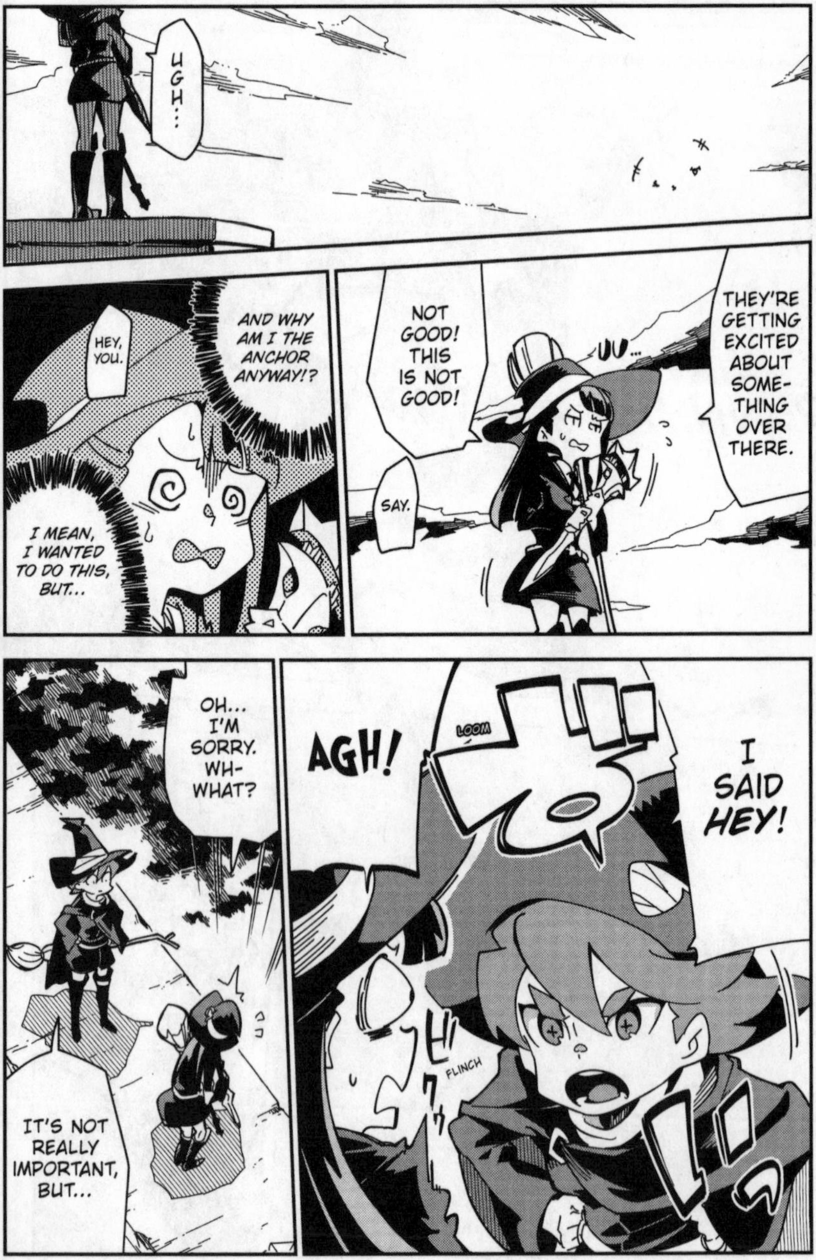
UGH...
THEY'RE GETTING EXCITED ABOUT SOME-THING OVER THERE.
UU...
NOT GOOD! THIS IS NOT GOOD!
SAY.
AND WHY AM I THE ANCHOR ANYWAY!?
HEY, YOU.
I MEAN, I WANTED TO DO THIS, BUT...
I SAID HEY!
LOOM
AGH!
FLINCH
OH... I'M SORRY. WH-WHAT?
IT'S NOT REALLY IMPORTANT, BUT...

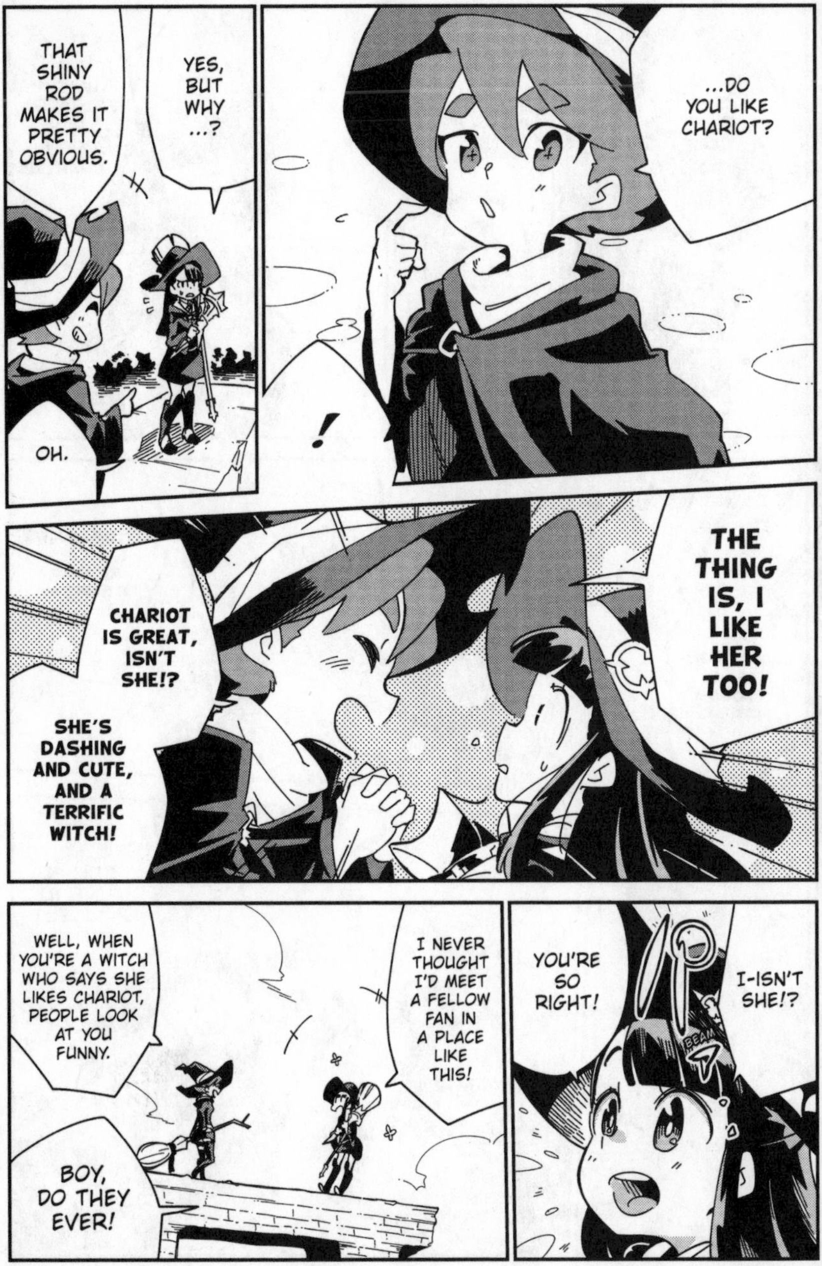
...DO YOU LIKE CHARIOT?
!
YES, BUT WHY ...?
THAT SHINY ROD MAKES IT PRETTY OBVIOUS.
OH.
THE THING IS, I LIKE HER TOO!
CHARIOT IS GREAT, ISN'T SHE!?
SHE'S DASHING AND CUTE, AND A TERRIFIC WITCH!
I-ISN'T SHE!?
BEAM
YOU'RE SO RIGHT!
I NEVER THOUGHT I'D MEET A FELLOW FAN IN A PLACE LIKE THIS!
WELL, WHEN YOU'RE A WITCH WHO SAYS SHE LIKES CHARIOT, PEOPLE LOOK AT YOU FUNNY.
BOY, DO THEY EVER!

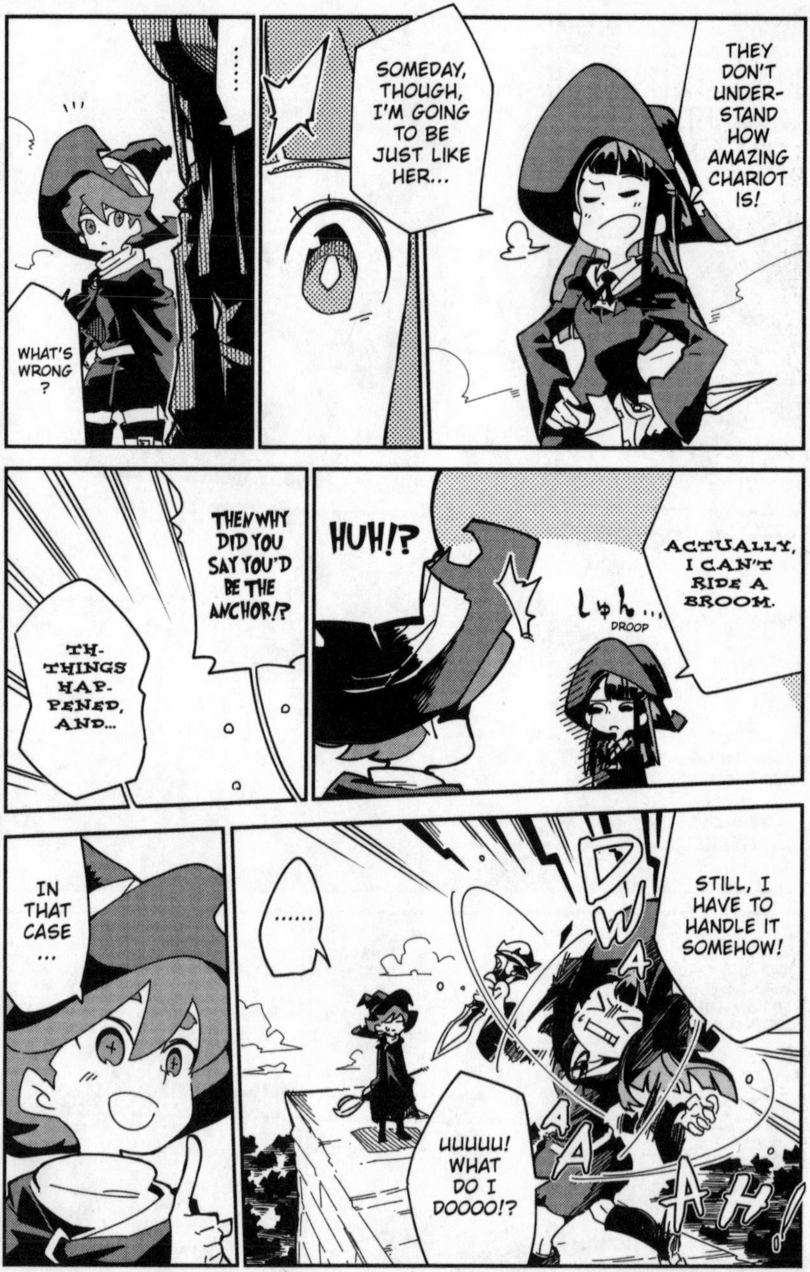
THEY DON'T UNDER-STAND HOW AMAZING CHARIOT IS!
SOMEDAY, THOUGH, I'M GOING TO BE JUST LIKE HER...
......
WHAT'S WRONG?
ACTUALLY, I CAN'T RIDE A BROOM.
しゅん...
DROOP
HUH!?
THEN WHY DID YOU SAY YOU'D BE THE ANCHOR!?
TH-THINGS HAP-PENED, AND...
STILL, I HAVE TO HANDLE IT SOMEHOW!
DWAAAAH!
......
UUUUU! WHAT DO I DOOOO!?
IN THAT CASE...

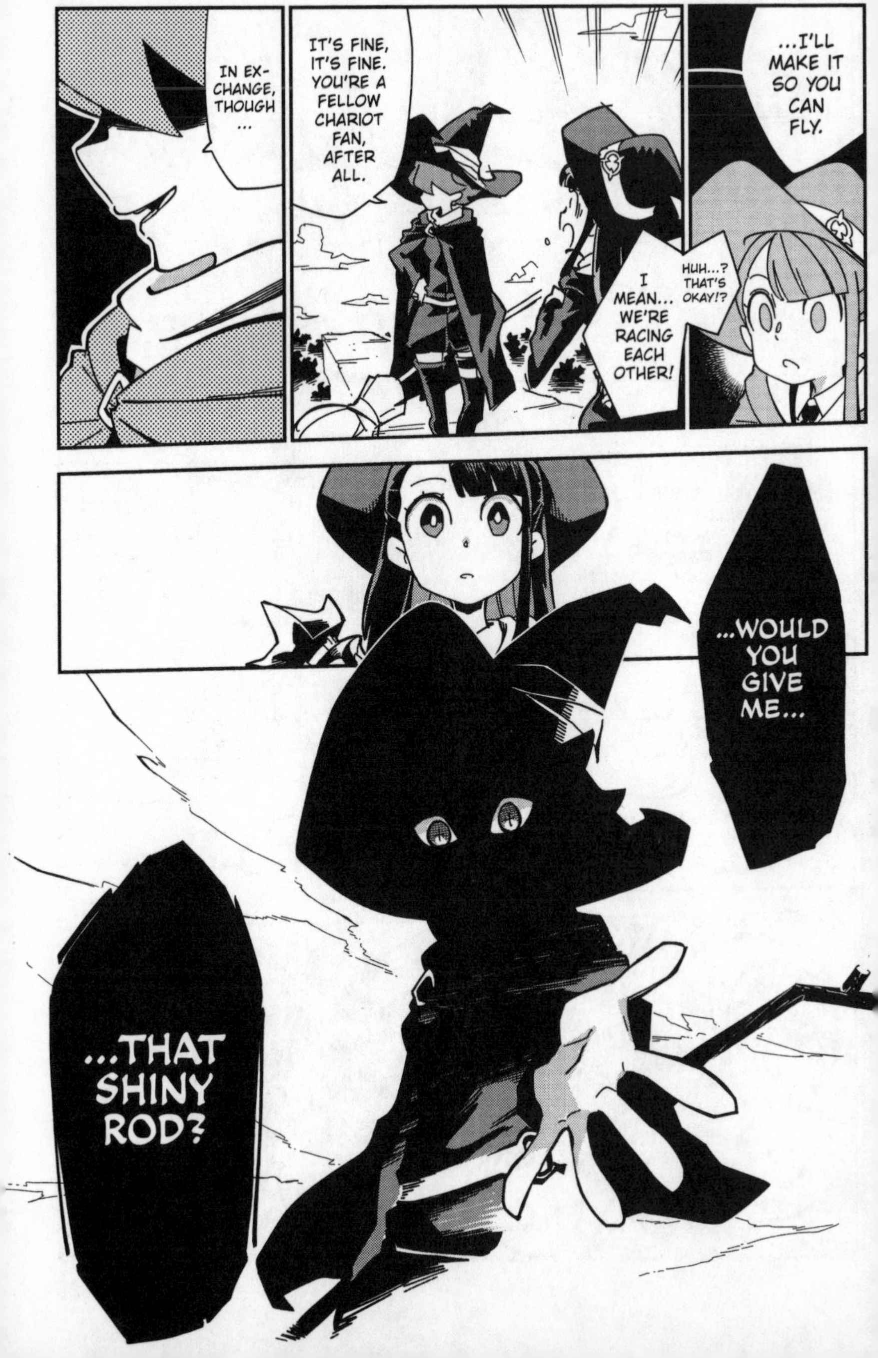
...I'LL MAKE IT SO YOU CAN FLY.
HUH...? THAT'S OKAY!?
I MEAN... WE'RE RACING EACH OTHER!
IT'S FINE, IT'S FINE. YOU'RE A FELLOW CHARIOT FAN, AFTER ALL.
IN EX-CHANGE, THOUGH...
...WOULD YOU GIVE ME...
...THAT SHINY ROD?

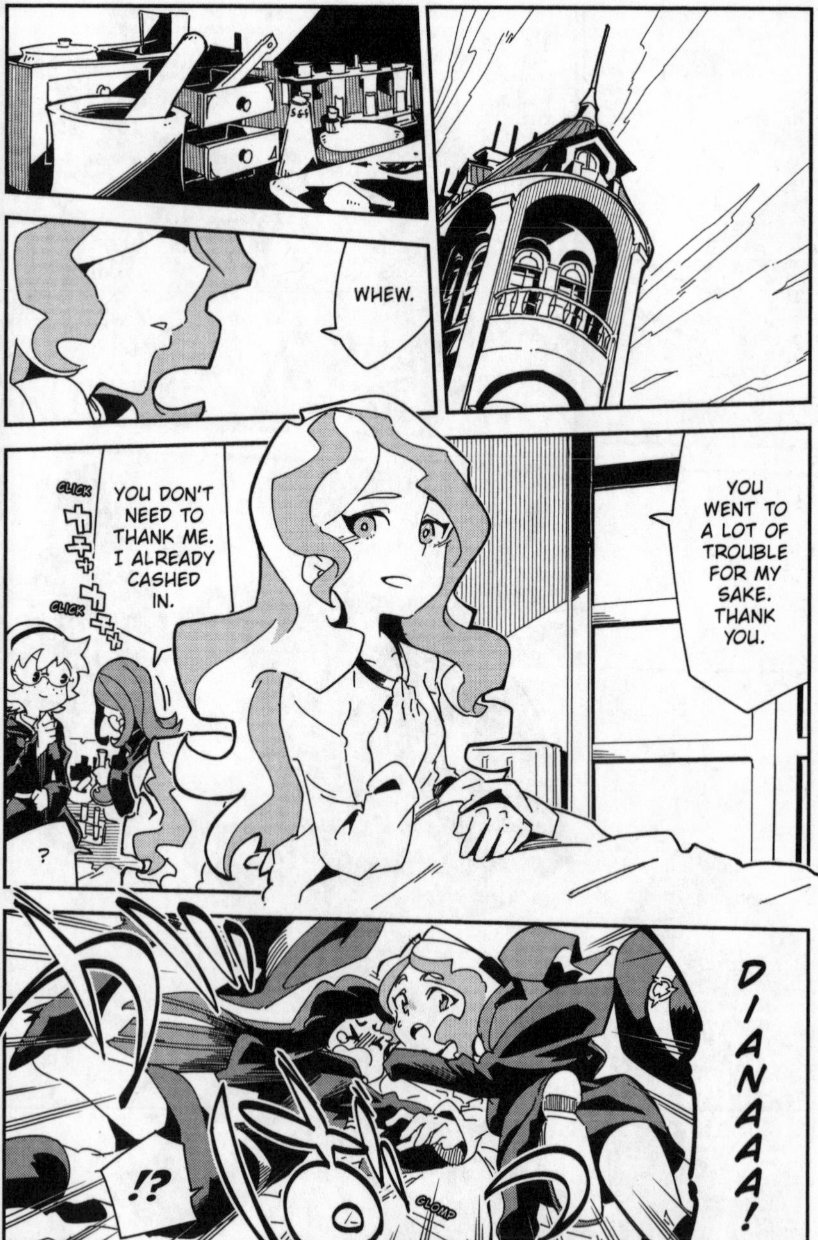
WHEW.
YOU WENT TO A LOT OF TROUBLE FOR MY SAKE. THANK YOU.
YOU DON'T NEED TO THANK ME. I ALREADY CASHED IN.
CLICK
CLICK
?
DIANAAA!
!?
GLOMP

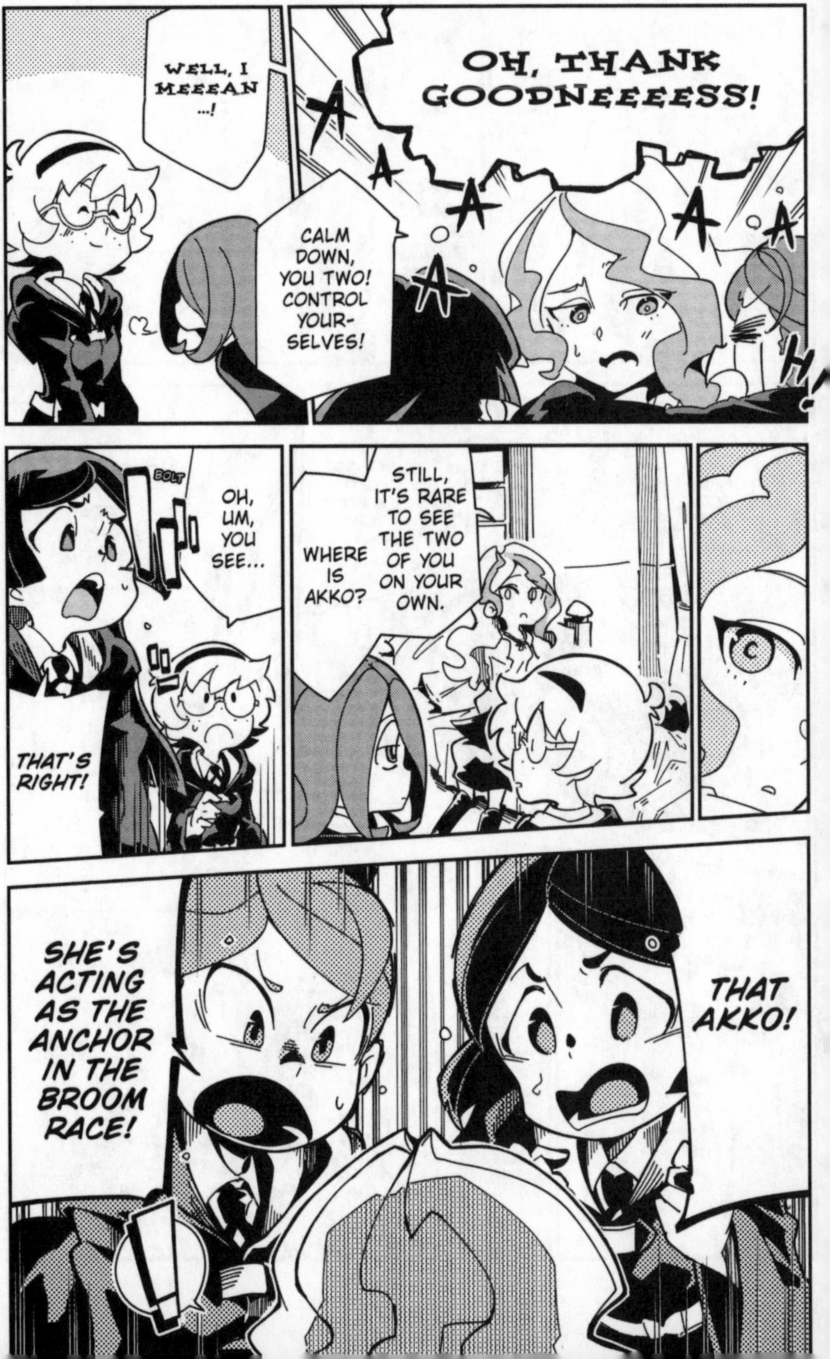

OH, THANK GOODNEEEEESS!
A A A A A A H!
CALM DOWN, YOU TWO! CONTROL YOUR-SELVES!
WELL, I MEEEAN ...!
STILL, IT'S RARE TO SEE THE TWO OF YOU ON YOUR OWN.
WHERE IS AKKO?
BOLT
OH, UM, YOU SEE...
THAT'S RIGHT!
THAT AKKO!
SHE'S ACTING AS THE ANCHOR IN THE BROOM RACE!

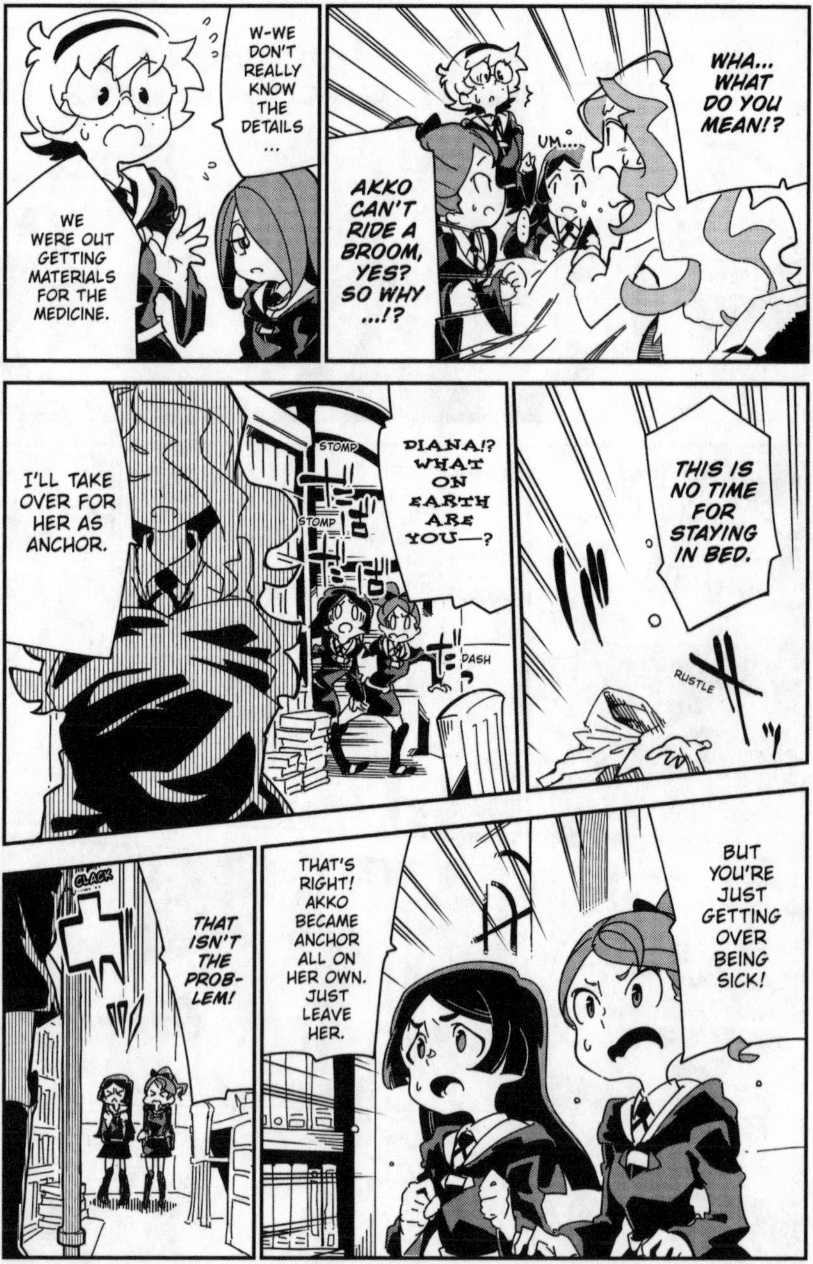
WHA... WHAT DO YOU MEAN!?
UM...
AKKO CAN'T RIDE A BROOM, YES? SO WHY ...!?
W-WE DON'T REALLY KNOW THE DETAILS ...
WE WERE OUT GETTING MATERIALS FOR THE MEDICINE.
THIS IS NO TIME FOR STAYING IN BED.
RUSTLE
DIANA!? WHAT ON EARTH ARE YOU—?
STOMP
STOMP
DASH
I'LL TAKE OVER FOR HER AS ANCHOR.
BUT YOU'RE JUST GETTING OVER BEING SICK!
THAT'S RIGHT! AKKO BECAME ANCHOR ALL ON HER OWN. JUST LEAVE HER.
CLACK
THAT ISN'T THE PROBLEM!

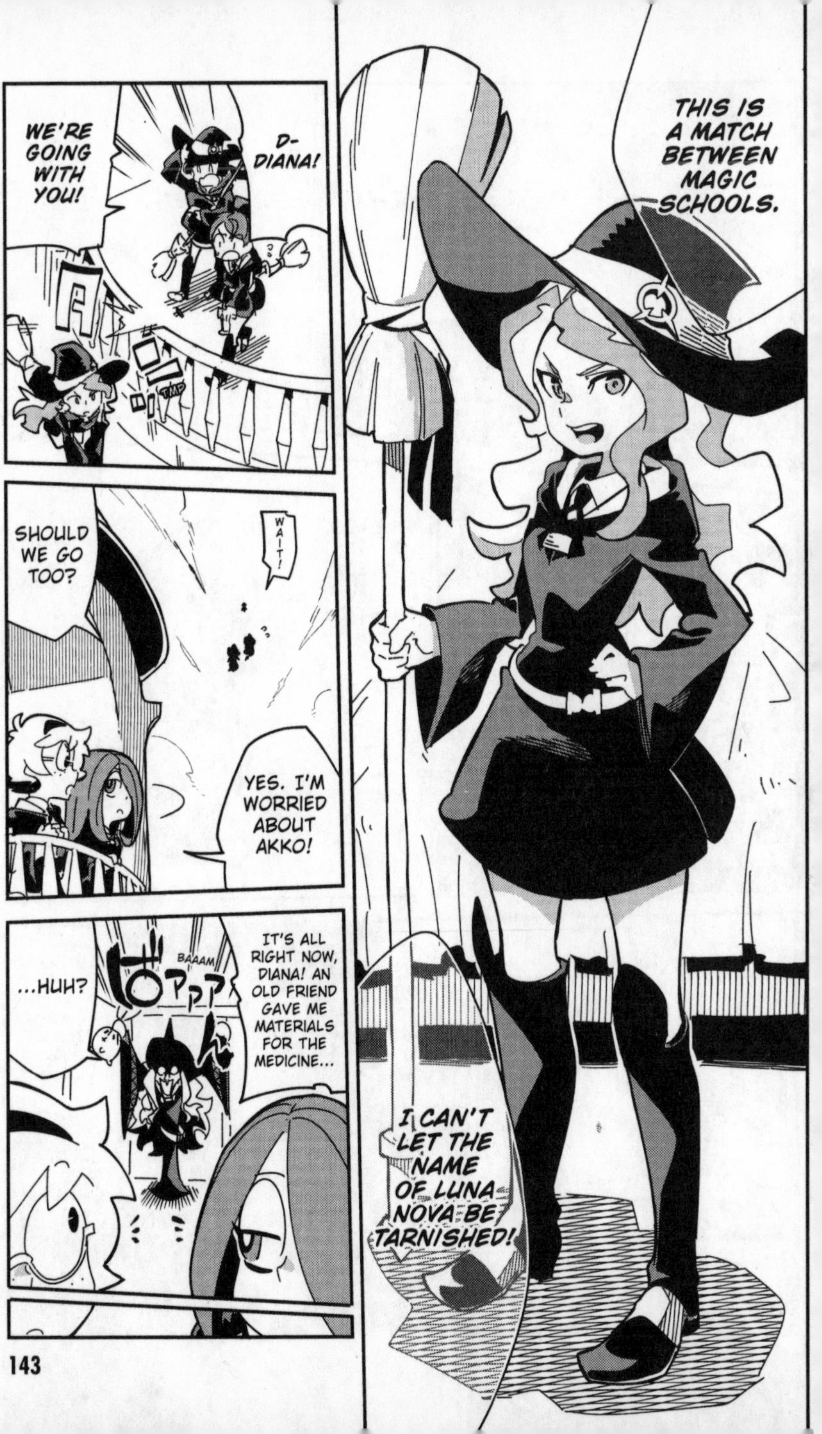
THIS IS A MATCH BETWEEN MAGIC SCHOOLS.
I CAN'T LET THE NAME OF LUNA NOVA BE TARNISHED!
D-DIANA!
WE'RE GOING WITH YOU!
TMP
WAIT!
SHOULD WE GO TOO?
YES. I'M WORRIED ABOUT AKKO!
IT'S ALL RIGHT NOW, DIANA! AN OLD FRIEND GAVE ME MATERIALS FOR THE MEDICINE...
BAAAM
...HUH?

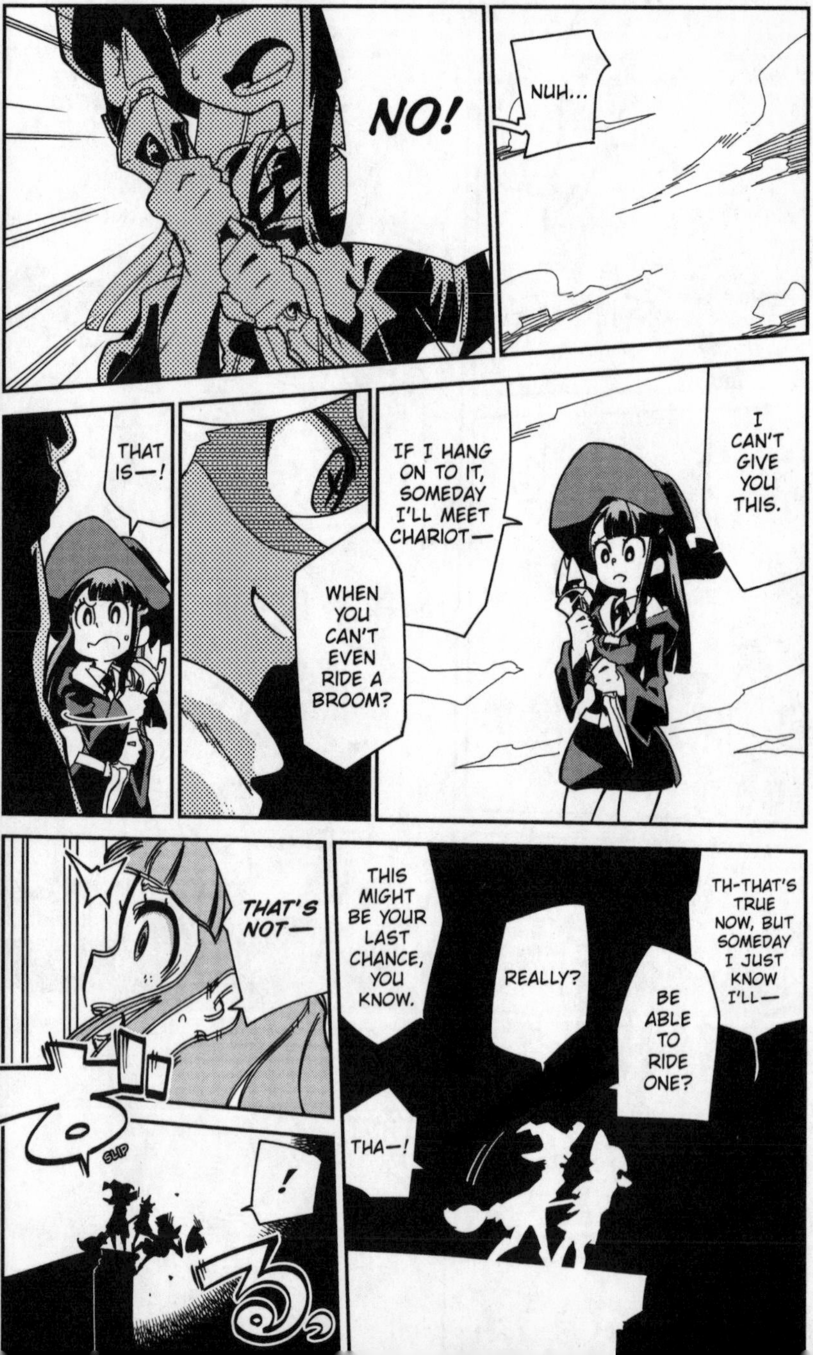
NUH...
NO!
I CAN'T GIVE YOU THIS.
IF I HANG ON TO IT, SOMEDAY I'LL MEET CHARIOT—
WHEN YOU CAN'T EVEN RIDE A BROOM?
THAT IS—!
TH-THAT'S TRUE NOW, BUT SOMEDAY I JUST KNOW I'LL—
BE ABLE TO RIDE ONE?
REALLY?
THIS MIGHT BE YOUR LAST CHANCE, YOU KNOW.
THA—!
THAT'S NOT—
SLIP
!

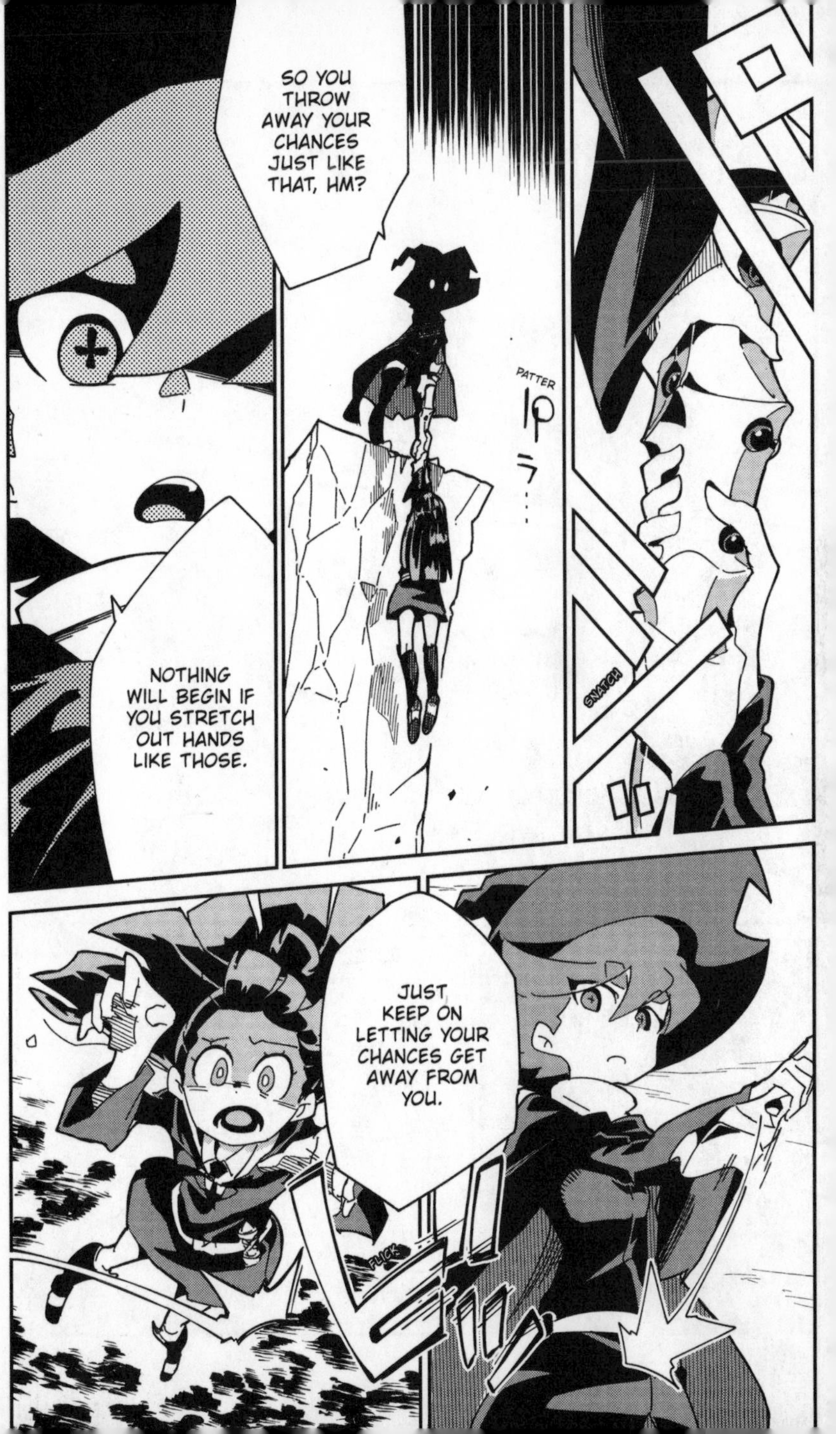
SNATCH
PATTER
SO YOU THROW AWAY YOUR CHANCES JUST LIKE THAT, HM?
NOTHING WILL BEGIN IF YOU STRETCH OUT HANDS LIKE THOSE.
JUST KEEP ON LETTING YOUR CHANCES GET AWAY FROM YOU.
FLICK

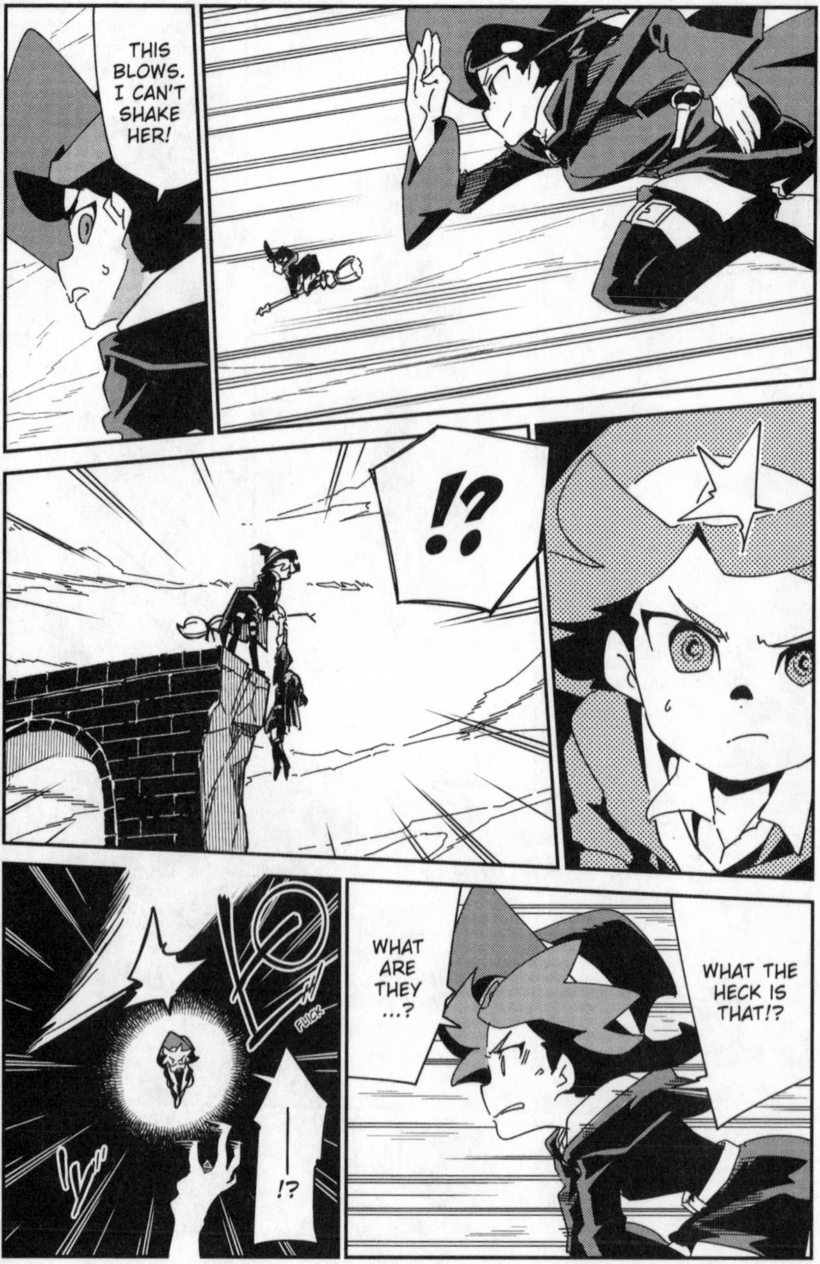
THIS BLOWS. I CAN'T SHAKE HER!
!?
WHAT THE HECK IS THAT!?
WHAT ARE THEY ...?
FLICK
!?

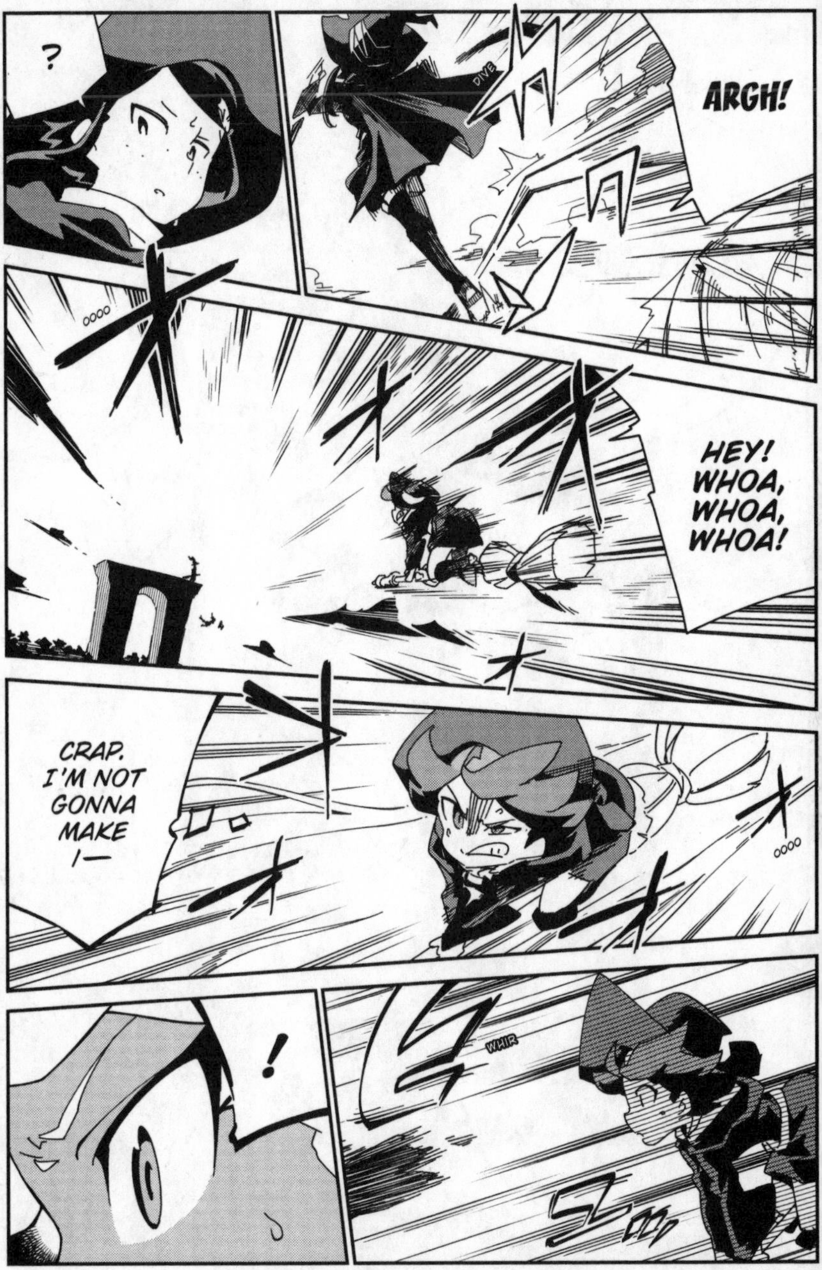
ARGH!
DIVE
?
HEY! WHOA, WHOA, WHOA!
OOOO
OOOO
CRAP. I'M NOT GONNA MAKE I—
WHIR
!

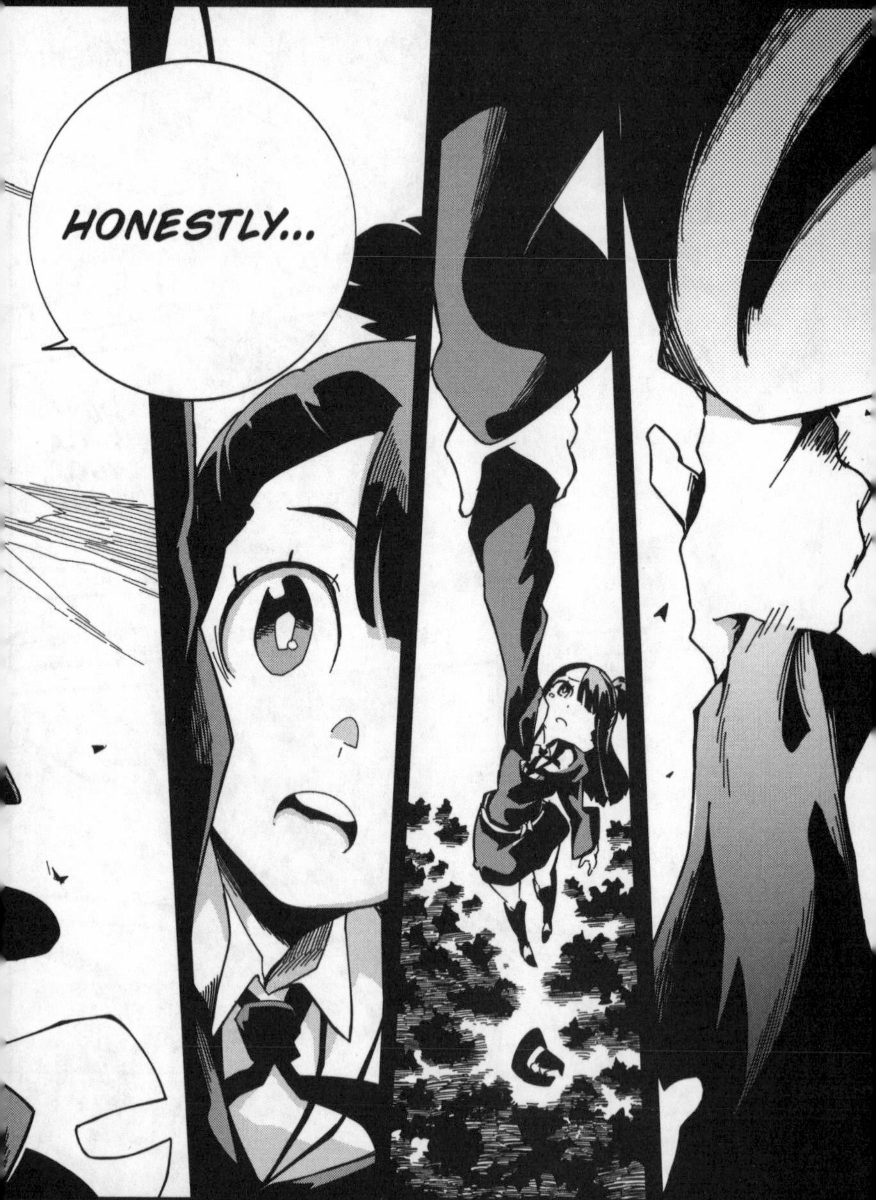
HONESTLY...

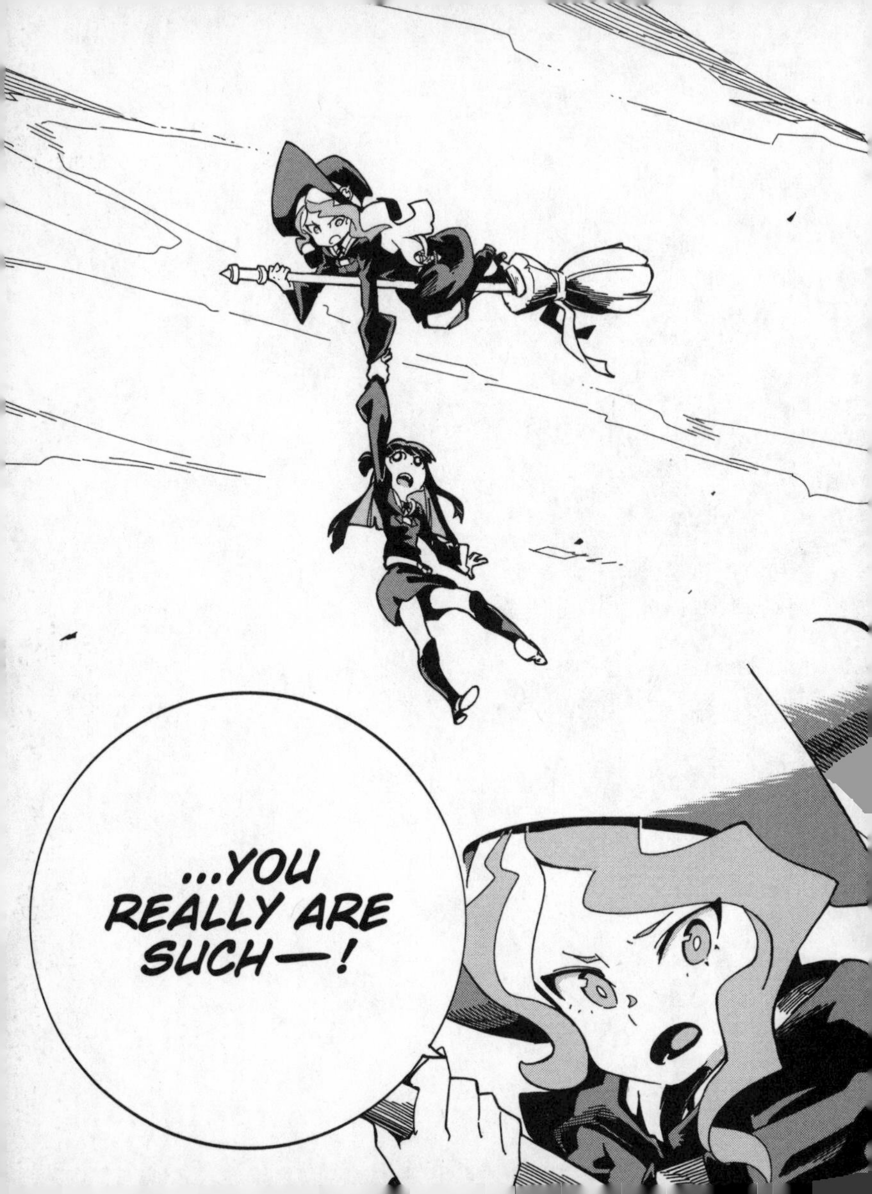
...YOU REALLY ARE SUCH—!

Little Witch Academia

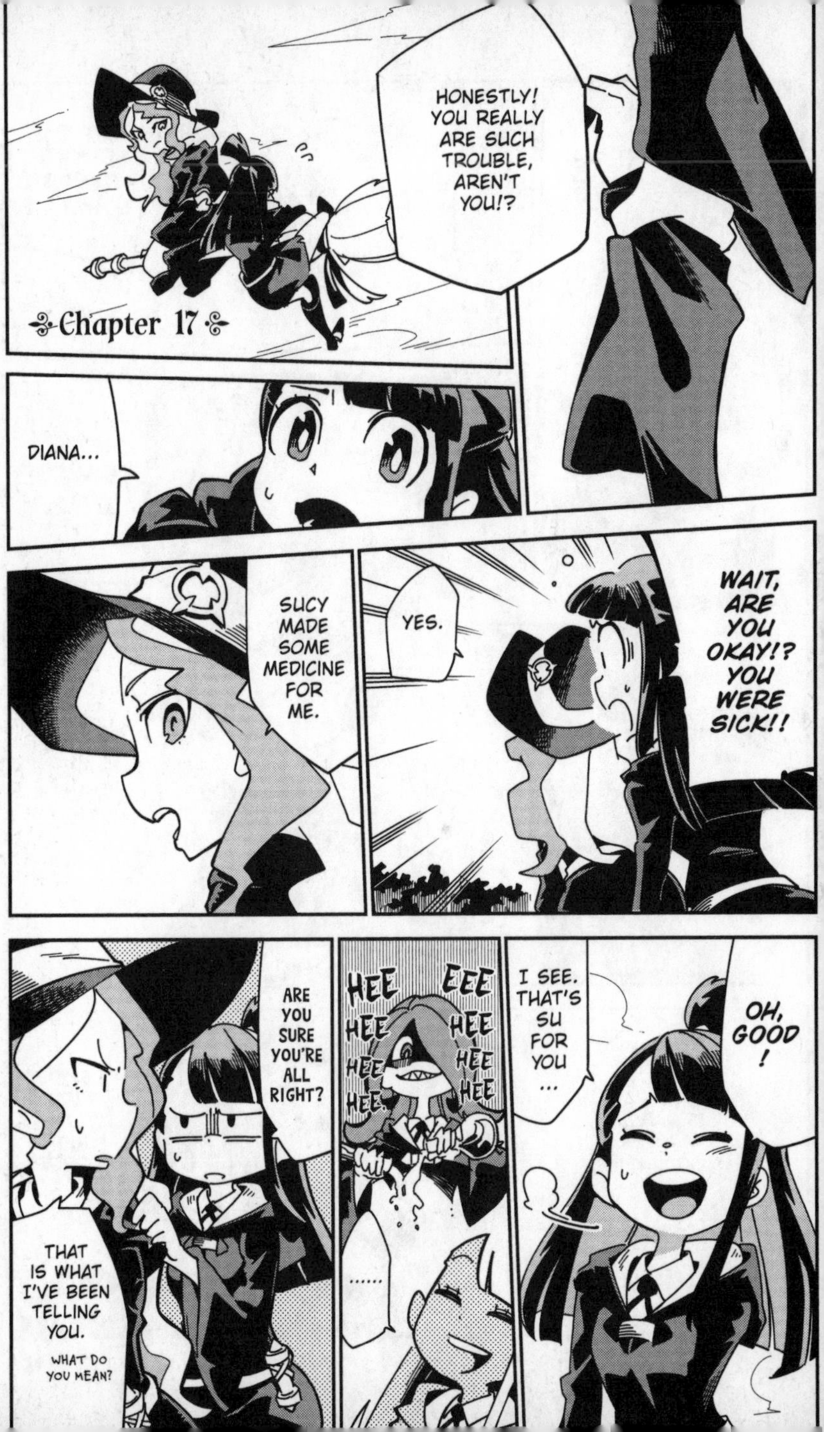
HONESTLY! YOU REALLY ARE SUCH TROUBLE, AREN'T YOU!?
Chapter 17
DIANA...
WAIT, ARE YOU OKAY!? YOU WERE SICK!!
YES.
SUCY MADE SOME MEDICINE FOR ME.
OH, GOOD!
I SEE. THAT'S SU FOR YOU...
HEE HEE HEE HEE EEE HEE HEE HEE
......
ARE YOU SURE YOU'RE ALL RIGHT?
THAT IS WHAT I'VE BEEN TELLING YOU.
WHAT DO YOU MEAN?

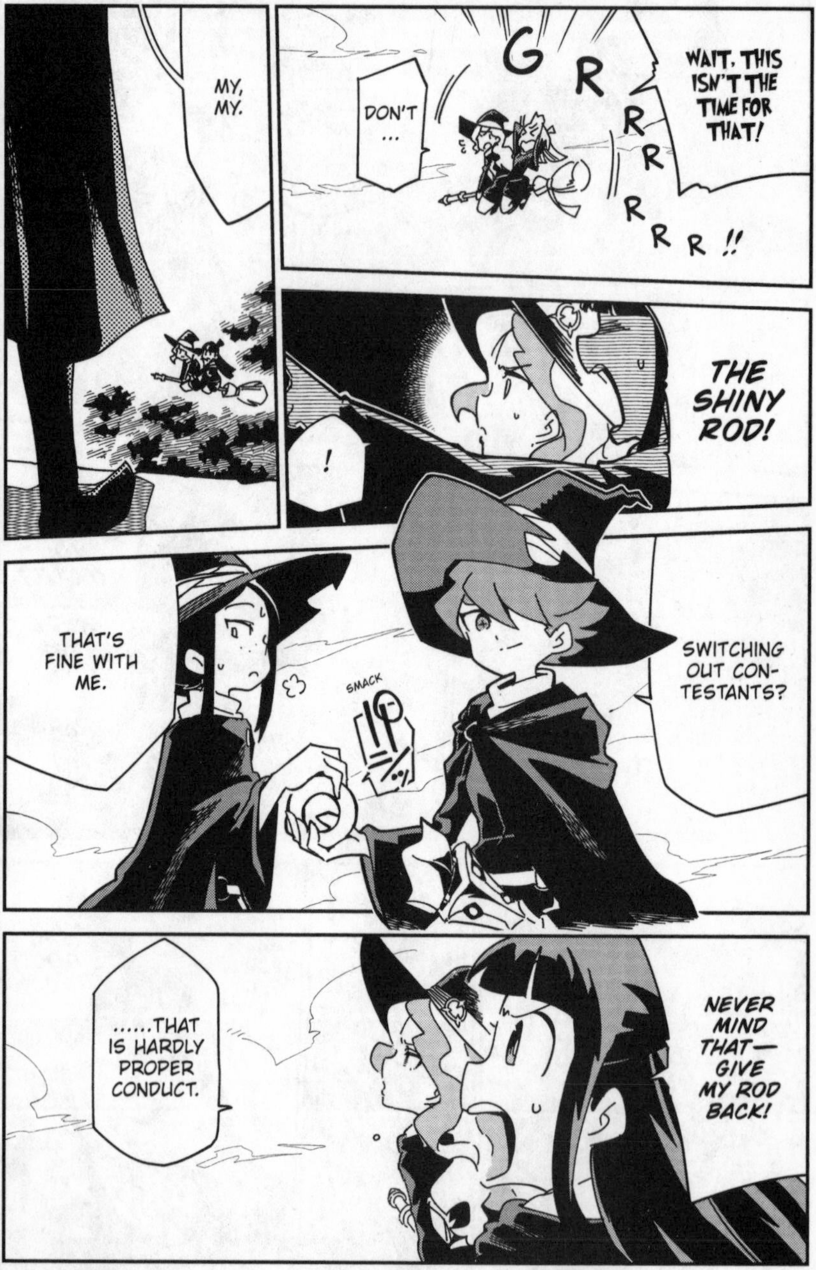
WAIT, THIS ISN'T THE TIME FOR THAT!
GRRRRRR!!
DON'T ...
THE SHINY ROD!
!
MY, MY.
SWITCHING OUT CONTESTANTS?
SMACK
THAT'S FINE WITH ME.
NEVER MIND THAT—GIVE MY ROD BACK!
......THAT IS HARDLY PROPER CONDUCT.

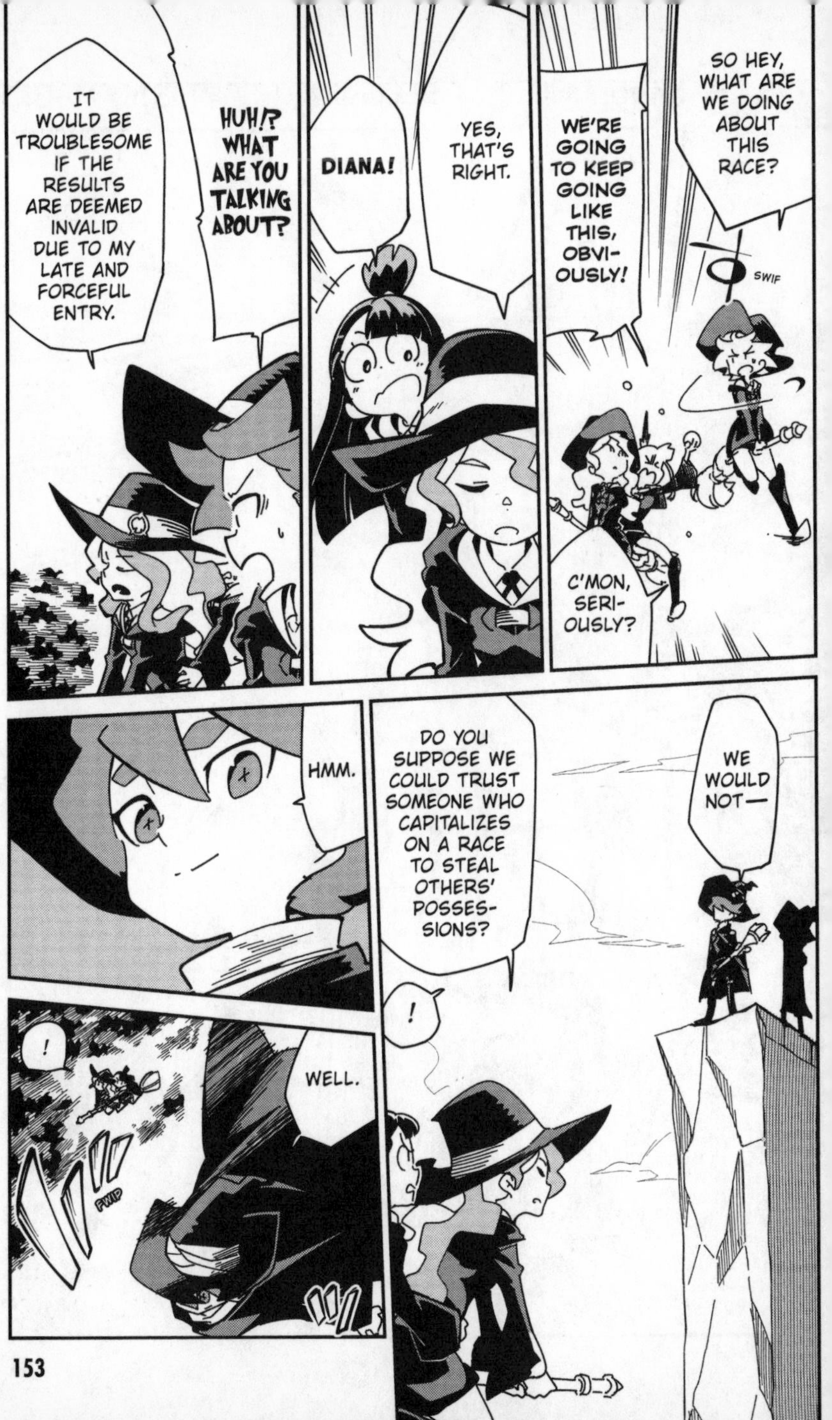
SO HEY, WHAT ARE WE DOING ABOUT THIS RACE?
WE'RE GOING TO KEEP GOING LIKE THIS, OBVIOUSLY!
SWIF
C'MON, SERIOUSLY?
YES, THAT'S RIGHT.
DIANA!
HUH!? WHAT ARE YOU TALKING ABOUT?
IT WOULD BE TROUBLESOME IF THE RESULTS ARE DEEMED INVALID DUE TO MY LATE AND FORCEFUL ENTRY.
WE WOULD NOT—
DO YOU SUPPOSE WE COULD TRUST SOMEONE WHO CAPITALIZES ON A RACE TO STEAL OTHERS' POSSESSIONS?
HMM.
!
WELL.
!
FWIP

Chapter 17 A BELIEVING HEART IS MY MAGIC

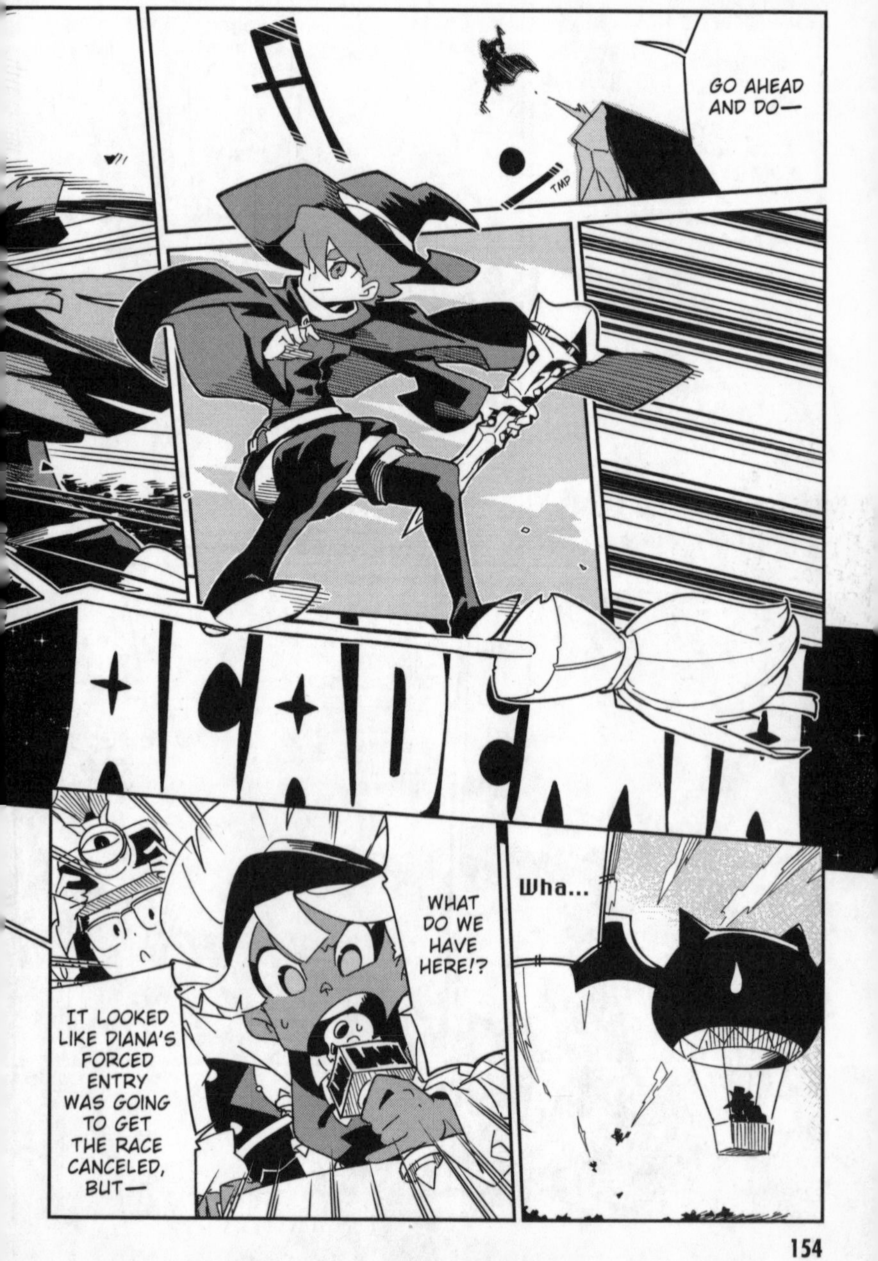
GO AHEAD AND DO—
TMP
Wha...
WHAT DO WE HAVE HERE!?
IT LOOKED LIKE DIANA'S FORCED ENTRY WAS GOING TO GET THE RACE CANCELED, BUT—

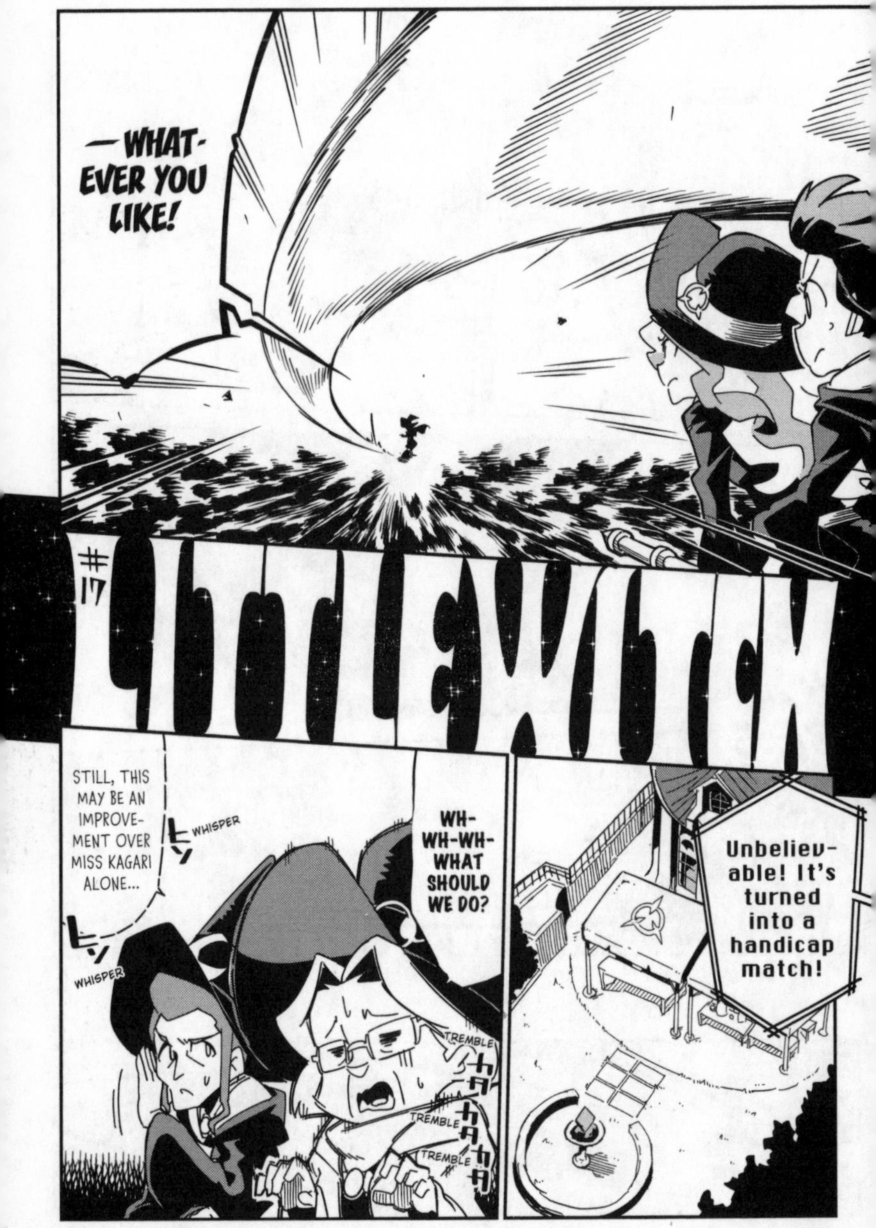
—WHAT-EVER YOU LIKE!
#17
Unbeliev-able! It's turned into a handicap match!
WH-WH-WH-WHAT SHOULD WE DO?
STILL, THIS MAY BE AN IMPROVE-MENT OVER MISS KAGARI ALONE...
WHISPER
WHISPER
TREMBLE
TREMBLE
TREMBLE

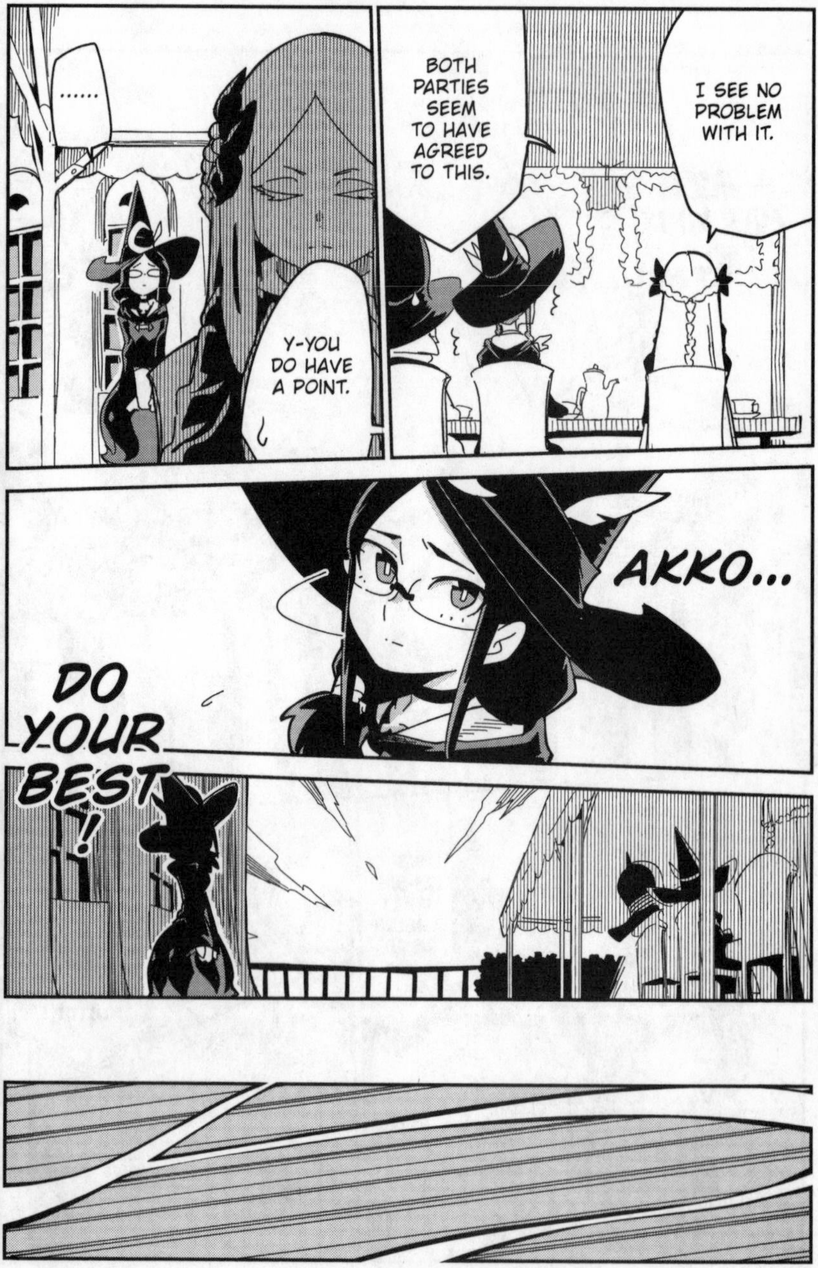
I SEE NO PROBLEM WITH IT.
BOTH PARTIES SEEM TO HAVE AGREED TO THIS.
......
Y-YOU DO HAVE A POINT.
AKKO...
DO YOUR BEST!

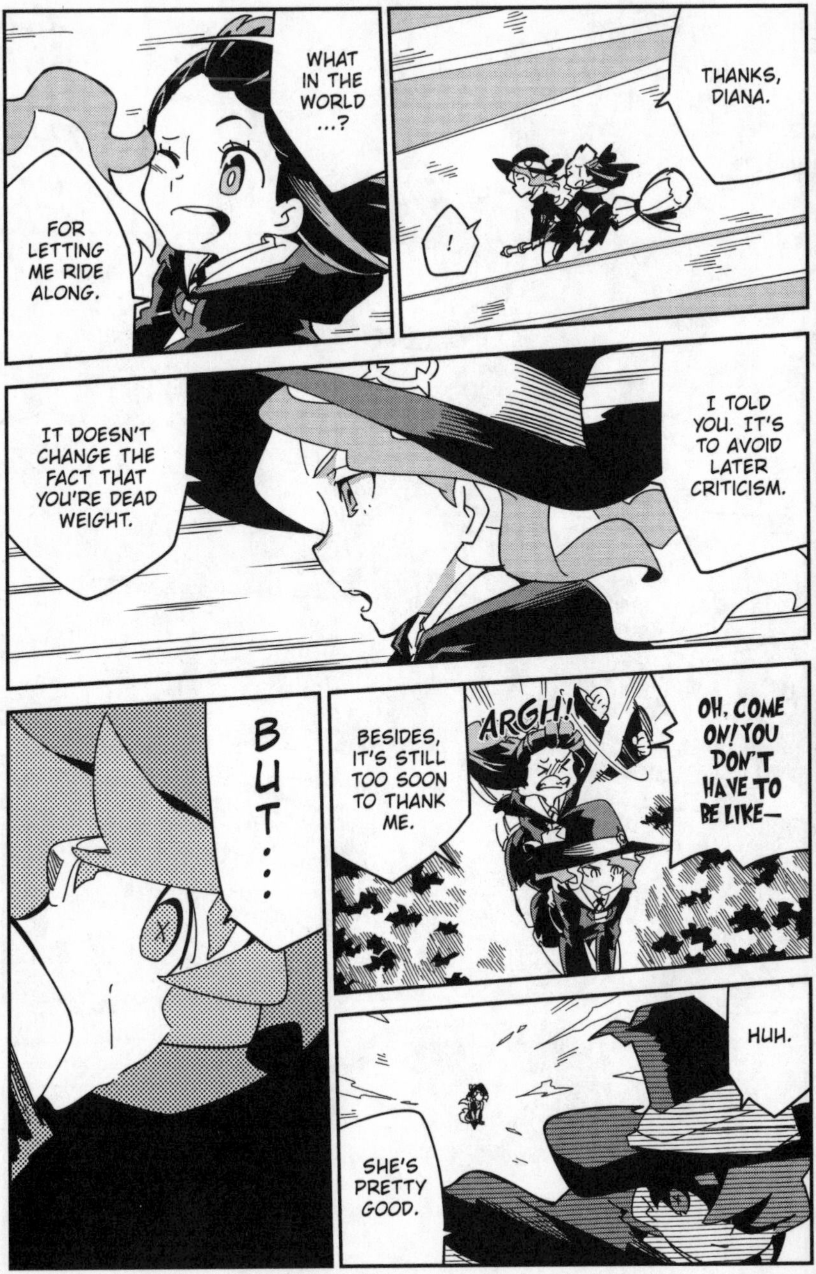
THANKS, DIANA.
!
WHAT IN THE WORLD ...?
FOR LETTING ME RIDE ALONG.
I TOLD YOU. IT'S TO AVOID LATER CRITICISM.
IT DOESN'T CHANGE THE FACT THAT YOU'RE DEAD WEIGHT.
OH, COME ON! YOU DON'T HAVE TO BE LIKE—
ARGH!
BESIDES, IT'S STILL TOO SOON TO THANK ME.
HUH.
SHE'S PRETTY GOOD.
BUT...

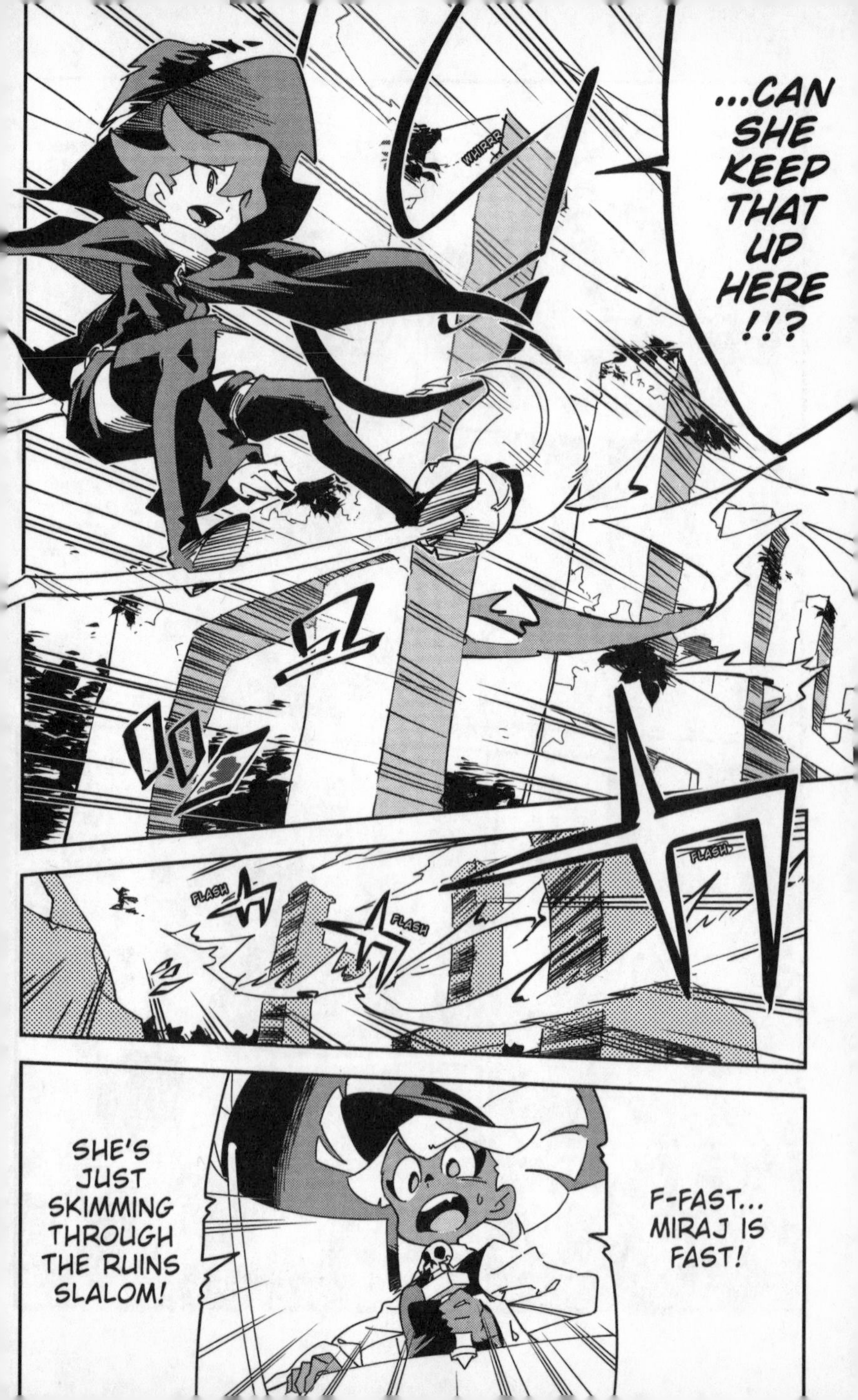
...CAN SHE KEEP THAT UP HERE!!?
WHIRRR
FLASH
FLASH
FLASH
F-FAST... MIRAJ IS FAST!
SHE'S JUST SKIMMING THROUGH THE RUINS SLALOM!

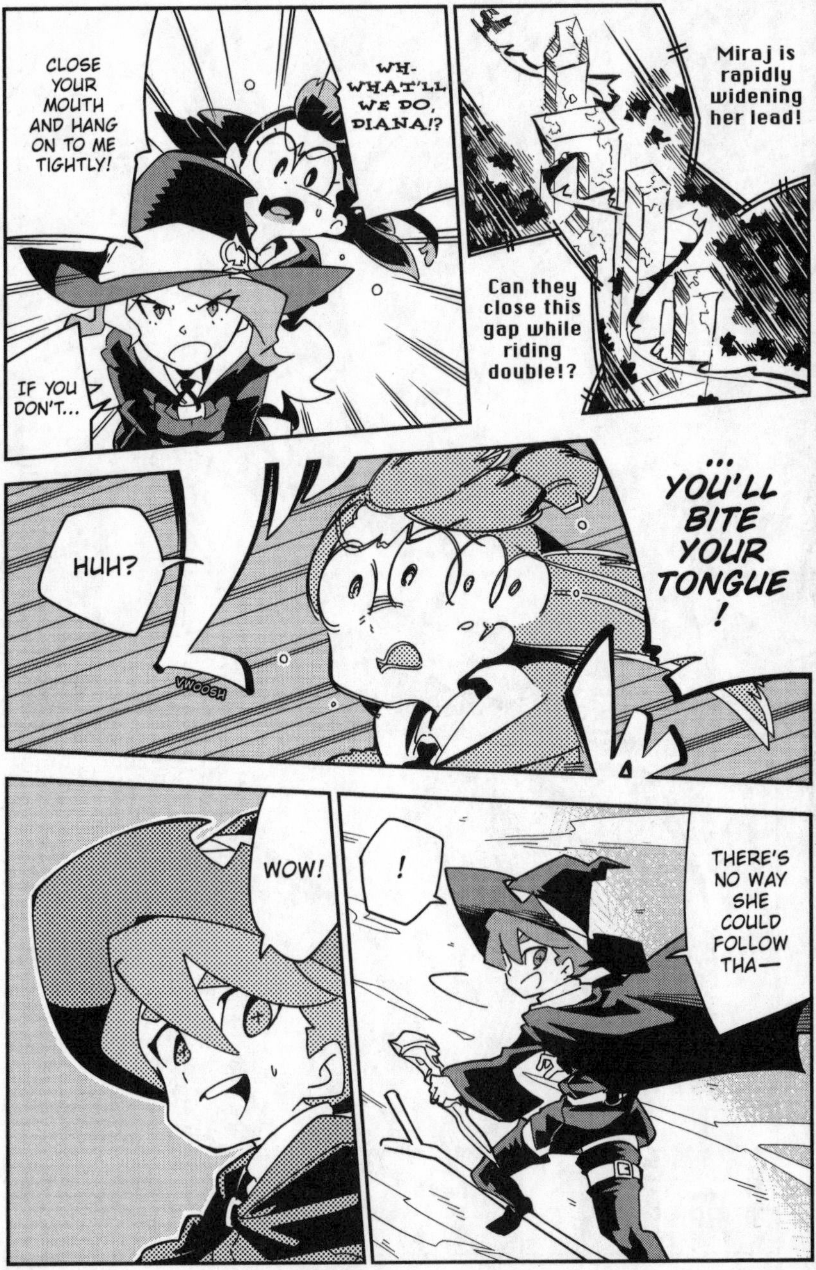
Miraj is rapidly widening her lead!
Can they close this gap while riding double!?
WH-WHAT'LL WE DO, DIANA!?
CLOSE YOUR MOUTH AND HANG ON TO ME TIGHTLY!
IF YOU DON'T...
...YOU'LL BITE YOUR TONGUE!
HUH?
VWOOSH
THERE'S NO WAY SHE COULD FOLLOW THA—
!
WOW!

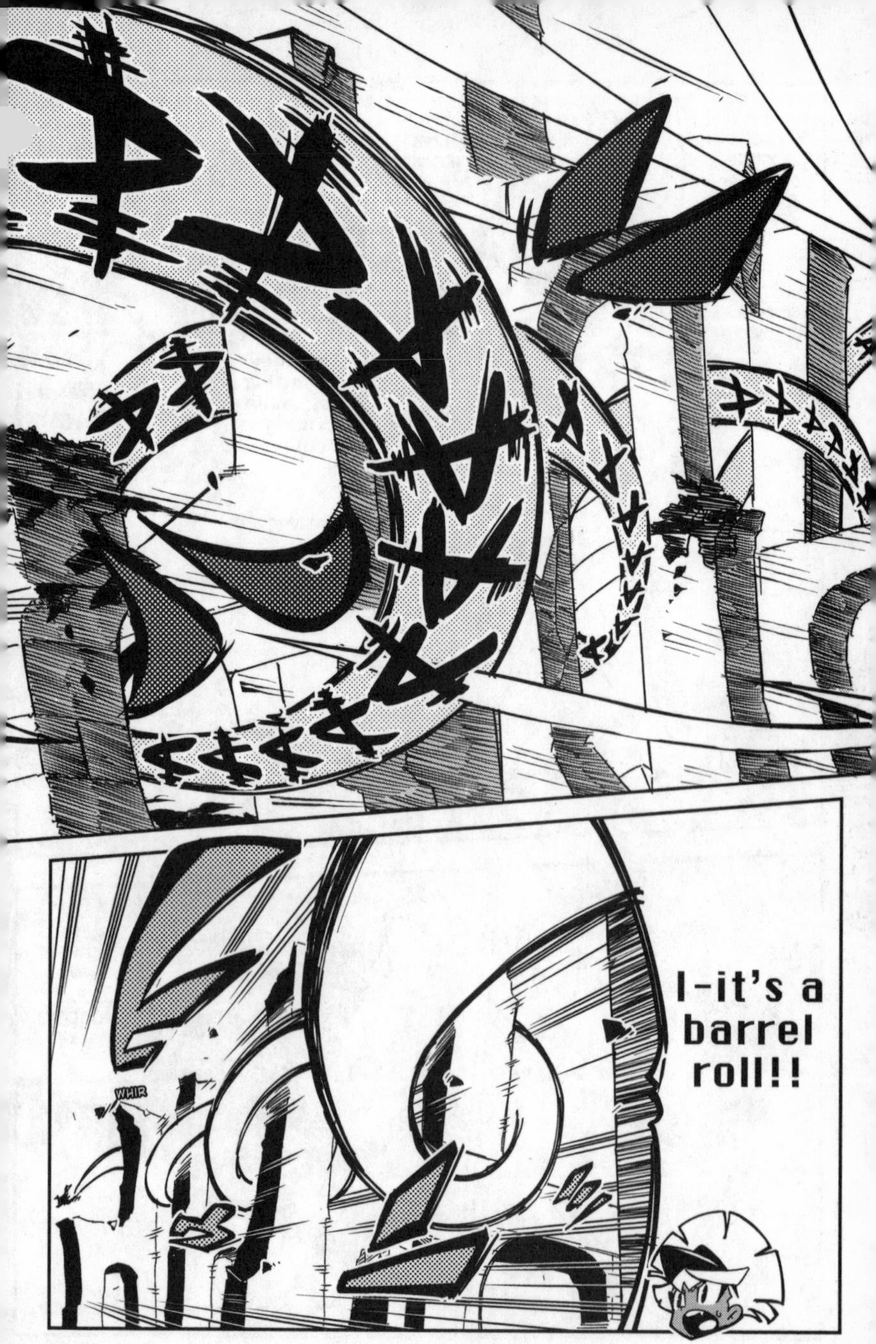
I-it's a barrel roll!!
WHIR

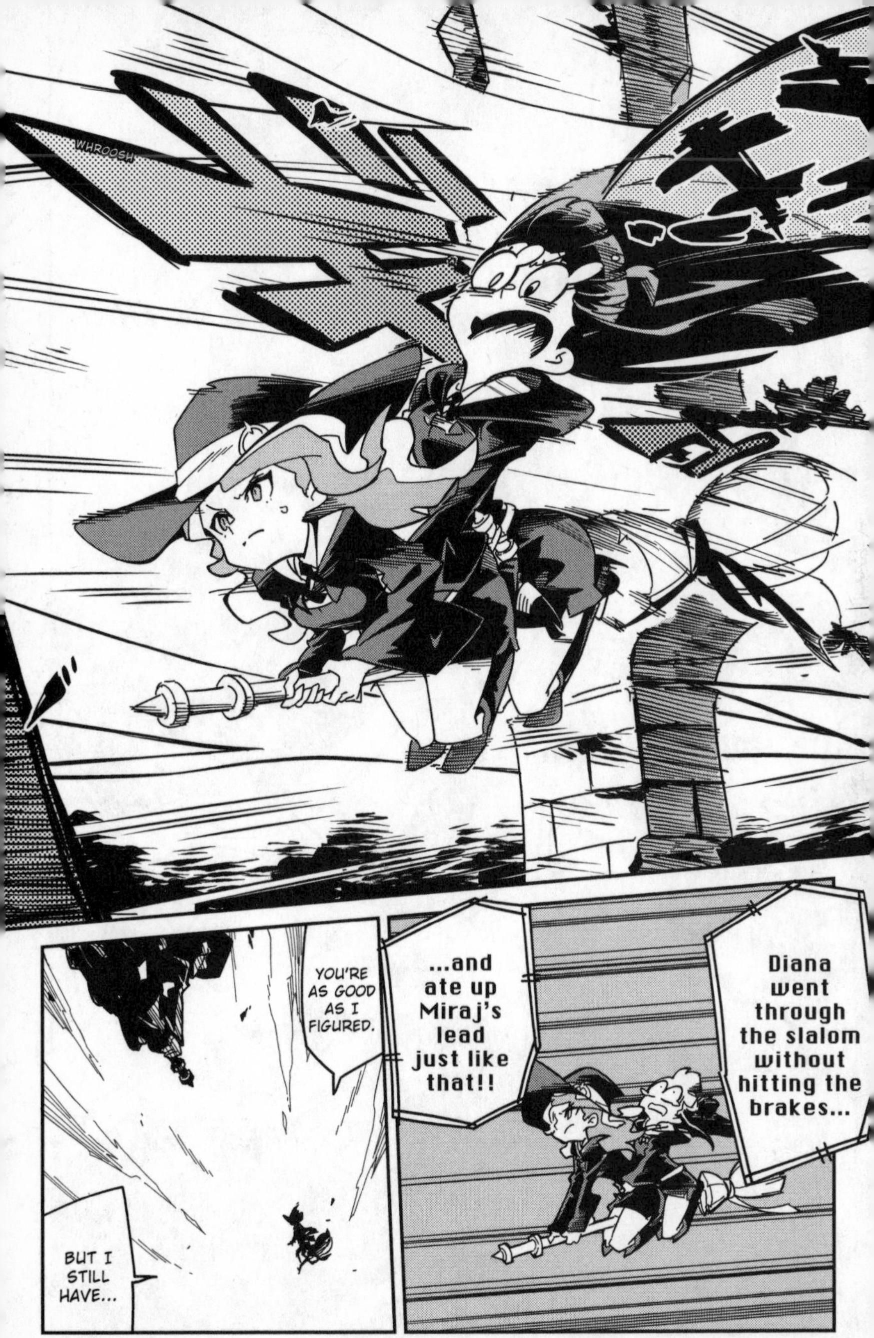
WHROOSH
Diana went through the slalom without hitting the brakes...
...and ate up Miraj's lead just like that!!
YOU'RE AS GOOD AS I FIGURED.
BUT I STILL HAVE...

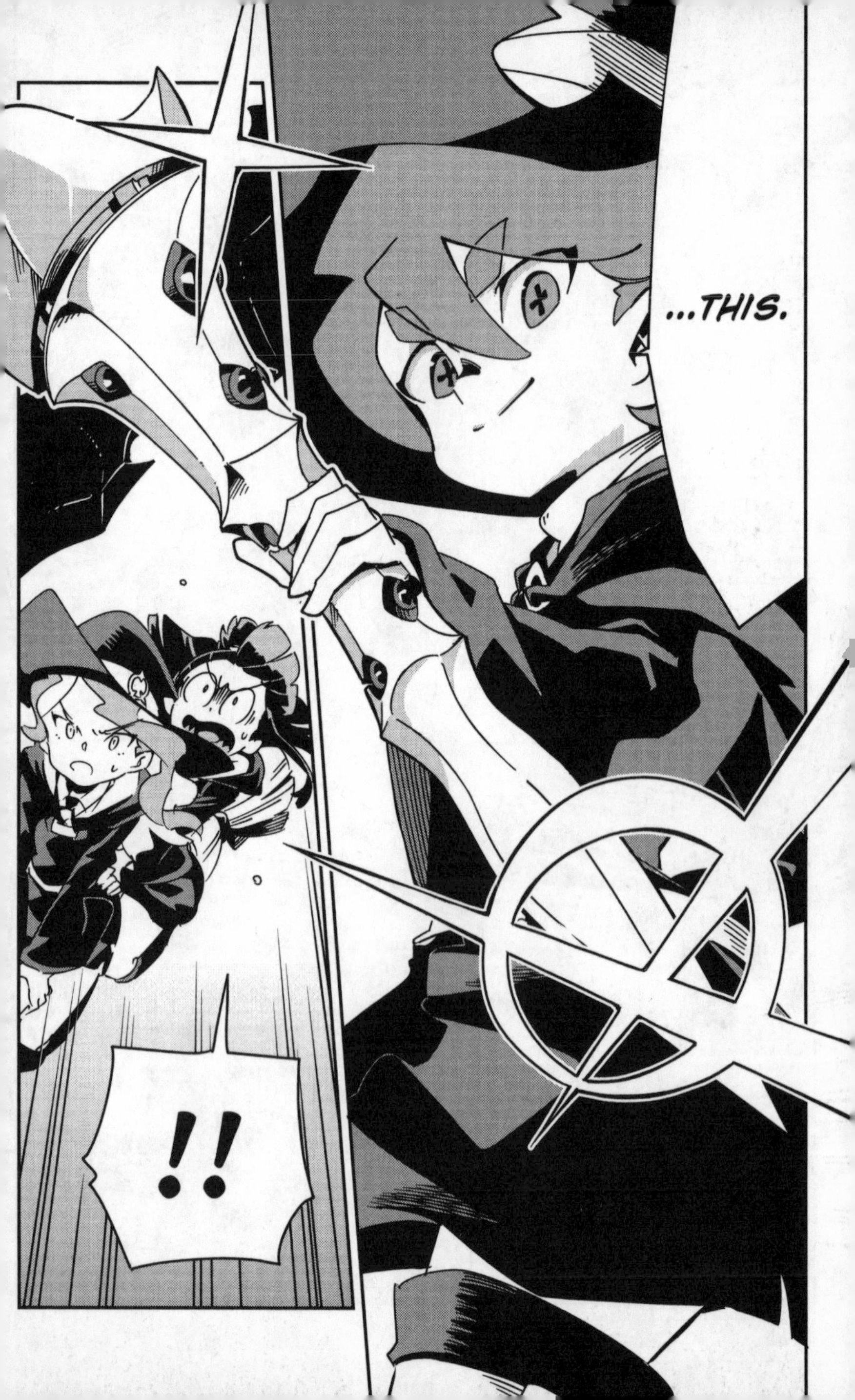

...THIS.
!!

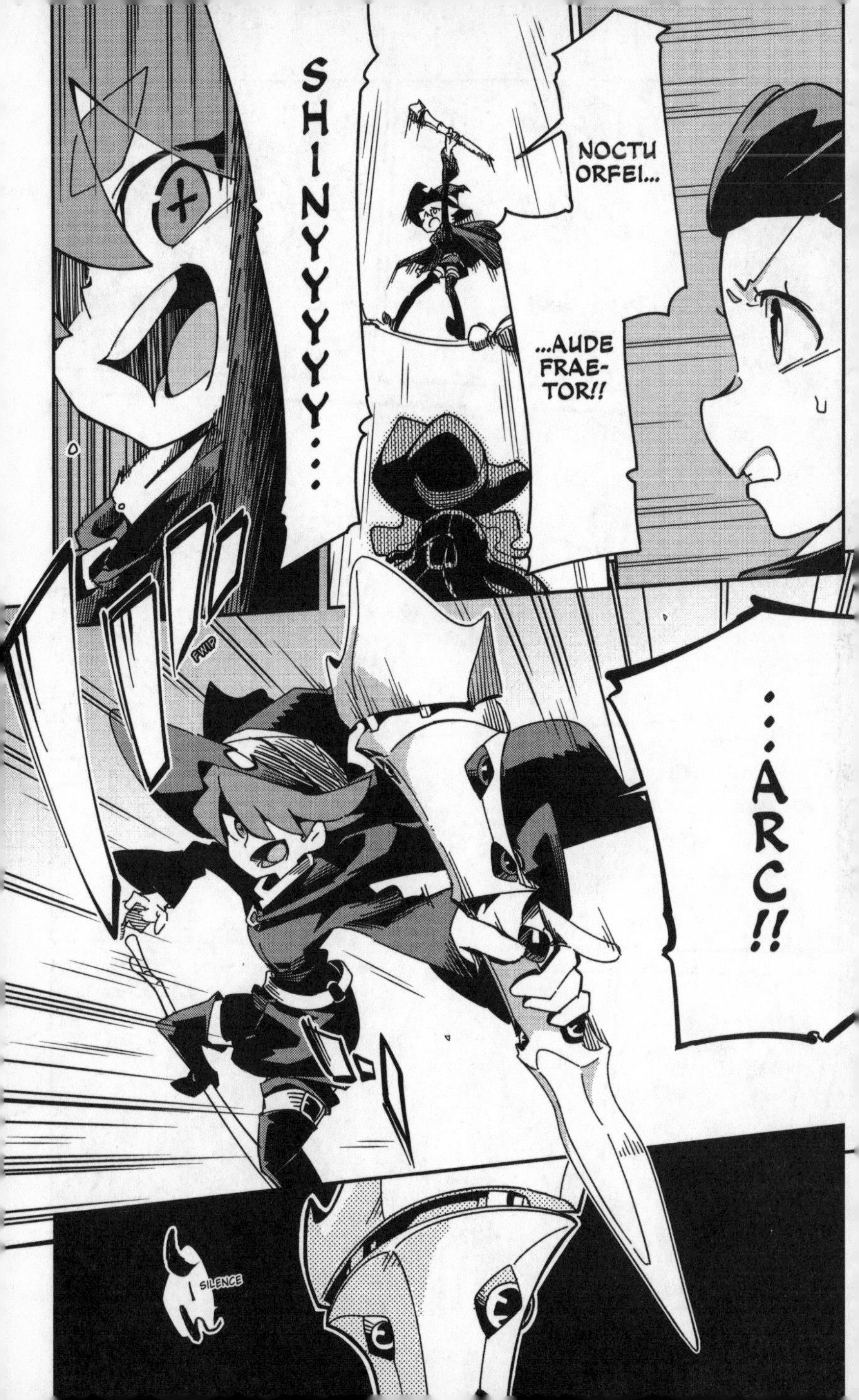
NOCTU ORFEI...
...AUDE FRAETOR!!
SHINYYYYY...
...ARC!!
FWIP
SILENCE

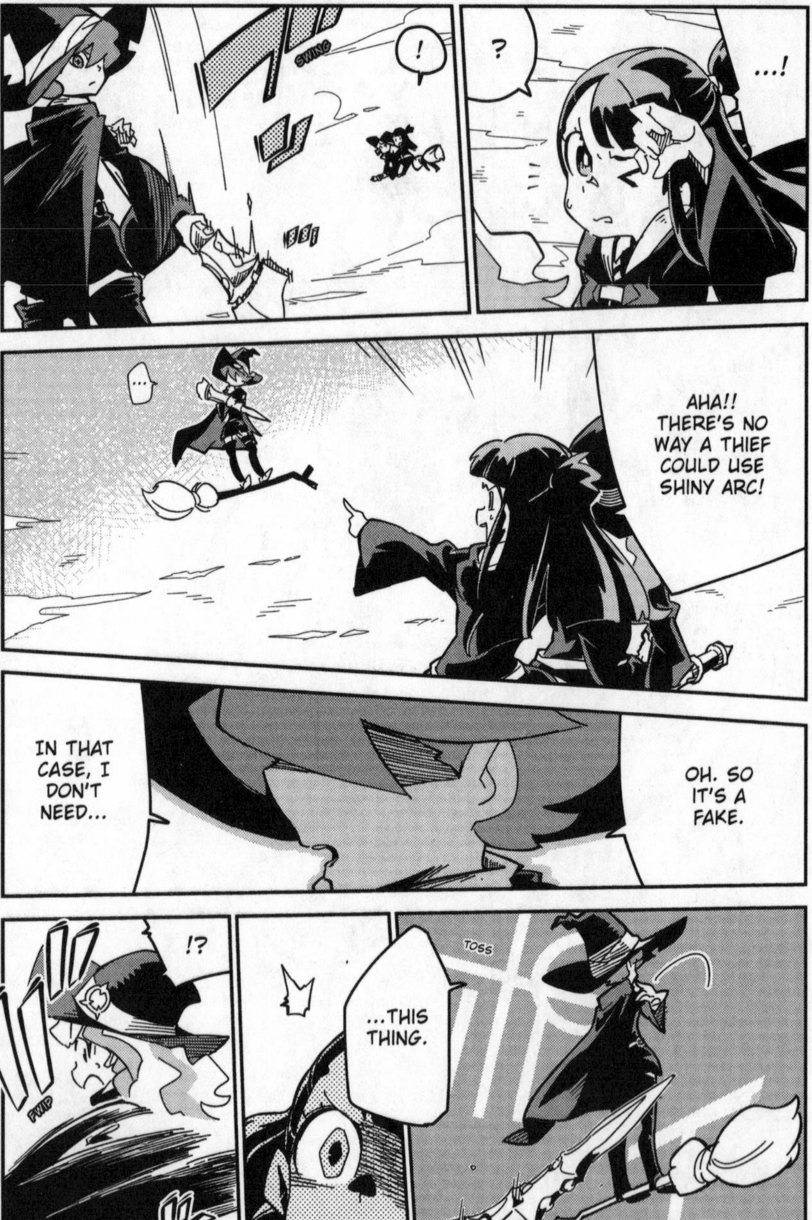
?
...!
!
SWING
AHA!! THERE'S NO WAY A THIEF COULD USE SHINY ARC!
...
OH. SO IT'S A FAKE.
IN THAT CASE, I DON'T NEED...
TOSS
...THIS THING.
!?
FWIP

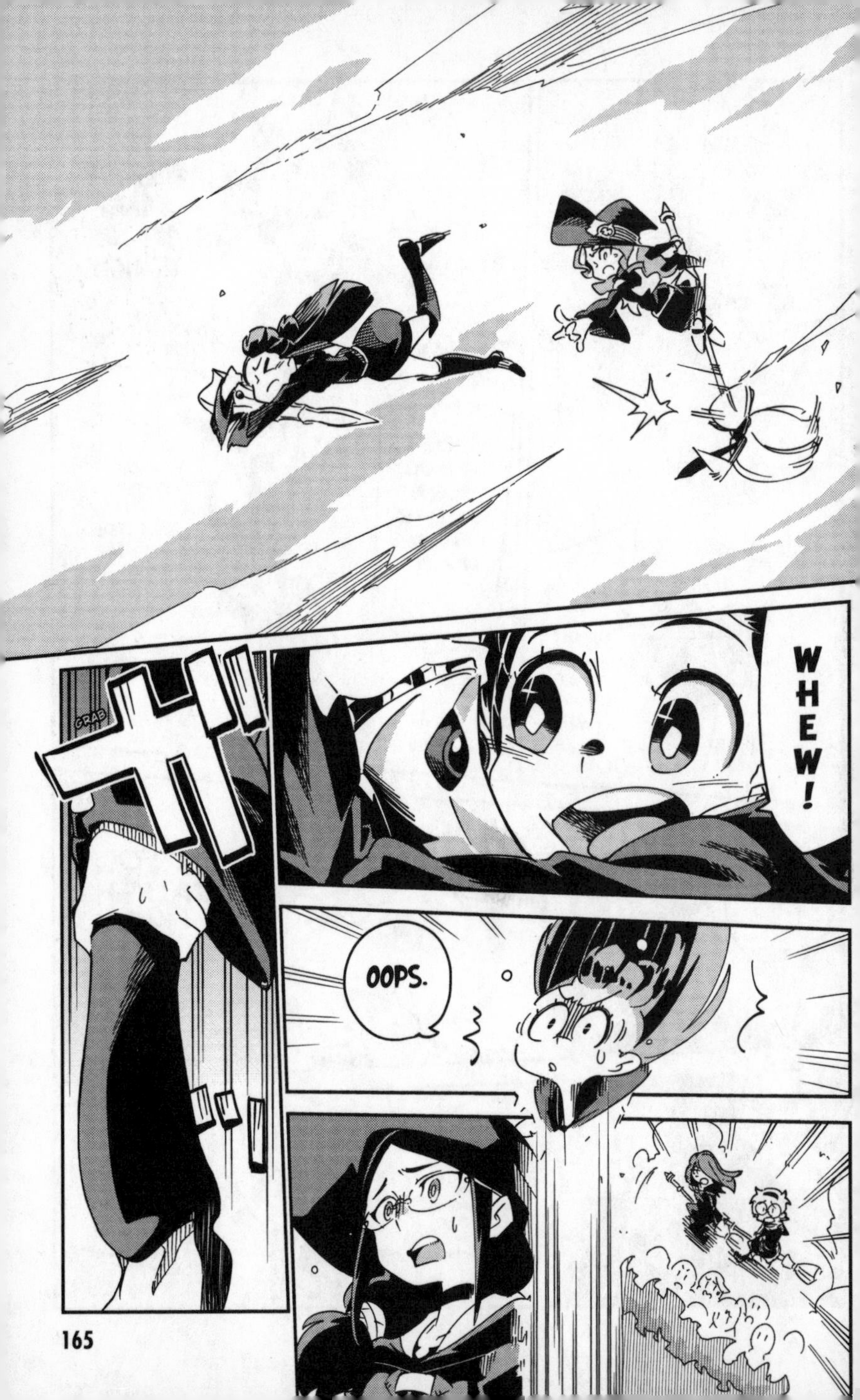
WHEW!
OOPS.
GRAB
ガッ

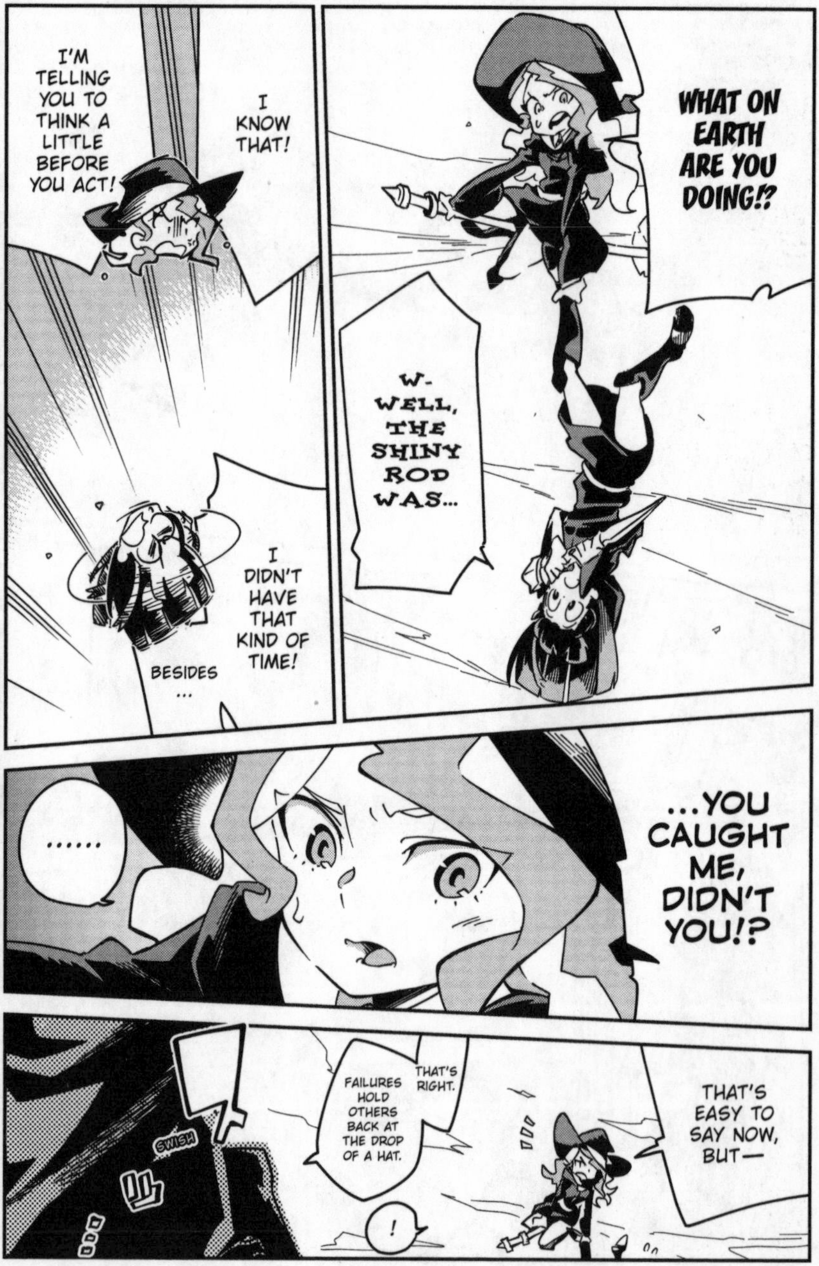
WHAT ON EARTH ARE YOU DOING!?
W-WELL, THE SHINY ROD WAS...
I'M TELLING YOU TO THINK A LITTLE BEFORE YOU ACT!
I KNOW THAT!
I DIDN'T HAVE THAT KIND OF TIME!
BESIDES...
...YOU CAUGHT ME, DIDN'T YOU!?
......
THAT'S EASY TO SAY NOW, BUT—
!
THAT'S RIGHT.
FAILURES HOLD OTHERS BACK AT THE DROP OF A HAT.
SWISH

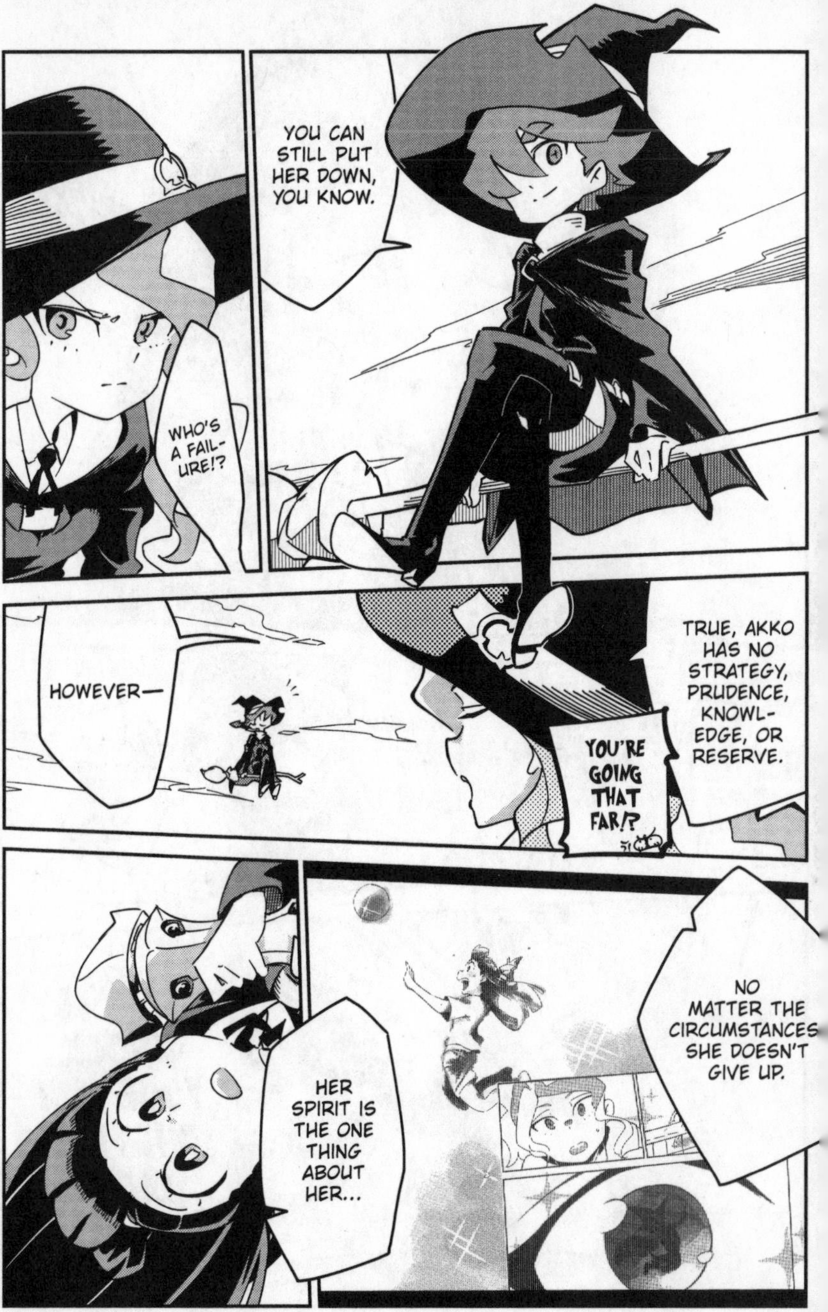
YOU CAN STILL PUT HER DOWN, YOU KNOW.
WHO'S A FAIL-URE!?
TRUE, AKKO HAS NO STRATEGY, PRUDENCE, KNOWL-EDGE, OR RESERVE.
YOU'RE GOING THAT FAR!?
HOWEVER—
NO MATTER THE CIRCUMSTANCES SHE DOESN'T GIVE UP.
HER SPIRIT IS THE ONE THING ABOUT HER...

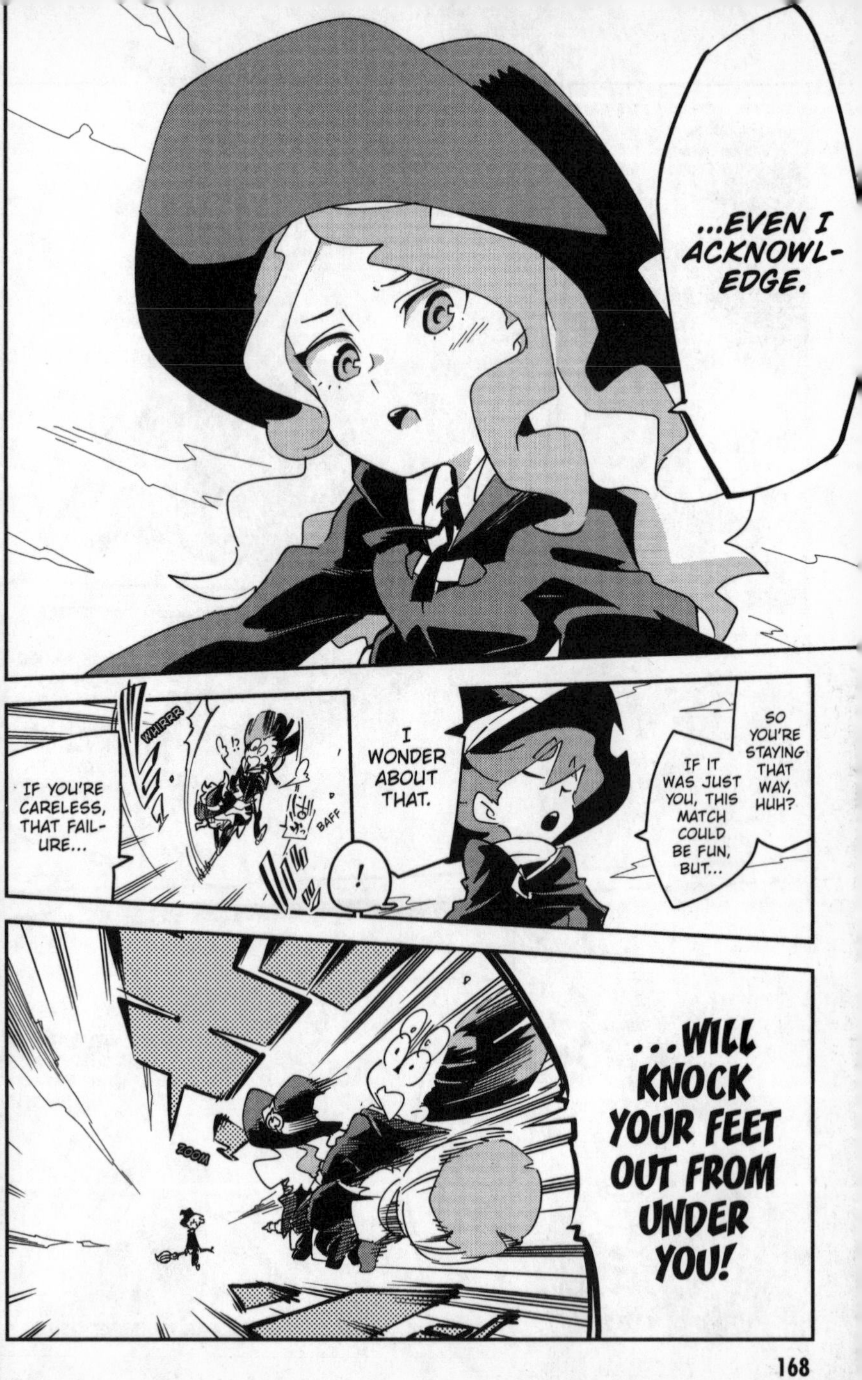
...EVEN I ACKNOWL-EDGE.
SO YOU'RE STAYING THAT WAY, HUH?
IF IT WAS JUST YOU, THIS MATCH COULD BE FUN, BUT...
I WONDER ABOUT THAT.
!
WHIRRR
BAFF
IF YOU'RE CARELESS, THAT FAIL-URE...
...WILL KNOCK YOUR FEET OUT FROM UNDER YOU!
ZOOM

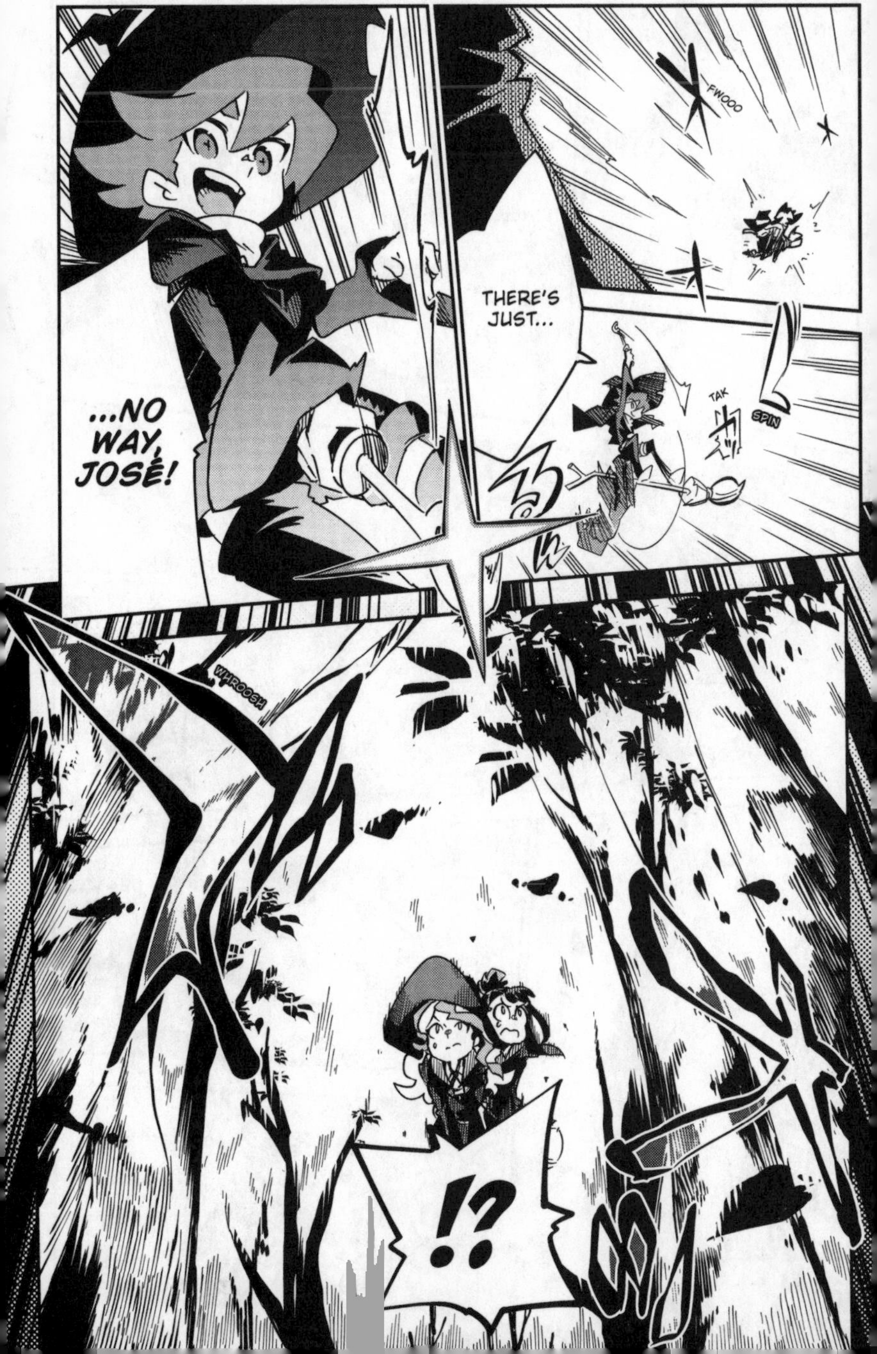
FWOOO
THERE'S JUST...
SPIN
TAK
...NO WAY, JOSÉ!
WHROOSH
!?

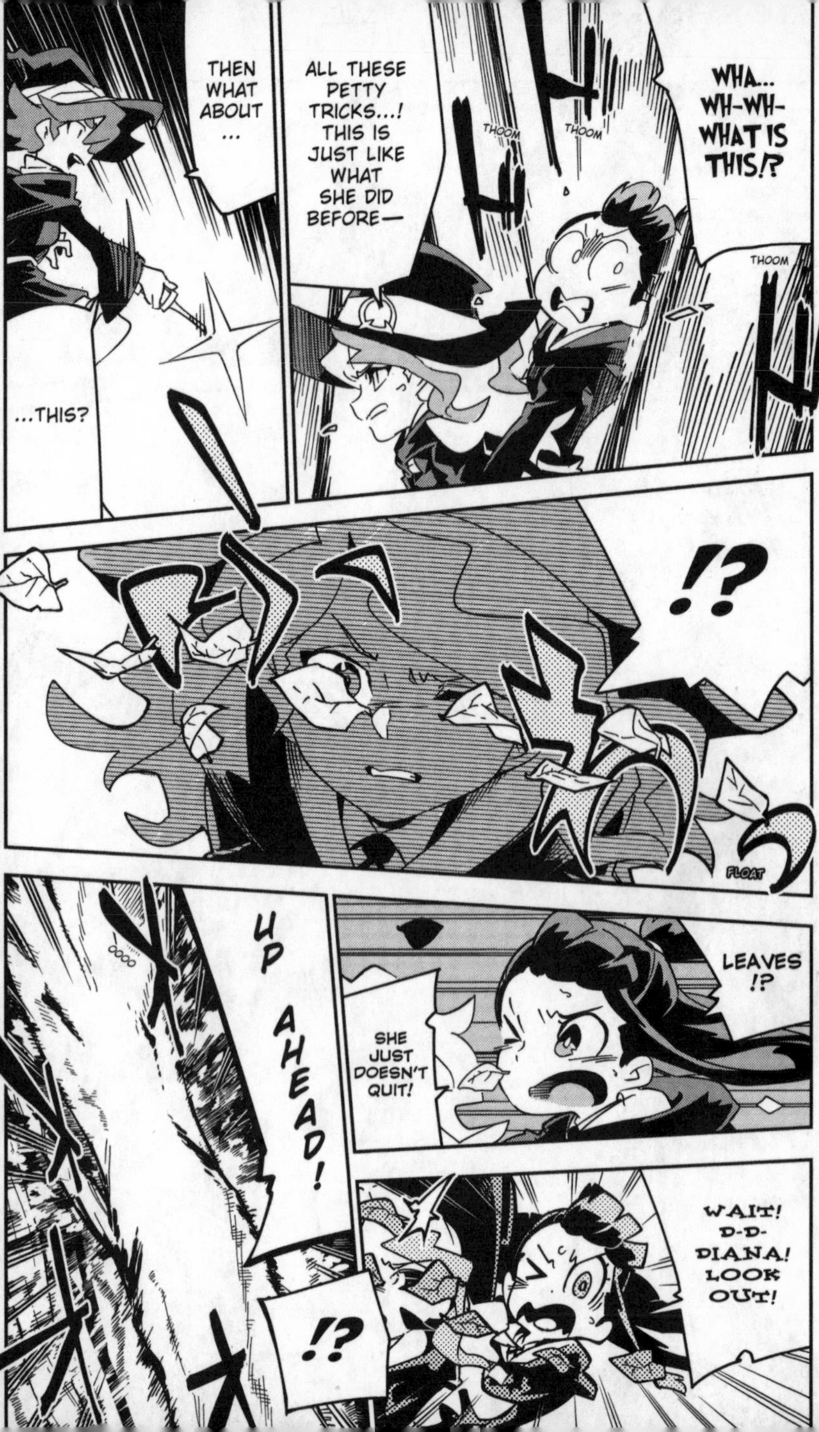
WHA... WH-WH-WHAT IS THIS!?
THOOM
THOOM
THOOM
ALL THESE PETTY TRICKS...! THIS IS JUST LIKE WHAT SHE DID BEFORE—
THEN WHAT ABOUT ...
...THIS?
!?
FLOAT
LEAVES !?
SHE JUST DOESN'T QUIT!
WAIT! D-D-DIANA! LOOK OUT!
!?
UP AHEAD!

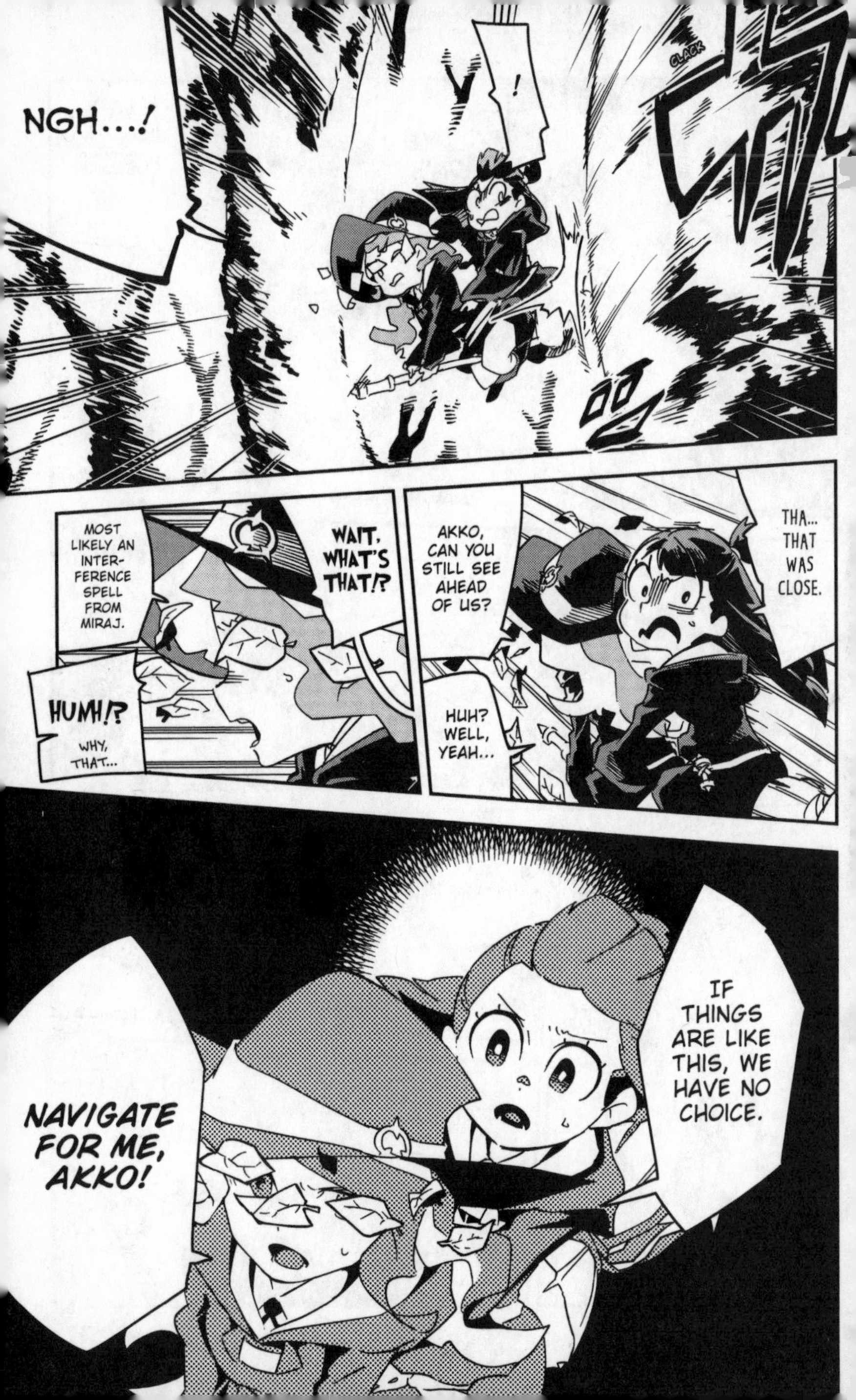
CLACK
Y !
NGH...!
THA... THAT WAS CLOSE.
AKKO, CAN YOU STILL SEE AHEAD OF US?
HUH? WELL, YEAH...
WAIT, WHAT'S THAT!?
MOST LIKELY AN INTERFERENCE SPELL FROM MIRAJ.
HUMH!?
WHY, THAT...
IF THINGS ARE LIKE THIS, WE HAVE NO CHOICE.
NAVIGATE FOR ME, AKKO!

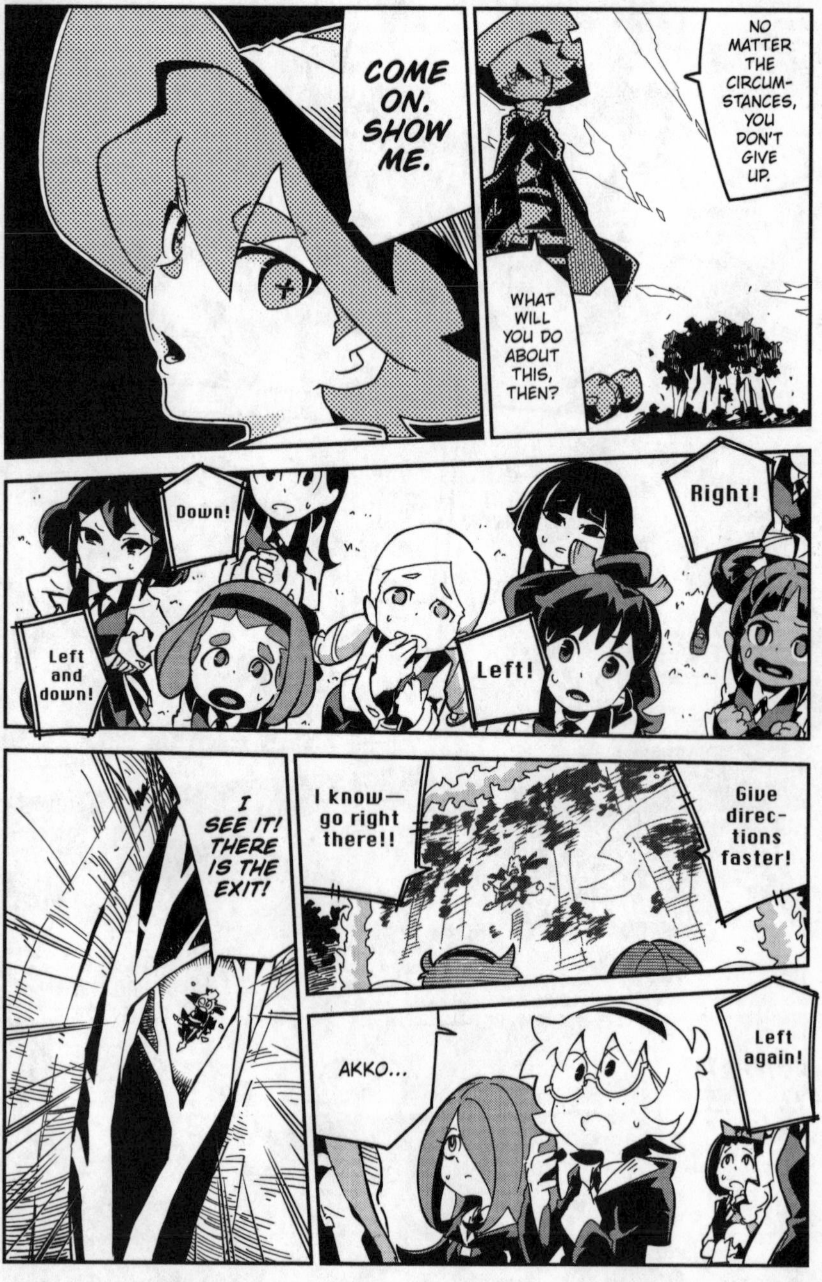
NO MATTER THE CIRCUMSTANCES, YOU DON'T GIVE UP.
WHAT WILL YOU DO ABOUT THIS, THEN?
COME ON. SHOW ME.
Right!
Down!
Left!
Left and down!
Give directions faster!
I know—go right there!!
Left again!
AKKO...
I SEE IT! THERE IS THE EXIT!

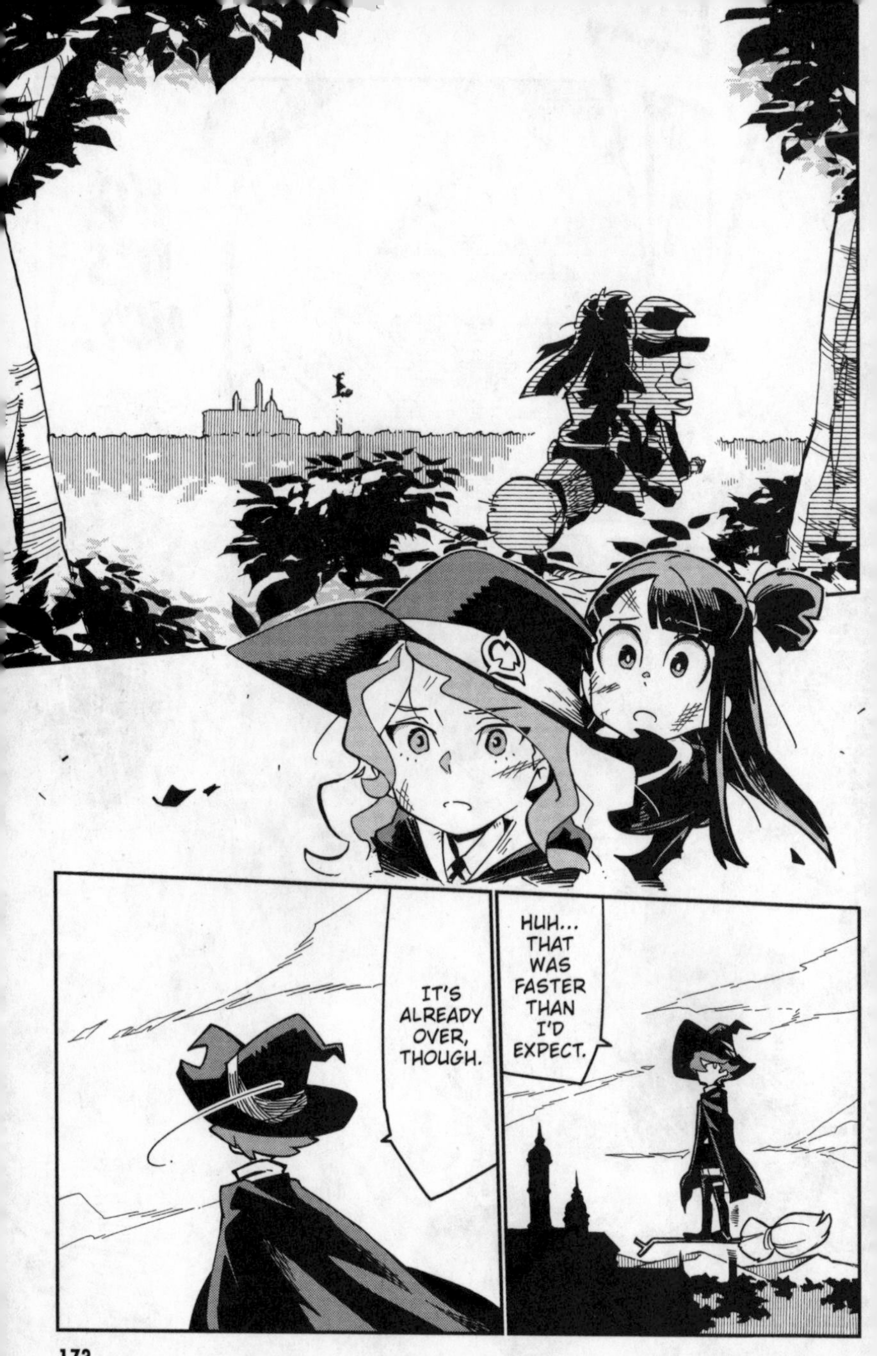
HUH... THAT WAS FASTER THAN I'D EXPECT.
IT'S ALREADY OVER, THOUGH.

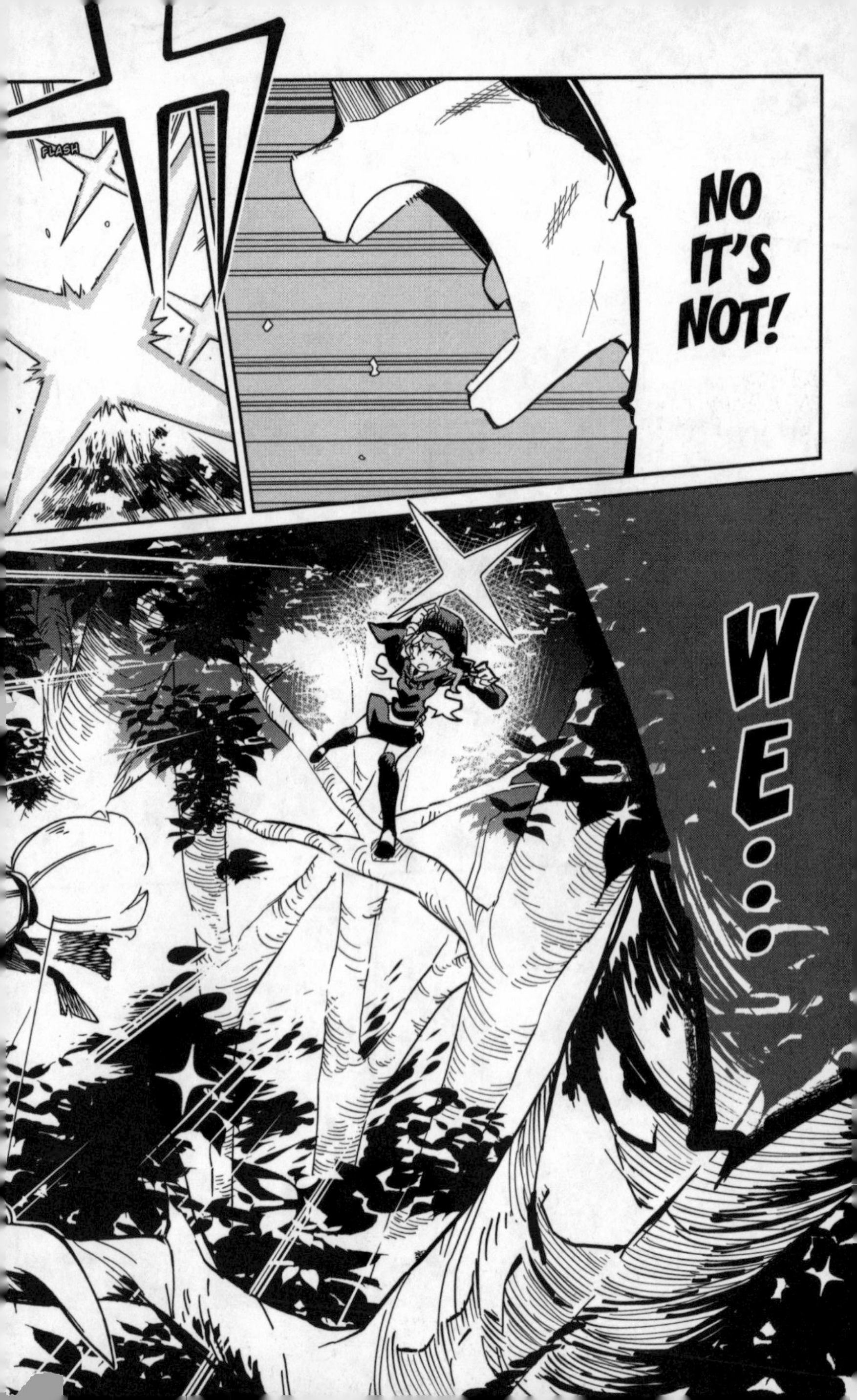
NO IT'S NOT!
FLASH
WE...

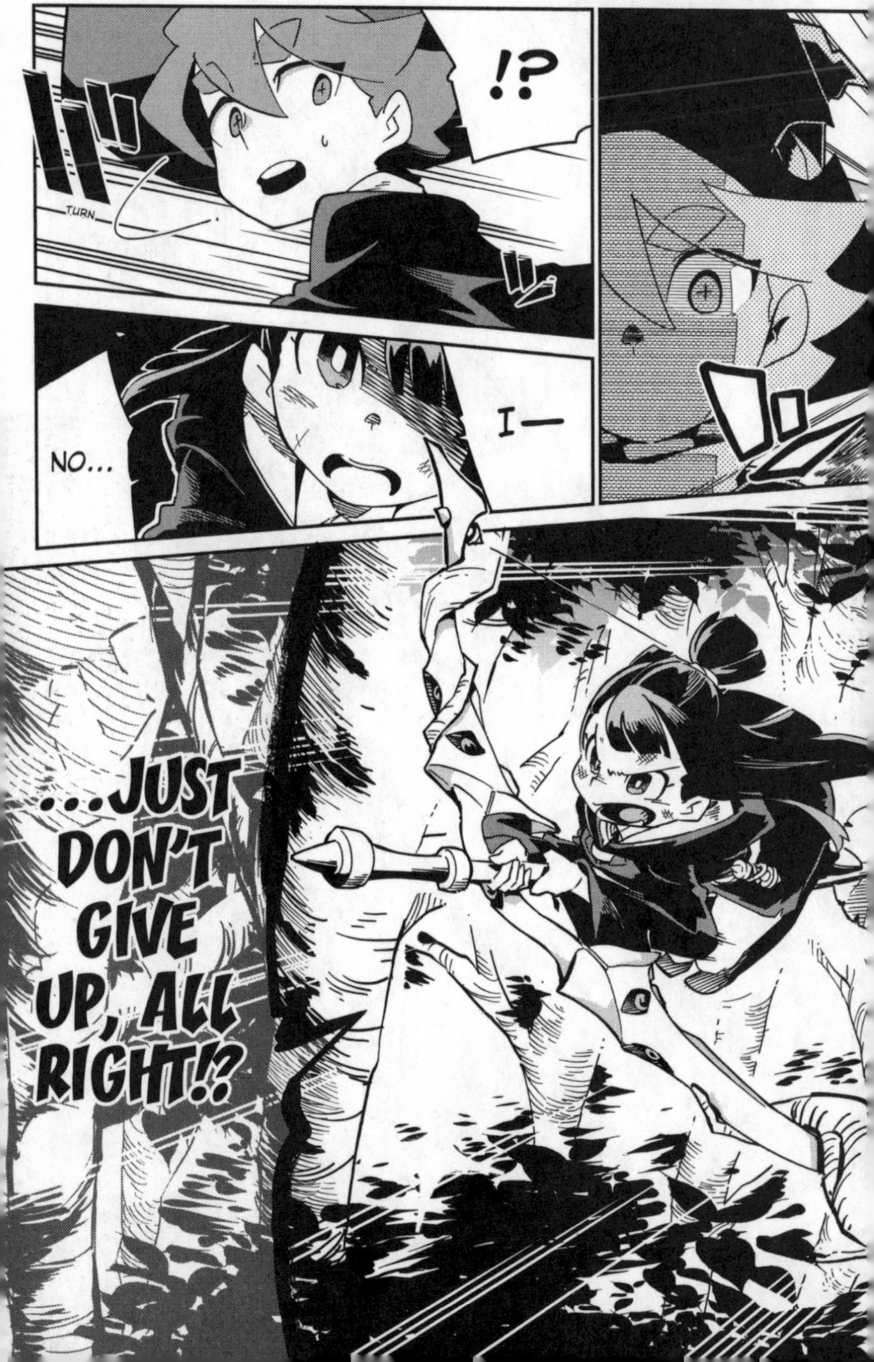
TURN
!?
I—
NO...
...JUST DON'T GIVE UP, ALL RIGHT!?

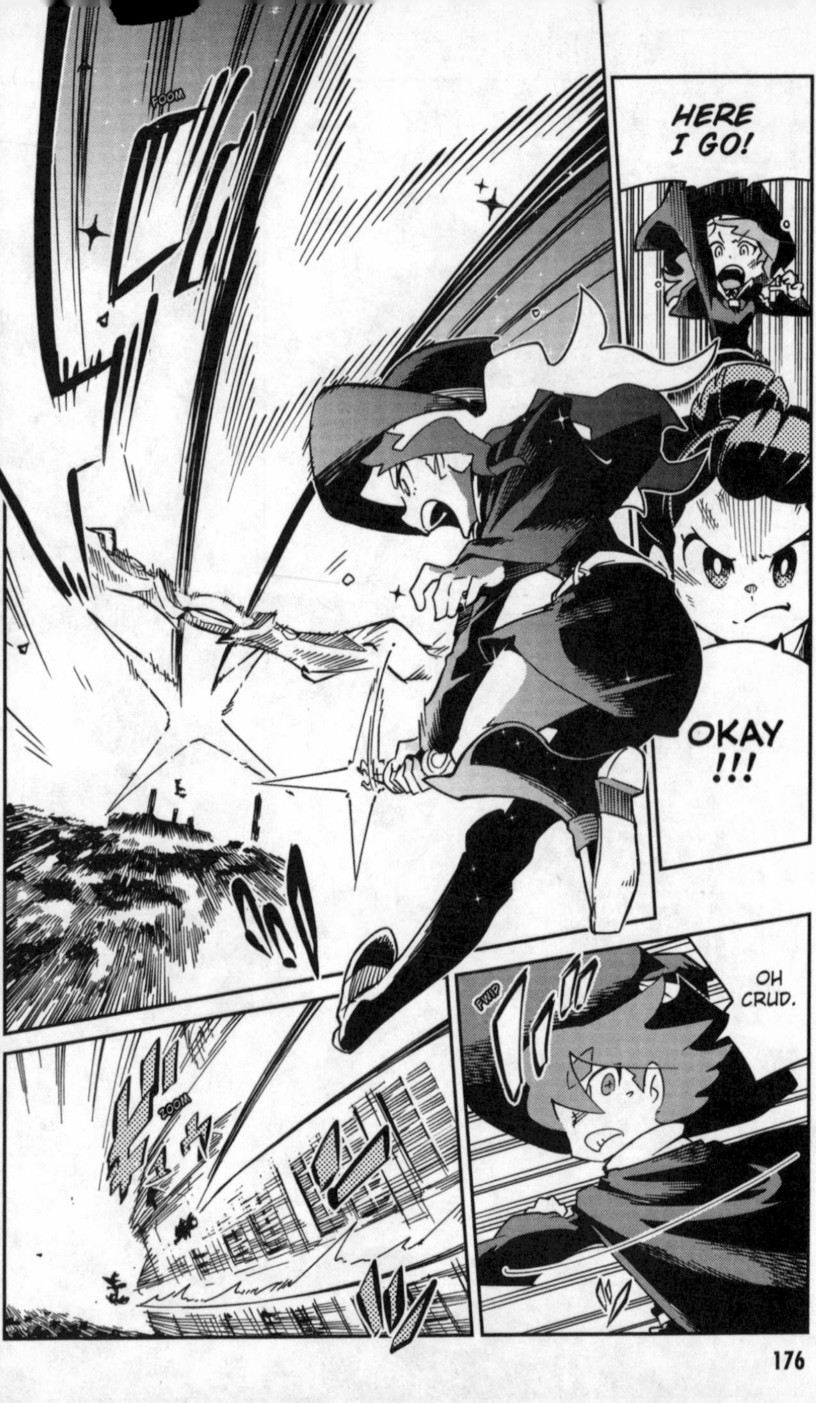
HERE I GO!
OKAY !!!
FOOM
OH CRUD.
FWIP
ZOOM

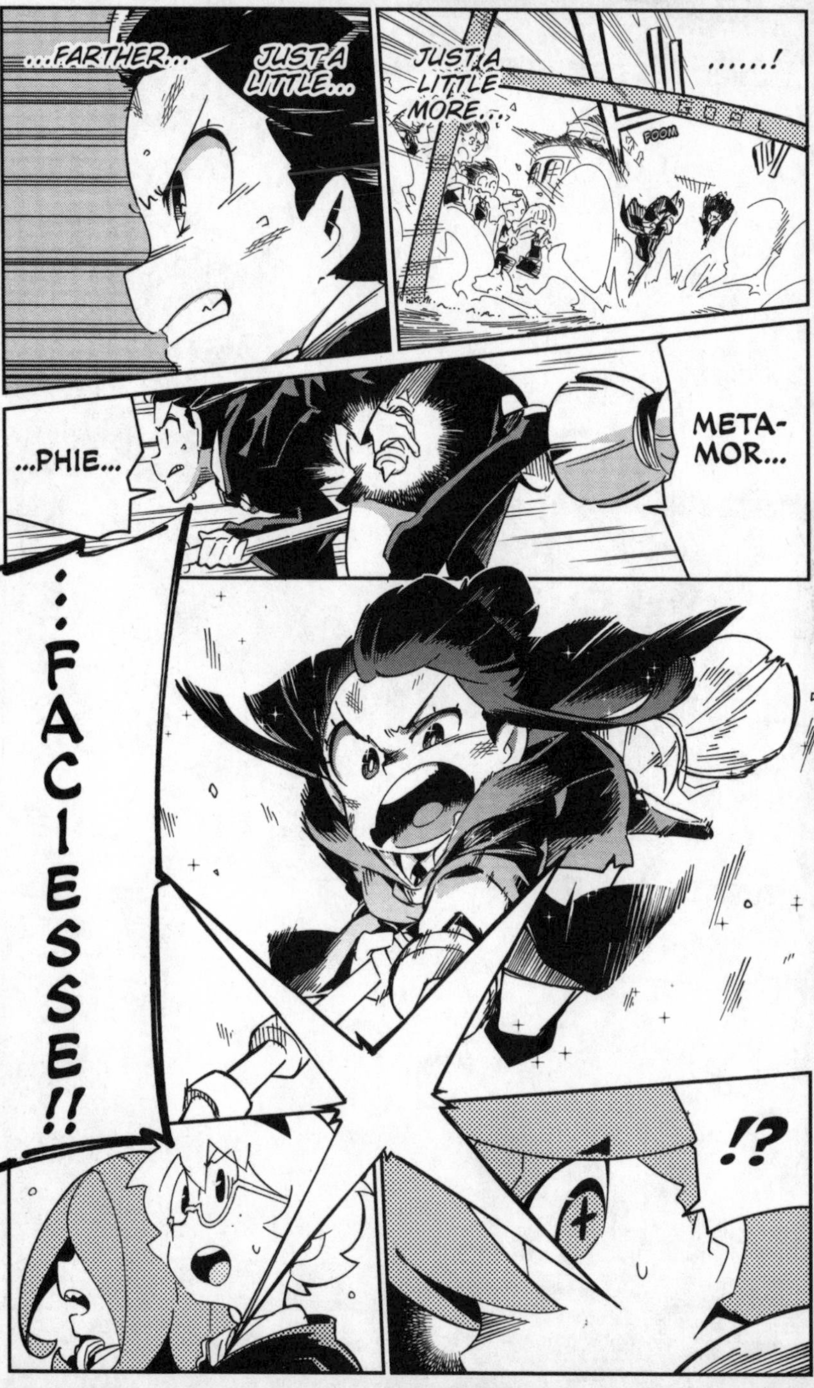

......!
JUST A LITTLE MORE...
GOAL
FOOM
JUST A LITTLE...
...FARTHER...
METAMOR...
...PHIE...
...FACIESSE!!
!?

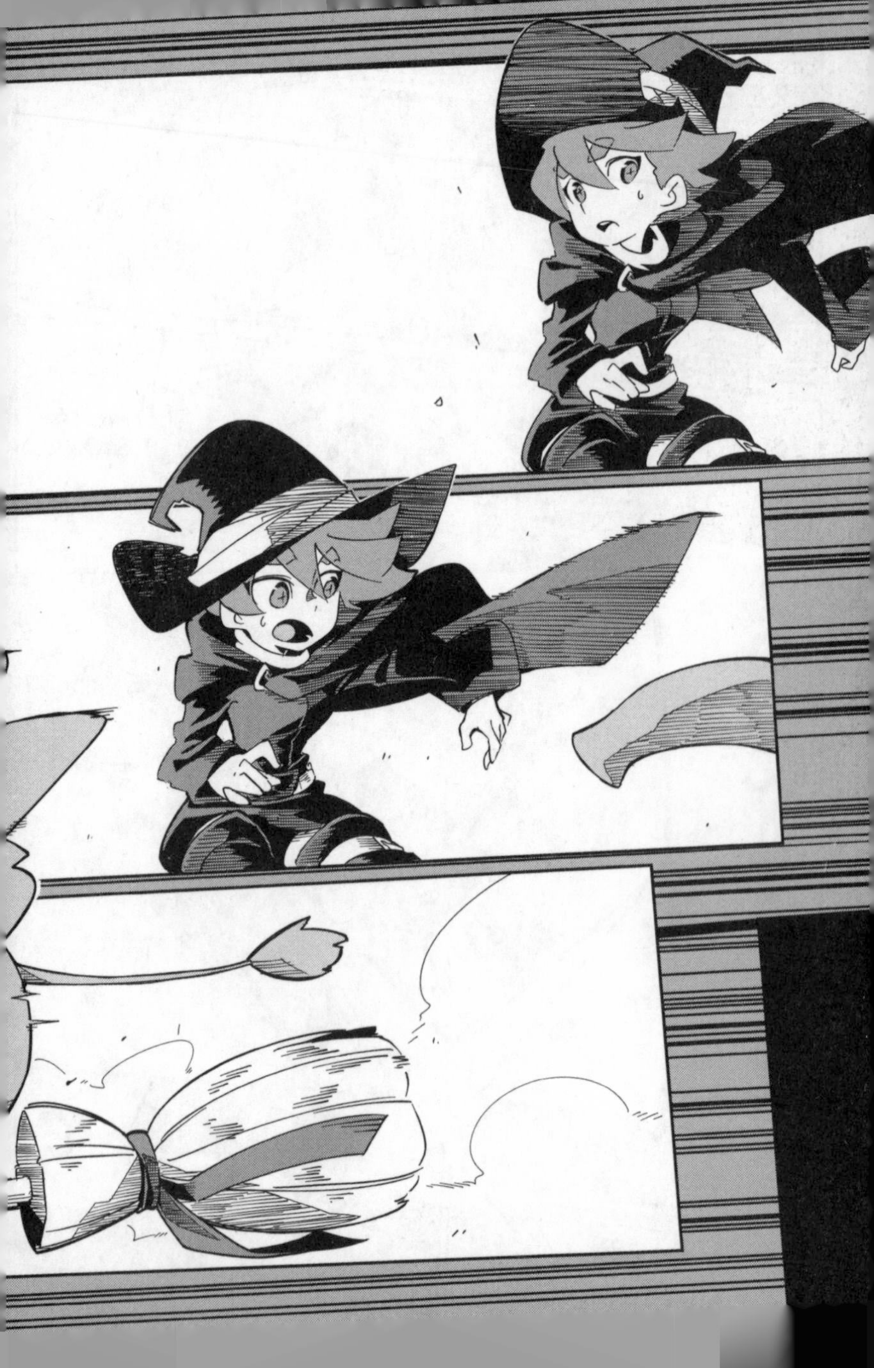

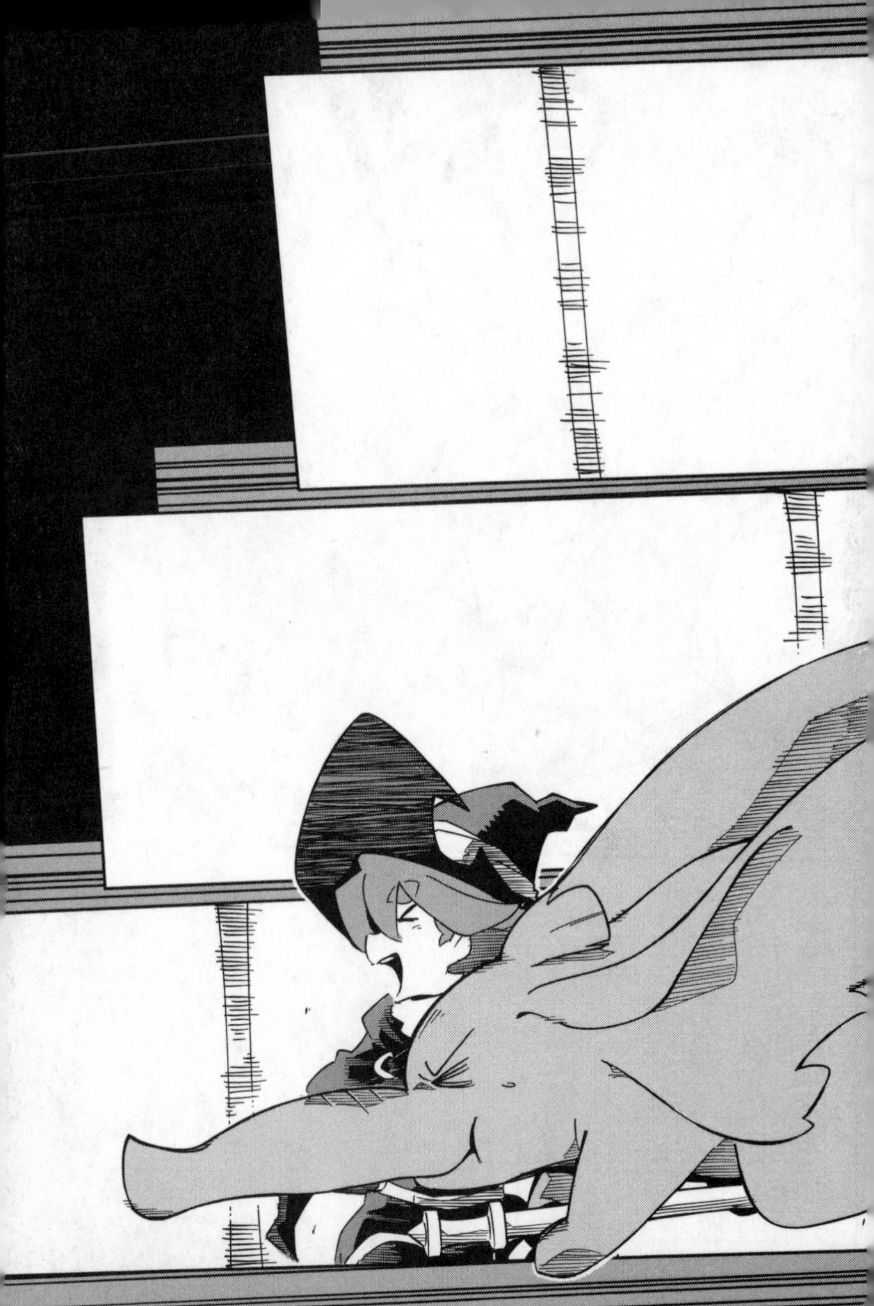

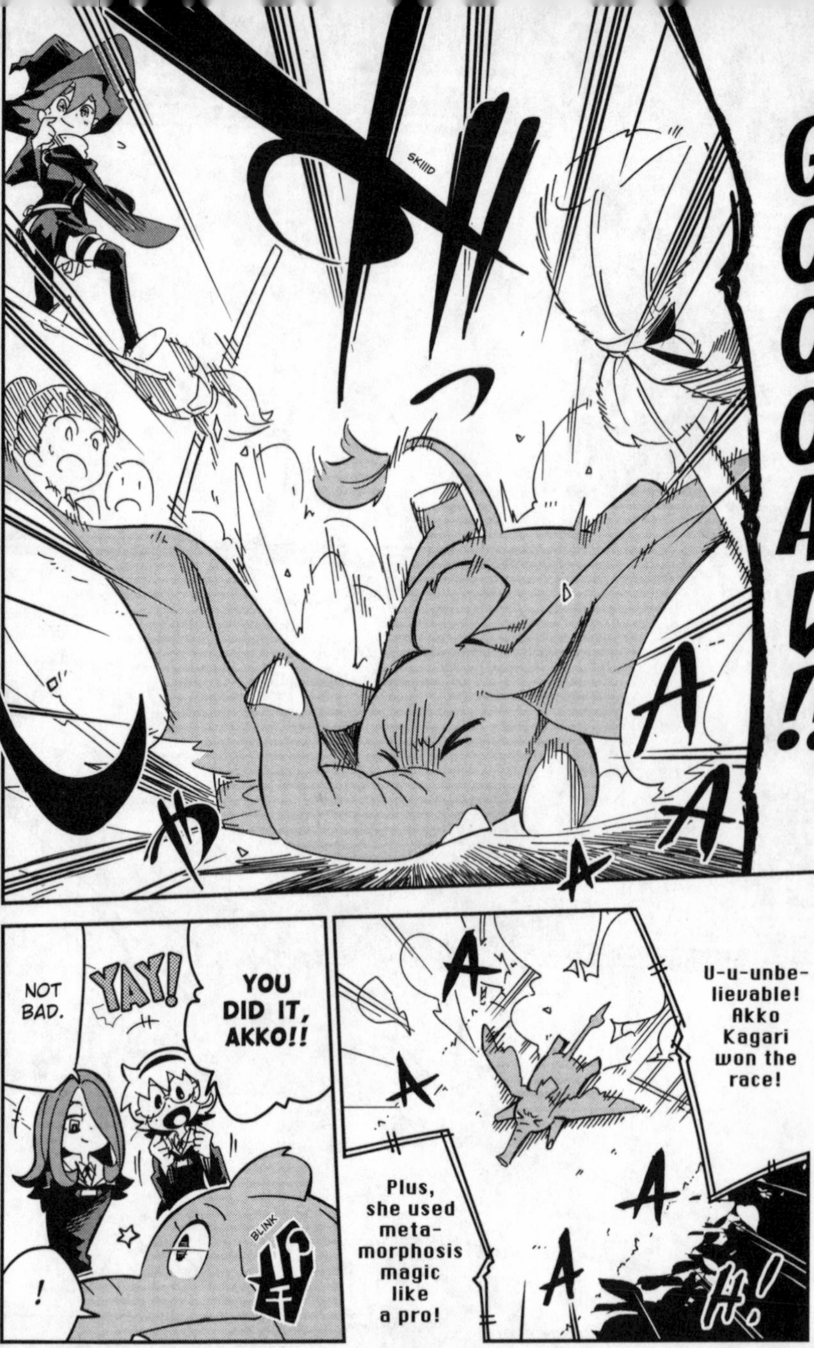
GOOOAL!!
SKIIID
U-u-unbe-lievable! Akko Kagari won the race!
Plus, she used meta-morphosis magic like a pro!
YOU DID IT, AKKO!!
YAY!
NOT BAD.
BLINK

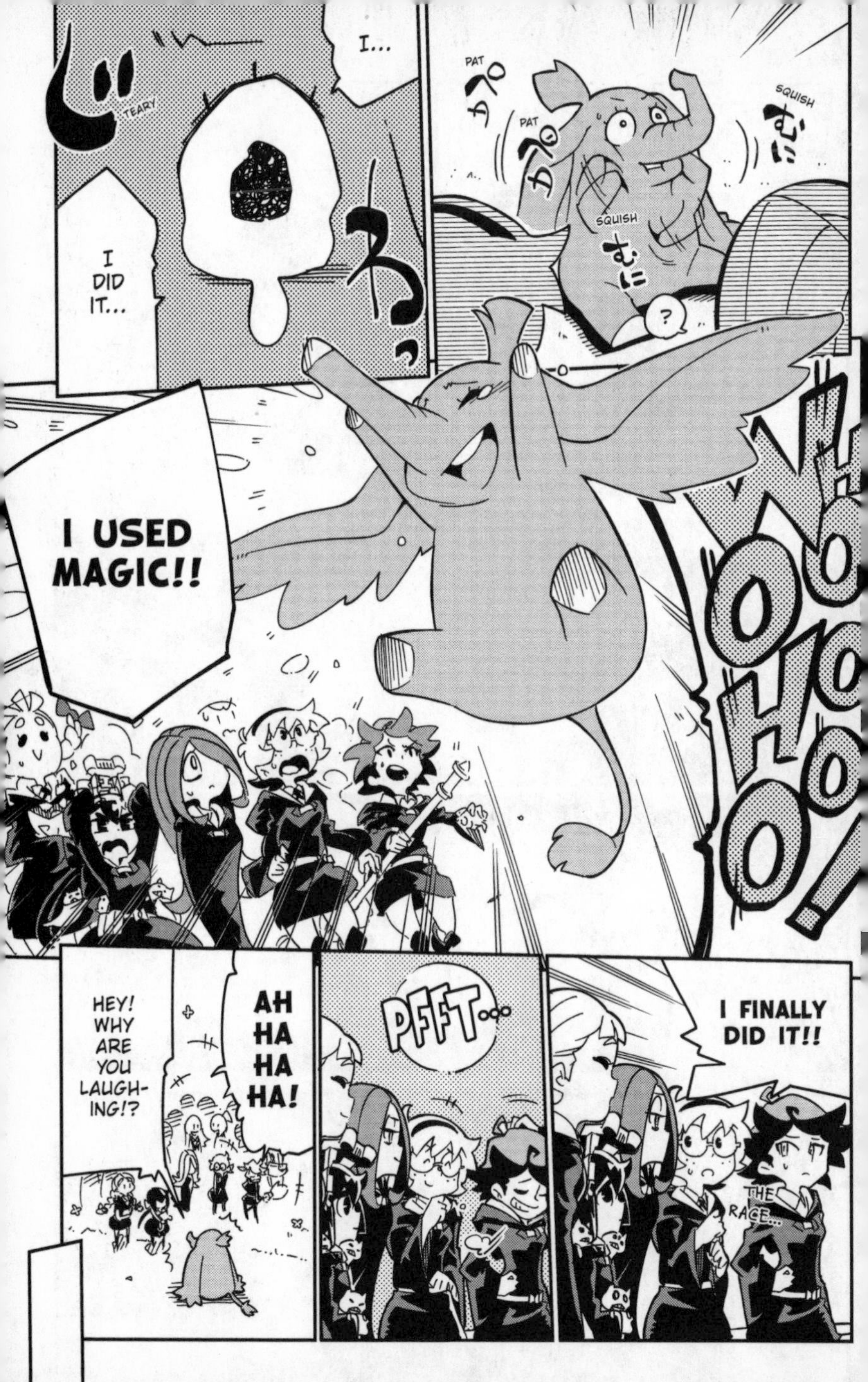
PAT
PAT
SQUISH
SQUISH
?
I...
TEARY
I DID IT...
WOOHOOOO!
I USED MAGIC!!
I FINALLY DID IT!!
THE RACE...
PFFT...
AH HA HA HA!
HEY! WHY ARE YOU LAUGHING!?

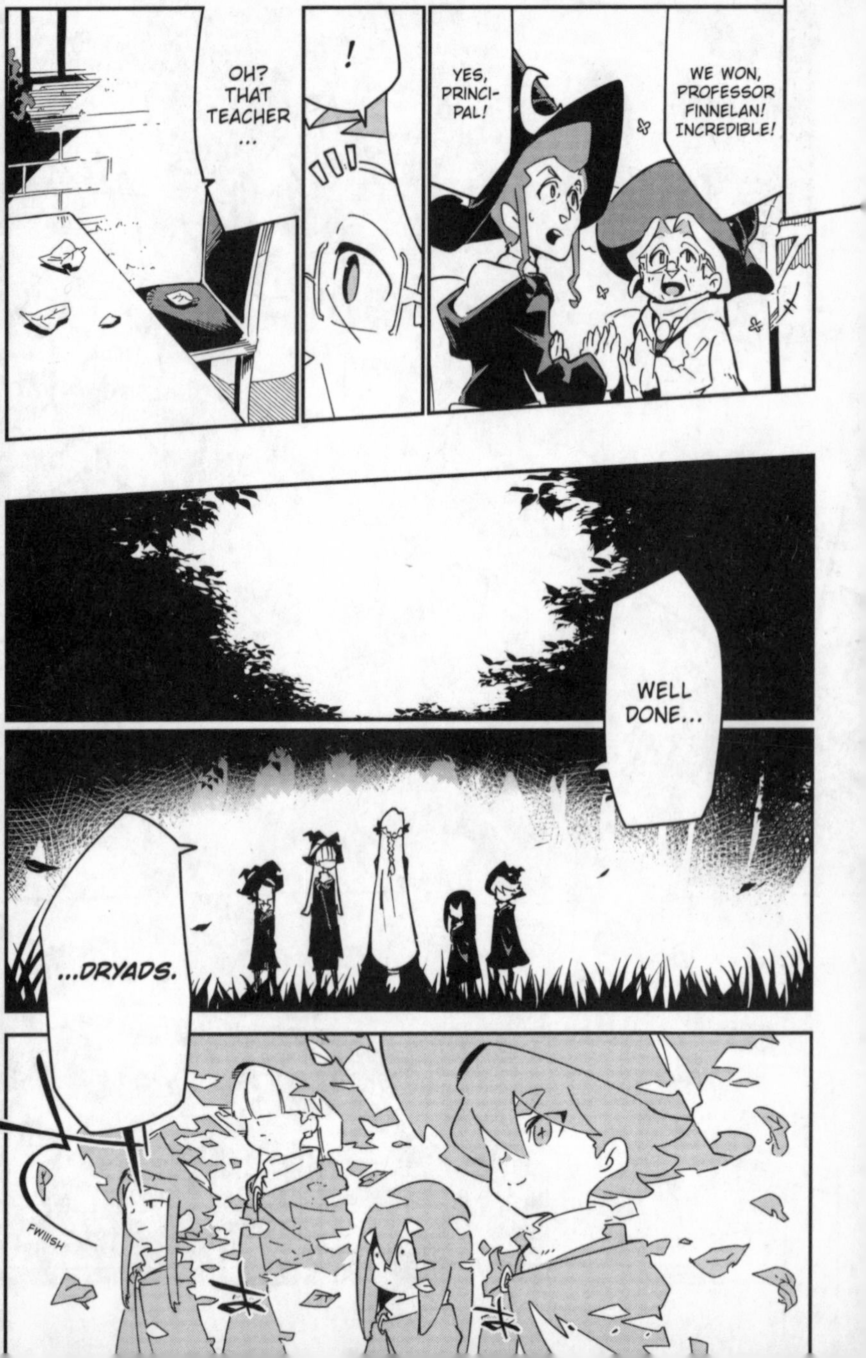
WE WON, PROFESSOR FINNELAN! INCREDIBLE!
YES, PRINCIPAL!
!
OH? THAT TEACHER ...
WELL DONE...
...DRYADS.
FWIIISH

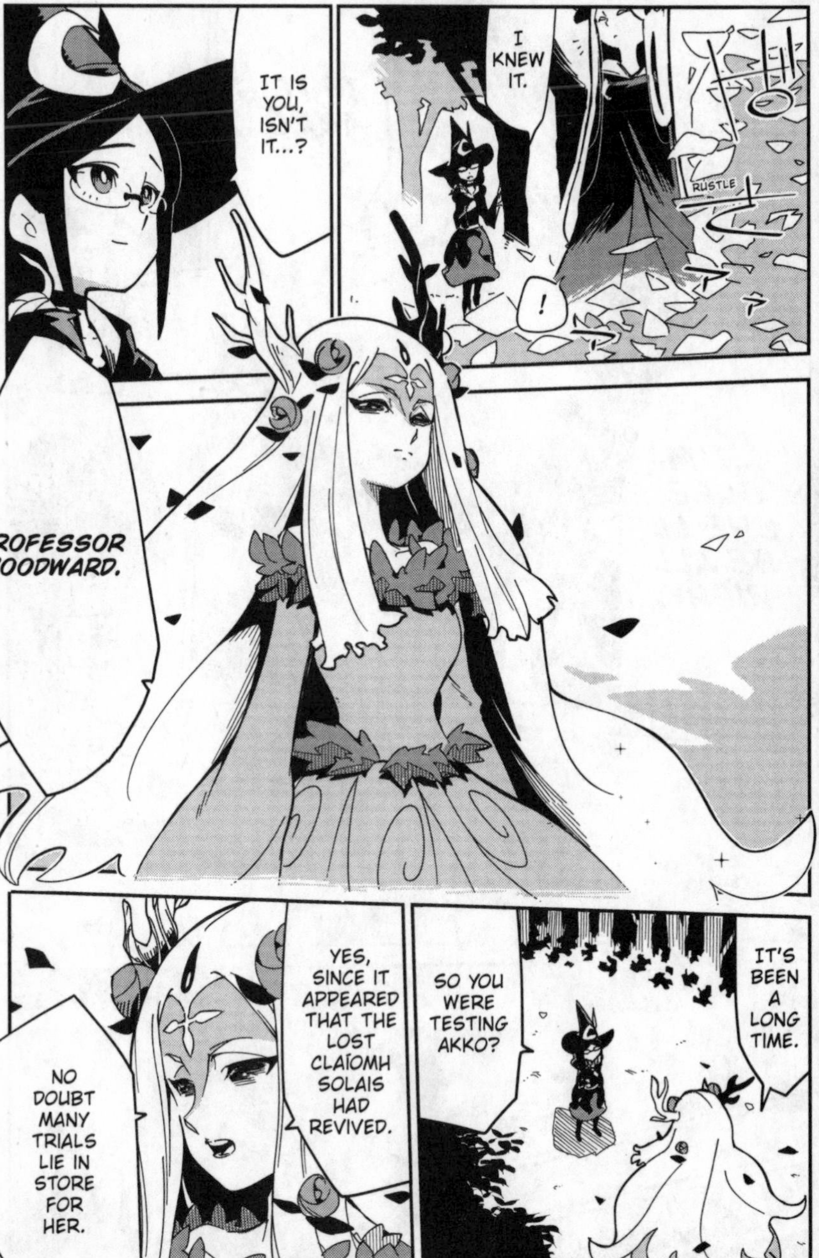
I KNEW IT.
RUSTLE
!
IT IS YOU, ISN'T IT...?
PROFESSOR WOODWARD.
IT'S BEEN A LONG TIME.
SO YOU WERE TESTING AKKO?
YES, SINCE IT APPEARED THAT THE LOST CLAÍOMH SOLAIS HAD REVIVED.
NO DOUBT MANY TRIALS LIE IN STORE FOR HER.

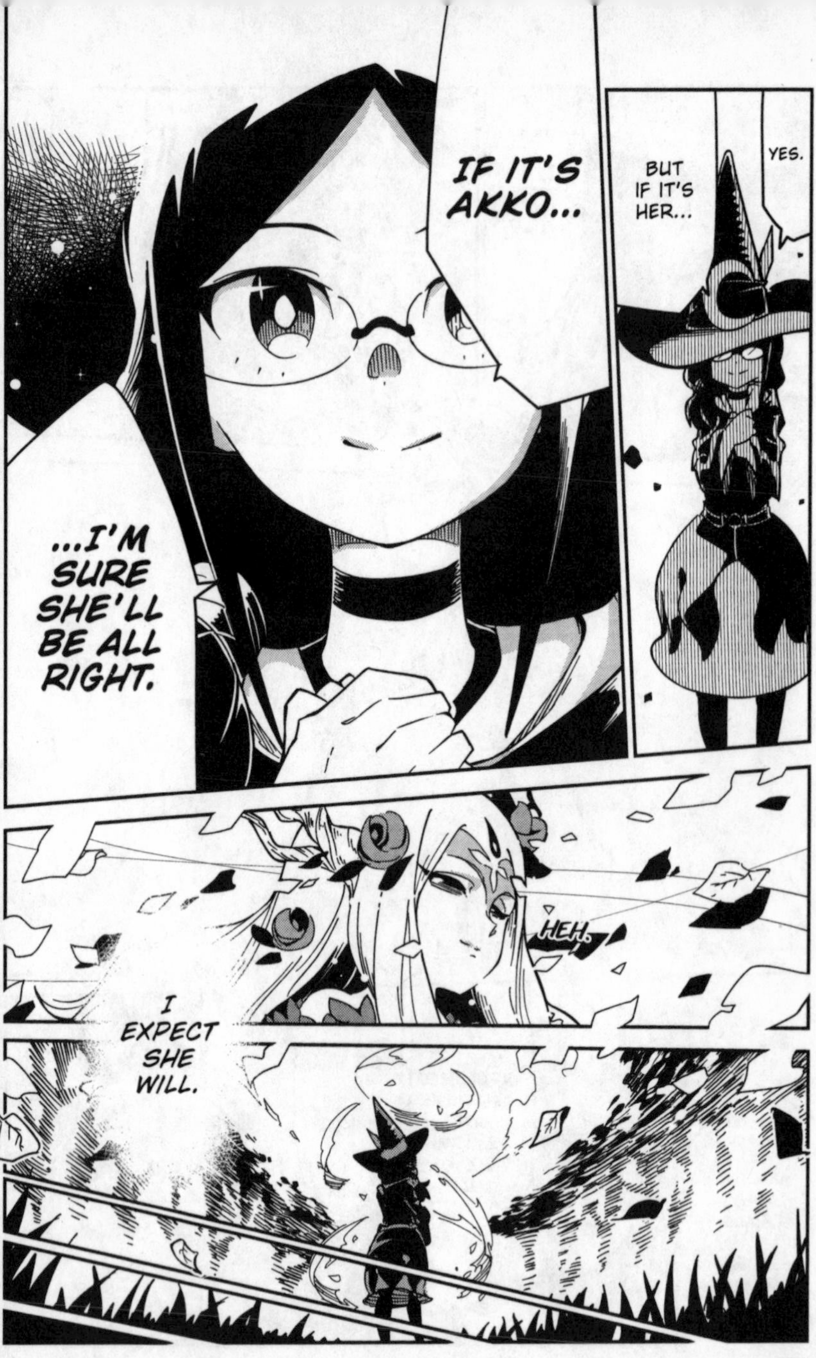
YES.
BUT IF IT'S HER...
IF IT'S AKKO...
...I'M SURE SHE'LL BE ALL RIGHT.
HEH.
I EXPECT SHE WILL.

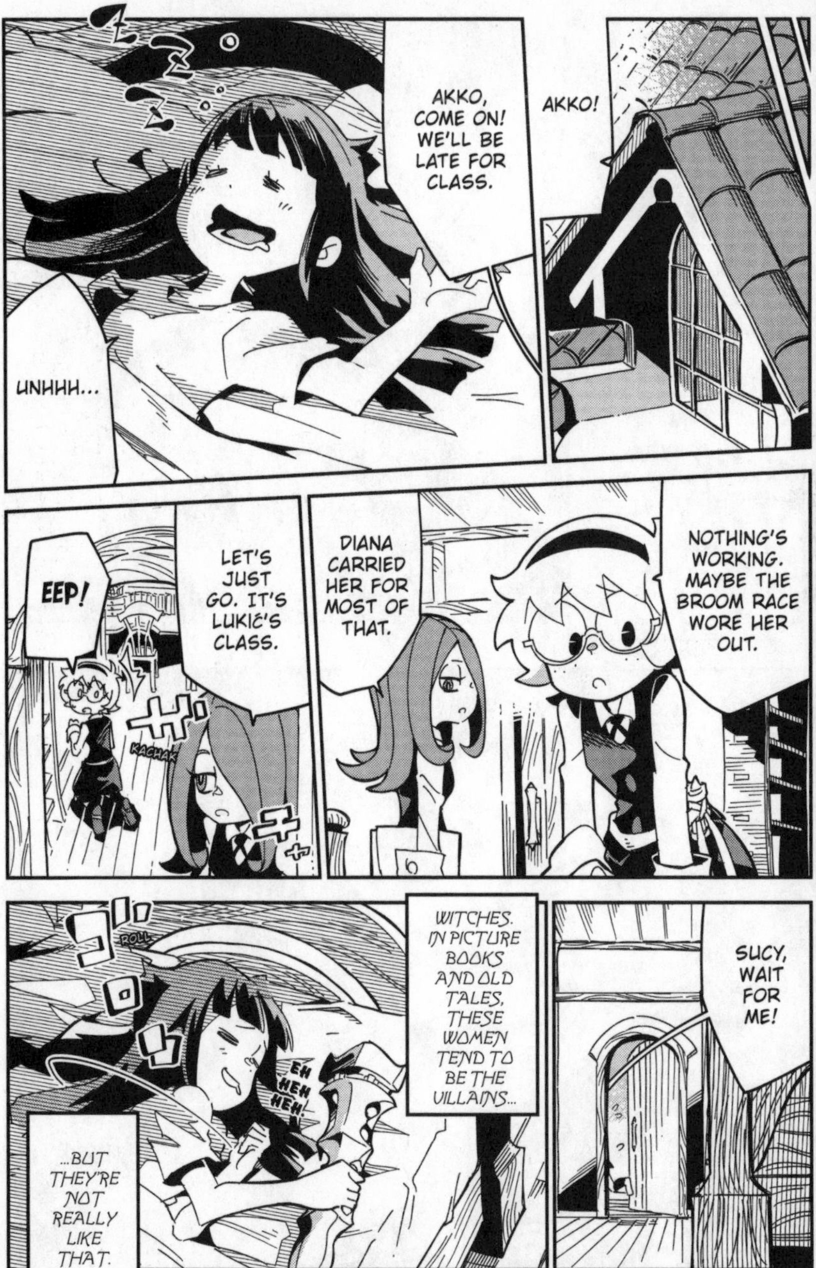
AKKO!
AKKO, COME ON! WE'LL BE LATE FOR CLASS.
UNHHH...
NOTHING'S WORKING. MAYBE THE BROOM RACE WORE HER OUT.
DIANA CARRIED HER FOR MOST OF THAT.
LET'S JUST GO. IT'S LUKIĆ'S CLASS.
EEP!
KACHAK
SUCY, WAIT FOR ME!
WITCHES. IN PICTURE BOOKS AND OLD TALES, THESE WOMEN TEND TO BE THE VILLAINS...
ROLL
EH HEH HEH!
...BUT THEY'RE NOT REALLY LIKE THAT.

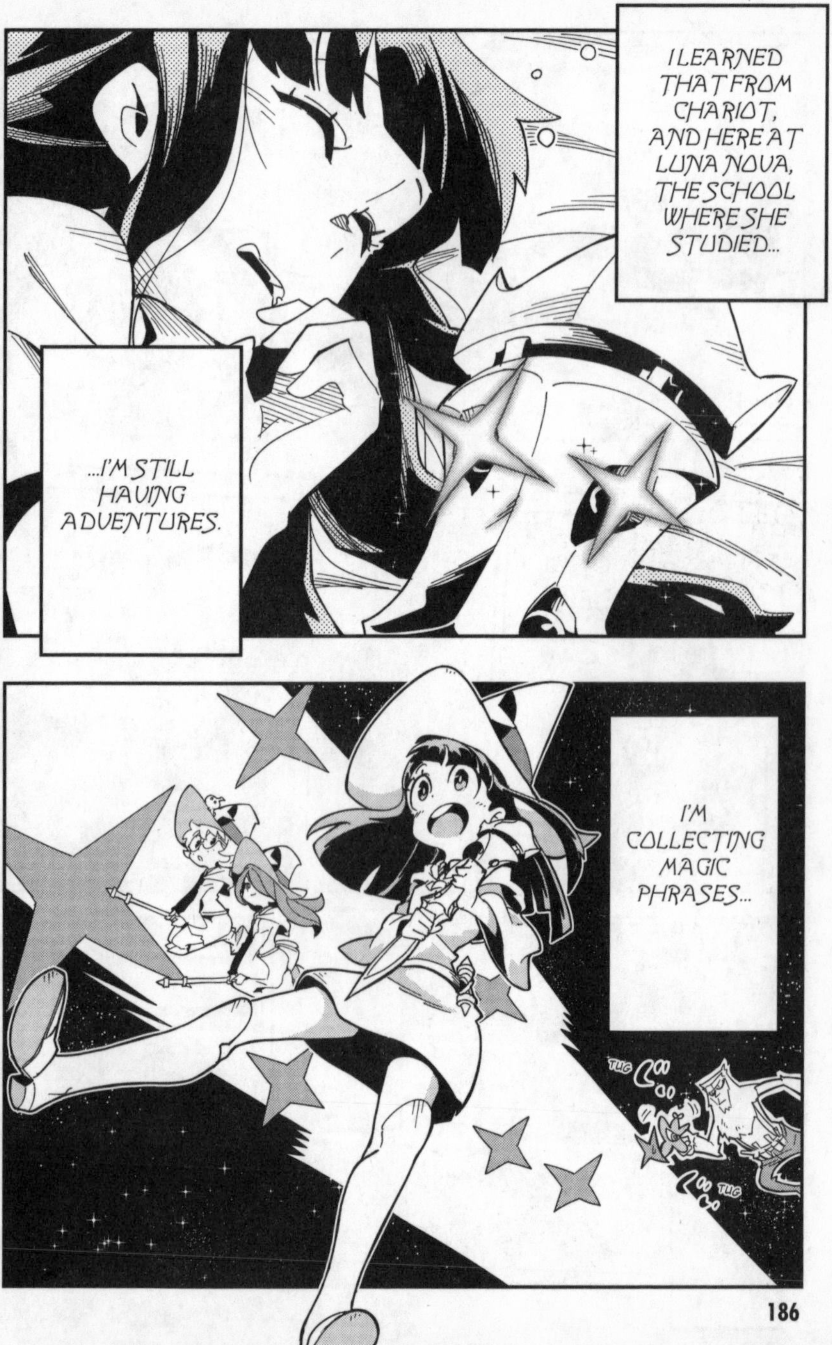
I LEARNED THAT FROM CHARIOT, AND HERE AT LUNA NOVA, THE SCHOOL WHERE SHE STUDIED...
...I'M STILL HAVING ADVENTURES.
I'M COLLECTING MAGIC PHRASES...
TUG
TUG

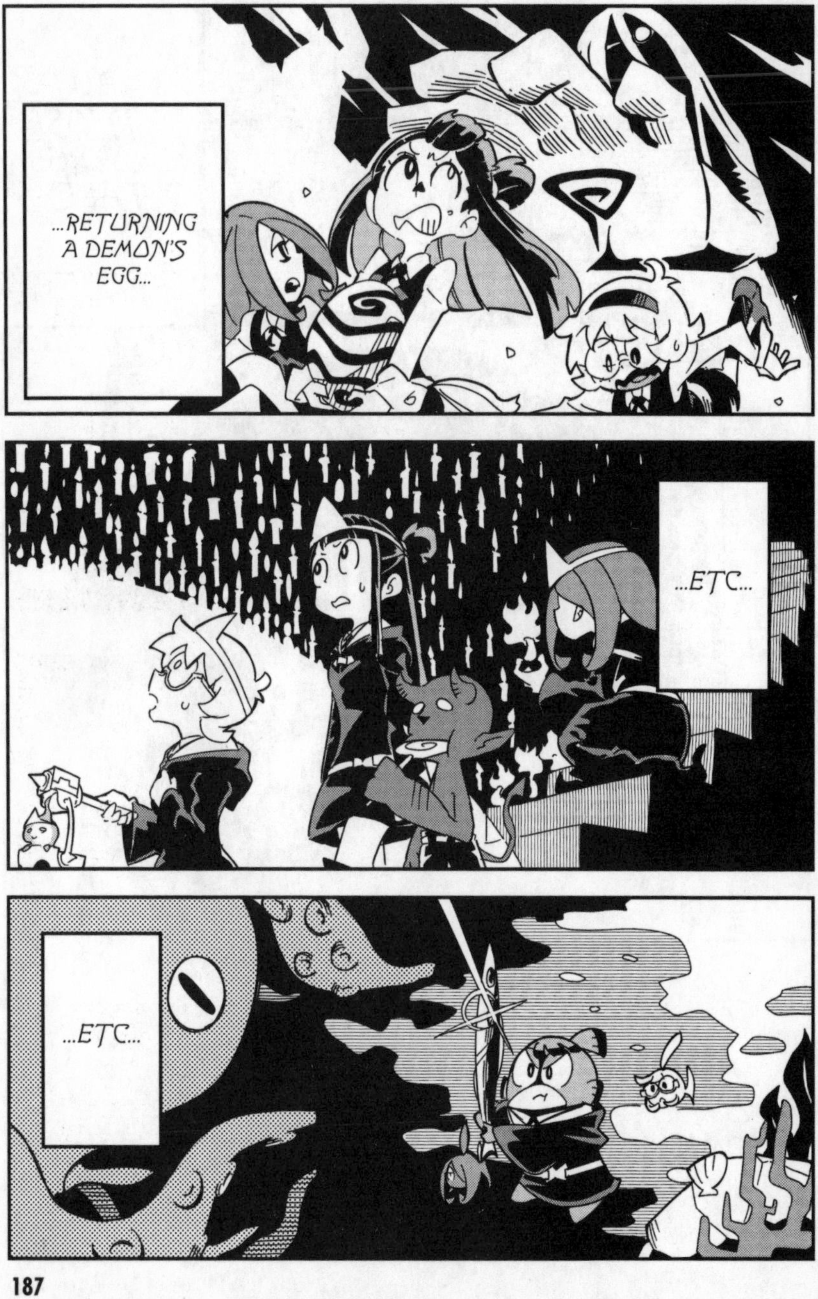
...RETURNING A DEMON'S EGG...
...ETC...
...ETC...

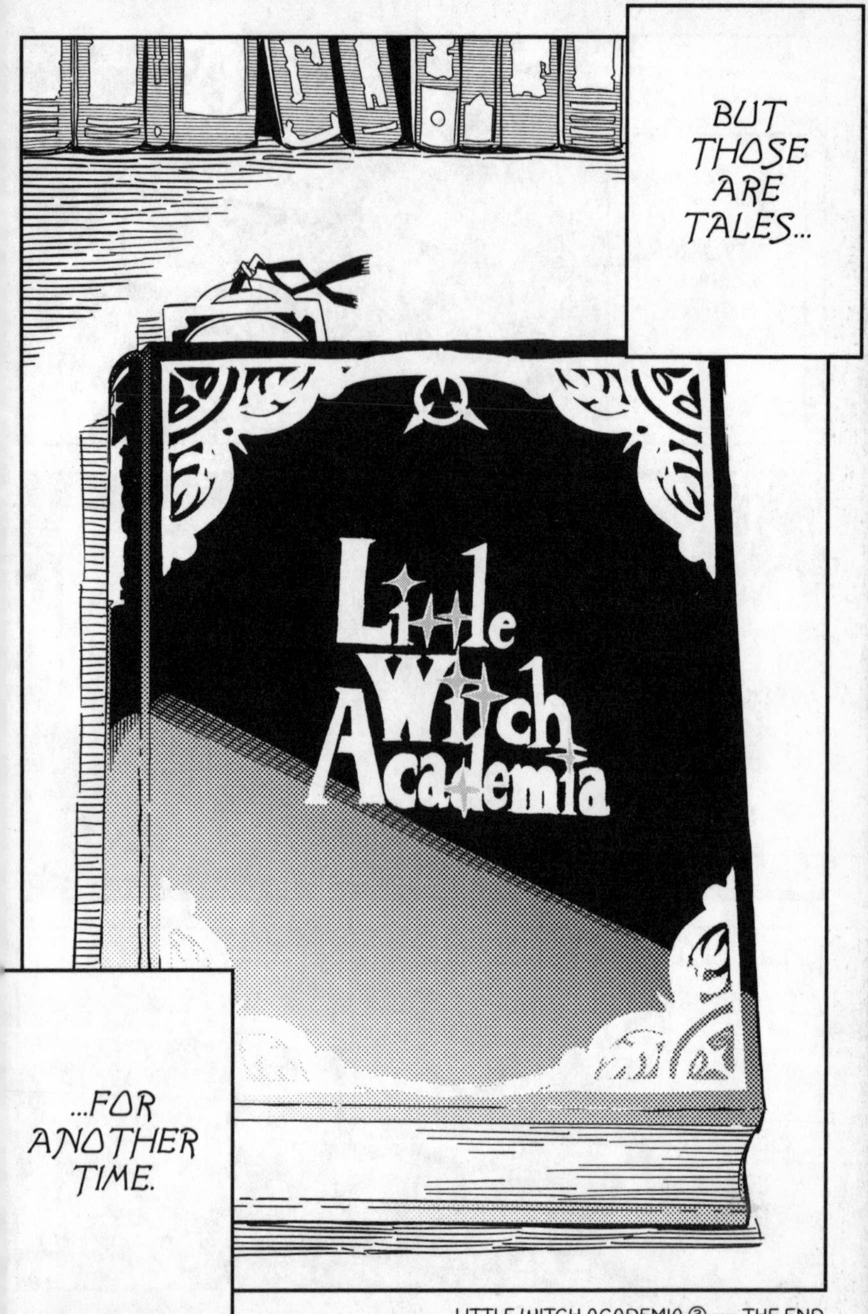
BUT THOSE ARE TALES...
Little Witch Academia
...FOR ANOTHER TIME.

LITTLE WITCH ACADEMIA ③ ...... THE END

WOODWARD'S HOBBY

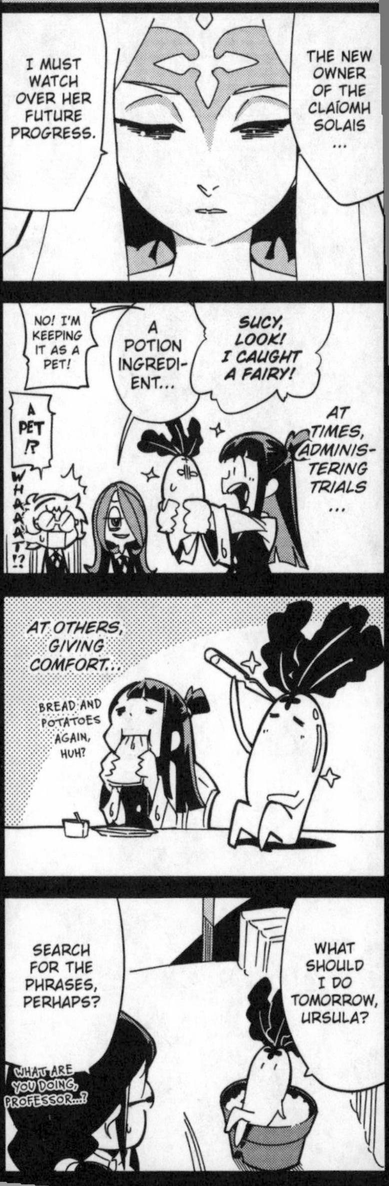
THE NEW OWNER OF THE CLAÍOMH SOLAIS ...
I MUST WATCH OVER HER FUTURE PROGRESS.
AT TIMES, ADMINISTERING TRIALS ...
SUCY, LOOK! I CAUGHT A FAIRY!
A POTION INGREDIENT...
NO! I'M KEEPING IT AS A PET!
A PET!?
WHAAAAT!?
AT OTHERS, GIVING COMFORT...
BREAD AND POTATOES AGAIN, HUH?
WHAT SHOULD I DO TOMORROW, URSULA?
SEARCH FOR THE PHRASES, PERHAPS?
WHAT ARE YOU DOING, PROFESSOR...?

URSULA'S WORRY

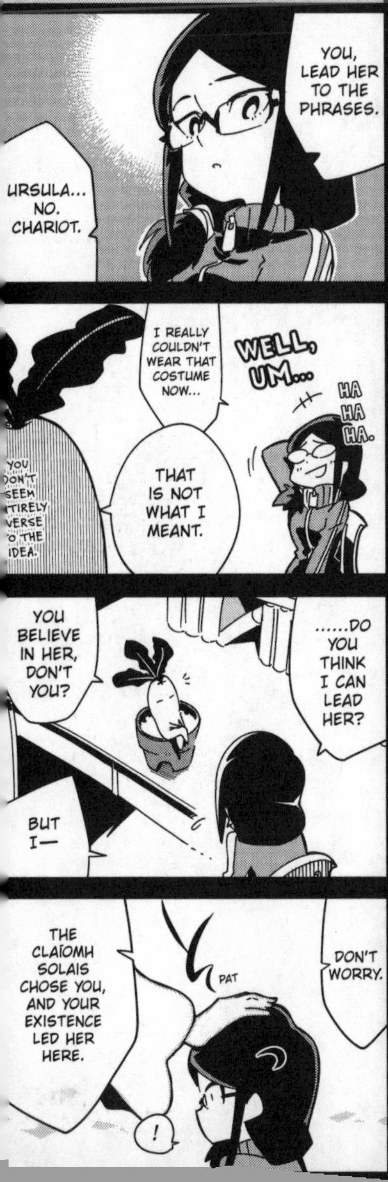
YOU, LEAD HER TO THE PHRASES.
URSULA... NO. CHARIOT.
I REALLY COULDN'T WEAR THAT COSTUME NOW...
WELL, UM...
HA HA HA.
THAT IS NOT WHAT I MEANT.
YOU DON'T SEEM TIRELY VERSE O THE IDEA.
......DO YOU THINK I CAN LEAD HER?
YOU BELIEVE IN HER, DON'T YOU?
BUT I—
DON'T WORRY.
PAT
THE CLAÍOMH SOLAIS CHOSE YOU, AND YOUR EXISTENCE LED HER HERE.
!

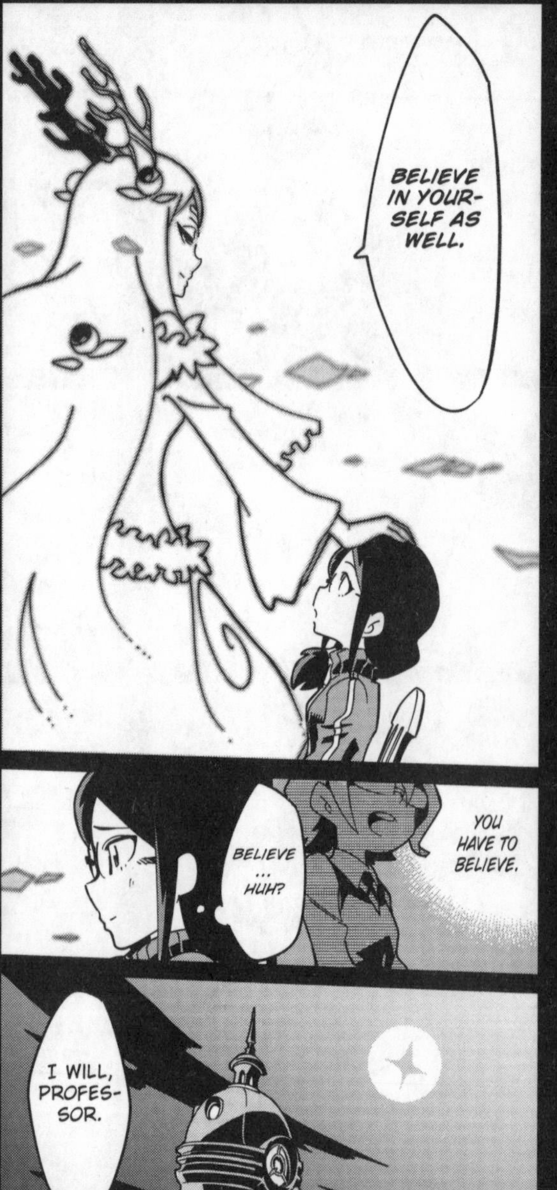
BELIEVE IN YOURSELF AS WELL.
YOU HAVE TO BELIEVE.
BELIEVE ... HUH?
I WILL, PROFESSOR.

Staff

MANGA: **Sato**

COLORIST: **uku-san**

DESIGN: **Kubo-san**

EDITOR: **Katsumura-san**

With gratitude to everyone who was involved in this series. And with great gratitude to everyone who read it!

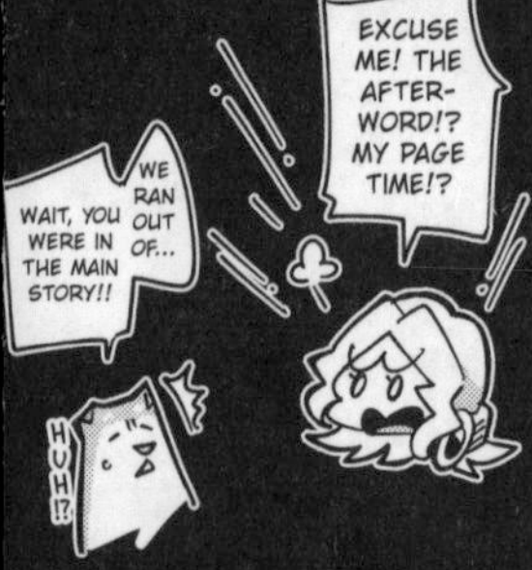
EXCUSE ME! THE AFTERWORD!? MY PAGE TIME!?
WE RAN OUT OF...
WAIT, YOU WERE IN THE MAIN STORY!!
HUH!?

See you Again! SOMEWHERE...!

Sato

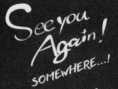

Little Witch Academia

Little Witch Academia

③ Original Story: TRIGGER / YOH YOSHINARI
Art: KEISUKE SATO

Translation: TAYLOR ENGEL ✦ Lettering: ROCHELLE GANCIO

Little Witch Academia Volume 3
©2018 TRIGGER / Yoh Yoshinari / "Little Witch Academia" Committee
©Keisuke SATO 2018
First published in Japan in 2018 by KADOKAWA CORPORATION, Tokyo.
English translation rights arranged with KADOKAWA CORPORATION, Tokyo
through TUTTLE-MORI AGENCY, INC., Tokyo.

English translation © 2019 by Yen Press, LLC

JY
1290 Avenue of the Americas
New York, NY 10104

Visit us at jyforkids.com ✦ facebook.com/jyforkids ✦ twitter.com/jyforkids ✦
jyforkids.tumblr.com ✦ instagram.com/jyforkids

First JY Edition: May 2019

JY is an imprint of Yen Press, LLC.
The JY name and logo are trademarks of Yen Press, LLC.

The publisher is not responsible for websites
(or their content) that are not owned by the publisher.

Library of Congress Control Number: 2018935620

ISBNs: 978-1-9753-5742-9 (paperback)
978-1-9753-5743-6 (ebook)

10 9 8 7 6 5 4 3

WOR

Printed in the United States of America